via her website, Twitter and Facebook page.

@ChristieJBarlow

w[...]

Also by Christie Barlow

A Year in the Life of a Playground Mother
The Misadventures of a Playground Mother
Kitty's Countryside Dream
Lizzie's Christmas Escape
Evie's Year of Taking Chances
The Cosy Canal Boat Dream
A Home at Honeysuckle Farm

Christie Barlow

Love Heart Lane

A division of HarperCollins*Publishers*
www.harpercollins.co.uk

Harper*Impulse* an imprint of
HarperCollins*Publishers*
The News Building
1 London Bridge Street
London SE1 9GF

www.harpercollins.co.uk

This paperback edition 2019

First published in Great Britain in ebook format by
HarperCollins*Publishers* 2019

Christie Barlow asserts the moral right to
be identified as the author of this work

A catalogue record for this book
is available from the British Library

ISBN: 9780008319700

This novel is entirely a work of fiction.
The names, characters and incidents portrayed in it are
the work of the author's imagination. Any resemblance to
actual persons, living or dead, events or localities is
entirely coincidental.

Typeset in Birka by Palimpsest Book Production Ltd,
Falkirk, Stirlingshire

Printed and bound in Great Britain by CPI Group (UK) Ltd,
Croydon CR0 4YY

For Roo, Mop, Missy & Mo,
It's the circle of life.
It's not negotiable.
Where's my woodland outfit?
Operation Miaow.
Walnut Wendy.
Thank you all for the best week of summer 2018!

Chapter 1

Staring out of the window, Felicity Simons sat nervously at her boss's desk. As she admired the view across the city of London, she wasn't in any doubt that this was the best seat in the building.

It was only a few seconds later that she spotted her boss through the glass walls of the office, her size-eight figure tottering along the plush red carpet on her high heels, wearing the usual well-tailored suit with distinctive buttons that oozed designer brand. Her crimson blouse matched the colour of her nails and made Felicity feel unrelentingly beige in her dowdy brown tunic and scuffed patent shoes.

Eleanor Ramsbottom had arrived at Little Browns department store six months ago, and Felicity had always felt inferior in her boss's company, knowing from the outset that there was no chance they'd ever hit it off. After sixty years of steady trade, the store had landed itself in financial difficulty and Eleanor, the daughter of a rich businessman, had rescued the store from closing. At the time everyone had been grateful, all the staff thankful that their jobs had been saved – until they'd had to work under Eleanor Ramsbottom, who lacked warmth, compassion and basic people skills.

The second Eleanor glided into the room Felicity bristled. She was aware that she was forcing a smile, putting on a happy face, but she needed this conversation to go in her favour. Under the desk, Felicity had her fingers firmly crossed. She watched as Eleanor pulled out a chair and shuffled some papers into a neat pile before finally settling down at the desk. Clasping her hands in front of her, she stared towards Felicity.

'My secretary said you needed to see me urgently. It must be urgent to want to see me at 5 p.m. on a Friday night, have you no home to go to?' Eleanor asked, as she flicked a glance towards the clock on the wall.

Felicity took a breath, knowing home was exactly where she *didn't* want to be, because right at this moment in time Adrian would be moving out. They'd lived together for six months, but Felicity had known within hours of him moving into her flat that she'd made a huge mistake.

Initially, Felicity had been swept away on a tide of passion – Adrian was overwhelmingly sexy, after all – but the second she found herself picking up his dirty laundry despite the washing basket being within reaching distance, the lust had worn off and real life had smacked her right between the eyes.

'I would like ... if at all possible...' She paused. '... Some time off.' Felicity was relieved to finally get the words out in the open.

'You don't see me to book time off.' Eleanor's manner was curt. 'You know what to do, fill in your request form and pass it to your team leader and I will authorise it within due course, after I've checked the chart.'

Eleanor was always about the charts.

'Unfortunately, that's not possible; I would like two weeks off from Monday.' Felicity was thankful her voice was steady because inside she felt all jittery and even more so when Eleanor released a long, shuddering sound underneath her breath. Felicity could already feel the disapproving tension in the room. She watched Eleanor slouch back in her chair, twisting her wedding ring round and round before letting out a half laugh then fixing a serious expression back on to her face.

'For a second there, I could have sworn you asked for two weeks off from Monday, and with it being Friday afternoon ... not to mention the January sales, one of the store's busiest times, where we need every hand on deck to reach our targets, and that includes yours, Felicity – both hands.'

Felicity shifted uncomfortably in her seat. 'I wouldn't ask ... but...'

'The implication ... leaving us in the lurch.' Eleanor was a trifle short. 'What's so important you need time off at such short notice?'

Felicity swallowed the lump in her throat and hoped the tears wouldn't cascade down her face. 'My grandmother has passed away and I need to go home, to my family.'

As conversation stoppers go, this one threw Eleanor for a second.

'I wouldn't ask if it wasn't important and I have enough annual leave for two weeks,' added Felicity quickly.

'I'm sorry to hear your sad news,' Eleanor finally offered, keeping her gaze fixed on Felicity. There was a veil of politeness, covering up disappointment at the loss of potential drama.

'Thank you,' replied Felicity.

'Where is home?' That was the first personal question Eleanor had ever asked Felicity.

'The Scottish Highlands,' replied Felicity taken aback. 'A little village called Heartcross.'

Eleanor sighed and made a vague despairing gesture with her hand. 'If you need anything, please don't hesitate to call and we will see you back here two weeks on Monday.' There was nothing in Eleanor's tone that offered any real compassion; her face was expressionless. Felicity watched Eleanor stand up, a clear indication this conversation was over and that this was her cue to leave.

Felicity forced her lips into a smile and couldn't get out of the office fast enough. She grabbed her coat from her locker and paused only briefly on the steps outside the department store. The sign illuminating 'Little Browns,' had once held a special place in her heart. A family-run business that had cared, this store had given her a chance and provided her with an opportunity. She'd worked here for nearly the last eight years after arriving in London on a whim, ready for a change from village life. She'd had grand ideas of seeking her fortune, bright-eyed and bushy-tailed, looking for adventure. But things hadn't been easy. She'd left Heartcross under a cloud and had spent much of her time in London trying to block out the past, especially Fergus. But it was always there. *He* was always there in the back of her mind.

Recently, when things had changed at work and Eleanor Ramsbottom had arrived on the scene, the days had become even less enjoyable and now Felicity was questioning what she was actually doing here. She found herself thinking about home more and more, and how she'd distanced herself from that life. She came to realise that she missed Heartcross, the good friends she'd left behind and of course, her mum and her gran.

Feeling glum and seriously hankering after a gin and

tonic, she turned and weaved in and out of the masses of people who were powering up the busy high street towards the tube station. Felicity dug her hands deep in the pockets of her coat and fought back the tears of sadness as a pang of guilt hit her hard. As she jumped onto the packed tube and headed towards her flat, thoughts of Heartcross were still very much on her mind; memories of the small bustling village in the Scottish Highlands where she'd grown up, the place she had wanted to escape from, suddenly enveloped her and gave her an overwhelming feeling of comfort and belonging.

In the last eight years Felicity had been home on numerous occasions, but they were always fleeting visits with excuses that she couldn't take time off work. And that's exactly what they were – excuses. She knew the real reason why she couldn't spend time there, but now she felt things were changing.

Felicity had fallen out of love with her job and her man, if she'd ever been in love with him at all, and even though she had friends in London, she didn't have friends like the ones she'd had in Heartcross ... solid friends that would have your back, look out for you no matter what.

Why hadn't she gone home for Christmas? As the tube rumbled on, the conversation with her mum played on Felicity's mind.

'Please come home soon, your grandmother's health is deteriorating, she misses you Flick, and I do too.'

'Mum, I live in London, it's difficult to get time off. Do you know how far away Scotland is?'

It was five hundred and eighty-six miles to be precise and ten hours in the car, not including toilet stops. In the last few weeks the weather had been unpredictable, planes and trains had been cancelled due to severe weather conditions and more snow was predicted soon.

But her mother's words played on her mind now. 'Your grandmother won't be around forever, Felicity.' And, of course, her mother, Rona Simons, had been right. Bonnie Stewart had passed away at the age of eighty a little over a week later.

Felicity held on tightly to the aluminium pole in the tube carriage and watched the stations whizz by. This journey was never one she relished, especially during rush hour on a Friday when the tube was packed to the rafters with everyone jostling for their own little space. Life had seemed so exciting when she'd first arrived in the big smoke, but now she was tired of the busy pace of life.

Finally, Felicity jumped off the tube at Leicester Square and pushed her way in the direction of one of the side streets towards The Chatty Banker pub. She pushed open the outer door and saw her friend Polly behind the bar, thoroughly at home with all the regulars.

She was leaning against the pump, all her usual confidence on display.

'Felicity! I didn't expect to see you tonight.' Polly glanced sideways and beamed towards her friend; she was invincibly cheerful as ever but Felicity thought she looked exhausted.

'I'm hungry, don't feel like cooking and could murder a double gin... and when your good friend is the manager of such a good establishment, then it's a no brainer.'

'You can't say fairer than that,' smiled Polly, immediately sliding a glass towards Felicity who balanced on the bar stool in front of her.

'Are you okay? You're looking tired.'

'I'm all right, I've just been run off my feet today ... no rest for the wicked.'

'And you are very wicked.' Felicity smiled.

'How was New Year? I thought you and Adrian would be in.'

New Year's Eve was overrated where Felicity was concerned. As far back as she could remember there had been nothing special about that date, and she'd automatically blocked out the last New Year she'd spent at Heartcross, eight years ago. It still pained her to remember the look on Fergus's face, the pleading tone in his voice begging her not to leave as she'd turned and walked away, shutting the cab door behind her. Felicity had never forgotten that night, but as time went on, she'd regretted it more and more. She drew her glass towards her and drained the contents of it slowly.

Polly narrowed her eyes at Felicity. 'Bad day?'

Where do I start? Felicity thought to herself blowing out a breath. 'You could say that. Adrian and I weren't around New Year's Eve, because that's when I decided we were no longer a "we".' She shifted the glass to one side to make room for her elbows on the bar. 'As we speak he should be moving out of the flat.'

At first, she'd thought he was shocked when she'd asked him to leave, but then he'd retaliated and had the audacity to tell her she wasn't all that. Felicity had fought the desire to argue with him – after all, what was the point? Adrian's expectations of their relationship had differed greatly to hers, and he had basically treated her like his mother, not his girlfriend. Now she just wanted her own space back.

'Oh Flick, what happened?'

'I just realised he wasn't the one for me.'

'You'll be fine,' reassured Polly in a soft tone. 'There are heaps of nice men you could go out with.'

'I think I'll give it a miss for a while,' said Felicity, with tears welling up in her eyes. 'But that's not all, Pol. I've been the worst daughter in the world,' Felicity said as sadness overwhelmed her. Her heart sank, and her shoulders heaved, 'My grandmother has passed away, and I didn't get to say goodbye.'

Without hesitation, Polly reached across the bar and squeezed her friend's hand. 'I'm so sorry to hear that,' she said in a soft soothing tone.

Without warning the tears rolled down Felicity's cheek. She felt ashamed that she'd been selfish and put her own self-importance and feelings before her mum's and now she truly regretted it.

Felicity thought back to her life at Heartcross and memories of her grandmother flooded her mind; the times they'd spent together in the family teashop and the love they'd shared. Bonnie Stewart had lived her whole life in the Scottish Highlands, and sadness flooded Felicity's veins again as she remembered the way her grandmother's cheeks had dimpled with her smile, the way she'd planted noisy kisses on the top of her head and the way she'd always smelled of scrumptious baking.

Heartcross village was a tranquil place off the beaten track, surrounded by majestic mountains, heather-wreathed glens and beautiful waterfalls – place untouched by time. Bonnie's heart-warming traditional stone cottage was snuggled away next to the trim necklace of whitewash houses on Love Heart Lane and had become the hub of the community when she'd turned her front living room into a tearoom over fifty-five years ago. The place had welcomed villagers and passing ramblers walking in the area, and working in 'Bonnie's

Teashop' alongside her grandmother still held happy memories for Felicity. Again, she was beginning to question why she'd been so eager to leave it all behind.

'I should have made more of an effort,' Felicity said to Polly regretfully. 'I thought she'd be around forever, but time runs away, and now ... and now...' Felicity couldn't finish her sentence, her heart was breaking so badly.

'Flick, you need to go home,' Polly said gently as she comforted her friend.

Felicity nodded, 'I know, I am ... I leave first thing tomorrow, flying to Inverness ... it should only take an hour and half.' The guilt ricocheted through her body again. She had only ever been an hour and half away by plane so why the fleeting visits home? She knew exactly why – Fergus.

'How long are you going for?'

'Two weeks,' answered Felicity, dabbing her eyes with the back of her hand. 'I'll be fine,' she said, pasting on a smile, but deep down she knew it wasn't fine.

Taking a second to compose herself, she scanned the menu and ordered a bowl of chips before checking her phone. No word from Adrian but what was she expecting, a farewell text?

Just at that moment a gust of air rushed in as the pub door swung open and to Felicity's shock, in walked Adrian with a girl she didn't recognise by his side. His eyes widened the second he set eyes on Felicity and he turned towards the girl, speaking to her briefly, before she nodded and disappeared towards the far end of the pub.

Felicity couldn't help feeling a little miffed. 'Moved on already?' she asked, knowing it was none of her business.

There was an uncomfortable silence before Adrian shrugged sheepishly. 'Just a friend from work.'

'Yeah right.' The words were out before Felicity could stop them.

He appeared indignant. 'And you care because?'

'It's fine, I'm sure you need a friend right now,' she reasserted herself quickly.

He nodded and Felicity felt the sudden urge to extract herself from this situation. 'While you're here, can I have the keys?' She held out her hand while Adrian dug into his pocket and placed the bunch of keys into her hand.

'Take care of yourself,' he said, before turning and walking away to join the girl.

'Goodbye Adrian,' she managed, before twisting back on her stool towards Polly. 'I think I'll give the food a miss, I just want to go home.'

'Are you sure?'

Felicity was absolutely sure. Her appetite had diminished further and even though she knew it had been over with Adrian for a while she still didn't need to watch him have dinner with another woman, friend or no friend.

Polly lifted up the hatch to the bar and walked towards Felicity, her arms open wide, waiting to swathe her in the biggest hug.

'You have a safe trip and call me when you arrive,' she insisted, hugging her hard. 'I'll see you in a couple of weeks ... and make sure you FaceTime me.'

'I will,' Felicity promised, pressing a kiss to Polly's cheek before walking out of the pub towards the tube station.

It was time to go back to Scotland and set aside her personal hang ups to support her mum at such a sad time. At the time she'd thought she'd left with an air of elegant sophistication, but it was only recently she had begun to realise the hurt she'd left behind.

She knew arriving back at Heartcross wouldn't be easy. In fact, it would be the hardest thing she'd ever done.

Chapter 2

At the airport, the buildings were still shrouded in Christmas decorations and the ten-foot tree sparkled in all its glory. The morning was cold, freezing in fact, with temperatures dropping to minus one, and Felicity had wrapped up warm. Pulling down her unflattering woolly hat over her ears, and with the cold biting the tip of her nose, she wandered towards the glass revolving doors and stood inside Heathrow airport. She was wearing tights as well as socks, two jumpers and a thermal vest. She knew that once the plane landed in Inverness the temperature would be even colder than in London.

After skimming the departures board, she was thankful the flight was on time. She checked in at the desk, then made her way to the lounge area and purchased a skinny latte alongside a ham salad baguette; her appetite was back and finally her fierce hunger was satisfied. Last night, when she'd arrived home Felicity hadn't felt much like eating. Instead, she'd poured a large glass of wine and soaked in a hot bubble bath. All of Adrian's belongings had disappeared, and for the first time ever, he'd managed to pick up his dirty underwear off the floor. She was thankful he'd gone; he just hadn't been her happy ever after.

She'd soaked in the bath for over an hour, until the water was barely warm, her mind whirling. When she'd got out, she'd telephoned her mum to let her know what time she'd be arriving, but there had been no answer. It was more than likely her mum was over at The Grouse and Haggis, the local pub situated in the middle of the village which offered a warm welcome to all with its flagstone floors, wooden pews and roaring log fires. It was the hub of the community, especially during the harsh winter months. The locals all huddled together after work, sharing stories, while sampling the local ales and whiskies. Without fail Hamish would play his fiddle, adding to the good-humoured atmosphere. The pub was run by Meredith and Fraser Macdonald and their daughter Allie had been Felicity's best friend from school before she'd moved to London.

Up until their early twenties the two girls had been as thick as thieves, and Allie had been the kind of friend that Felicity could always be herself with. But Felicity knew she'd let Allie down. She sighed to herself, feeling glum. Allie had every right to be mad with her. Felicity had never confided in her that she planned to leave for the big city. Looking back now, she knew her actions had been underhand, but at the time she'd known that Allie would have tried to talk her out of it. And after everything that had happened with Fergus, Felicity had needed to escape with minimum fuss. She knew on her return she'd have many bridges to build and even though Felicity had made friends in London, nothing had come close to the bond she'd had with Allie. She missed her and their friendship and hoped things were fixable between them.

Finally, trying to shrug off the guilt, Felicity had packed her suitcase and snuggled inside her grey fleecy PJs, determined to get a good night's sleep to be fresh and ready for her trip back to Scotland.

The airport was busy and while waiting for her flight to be announced Felicity buried her head in a book, but after reading the same sentence over and over she realised she wasn't concentrating at all; her mind was on other matters. Lifting her head, she watched a young couple gently chastise their son who was running around leaving a trail of crisps behind him. He hovered in front of Felicity and lifted his blue eyes to meet hers. He was adorable and by her reckoning must have been around three years old. He offered her a crisp with a cheeky smile. Felicity hesitated for a millisecond before accepting. 'Why thank you, young man,' she said with gratitude before his expression knotted with concentration and he ran off with his arms stretched out wide pretending to be an aeroplane. The parents' annoyance now softened as he giggled.

Watching that tiny boy, Felicity felt another pang of sadness. If only things had been different, she thought, blinking away the sudden tears that sprang from nowhere. The pain of the past still twisted in her stomach, and the fear of seeing Fergus again never went away, but over time she'd learnt to cope as best she could. With her heart thumping anxiously in her chest, Felicity shut her eyes briefly, trying to compose herself. As she calmed herself, a voice over the tannoy announced her flight and within seconds a surge of passengers stood up and began to make their way towards the gate clutching their passports and boarding cards. Felicity took in a breath and glanced towards the window. Outside, the sky had darkened and threatened snow. This was it, she thought to herself. She had no idea how people were going to react to her homecoming. All she could do now was hope for the best. Feeling anxious, she squeezed out a wobbly smile at the small boy who was now standing in the queue, grasping his mother's hand and pointing towards the aircraft they were just about to board through the window.

Felicity's chest heaved, and she couldn't bear to think about it anymore. Keep breathing, she told herself, there's no turning back. It's time to go home.

Chapter 3

'Where to?' asked the taxi driver after he'd placed Felicity's suitcase in the boot of the cab and climbed behind the wheel.

'Heartcross,' replied Felicity, pulling the gloves from her hands and resting them on her lap.

The driver turned and looked over his shoulder. 'Heartcross? The track will be treacherous over the bridge and these flakes are falling fast.'

The moment Felicity had stepped off the plane she'd known this might be a problem. 'I kind of gathered that may be the case. How close can you get me?'

The driver raised a sceptical eyebrow. 'Maybe just before the bridge? I don't want to be stranded.'

'As close as you can then,' Felicity replied, knowing she was in for a short trek up the track in severe weather conditions.

Heartcross was separated from the local town of Glensheil by a Grade II listed bridge that had arched over the River Heart for nearly two hundred years. The only way into the centre of the village was by a steep, mountainous track, approximately half a mile long. In the summer it was the most beautiful track to walk along, easily accessible by foot and four-wheel drives, but it was trickier in winter when the snow hit. The village was compact, home to approximately two hundred cottages, but with every amenity you might need.

Fifteen minutes later the cab began to crawl along, the wipers moving frantically and the wheels finding it difficult to turn in the snow. 'This is about far as I can get you,' the driver said, pulling the cab to a halt and climbing out to retrieve Felicity's suitcase from the boot of the car.

Reluctantly, Felicity opened the door and shivered before paying the driver and taking the case from him.

She watched enviously as he clambered back into the warmth of his cab and slowly began to manoeuvre the car in the snow, the wheels spinning momentarily before they regained traction. The taxi driver appeared almost sympathetic as he wound down his window. 'You'll need to get a shifty on up that track, otherwise you'll be stranded.'

Felicity nodded, clutching the handle of her suitcase tight. No sooner had the car's icy tracks imprinted on the road, they were covered by a fresh onslaught of snow. Felicity knew it would be impossible to drag the wheels of her suitcase up the path in the snow for over half a mile and it was too heavy to carry. There was only one thing for it. She sighed as she abandoned the case under a tree before she began trudging through the snow.

Huddled deep inside her parka, Felicity clutched her handbag and raised a gloved hand to shield her eyes from the oversized snow confetti flying towards her. She'd prepared for the drop in temperature but as the ferocity of the snow stung her face she bowed her head and kept walking.

Twenty minutes later the blizzard was so strong the path of footprints she'd followed for a short while were already covered and the familiar sight of Love Heart Lane had nearly been erased. Her fingers and face stung but she allowed herself to be shoved along by the wind and snowstorm.

Finally, she reached the row of whitewashed cottages and heaved a huge sigh of relief when she noticed she'd nearly arrived home, at Heartwood Cottage. Even in the bleak mid-winter, the cottage looked as if it had come straight out of a fairy tale. On the solid oak door there was a heart carved in the middle, whittled by Felicity's grandad on the day he'd moved in with his newly beloved wife Bonnie. It was a cosy dwelling and in the summer its hedges and oak beamed porch were entwined with pink clematis.

There wasn't a soul in sight as Felicity slugged up the path towards the door. She stopped for a second and stared at Bonnie's Teashop, thinking fleetingly that it seemed a little run down, until she remembered she was standing in a middle of a snowstorm and the flakes were blurring her vision.

She twisted the knob on the front door and was thankful it opened. Grateful to leave the blizzard behind, Felicity stamped her feet on the mat outside and closed the door behind her.

'Mum, are you home?' Felicity shouted up the hallway, peeling the sodden gloves from her bitterly cold hands and hanging her coat over the banister. 'It's only me.'

Felicity heard movement and startled eyes peered around the door of the living room. 'Felicity? Oh my! It is you ... come here!' Rona hurried up the hallway with her arms flung wide open and Felicity fell into them. The familiarity and warmth of the hug brought fresh tears to Felicity's eyes and she suddenly realised how much she had missed her mum, this place. She was glad to be home.

'I can't believe you're here.' Rona pulled away and held both of her daughter's hands, kissing her cheeks, as she too shed a tear. 'You don't know how happy I am to see you ... you're freezing ... let me get you a warm drink.'

Felicity wasn't about to argue, she was frozen to the

core. She followed her mum into the living room and took another moment to cast her gaze around. This time she was more certain that something had changed. Everything suddenly seemed so tired at Heartwood Cottage ... so tattered. Even the curtains were hanging off the rail and there weren't any blooms in sight. Back in the day, Rona would always display flowers in the front window, every week without fail.

'How have you got here? The weather warnings are severe, surely no car could cross the bridge?' Rona's eyes were wide as she plumped up the cushions so Felicity could sit down.

'The cab couldn't cross the bridge, it was too treacherous. I had to walk the next half mile.'

'Oh my, you should have rung, I could have sent Drew down with the tractor to fetch you.'

'Mum, the mobile signal is virtually nothing.' Felicity glanced at her phone. 'See ... no service.' She held the phone up.

'And where's your suitcase?' Rona gave a puzzled look all around.

'I couldn't drag it through the snow. I abandoned it under a tree ... this side of the bridge though.'

'It can't stay there, you'll never find it again. This snow is going to fall all night, maybe for the next few days. Ring the farm. The number is by the phone,' Rona insisted, before poking the embers of the fire. Felicity hesitated and felt a wave of uneasiness pass through her.

'Go on, the phone is where it's always been,' Rona continued brightly and shooed Felicity out into the hallway.

Foxglove Farm was owned by Isla and Drew Allaway. Felicity had known them all her life, and they had all once been the best of friends. Isla and Drew were childhood sweethearts who had married and took over the farm from Drew's dad when his wife had sadly passed away. Even though over the years Felicity had taken short trips back home, she'd not seen or spoken to either Isla or Drew in all that time. She had no clue how they were going to react to her homecoming.

Hesitantly, she picked up the olive-green phone and began to dial the number. As soon as the phone connected it only took two rings before it was picked up. 'Hello, Foxglove Farm.' Even after all this time she instantly recognised Drew's voice.

Felicity took a deep breath, 'Hi Drew … it's me … Felicity.'

There was a short pause on the other end of the line. 'Flick! … Welcome home! It's been a while.'

He sounded pleased to hear from her which was a relief. 'Yes, it has. How are you?'

'Good thanks, we are all good. But I'm sorry to hear the sad news about your grandmother.'

'Thanks Drew ... me too.' There was a slight pause.

'What can I do for you? Rona's okay for wood, isn't she?' he asked with concern. 'She doesn't want to be stranded for warmth in this weather.'

'I'm not sure ... wait there ... Mum!' bellowed Felicity from the hallway. 'Are you okay for wood?'

Immediately Rona appeared in the doorway. 'That's nearly the last of the logs on the fire. With everything ... I've not had much time to re-stock. It's all been quite difficult.'

'Drew, are you okay to bring some logs up?'

'Yes, of course ... and what was it we can do for you?'

For a second, Felicity had forgotten why she was ringing. 'My suitcase ... it's my case. It's stranded by the bridge at the bottom of the track ... under the tree. The wheels wouldn't turn in the snow and it was too heavy to lift. Mum thought you might...'

'Don't worry, I'll come now Felicity,' he responded valiantly, 'before it's buried forever. Well, until the snow thaws anyway.' He gave a small chuckle.

'Thanks Drew,' she said, before hanging up and joining her mum back in the living room.

'I've made tea ... help yourself,' said Rona, 'and have a flapjack.' She pointed to the plate on the coffee table. 'We always had a slice of flapjack at this time, most days.' Her voice suddenly wavered and Felicity felt a pang of sadness as her mother glanced towards the empty rocking chair which displayed her grandmother's hand-crocheted, multi-coloured blanket draped over the back of it.

Felicity instantly felt guilty for not being around to help her mum during her grandmother's illness. The tiredness and grief in her mum's eyes were apparent.

Out of every inch of Felicity's body poured the memories of her grandmother, magical moments she'd never forget. She could still remember the hours she'd spent in the teashop at the weekend mirroring her grandmother while she helped to bake all the delicious cakes and scones.

'I'm so sorry, Mum, for not coming home at Christmas,' Felicity said, genuinely remorseful.

'It's not that easy to just up and leave your job, especially working in the department store. It must be one of the busiest times of the year. And how is Adrian? I thought I might finally get to meet him.'

Felicity exhaled. 'It's over Mum ... we've finished. He's moved out.'

'Oh Felicity, why didn't you say?' Rona's voice was earnest.

'Because it was my choice. Honestly, he just wasn't my happy ever after ... that's all there is to it.'

Rona gave Felicity a knowing look.

'Mum, don't give me that look,' she exclaimed.

'You do know you're going to have to face your happy ever after at some point.'

Felicity protested. 'I don't know what you mean.'

But she knew exactly who her mum was talking about ... Fergus.

She and Fergus had made plans, they'd promised each other they'd be together forever. Felicity had thought their love was unbreakable until tragedy had struck... twice. Then Felicity had convinced herself she'd never be enough for him, and she'd upped and left for London, breaking his heart as well as her own.

She took a second to remember their first kiss. Her knees had actually trembled like in the movies and goose bumps had prickled over every inch of her skin. She remembered the feeling like it had only happened yesterday. Felicity knew that being back for two whole weeks, she was bound to bump into Fergus at some point. She wasn't sure how he was going to react to seeing her after all this time or how she was going to feel.

Hearing the drone of the tractor outside, Felicity thankfully abandoned her train of thought. She shifted to the edge of the settee and flicked a glance out of the window. There was Drew waiting outside. He noticed her and gave her a quick wave above his head as Felicity stood up.

'I've brought your old snow boots in from the shed, you'll need them out there on a day like today.'

'Thanks Mum.'

Felicity thrust her feet into her old boots and slipped

her arms into her coat. 'I won't be long,' she said, closing the cottage door behind her.

Since her arrival, the snow hadn't given up for a second and already Love Heart Lane was covered in a thick blanket, inches deep. Felicity had barely seen snow in London – the odd flurry here and there, but nothing that ever stuck.

But Heartcross was used to this kind of weather, they were prepared. The route into the village would be restricted and depending on the snowfall some vehicles might find it difficult to climb the half mile track but when they knew the bad weather was coming the delivery drivers always doubled up on supplies.

Felicity pulled open the door of the tractor to be greeted Drew's huge beam. 'Hi Flick, jump in. It's great to see you.'

Drew hadn't changed a bit. His blond tight corkscrew curls were still as springy as the last time she'd set eyes on him.

'How are you?' asked Felicity. 'And Isla?'

Drew started the engine, and the tractor began to move through the snow with ease.

'She's fed up, but not long to go now until the baby's arrival.'

Felicity swung a glance towards Drew. 'Baby?'

'Aye, a baby brother for Finn, due in the next few weeks.'

Felicity had had no idea. 'Congratulations!' She was

genuinely chuffed for them both. The pair had been inseparable since high school and had married at the age of nineteen at the small church in Heartcross. Their wedding had been beautiful, and all they'd ever wanted was to be together, a family.

'We are all ready for the little fellow, but this weather is a worry if Isla goes into labour. I can see her arriving at the hospital in this tractor—' he gave a small chuckle '—and she won't be best pleased about that.'

Felicity smiled. 'Any names?'

'Angus,' said Drew proudly, 'after my father.'

'Great name.'

'How's the big city?' he asked, changing the subject while carefully steering the tractor down the steep slope towards the bridge.

'Not how it used to be.' The words were out of Felicity's mouth before she could stop them.

He snagged her eye. 'Everything okay? That doesn't sound good.'

'It's just work, I'm not as enthusiastic about it as I once was.'

'I know that feeling. If you need a shoulder, Isla's going nowhere. She's always been a good listener,' he offered with a smile, halting the tractor. 'She'd love to see you. How long are you around for?'

'A couple of weeks.'

'In fact,' he said, opening the door and jumping to

the ground, 'come back with me now to the farm. I need to load up Rona's wood – say hello to Isla and then I'll give you a lift back.'

Felicity thought about it for a second. It had been eight years since she'd set foot on Foxglove Farm. The very last time was the night she'd upped and left.

'Yes, you know, I will. It will be great to see Isla.'

'She's missed you, you know ... but understands you've had a lot to deal with. Now where's this suitcase of yours?'

'Just there, under the tree,' answered Felicity, her thoughts turning to Isla. She'd missed Isla too, and all of a sudden she felt a tiny pang. True friendship was hard to find and Felicity knew she had a great deal of apologising to do. Of course in London she'd hung out with people, and she socialised with many work colleagues from the department store – but her only real friend was Polly from the pub. And no one had come close to the friendship she'd once shared with her two oldest friends Isla and Allie. They'd always been a close-knit group until Felicity had decided she needed to escape the pressures of a small village, spread her wings and escape into the world beyond Heartcross.

The snow crunched under Drew's boots as he quickly retrieved the suitcase and threw it into the tractor before turning around and driving the short journey back to Foxglove Farm.

'So, were you prepared for this weather?' asked Felicity, holding onto her seat as they bounced along the snowy rocky track.

'We knew it was coming but didn't expect it to descend so quickly and it's here for the foreseeable. Apparently, according to the predictions, this is going to be the worst snowfall we've had in twenty years.' Drew cocked an eyebrow.

Felicity hadn't realised this when she'd jumped on the flight from London, and she suddenly panicked. 'Has the village already made provisions?'

'The last trucks came over the bridge this morning and stocked up Hamish's shop. It may be a few days before they can get through again.'

'How is Hamish?'

Hamish and his wife Ava had owned the village shop for as long as Felicity could remember. They were lovely down-to-earth people in their mid-sixties, who had never set foot outside of Scotland. Felicity had fond memories of them both. After school her grand-mother used to give her a handful of pennies – the local shop always had the best collection of penny chews, and Hamish would often throw in extras for Felicity. But two years ago, Ava had passed away, leaving Hamish completely devastated and struggling to cope without the woman he'd loved for all those years by his side. The village community had rallied around him, helping to keep the shop running until he was back on his feet.

'He's doing okay now. It took him a while but recently he's joined numerous clubs in the village from the ramblers, which keeps him fit, to playing bowls.'

'Good for him.'

'He'll be happy to see you. He always had a soft spot for you. Everyone in the village was deeply saddened by your grandmother's death. The village is definitely not the same.' His voice faltered. 'She was always kind to me. As a wee kid, I used the shortcut at the back of your house on the way to school and your grandmother was always waiting at the garden gate with a sausage roll or a slice of homemade cake for my lunch box. She was an absolute gem. It's a shame to see the teashop close after all this time though. Isla used to love to escape there for a slice of cake and a cup of tea on the way back from the village.'

Felicity swung round towards Drew. 'What do you mean, the teashop has closed?' Surely Drew had got that wrong.

'Have I said something out of turn?' asked a surprised Drew. 'Didn't you know?'

Felicity shook her head. 'Mum hasn't said a thing, well, not to me anyway.' She felt sad that the teashop hadn't been open and perplexed as to why she hadn't been told. 'How long?'

'I'd say a good six months. It's been difficult since your grandmother became ill. Your mum couldn't keep everything going.'

Felicity's eyes became glazed with a layer of glassy tears. She brushed them away with her glove. Why hadn't her mum told her how difficult things had become? 'I didn't know Drew, I really didn't.'

'Allie thought you may be back sooner to give a hand, but then we all realised it's not that easy when you have your own job to do and a life in London.'

Felicity nodded, but no words came out. Why hadn't she come back at Christmas? But in her heart of hearts she knew why – that time of year was always too painful for her.

'Working in a department store it's always busy in the lead up to Christmas and then there's the sales.' Felicity knew she was saying the right things, but it didn't sit right with her. Deep down, she knew she'd let her mum down and wished she could turn back time.

Drew nodded, 'Here we are, Foxglove Farm. It's been a while since you've seen this place.'

'Too long,' Felicity whispered under her breath, looking out of the windscreen at the swirling storm of white that was being battered away by the wipers. The usual sight of the farmhouse was nearly hidden by the snow that now swirled densely.

'What on earth?' A sudden movement in the bottom

field caught Drew's eye. Felicity shot a look towards Drew, then followed his gaze.

And suddenly, there he was in the distance, waving his arms frantically towards the tractor. Fergus. Felicity's breath caught in her throat as she recognised him instantly, her heart pounding faster against her chest. She'd never anticipated that he would be here, at the farm, and she had no idea how he was going to react to seeing her for the first time in eight years. This wasn't how she'd planned it out in her head.

Drew flounced out of the tractor leaving the engine running, bellowing to Felicity to follow him. Before she had time to think she trailed Drew through the blanket of snow, her legs trembling. Snowflakes pelted against her face as she struggled to keep up with him.

'Drew ... I need help.' Fergus Campbell's voice was fraught. 'The Shetland is stranded in the icy water.'

Drew stopped for a second to assess the situation, raking his wet hands through his hair. The pony was struggling to climb up the bank of the river. Each time it tried it slipped back down into the water.

'We need a rope ... wait there, and I'll bring the tractor back down,' he cried, turning and striding back past Felicity quickly. 'You stay with Fergus,' he instructed with authority.

Fergus hadn't spotted Felicity yet but it was only a matter of time. Felicity felt anxious, the past dominating her mind. As she moved closer, she could see the panic-stricken face of Fergus, and her nerves jumped all together in every direction. She'd no idea how Fergus was going to react to her arrival back in Heartcross but any second now she was about to find out.

Felicity looked nervously in his direction, and finally Fergus met her gaze. For a split second he narrowed his eyes and remained silent.

She swallowed. 'Hi Fergus.' As much as Felicity didn't want her voice to sound shaky, she faltered.

Fergus just stared at her, then gritted his teeth. There was no welcoming smile, more of a '*What are you doing here*' grimace.

Felicity felt her cheeks colour fast and that was down to the look on Fergus's face, not the cold white flakes stinging her face.

'Well, you crop up in the most unexpected places,' he said gruffly.

Felicity flinched at his words. She'd dreaded this moment and didn't know what to say as she swallowed a lump in her throat. The snowflakes continued to pelt against her frozen cheeks, clinging to her eyelashes forcing her eyes into a squint.

'And don't look at me like that; what did you expect, that you'd be welcomed back with open arms?'

The tension between them could be cut with a knife. Felicity felt wretched. She'd not prepared for this meeting and had thought she'd at least have a couple of days to catch up with Allie and Isla first and gauge how the land lay.

'It doesn't have to be like this,' said Felicity, knowing it wasn't going to be easy.

'So, you're finally back then? How long has it been?' His dark brows sloped downwards in a serious expression and the playful smile she once knew had drawn into a hard line across his face.

Feeling a tug at her heart, Felicity felt shameful. Fergus was a decent man and she knew she hadn't been fair to him. He'd needed her, but she hadn't been able to cope. Call it self-preservation but the only person she could concentrate on at the time was herself. She'd been young, but she'd treated him badly, and he had every right to speak to her this way even though it saddened her that it had come to this.

'Eight years,' she said regretfully.

Fergus's hazel eyes didn't look any different from all those years ago, and she could still sense a sadness in them. He stood and raked the snow from his swooping fringe that revealed the kind face Felicity had once loved to kiss. He was handsome all right, but his character was also beautiful on the inside. He was slim yet muscular and his face almost symmetrical with his sharp jawline and chiselled cheekbones. She felt a pang in her heart and wished she could turn back time.

To Felicity's relief, the icy silence was interrupted by the drone of the tractor making its way back through the snow towards them.

Once at the river bank, Drew jumped out, leaving the engine running. In his hands he grasped a rope.

'I'm not sure how we're going to do this?' Drew shouted down the bank, the blizzard now coming down thick and fast.

Fergus looked between him and the Shetland. 'I'm not sure how close I can get.'

The river ran along the bottom of Foxglove Farm's boundary. Felicity remembered many hot summers swinging on the rope swing with Isla and Allie, all of them without a care in the world. The banks had been alive with nestling ducks taking advantage of the tall reeds providing shade but today everywhere was stripped bare. The river had an eerie feeling about it, and was wider than she ever remembered, flowing swift and strong.

Drew threw the rope down the bank towards Fergus who gradually began making his way into the water. The Shetland pony was now wedged against an old oak tree that must have fallen into the water after a storm.

Felicity shivered at the very thought of the icy coldness of the water against Fergus's skin.

'I'm going to tie this end to the tractor mate, keep hold of the rope and we'll pull you out.'

Fergus nodded, taking in the instructions as he stumbled into the fast-flowing freezing water, which was now attempting to knock him off his feet. Suddenly he lost his footing, the water gushing over his head. Without thinking, Felicity let out a scream. She watched on in horror, her heart banging against her chest willing Fergus to reappear, her brain now in full panic.

'There he is,' she exhaled with relief, pointing to where Fergus reappeared above the water line. The river was bashing against his body, as his head went underneath the water for a second time.

Drew cupped his hands around his mouth and shouted with all his might. 'FERGUS!' He turned to Felicity. 'I'll have to go in after him.'

'Wait ... look!' She pointed.

Fergus' limbs moved slowly through the water as he managed to claw himself back up and grasp on to the fallen tree strewn across the water. Felicity gasped in relief to see he'd managed to get himself upright. The river was flowing around his thighs, swirling around his stomach and splashing into his face as he waded towards the Shetland which was now within grabbing distance.

'The water is too fast ... I can't ... I can't...' His voice petered out as he slipped again under the fast-flowing water.

Felicity's heart was in her mouth. 'Please let him be

okay,' she whispered to herself as she saw Fergus fight to get to his feet once more, his exhausted but strong arms powering through the water.

They both watched in anticipation as Fergus looped the end of the rope and tied it securely.

'Throw it,' instructed Drew.

Fergus flicked a quick glance over towards Drew before taking a deep breath. He focused his gaze and threw the rope successfully over the little pony's head.

'Yes!' Drew shouted, triumphantly punching the air. 'Keep hold of the rope,' he shouted down the bank before turning towards Felicity. 'Can you remember how to drive the tractor?'

Felicity thought for a second. There had been many summers she'd helped out at the farm. 'Yes, I think I do.'

'You jump in and drive it slowly, and I mean slowly. I'm going down to the water,' Drew continued, beginning to clamber down the bank.

The snow wasn't slowing down, and thick flakes pelted against their cheeks, clinging to their eyelashes and hair. Even though Felicity was frozen to her core it was nothing compared to what Fergus must be suffering right that very second in the freezing cold river.

Climbing into the tractor, she was relieved to have shelter from the flakes. She started driving the tractor slowly.

She could hear Drew yelling behind her and opened the door quickly to make sure everything was okay. He was back on the top of the bank and gave her the thumbs up. She continued to drive forward. She'd no clue what was going on behind her but then suddenly Drew was at the side of the vehicle banging on the window. Immediately, Felicity came to a stop and turned off the engine.

'They're out.' The look of relief on Drew's face said it all. 'But we need to get Fergus back to the farmhouse ASAP. I'm going to take the pony over to the stable block, but I need you to drive him back. He needs to get out of those wet clothes and get warmed up. His body temperature has dropped considerably.'

Just as Drew was talking, the passenger door opened, and an exhausted Fergus wearily climbed into the tractor and slumped into the seat. He was soaked to the bone, his head bent low, his lips blue and he couldn't stop shivering.

Felicity's heart began to race as she took him in. She knew this didn't look good.

'Felicity,' Drew said in a stern tone. 'He needs to get out of those clothes, wrap him in blankets and put him in front of the fire. He needs a warm drink and make sure he can swallow properly. Any concerns, ring the emergency services.'

Felicity nodded, taking in every instruction even

though she knew in this weather there was no ambulance getting over the bridge and up the track into Heartcross today.

Her gaze slid to Fergus again. No matter the distance and time that was between them, Felicity's attraction towards him had never wavered. His eyes, his skin and his toned muscles still made her pulse race and as much as they had their differences, Felicity didn't like seeing him like this. She felt worried and knew there was every possibility his condition could worsen. They didn't speak as Felicity ploughed the tractor through the snow and pulled up outside the farmhouse.

Almost immediately the solid oak door swung open and a very pregnant Isla was standing in the doorway. Felicity jumped down from the tractor while Isla did a double take.

'Felicity, is that you? It is!' Isla swooped out of the doorway.

'Isla, we need to get Fergus inside quick. He's been in the river.'

Isla stopped in her tracks and glanced towards the passenger side. 'The river?' she questioned. 'In this weather?'

'A Shetland was stranded in the water. We've just rescued it. Drew's seeing the pony into the stable.'

Fighting against the snow that was still falling heavily to the ground Isla flung open the tractor door with vigour. Taking one look at Fergus, she assessed the situation, knowing that the circumstances were serious, and began to coax Fergus down from the tractor, his body limp and shivering.

Felicity felt heartbroken and hated seeing him like this. He'd put himself in danger and was now paying the price. She knew they needed to act fast so he didn't deteriorate any more.

'Can you speak?' Felicity asked softly.

His words were slurred and his teeth were chattering, 'I'm freezing,' he managed to say.

'He's not in a good way,' Isla quickly observed. 'Help me get him inside.'

Felicity didn't hesitate and hurling his arms over each one of their shoulders, they helped carry Fergus into the farmhouse.

The second they were inside, Felicity supported his weight, while Isla skinned the sodden shoes and socks from his feet before leading him into the kitchen.

With the welcoming heat from the Aga and the log fire roaring, the kitchen was toasty warm. 'Peel those clothes off him now,' instructed Isla, 'while I grab some towels, blankets and some of Drew's clothes.'

Felicity hesitated, her face heated.

'Now Felicity—' Isla's tone was firm '—time is precious, and it's not as though you haven't seen it all before.' With that, she hurried out of the kitchen.

Inside her head, Felicity gave herself a talking to. Isla was right, there was no time to lose.

'Is that okay ... Fergus?'

With his teeth still chattering he just nodded and Felicity guided him to the rug in front of the fire. He continued to shiver and didn't object to Felicity helping him out of his clothes, but he avoided eye contact with her at all costs. As she stripped off his damp clothes the familiarity was all too much for Felicity. She gently touched a body that she'd spent time loving but now, he was a distant stranger. She ran her hand over the scar on his shoulder and for a second, he allowed her a moment's eye contact before quickly looking away.

Suddenly, it hit her hard how much she'd missed him, and a twinge of sadness ricocheted through her body. He was still overwhelmingly sexy, and she knew the second she set eyes on him she was still attracted to him. But there was no going back. She knew from past conversations with her mum that Fergus had moved on and had a family of his own now. These feelings for him were ones she needed to curb for the two weeks she was back home in Heartcross, for everyone's sake. Fergus and Felicity had a past, as childhood sweethearts who had made plans and dreams. But that was over now.

Felicity sighed inside. What was the point in raking up the past? It wasn't going to help either of them.

Isla returned a few minutes later, armed with blankets

and a set of Drew's clothes, and while Felicity held a towel around Fergus's waist Isla quickly began to dress him then draped the blankets over his shoulders. Once he was safely in the old battered armchair in front of the fire she put the kettle on the hotplate of the Aga.

'He needs warm sweet tea.'

Felicity perched on the edge of the small coffee table next to him and automatically placed her hand lightly on his knee. His eyes skimmed hers for a split second. 'Are you feeling any better?' she asked, trying to keep her voice bright.

Fergus looked up as Isla placed a steaming mug of tea in his hand and one in Felicity's too. 'Drink this slowly,' she said to Fergus. 'There's a couple of sugars in that.'

He nodded and took small sips.

Isla turned back towards Felicity. 'I'll finally say my hellos,' she said, with her arms open wide. Felicity stood up and hugged her as best she could with Isla's heavily pregnant stomach in the way.

'Good grief, you're sodden too,' she said, pulling away quickly. 'Do you need a change of clothes?'

'Honestly, I'm fine. Don't worry about me,' Felicity said, not wanting to make a fuss. 'I'll sit here and get warm by the fire. And congratulations! Look at you, all blooming. I believe it's any minute now for this little one to make an appearance.'

Isla patted her stomach. 'Blooming fed up. I'm more than ready for this wee one to come out now, and me, you and Allie, we need a proper catch up. I'm so glad you're home.' Isla pulled Felicity in for another quick hug.

Felicity felt relieved there was no awkwardness between her and Isla. It was like they'd never been apart. Isla had always been the calm friend, the voice of reason. She always saw the good in everyone and Felicity was thankful she'd welcomed her back with open arms.

Then, her thoughts turned to Allie. She knew it might not be as easy to build bridges with her. Allie was without a doubt the friend with lots of character, the feisty friend, who could hold a grudge until the cows came home ... stubborn beyond belief. But even though the three of them had had their spats over the years they'd always stuck by each other no matter what ... until Felicity had left the village. It was safe to say Felicity felt nervous at the thought of catching up with Allie.

'How will Allie feel about that?' asked Felicity, with a worried expression etched on her face.

Isla took a moment to answer. 'I won't try to hide the fact she was mad when you left without telling her. In fact, imagine one of those cartoon characters with steam shooting out of their ears, stomping around ... I'm only joking,' laughed Isla seeing the look of horror on Felicity's face then taking a swift glance towards Fergus suddenly realising he'd been the reason Felicity had fled so suddenly in the first place. 'But we know her from old, she'll be fine,' she quickly added, giving Felicity a knowing look with a tilt of the head towards Fergus.

Isla knew the heartache and devastation that Fergus had gone through after the tragedy; she and Drew had been left to pick up the pieces. But Felicity had no idea the effect her leaving had had on Fergus. Isla and Drew had never seen him so low, and he'd been lost without Felicity.

Fergus coughed and they both spun around towards him.

'How're you doing, Fergus?' Isla asked, tentatively.

'I'm okay, I'm just starting to feel a little normal again.' They both noticed his teeth had finally stopped chattering and it was also a good sign that Fergus's speech was normal, the colour of his lips gradually returning to a pinkish colour.

'Is there anything I can get you?' Isla asked, but before Fergus could answer Drew bounded through the kitchen door, stripping off his own wet coat from his back.

'How are you?' Drew placed a hand on his mate's shoulder.

'I'm doing okay, the cold was just a bit of a shock.'

'He looks surprisingly good compared to the way he looked about ten minutes ago,' Isla added, looking between Drew and Fergus.

'There was a split second I didn't think we'd get the pony out of there – or you for that matter.'

'How is the pony?' asked Isla placing the biscuit barrel on the table. 'You need sugar,' she said to Fergus passing him a biscuit before turning back towards Drew.

'I've dried her off, put the heat lamps on in the barn and buckled on two fleece coats to warm her up, but with her thick coat we shouldn't have any problems. She's got plenty of hay. I'll check on her again after I've taken Flick home and picked up Finn.'

'Or you could stay for tea,' suggested Isla, looking at Felicity. 'There's last night's leftover curry and Finn would love to meet you.'

Felicity swallowed and shot a quick look over at Fergus, who wasn't forthcoming with any encourage-ment – but why would he be? She was probably the last person he wanted to spend any time with.

'I'd love to, but I've only just arrived home and Mum will be expecting me and the logs.'

'The logs!' Drew threw his hands up the air. 'I've forgotten the logs with everything. I'll load them up now and get you home to Rona.'

'Thanks Drew, I'll come and help. We'll do it in half the time.'

'If you're sure?'

As Felicity stood to leave, she hovered at the side of Fergus. Her mind was in complete overdrive. She knew there was unfinished business between them, but this wasn't the right time to bring any of it up.

'Fergus...' Felicity took a breath. 'Can I come and see you?' Feeling the emotion rise up inside her, she swallowed hard. Fergus didn't look up but stared into the fire with the blankets still firmly wrapped around his shoulders. His features had suddenly become expressive. Disapproval was etched into every line, but he didn't respond, leaving Isla and Drew exchanging uncomfortable looks.

Felicity's lower lip quivered as she followed Isla into the hallway. As soon as they were out of ear shot of Fergus, Isla spoke. 'He'll come round, it's just the shock of seeing you again,' she said softly, giving her hand a reassuring squeeze.

Felicity tried for a smile; the sad thing was that deep down she knew Fergus was still hurting. She was still hurting too. At one time Fergus would have given her the world but now he could barely make eye contact with her. She'd thrown away everything.

'I hope so Isla, I really hope so.'

Chapter 4

Back at the cottage the fire was nearly out when Drew and Felicity arrived. Fighting against the blizzard outside, Drew kindly loaded all the wood into the log shed and hauled in a huge basket of wood and placed it by the fire.

'This should keep you going until morning,' he said, bending down and poking the embers of the fire before throwing a few more logs into the grate. Within no time at all the fire was thankfully roaring once more.

Rona was more than thankful to Drew and offered him a cup of tea and slice of cake which he was grateful for.

'Meredith has invited everyone over to the pub tonight for chilli. Are you and Isla going?' asked Rona turning towards Drew.

'It's the first I've heard of it but if it's an open invitation I'm not one to pass up on Meredith's chilli, and I think it will do Isla good to get out for a while.'

'Yes, it's an open invitation. I think she thought everyone would have had quite a day of it with the weather and wouldn't feel much like cooking.'

'And she is right, we were having leftover curry. God love that woman, always thinking of others. I'll pick up Finn from his friend's and we'll see you over the pub in about an hour,' he said, finishing his tea and cake before pulling on his coat that had been warming on the armchair in front of the fire.

'Good, good,' said Rona, showing Drew to the front door after Felicity thanked him for rescuing her suitcase and bringing her home.

While she could still hear Rona chatting away to Drew, Felicity wandered through to the kitchen and placed the kettle on the hotplate of the Aga. The sound of the constant dripping from the tap caught her attention but however hard she tried she couldn't get it to stop. Taking a look around the room she noticed that the place not only seemed tired, but the room felt quite chilly too. She placed her hand on the radiator. It was stone cold and she shivered. The only heat was coming from the Aga. She wandered over to the pantry and opened up the door, astonished to find the shelves near enough bare, when they'd always been packed to the brim with baking ingredients for the teashop cakes.

Felicity could still hear her mum and Drew talking so unlocked the duck-egg coloured door next to the pantry which led into the teashop. She switched on the light and stood and stared.

Drew had been right; this place looked like it hadn't been in use for a while. Everywhere seemed worn, tired and washed out. Felicity brushed her hand over the counter and a mushroom of dust danced before her eyes. The whole place seemed so lifeless, so colourless. Even the shabby chic coloured bunting that criss-crossed the ceiling looked drab; it had definitely seen better days.

Felicity walked past all the chairs neatly pushed underneath the tables towards the front of the shop. She could visualise her grandmother standing in the front window smoothing down her white pinny before waving madly at her as she walked home from school along Love Heart Lane. Every night, without fail she'd waited in the window at the same time.

Felicity couldn't help but wonder what had happened here and began to feel guilty and confused. How did she not know the shop had closed? This was her mum's livelihood.

Through the window Felicity watched Drew climb into his tractor and wave goodbye to Rona as he drove off back home towards Foxglove Farm. The rest of the lane was silent. The line of houses on Love Heart Lane looked like a picturesque snowy Christmas card, with some of the cottages in complete darkness while others were lit up. There was a romantic feel about the place.

Felicity watched Rory, who lived opposite, as he stood in the middle of his living room hugging a mug. She and Rory had grown up together in the village and like everyone else in Heartcross, they had once been good friends. Rory had always known from an early age that he wanted to be a vet. His parents Stuart and Alana Scott ran the veterinary surgery in the village, and Rory was now in partnership with them.

Felicity heard a noise behind her and spun round as Rona appeared by her side. 'I wondered where you'd got to.'

'Mum, what's happened to this place? Why didn't you tell me the teashop wasn't up and running?'

The teashop was a place where Felicity had spent most of her free time as a young girl, especially in the school holidays. She'd worked alongside her mum and grandmother helping to bake the scrumptious cakes Bonnie was famously known for, and when she was in her teens she'd waited tables. Early mornings had always been Felicity's favourite time. The mouth-watering aromas that had drifted from Bonnie's kitchen were a great start to the day. Before school, Felicity had always helped to arrange the home-baked pastries and cakes in the open counter and on the numerous glass-domed cake stands in exchange for her daily gingerbread man that she took to school without fail.

Most weekends this small teashop would be jam-packed with passing ramblers who'd trek through the mountainous terrain of Heartcross and sample the delicious delights of Bonnie Stewart's baking. Her grandmother had opened the tearoom on a whim. Her cottage was the last stop on Love Heart Lane before the hikers ventured on the three-hour rocky trek to reach the summit of Heartcross Mountain. It was a great last stop to fuel the body and grab a cuppa and of course use the bathroom facilities.

As Rona pondered the answer to the question a look of pain crossed her face. 'It's not been that easy, Felicity.' Her voice was low and shaky taking Felicity by surprise. Her mum had always been a tower of strength and seeing the look on her mother's face, she felt numb, an entire stock of emotions running through her body. 'What do you mean?' she asked hesitantly.

'I tried my best,' said Rona, holding on to the last trace of pride.

Felicity's heart sank.

'I couldn't do everything.'

Feeling wretched, Felicity blinked back the tears that brimmed in her eyes. The business her grandmother had worked so hard for lay in ruins. What had her grandmother thought? The teashop closed, her hopes and dreams dashed. Felicity swallowed hard. She'd never thought in a million years that this place would close.

Add in the factor that her mum was clearly struggling, and Felicity felt shaken by it all.

'I tried to keep things afloat but everything just spiralled out of control. It all got a bit too much for me.'

The comfortingly familiar life and beloved teashop had folded around Rona and Felicity had been none the wiser. She was devastated that she'd been caught up in her own little world and never realised how bad things had got back home. This place had been the heart of the community for decades, and this was a hurdle that they needed to get over. This place couldn't stay shut. In deep thought, Felicity linked her arm through her mum's and turned to slowly walk back into the kitchen of the cottage.

'I'll make us a hot drink and bring it through. You go and sit down.'

Rona nodded and settled down on the wingback chair in front of the fire. As soon as the drinks were made Felicity slid herself on to the battered old chesterfield.

'How long has the shop been closed?'

Rona looked up at her daughter. 'About eight months.' She let out a breath. 'Everything seemed to all go wrong at once.'

'You mean with Grandma being ill.'

Rona nodded. 'That was the start of it, but not just

that, there was this place too. Everything seemed to break at once. The boiler packed up, the tap's beginning to leak and looking after your grandma full time meant I couldn't juggle the shop.' The tone to her voice was sad.

Felicity sat back and digested this information, 'Did you get any help with Grandma?'

Rona shook her head and took a sip of her drink. 'No, all those years ago we'd made a pact; when the time came, she never ever wanted to go into a home. I promised I would care for her until the very end and that's what I did. She dedicated her life to looking after me, looking after us when you were growing up. I couldn't even afford my own house after your father died, there was no life insurance or any spare cash. We'd always lived here with Mum and after putting a roof over our heads all this time it wasn't a big ask. I kept my promise.'

A small tear slid down Rona's face. 'I miss her so much. And there's still so much to sort out, her clothes and belongings, but I just can't face it all at the minute.'

'I can help with all that while I'm here.'

Rona smiled with appreciation towards her daughter.

'Mum, I'm so sorry.' Felicity was heartbroken and surprised to discover how hard things had become for her mum.

'It's not your fault, you have your own life, and your

grandmother wouldn't have wanted you to come home just for her.'

Felicity knew her life hadn't been all that in the past year. She could have come home at any time to help and felt disappointed in herself that she hadn't supported her mother more.

'And the boiler, is that fixed? It does seem awfully cold in the cottage.'

Rona regretfully shook her head, 'Unfortunately, with the teashop being shut I've lost my income and just didn't have the money to get it fixed. Any savings I had, I used them to get by … to live on for the last eight months.'

Felicity stared at her mum. She couldn't believe for all this time she had been struggling by herself. 'How are you heating the water?'

'With the kettle. I've been boiling the water on the Aga to have a wash. It's going to be all right,' Rona quickly added with a wan smile.

Felicity's eyes widened; she couldn't believe her mum was living like this. Twelve months ago, this cottage had been spick and span, everything gleamed, and the teashop had been packed to the brim with customers, and now everything had changed in such a short space of time.

'Why didn't you ask for help, surely Drew would have taken a look at the boiler for you?'

'I don't like to bother people and anyway he's got enough on his plate with the new baby on the way.'

'Mum, you wouldn't be bothering them. They'd be upset knowing you've been living like this; they would never ever see you in a pickle and without a proper source of heat, especially in the winter months.'

Rona sipped her drink. She was a proud, strong, independent woman and had always been in control, but things had begun to slip when Bonnie had become ill.

'There's also Rory – and even Fergus wouldn't see you struggling surely.'

Now it was Rona's turn to stare at her daughter. 'That's the first time I've heard you mention his name in a long time,' she said in astonishment.

Felicity had avoided saying Fergus's name out loud for years; the memories were too painful, and she thought if she pretended he didn't exist it would all go away, but of course it was never going to go away. It was always going to be there.

Felicity exhaled. 'I've seen him.'

Taking Rona by surprise she sat up straight. 'You've seen Fergus? When? Where?'

'Today, up at the farm. One of Drew's Shetlands was stranded in the river. Fergus went in after it and Drew and I helped to rescue them.'

'In this weather? He'd catch his death.'

'He nearly did.' The pang of worry was still firmly in the pit of her stomach.

'How is he?'

'He's okay now,' answered Felicity, thinking of a cold Fergus shivering out of control.

'And how did that go down ... seeing you?'

Felicity sighed. 'Difficult, he wasn't over the moon to see me, which of course is understandable.'

'Did you talk?'

Felicity shook her head. 'Not really, it wasn't the time or the place, but I will. And anyway—' she attempted to change the subject '—what are we going to do about this boiler? We can't go on boiling kettles on the Aga.'

Rona sighed. 'There's a quote on the dresser, but it's over a thousand pounds for a new one.'

Felicity stood up and wandered over to the stack of papers piled up and stared down at the quote. 'Mum, let me help. I can pay this.'

'That's very kind of you but...'

'But nothing, I insist. I've a little saved up with all the extra work over Christmas and there's no way I'm going back to London leaving you here with no hot water or heat.' Felicity flicked a glance towards the living-room clock – it was now past five o'clock. 'I'll give them a ring first thing in the morning.'

Rona blinked back her tears and her face brightened. 'Thank you.'

'You don't need to thank me and please talk to me in the future. Let me know if you need help.'

Rona nodded. 'I will, I promise.' She got to her feet and enveloped her daughter in a hug. 'It's good to have you home, even if it's only for a little while.'

Felicity felt the love and warmth from her mother as she wrapped her arms tightly around her. She made a promise to herself there and then that she would come home more and ring as often as possible.

'What time do we need to be at the pub?' asked Felicity, releasing herself from her mother's arms and suddenly feeling ravenous.

'Anytime now,' answered Rona, looking towards the window. The snow was still coming down thick and fast. 'Everyone will be there, you know.' Rona held her daughter's gaze and Felicity nodded her understanding.

'Might as well get it over with.'

'How are you feeling?'

'A little apprehensive. I know it sounds daft but maybe a little scared of seeing Allie again ... I caught up with Isla this afternoon, she was lovely to me. It was like I'd never been away. But I'm not sure how Allie is going to react. She took it badly when I left ... and she's not as forgiving as Isla.'

'And there's Aggie too.' Rona cocked an eyebrow.

Every time Felicity had come back to the village for a brief visit she'd tried not to think about bumping into

Aggie but she knew it was going to happen sooner rather than later and it was something she wasn't looking forward to.

Aggie Campbell was Fergus's mother, and he lived with her in Fox Hollow Cottage, just at the bottom of Love Heart Lane. Aggie was without a doubt a kind woman, but she had strong opinions, especially when it came to her only son whom she doted on.

'I know.'

'And it's more than likely Fergus will be there. If he's okay after today.'

Every time Felicity thought of Fergus she felt a tremor of emotion that she couldn't quite place. She closed her eyes for a split second, the image of him and his soft smile firmly on her mind. If she closed her eyes tight enough she could still feel his strong arms around her and his woody, manly smell as she snuggled into his chest all those years ago. There was a time she'd thought Fergus would always be by her side, every step of the way, growing old together – but she'd messed that up. She gave herself a little shake. All that was in the past. She needed to accept that.

'It will be okay, you know. I'm sure there will be a time when you can be civil together.'

Felicity really hoped so. She'd never admitted it to anyone before but there were times when she suffered bouts of depression, wondering what her life would have been like if she'd stayed in Heartcross. Would she and Fergus still be together? Would they have gotten over the heartache? Would she have been enough for him? She would never know the answers to those questions. In fact, she'd cried a lot in London, pretending to be perfectly happy, creating a new existence that was basically a pretence.

Of course there had been good times but once the initial excitement and adventure had worn off she'd wanted to go back home on numerous occasions. However, her pride had always stopped her. She'd suffered for her actions and seeing the look Fergus had given her today, it was clear he'd suffered too. She knew him from old and he was still hurting. Over time, Felicity had learnt to block out her deep sadness, but seeing Fergus again, she knew the feelings she'd once had for him were still very much there.

Chapter 5

After stamping her snowy boots on the mat outside, Felicity's nervousness peaked the second she walked through the door of The Grouse and Haggis, the pub owned by Meredith and Fraser, Allie's parents. This was the first time she'd stepped inside the pub for a very long time but it was exactly how she remembered it. The oak beams ran right across the low ceiling, the private alcoves were still plumped with bright-coloured cushions and the log fire roared.

Huge aluminium pots of chilli and baskets of crusty bread lay on a long trestle table stretched out at the side of the bar ready to feed the hungry villagers.

'How're you feeling?' Rona whispered under her breath.

'Nervous,' mumbled Felicity locking eyes with Meredith who was serving Heather the postmistress with a drink.

Immediately, Meredith hitched a smile on her face

and scuttled around the bar with her arms flung open wide, hugging Felicity like she was a long lost relative. 'Felicity ... Felicity, my dear girl, it's great to have you home. It's been too long.' If anyone hadn't spotted Felicity walking into the pub, they certainly knew of her arrival now – she felt like the whole pub was looking her way. Felicity was very fond of Meredith and Fraser; in fact, they used to call her their second daughter. As children, Felicity and Allie had been inseparable and even through their teenage years they had been as thick as thieves.

Felicity pulled gently away from Meredith's hug to find Fraser now standing next to his wife. 'Welcome home, Felicity, let me get you a drink. What would you like?' he asked.

'Thanks Fraser, a gin and tonic please, and for you, Mum?' Felicity turned towards her mum.

Meredith touched Rona's arm. 'The usual?' She smiled and Rona simply nodded.

'Wait until Allie sees you, she's just collecting the wood from the shed to keep these fires going. She'll be back in in a minute.'

Felicity felt a little uneasy watching Meredith and Fraser disappear back behind the bar. Meredith seemed unaware of the possible friction between Allie and herself or maybe she'd just forgotten over time.

'Why don't you go out the back and catch up with

her?' Meredith suggested, passing the drinks over the bar.

Felicity hesitated and looked towards her mum. She'd no clue how Allie was going to react to her homecoming but she knew she was going to have to face her at some point. Maybe it would be better to slip out the back to see Allie for the first time without a group of lookers watching their every move. 'Are you going to be okay?' Felicity asked her mum.

'Why wouldn't I be okay? I've been drinking in this pub on my own for as long as I can remember,' she said, with a small chuckle. 'You go and see Allie, see how the land lies … try and put things right.'

Fraser nodded towards the oak door at the far end of the pub. 'You know the way.'

Feeling apprehensive, Felicity clutched her drink and weaved her way through the villagers. The pub was full to the brim and despite the bad snowfall everyone seemed in good spirits. Felicity spotted Hamish from the village shop who tilted his flat cap and gave her a wave, and then she noticed Rory slipping in through the side door. As soon as he spotted her he stopped dead in his tracks. 'Hey, Flick!' He flashed her a grin. 'You're home! Welcome back.'

Rory hadn't changed a bit. He was slim, clean shaven and his dark hair with a hint of auburn was still styled in the same way. His pale blue eyes glinted back at her.

'I am indeed! How are you?'

'Me ... I'm good, same old, same old ... working hard as usual. I'm sorry to hear about Bonnie.' He quickly gave his condolences before carrying on, telling Felicity that all was good in the land of animals except for the snowy weather that was forecast for the next few days.

'Have you seen Allie yet?' he asked.

'I'm just going through to the back now,' Felicity answered, feeling her heart thump a little faster.

Rory must have noticed the uneasy look on Felicity's face. 'Don't worry ... we both know her bark's worse than her bite. She's actually missed you, you know.'

'How would you know?' Felicity narrowed her eyes at him.

'Because we've talked about it ... and she still talks about you a lot.'

'We?'

Rory gave Felicity a grin.

'You and Allie are together?'

He nodded. 'Yes, just under twelve months now.'

Elated by the thought of them being together, Felicity couldn't help but give Rory a quick hug. As teenagers, Felicity had teased Allie that they would make the perfect couple, but Rory had gone off to university while Allie had stayed in Heartcross working alongside her parents in the pub.

'I always said you were made for each other.' She grinned.

'You did, that.' Rory touched Felicity's arm tentatively before spotting his parents at the bar.

Taking a deep breath, Felicity turned the wrought iron ring of the pub's oak back door and stooped her head under the low frame, stepping down the stone steps into the pub's living quarters. She could hear footsteps from the backyard and spotted Allie lugging wood in from the shed, placing the logs in large wicker baskets. The last time she'd seen Allie was the night she'd left Heartcross. Felicity truly regretted cutting out everyone from her life, but it had been the only way she could cope at the time. Standing there, she suddenly yearned for her old friendship. A friendship that had stood the test of time until she'd taken herself off to London.

Felicity took a deep breath before speaking. 'Hey,' she said softly, causing Allie to jump and spin round. 'I didn't mean to startle you.'

For a brief moment, Allie just stared at her which left Felicity unsure of what to say next.

'You okay?' added Felicity quickly.

'I didn't expect to see you ... it's been a while,' Allie answered as she carried on throwing logs in to the basket and looked away.

Felicity walked towards her and leant against the door frame.

'I'm back to see Mum after Grandma...' Felicity's voice faltered.

'I'm sorry about Bonnie, we all are. Everyone really misses her.' Allie's tone was sincere and she softened for a moment.

'Thanks, it's a difficult time, especially for Mum.'

Feeling emotional, tears welled up in Felicity's eyes and there was a distinctive wobble in her voice. They both stared at each other for a moment in an awkward silence.

Felicity was hoping that Allie would step forward with her arms open wide, but it wasn't forthcoming. She knew she'd treated her friend appallingly in the past but she hadn't been thinking about anyone else when she'd left Heartcross. Only about protecting herself.

'Allie...' Felicity took a breath. 'I'm—'

'Let's not do this now,' Allie interrupted. 'There's a pub full of hungry people, and I really need to help Mum behind the bar.'

Felicity nodded. 'Soon?'

'Soon.'

Allie carried one of the baskets of logs and Felicity grabbed the other before following Allie back through the oak door and into the pub. 'Rory just told me you're together. I always said you were a match made in heaven,' said Felicity, trying to lighten the mood and make conversation.

Allie hitched a small smile on her face but didn't say

a word. Felicity could still feel a frosty tension between them. Allie wasn't as forgiving as Isla.

'You do make the perfect couple,' Felicity continued.

They placed the wicker baskets on each side of the log fire. 'Yes, we do. We all used to say the same about you and Fergus.' Allie's tone was curt.

Felicity did her best not to let it upset her, but she knew Allie was never going to be a pushover and let her back in like Isla.

'I've seen Isla too ... I didn't realise she had another baby on the way.' Felicity tried to soften the conversation.

'Well and truly on the way, in fact it could arrive at any time,' answered Allie, swooping up the empty glasses from the nearby table but not catching her eye.

Felicity swallowed and took a deep breath. 'Isla's suggested maybe we have a proper catch up ... that's if you're free?'

Allie thought for a second. 'We'll see... tomorrow is my night off,' she replied, giving Felicity a glimmer of hope.

Felicity watched as Allie spotted Rory and smiled before disappearing back behind the bar to serve the customers.

'So, how is life in the big city? Single, married...?' probed Rory as Felicity stood next to him at the bar.

Felicity let out a breath. 'Very much single.'

'Really?' His eyes widened.

'I know it's hard to believe,' joked Felicity, 'but really.'

'How's the job?' Rory perched on the stool and Felicity sat next to him.

'That's not going brilliant either,' she admitted. 'It's all doom and gloom in the life of Felicity Simons.'

'Really? Your mum seems to think everything is hunky dory, working so hard that you couldn't even have time off over Christmas.'

Instantly Felicity felt guilty once more. 'That's what I'd like her to think.' She took a swooping glance over towards her mum who was chatting away to Rory's parents, Stuart and Alana, at the other end of the bar.

'The department store where I work has been sold to a company that has new ideas and seems more interested in making money than any sort of decent customer service. Let's just say I don't exactly gel with the new boss.'

'One of those "let's stamp my mark and change every-thing" types?' asked Rory. 'What do you think you are going to do about it?'

'I've absolutely no idea,' she sighed. 'Going into work these days has had all the fun squeezed out of it. Time for a change I suppose ... but I need to work out what that change is. How's life at the practice?' asked Felicity, taking a swig of her drink.

'Good, really good. How long are you around for?'

'A couple of weeks.'

'Plenty of time to catch up then,' he said, touching her gently on the shoulder.

Felicity had always liked Rory. He was such a kind-hearted person, always there with a smile on his face – someone who would do anything for anyone. She took a moment to think about Fergus. Allie had a good man in Rory and she knew that she'd always had a good man in Fergus. If only...

Starting to feel peckish, Felicity glanced over her shoulder and noticed a queue forming at the end of the long trestle table. At that very moment, Allie rang the bell behind the bar and shouted, 'Help yourself to food!'

Within seconds, the lids of the aluminium pots were removed and the villagers began to spoon vast amounts of good wholesome food into their bowls.

Rona was near the front of queue. She made her way over to Felicity, offering her a bowl of chilli that Felicity gladly took from her mum's hand.

By now, Rory had joined Allie and they were chatting with some of the other locals who were staring out of the window to the white street. The snow was still falling thick and fast. Felicity sat by the window and watched the flakes as she ate the delicious food. There was something very romantic about the first fall of snow.

She remembered a time when she had been woken up by the sound of a thud on her window pane. Thinking that a bird had flown into her window, she'd jumped out of bed only to find that snow had fallen through the night, and there standing in her garden was Fergus grinning up at her. He'd built the biggest snowman she'd ever set eyes on and was throwing snowballs at her window. They'd spent the day sledging on Heartcross Hill along with the rest of the villagers. It had been such fun and that was when she'd realised how strongly she was attracted to him. He was her ideal man and she'd fallen hook, line and sinker for Fergus Campbell.

'Penny for them?' asked Rona, who sat down next to Felicity and took a fleeting glance outside at the freshly fallen snow.

'Ah, it's nothing,' Felicity replied, although she didn't sound convincing. She didn't want to admit how she'd messed up her life by running away to the big smoke, but sitting in the pub for the first time in a long time she realised she missed the familiarity of this place and the people who lived here.

She knew her time in London was nearly up and that she was falling out of love with the place. It had served a purpose at a time she needed it most but now she needed to make some tough decisions about her job and her life.

Rona didn't press her daughter. She took the hint and changed the subject, but not before saying, 'You know where I am if you want to talk.'

'Thanks Mum,' Felicity said, taking a sip of her drink.

Considering the number of villagers standing around, they were all relatively quiet while eating their food.

Felicity felt a slight draught as the pub door swung open. She didn't realise she'd let out a long shuddering sigh, until Rona looked up. 'You okay?'

Felicity didn't answer and Rona followed her daughter's gaze. Aggie Campbell had just walked into the pub.

Aggie hadn't changed a bit over the years. A thin woman, around five foot five, she had a slim build and long dark hair. She was dressed casually in jeans, a tweed jacket with a neck scarf, and she stamped her snow boots on the mat and took off her gloves before rubbing her hands together. Both Fraser and Meredith shouted a warm welcome over the bar to her.

Felicity knew her mum's relationship had suffered with Aggie when she'd ran from the village. Before that, they'd been good friends and often enjoyed nights out with each other. Aggie had even worked at the teashop when Rona and Bonnie had been short staffed. But then Felicity had broken her son's heart and everything had changed. Afterwards, their friendship had become very strained knowing the pain each of their offspring was suffering.

The second Aggie's eyes met Felicity's, they narrowed, and she stopped dead in her tracks. This was a moment Felicity hadn't been looking forward to and, feeling anxious, she shifted her bowl to make room for her elbows on the table and waited to see what would happen next. Her heart was thumping fast and she wondered frantically how she could make herself invisible, but it was too late. She could see Aggie walking over in their direction.

'Well, you're back then?' Aggie coughed, bringing her hand to her chest. She tried to compose herself and wiped her mouth with a tissue.

Felicity looked up at Aggie who was now standing at the side of the table, her expression revealing exactly how she was feeling.

'Aggie, we don't want any trouble. We are just grabbing some food like everyone else in the village.' Rona's tone was firm.

Felicity shifted uncomfortably in her seat.

Aggie coughed some more before attempting to speak again. 'I hope you have the good grace to stay away from Fergus while you're here.'

There was no sign of the friendly woman Felicity had once known. There'd been a time when Felicity would have considered Aggie a good friend, another mother figure in her life. Whilst Felicity had been with Fergus, she'd spent many a Sunday afternoon curled up on Aggie's sofa watching films after enjoying a huge roast dinner cooked by Aggie alongside a mouth-watering dessert. But once they'd split, Aggie had changed towards Felicity in a heartbeat, the relationship they once had completely evaporated. The last time Felicity had seen Aggie had been the night she'd left Heartcross, Fergus sobbing in her arms, screaming at the taxi for Felicity to stay. But Felicity had left, leaving a devastated Fergus standing on Love Heart Lane, his heart breaking and hers too.

Felicity knew Aggie had good reason to be cold and was obviously determined that Felicity should still suffer for her actions all those years ago.

Thankfully, Felicity and Rona didn't have a chance to respond.

'Grandma, Grandma,' an excited voice squealed. 'Have you seen the snow?' Esme appeared in the pub with a woman that Felicity had never seen before.

Aggie coughed again before she spun round to see her granddaughter running towards her. She opened her arms wide before the little girl launched herself at Aggie who spun her around a couple of times while she giggled. Placing her feet firmly back on the floor Aggie kissed the girl on both cheeks then grasped her hands.

'Let's get you something to eat and you know what, with all this snow still falling there will be no school tomorrow which means...'

'We can build the biggest snowman ever!' the girl shrieked.

Felicity watched Aggie wander over towards the food table still chatting away to her granddaughter and felt a tug at her heart. The little girl standing in front of her with a string of russet freckles scattered across her nose and those big brown eyes must be Fergus's daughter.

'Is that...'

'Yes, that's Esme,' said Rona, squeezing her daughter's hand.

All Felicity could do was stare at the beautiful little girl. Of course, she knew Esme existed and that Fergus was now a proud dad, but over the years she'd tried not to think about it. Esme must be around six years old now, and Felicity could still remember the night her mum had telephoned her in London to tell her the news that Fergus was expecting a child. Her heart felt as though it had been stabbed, it hurt that much. And although it had been her choice to leave Heartcross, she'd never thought that Fergus would move on so quickly. For her it had still been way too soon.

Felicity hadn't asked her mum for details. In fact, she told her mum that she didn't want any more updates from Heartcross, and that was when she'd cut herself off from everyone here.

She knew it wasn't going to be easy coming back. As

she finished her drink she spotted Isla and Drew who'd slipped in through the back door and tried to fix a smile on her face. Isla was clutching the hand of a handsome little boy, similar in age to Esme. The second he saw Esme he ran off towards her. Drew weaved his way to the bar leaving Isla to have a look around, and when she spotted Felicity and Rona sitting at the table in the window, she smiled and made her way over.

'Drew said you'd be here ... do you mind if we join you?'

'Be my guest,' answered Felicity, gesturing to the empty chair. She watched Isla slump into it.

'I'll be glad to get this little mite out, I feel like a barrel.'

Rona smiled. 'Then the fun really begins.'

'How's things?' Isla tactfully nodded her head towards Allie.

'A little frosty but I did mention about getting together very soon.'

'And...'

'And she didn't say no.'

'That's a start. I'll catch up with her in a minute and see when she's free, but with this weather I'm not sure I'm up to waddling very far. Maybe you could both come over to the farm? I'll get Finn into bed early and cook us something nice to eat.'

'Are you sure?'

'Absolutely.'

'Sounds like a plan,' said Felicity who also didn't want to venture out too far in this weather.

Drew appeared back at the table with a smile and handed a drink to Isla. 'Shall I get us some food?'

'That would be lovely.' Isla smiled up at him, not wanting to put any more weight on her feet just yet. Drew gave his wife a quick peck on the top of her head then disappeared off towards the table of food.

There was some sort of commotion going on in the far corner of the pub and raised voices could be heard. Rona strained her neck to see what was going on, before standing up and making her way over to the group of villagers that were huddled in the corner. Hamish was trying to calm things down and looked very official standing there with his pen poised against a clipboard.

'That all looks very serious,' commented Felicity to Isla. 'What's going on?'

'Urgent meeting, because of the snow. There's no deliveries scheduled now for a few more days and the bad weather has come early, taking everyone by surprise.'

Felicity knew the delivery trucks into Heartcross ran like clockwork, and everyone relied on them. Usually even in the bleakest mid-winters everything ran smoothly but for a meeting to be held, there must be real concerns.

'But Heartcross is used to this kind of weather and

is usually prepared,' said Felicity, still looking in the direction of Hamish.

'Usually, but we all thought we had a couple more days until the weather turned. Hamish had upped the grocery delivery to the shop but with this severe snow-fall no more trucks will be able to get through until the snow thaws,' said Isla with concern.

Drew appeared by Isla's side and handed her a bowl. 'Here, eat this.'

'Thanks. How's Hamish getting on over there? Have you listened in?' asked Isla, seeing even more villagers gathering around.

'Hamish is making it pretty clear he can't just sell the produce on the shelves to one person, and that it needs to be distributed fairly to each household until the delivery trucks can get through. But people are concerned and they're arguing amongst themselves, that's why I've escaped for a second ... taking a breather.'

'Any news on the school?' asked Isla, noticing Jessica, Finn's teacher, chatting to Rory.

Felicity looked up, Jessica was the woman who'd brought Esme into the pub.

'Not only is Jessica stranded in the village due to the weather, she's just announced the school is closed until further notice. She's had to rent a room with Julia at the B&B. There's no way she can drive her car down the track and over the bridge.' Drew placed his hand in the small of his wife's back. 'Which means Finn is going to be home from tomorrow but I promise I'll help out as much as I can.'

There was no hiding Isla's sigh, she barely had the energy to put on her own socks never mind entertain a six-year-old.

'Normally, I wouldn't mind. I enjoy him being home but it's just a little tiring at the moment waiting for this one to make an appearance.' She patted her stomach and felt a kick. 'He's being a little live wire tonight.'

'I can help out while I'm here. I had visions of me working in the teashop to pass some time but...'

'Give your mum some time, it's been difficult,' interrupted Isla. 'And thank you, I'd love to see as much of you as possible whilst your back.' Isla smiled at Felicity, meaning every word.

Their conversation was interrupted by the sound of Hamish raising his voice, 'If anyone would like to volunteer...' He looked hopefully at the crowd of people.

No one answered.

'You can't all stand here demanding to know how I'll allocate my produce when no one is willing to help.' He sounded exasperated.

Felicity stood up and wandered over to the crowd. 'What is it you need Hamish?'

'I need another pair of hands. Firstly, we need to concentrate on the perishable goods and make sure it doesn't go to waste and then we need to come up with a plan for the rest of the stock.'

Felicity determinedly stepped forward. 'I'll help you with that, no problem.' Felicity knew that with her own experience at work, she could easily scan through the stock lists and share out the food as fairly as possible. 'I've got time on my hands while I'm home.'

Hamish's face lit up. 'Felicity Simons, are you serious?'

'Deadly serious.'

'You are a gem.' He beamed, looking like a huge weight had lifted from his shoulders.

'What time do you want me in the morning?'

'Eight o'clock?'

'Eight o'clock it is.' She smiled at Hamish before noticing the proud smile on her mum's face. 'Can I make a small suggestion?'

'Of course,' answered Hamish, waiting to hear what Felicity had to say.

'Priority food maybe needs to go to the care home first, the elderly.'

'Indeed, we can draw up a list and hopefully the next truck will be able to get through as soon as the snow thaws.'

Everyone agreed, and Felicity joined Isla back at the table.

'Look at you,' grinned Isla as Felicity sat back down opposite her. 'Back in Heartcross two minutes and taking control. Hamish will never want to let you go if you can keep that lot in order.'

'Well, someone had to step in. Otherwise those perishable goods would be even more perishable by the time they sorted themselves out.'

Isla tried to laugh but her face paled. She clutched her stomach before letting out a tiny groan.

'What is it?'

'How are you at delivering babies?' She sucked in a breath and grimaced.

Instantly, Felicity felt her eyes well up with tears and swallowed down the lump in her throat. Her body surged with emotions she'd managed to keep locked away for a very long time, taking her by complete surprise. The guilt always hit first, wondering if she could have done something different – was the miscarriage down to her, could she have done anything else? The sense of loss never left her.

Isla noticed the colour had drained from Felicity's face.

'Oh my gosh, Flick, I'm so sorry, I really wasn't thinking,' said Isla, immediately reaching over the table and squeezing her hand.

'It's okay, really it is,' Felicity replied, her voice shaky. 'Shall I get Drew or even Rory?'

'Rory ... he's a vet!' Isla laughed, trying to lighten the mood but still clutching her stomach tightly.

'It's got to be the same difference, delivery of a baby or a lamb,' smiled Felicity.

'Luckily for everyone it's those Braxton Hicks, nothing to worry about. I'm sorry Flick, I really didn't mean to upset you.'

'I know you didn't. And I can't hide myself away from every pregnant woman I see,' said Felicity, even though she knew for a very long time she hadn't been able to even look at a pregnant woman.

'Are you going to try and talk to Fergus while you're back?'

'Aggie's already warned me off him.'

Isla rolled her eyes, 'She's been under the weather recently; she's got this cough that she can't shift so her mood is probably not the best, but you know Aggie from old … her bark's worse than her bite. Your reasons for leaving were about you. You were grieving and had to do what you needed to do. No one should judge you for it.'

Felicity was grateful that Isla understood.

'Aggie doesn't see it like that.'

'She didn't like to see her boy hurt but it still doesn't give her the right to treat you with a lack of respect. You both went through a difficult time. Time moves on, people move on.'

'Fergus has moved on,' added Felicity, glancing in Esme's direction.

Isla followed her gaze. 'She's a wonderful little girl, beautiful inside and out. You'll like her.'

'Fergus can't even bear to look at me.'

'He will, give it time. It's the first time he's set eyes on you since then. Even though I do know you've sneaked back a few times without seeing any of us.' Isla tutted playfully.

'I am sorry about that,' said Felicity regretfully.

'It's okay, honestly it is. There were a few people that were hurt when you upped and left including me and Allie but we knew why. We knew you needed space, we just didn't think it would be eight years of space.'

'Time drifted on but I don't think Allie will be as forgiving as you.' Felicity blew out a breath and glanced in her direction. She was standing by the bar laughing with Rory but caught her eye for a split second.

'We both know Allie from old, strong willed, stubborn but whatever she says, she's missed you like crazy. We all have. Grief is real and however long you needed, your crazy friends are still here. She'll come round ... we haven't gone anywhere.'

For a time, Felicity's life had descended into complete darkness. It had taken awhile but she had come a long way over the last eight years. Felicity's eyes glistened with tears as she felt an overwhelming feeling of love and belonging for her old village. She smiled across the table at her friend knowing that she had missed this place more than she wanted to admit. Everything felt right and familiar.

'Promise me one thing, Isla.'

'Go on,' Isla met her gaze.

'Just try and hold that baby in until we can get across the bridge and drive you to the hospital.'

'I'll try my very best for you. And I'm glad you've come home, I for one have really missed you.'

Felicity squeezed Isla's hand. She knew she had a few bridges to mend but having Isla back on her side gave her an overwhelming feeling of warmth. She'd missed Isla too.

Chapter 6

Felicity was up at the crack of dawn, woken by the chill in the air. She shivered and pulled the duvet up tight around her neck but it was no use, she couldn't get warm. Her feet felt like blocks of ice and her teeth were chattering. How could her mum live like this? She tossed and turned but it was no use, she couldn't get back to sleep. Slipping her socks onto her feet and a jumper over her head, she padded quietly downstairs in need of a warm drink. Everywhere was in complete darkness and Felicity looked up at the clock; it was only 6.30 a.m.

After placing the kettle on the Aga she pulled back the curtains and couldn't believe her eyes, the snow was actually still falling. There was no way the delivery trucks would be getting through until this began to thaw and Hamish had been right to think about rationing the food supplies in the village.

Felicity noticed the light was on in Rory's living room

opposite, but as she watched, it immediately turned off and his front door opened. As Rory stepped outside, his wellington boots disappeared under inches of snow. He didn't attempt to start his car; instead he clutched tightly on to his bag and with his head bent low, he ploughed through the snow in the direction of the veterinary practice. Hearing the kettle begin to whistle, Felicity made herself a coffee and made up the fire. Hopefully by the time her mum was awake there should be a little more warmth in the cottage. After the fire was lit and she'd drained her mug, she placed the kettle on the Aga once more, so she could use the warm water to have a wash. She didn't relish the idea of a cold shower in this weather. Before she could forget, she tucked the boiler quote into her bag, so she could arrange for them to come out to the cottage as soon as possible.

Within the hour, and with Rona still fast asleep, Felicity wrapped up warm, sank her feet inside her wellington boots and closed the front door quietly behind her. The whole of Love Heart Lane lay in complete darkness, everyone still fast asleep making the most of not going to school or work. The early morning chill instantly nipped at her face and she buried her chin under her scarf and clutched her bag against her body. Even though her thermal socks swathed her feet they instantly felt frozen. Her footsteps were small, the snow sinking halfway up her boots. It was difficult to walk in such conditions, and her legs felt heavy but she knew with each small step she was getting closer to Hamish's shop.

When she reached the shop the light was on and as she pushed open the door the bell tinkled above her head, alerting Hamish to her arrival. He looked up from behind the counter and smiled. 'You made it then! There's tea in the pot.'

'Thank you,' she answered, peeling the scarf from around her head and placing her white flaky sodden hat on top of the counter. 'Where do we start?' asked Felicity, skimming a glance around the shop before pouring herself a cup of tea.

'I've moved all the perishable goods into these boxes, and somehow we need to get these up to the care home.'

Felicity cocked an eyebrow. 'That's a half-mile climb up the hill.'

Hamish blew out a breath. 'I know – it's going to be a struggle but they will need the food for the residents.'

'We can do this, we won't be defeated,' answered Felicity with vigour and determination and a smile on her face.

'That's the spirit. The things over in that corner—' Hamish pointed '—are the tinned and packet items that go out of date first.'

Hamish had worked out what food was going where to keep the community fed over the next few days until the trucks could get through. All Felicity had to do was help to bag it up and get it delivered. They set to work and within thirty minutes there were carrier bags of food parcels lined up by the door ready and waiting to be delivered.

It was just at that moment the door opened and they both looked up to see a cold, red-faced Rory staring back at them.

'Good morning, how are the troops?'

Hamish smiled. 'Just preparing ourselves mentally and physically to begin the deliveries.'

'Mrs Hughes from the care home has just logged a call at the surgery. Remy the cat is a little under the weather so I'm off up there to take a look at him.'

'Does that mean what I think it means?' chipped in Felicity with her fingers firmly crossed behind her back.

Rory grinned. 'I'll take with me whatever you have.'

'You, my good friend, are a life saver,' said Hamish. 'Can you manage three carrier bags and this box?' Hamish looked hopeful while Rory began to juggle the food. 'If you get the door I should be okay.'

Hamish couldn't thank Rory enough as he set off towards the care home through nine inches of snow, with more flakes still falling.

'Are you okay delivering those bags to the residents of Love Heart Lane and I'll start at the opposite end of the village?'

'Of course,' answered Felicity, glancing at the clock. 'But can I use the landline before I go, I need to ring the plumber to arrange for Mum's boiler to be fixed.'

Hamish nodded towards the phone and while he bundled himself up in numerous layers Felicity made the call. As soon as she hung up, he noticed Felicity looked a little deflated. 'You all right?'

'I never thought, the plumber lives over the bridge in Glensheil, there's no way he's getting his van across the bridge and up the hill in this snow, but he's promised as soon as he can he will.'

'That's all you can ask for at times like this.'

Once Hamish and Felicity were ready, they each grabbed a handful of carrier bags and stepped outside into the freezing cold.

Hamish gave Felicity a nod of his appreciation and then they both battled through the snow. Hamish had stapled the names and addresses of the deliveries on to each bag. Felicity looked at the first one labelled Mr and Mrs Smith, an elderly couple she knew had been married for nearly fifty years. From what Felicity could remember they had numerous grandchildren.

The streets were silent and still in darkness as Felicity's feet crunched through the snow. No doubt by lunchtime the children would be out in full force sledging and building snowmen, enjoying the freedom from school.

As she approached the first house Felicity was relieved to see the light was on in Mr and Mrs Smith's living room and the second she knocked on the front door she heard a dog bark followed by the sound of keys being jangled. When the door swung open Felicity was met by Mrs Smith's rosy cheeks and beaming smile.

'Come on in, out of the cold.'

She wiped her hands down on her pinny and ushered Felicity into the warmth of the kitchen. She was amazed to find six pair of eyes sitting around the table staring back at her.

'It's lovely to see you back in Heartcross.' Mrs Smith patted Felicity's arm. 'We are so sorry to hear about Bonnie.'

'Thank you,' replied Felicity, touched by Mrs Smith's kindness. 'And look at all these little people. You've got your hands full today,' she said, changing the subject in an attempt to stop the tears instantly welling in her eyes at the mention of her grandmother.

'School's shut, which means Grandma here gets to look after all these bundles of joy today and believe me it's like a military operation to get them all fed. It's like my own little café,' she chuckled. 'But I'm not complaining, they keep me young.'

'This may help, a few supplies from Hamish – eggs, bread and a few essentials.' Felicity held up the carrier bag.

'He's a good one, that man.' Mrs Smith smiled, taking a quick peep inside the bag before laying it on top of the worktop. 'Please do thank him from us. Where are you off to next?'

Felicity looked at the name attached to the next carrier bag. 'Aggie's,' she said with a double take. She was sure that was one of Hamish's deliveries; she must have picked up the wrong bag by mistake. Felicity felt her heart beat a little faster. After Aggie's outburst in the pub last night she was sure the last person she'd want to see was Felicity, who felt the same.

'That poor woman hasn't been well,' Mrs Smith chipped in without noticing that Felicity's mood had suddenly slumped.

'Who, Aggie?' Felicity had noticed the cough in the pub and her wheezy chest.

'Terrible chest infection, I think it's the asthma, you see. She's not been able to shake it off for a while.'

'This weather won't help either,' said Felicity, making her way to the door after saying farewell to all the children who'd now finished their breakfasts and were busily putting their dirty bowls in the dishwasher.

'What's your plan of action for the rest of the day?' asked Felicity, watching the children pile in front of the log fire with a board game in hand.

'Keep warm.' Mrs Smith smiled. 'But I'm sure there will be an army of snowmen standing proud in the front garden by the end of the day, followed by a heap of soggy gloves and hats drying out on the Aga.'

Felicity said goodbye and after stepping back into the cold she took a deep breath and made her way towards Fox Hollow Cottage. Aggie and her husband Glen had lived in the cottage for all their married life but sadly he'd passed away nearly ten years ago after a short battle with cancer. Aggie had never remarried and as far as Felicity knew, Fergus still lived at the cottage with his new family.

As she trudged through the snow she saw a warm ribbon of smoke rising from the old chimney of the cottage which meant the fire was lit and someone was up. Felicity's heart pounded a little but, knowing that Fergus would have been up and out at the crack of dawn working at the farm, she knew it was unlikely she'd see him. It would just be Aggie's sharp tongue she'd have to deal with if last night was anything to go by. All she had to do was be polite, hand the bag over, and get on with the next delivery. She juggled the carrier bags in her hands before opening the garden gate. The way had been cleared and gritted and as Felicity carefully manoeuvred herself up the path, she noticed a pair of bright red wellington boots abandoned under the oak beam porch. She assumed they were Esme's.

Feeling a little apprehensive, she blew out a breath. Last night in the pub Aggie hadn't welcomed her home with open arms and Felicity didn't relish seeing her again so soon, but this was in in aid of the community and she'd offered to help Hamish. Felicity rapped on the lion door knocker and waited, but there was no reply. She tried once more before bowing her head and peering through the front window of the cottage. The fire was roaring and stretched out on the rug in front was Martha, the Campbells' black and white cat. There was no one else around but Felicity noticed the TV flickering away in the corner. Just at that second, movement caught her eye, and Felicity noticed Esme curled up on the old chesterfield. The little girl was crying, tears running down her cheeks. For a second, Felicity didn't know what to do. In spite of the past, Felicity couldn't leave the little girl crying. And where was Aggie? Without hesitation she turned the knob of the front door and immediately it clicked and opened.

Felicity stood in the hallway. The last time she'd been standing in this very spot was over eight years ago and she was surprised to see that everything seemed exactly the same. The wooden beams ran the length of the ceiling, the coat stand in the corner housed numerous jackets and hats and the antique dresser was jam-packed with family photographs.

'Hello,' Felicity shouted up the hallway towards the open door of the living room. She stayed rooted to the spot and called out again, then saw two startled, teary eyes peering around the doorway at her.

'Hello. It's Esme, isn't it? I'm Felicity.'

The wide-eyed little girl nodded and gulped back a sob.

'Hey, don't cry,' said Felicity softly. 'Where's your nana?'

Esme didn't say anything.

Felicity bent down to her level, and slowly stuck out her hand. Esme reached forward and politely shook it.

'I've brought some food for your nana from Hamish.' She held up the carrier bag. 'Where would you like me to put it?'

Esme shrugged.

'Is your nana here?'

This time Esme nodded and pointed towards the stairs. Felicity couldn't hear any movement and called out to Aggie.

'Is your nana okay?' asked Felicity, flicking a glance between the little girl and the top of the stairs.

'Nana's not well. She's asleep in bed.'

There was no denying the uneasy feeling in her stomach as Felicity quickly slipped off her boots and climbed the stairs. Felicity knew that Aggie's bedroom was the first door on the right at the top of the stairs. Slowly she pushed open the bedroom door and saw Aggie lying in bed.

'Aggie, it's me, Felicity. Are you okay?' She hovered nervously in the doorway.

Aggie didn't respond but Felicity could see the rise and fall of her chest. Feeling like she was intruding, she stepped into the room, not knowing how Aggie would react when she opened her eyes – but knowing there was a small child by herself it was a risk she was willing to take.

Felicity moved closer to the bed and was aware Esme was now right behind her. She turned towards the little girl. 'Is your daddy at work?'

'Yes, he's at the farm with Uncle Drew.'

Felicity knew that Drew wasn't a proper uncle, but it was lovely to hear him being referred to in that way.

'I'm going to check that your nana is okay, and then I'm going to ring your dad.'

Just at that second, Aggie's eyes opened.

'Aggie, it's me Felicity,' she said softly, trying not to frighten Aggie.

She looked up at Felicity pointedly, attempted to clear her throat but began to cough.

Immediately, Felicity grabbed the glass of water sitting on the bedside table and brought it up to her lips. Aggie took a sip and finally when she got her coughing under control, Felicity placed the drink back next to her bed.

'What are you doing here? In my house?' Aggie's tone was bordering on aggressive. She looked dreadful and pale.

'I don't mean to intrude,' Felicity approached with

caution, 'but I brought you food from Hamish and found Esme crying downstairs.'

Now it was Aggie's turn to look alarmed. 'What time is it?'

'Just before 10 a.m.'

'I must have drifted back off to sleep,' said Aggie, still spluttering.

Felicity quickly turned towards Esme. 'Your nana's feeling a little unwell and I'm going to make her as comfortable as possible. Would you go and put the food on the kitchen table for me, Esme?'

Esme nodded and Felicity could hear her footsteps echoing down the stairs and into the kitchen.

This time Aggie coughed up thick yellow-green, blood-stained mucus into the bowl next to her. Once she stopped Felicity took the bowl from Aggie and rinsed it out in the bathroom before placing it back at the side of her bed.

'You need to see a doctor. Have you rung Dr. Taylor?'

Aggie shook her head. 'I'm okay.'

Felicity knew she was far from okay. Aggie's breathing was rapid and shallow. Felicity pressed a hand to her forehead; she was burning up.

'You have a fever,' said Felicity, seeing that Aggie was sweating and shivering.

'Honestly, I'm okay,' she said in a tone that indicated she didn't want Felicity interfering.

Aggie began to cough again and clutched her chest. 'Whether you like me or not Aggie, I can't leave you like this – let me get help. What about Esme's mum?'

For a fleeting moment, Aggie looked like she was about to say something but didn't have the strength. 'Okay, if it's all right with you I'm going to take Esme with me,' said Felicity softly, not wanting to leave the little girl here by herself with Aggie in this state.

She shook her head. 'You can't, Fergus won't like that,' she wheezed.

'When he sees the bigger picture, he'll understand. I'm going to take Esme and drop her off with my mum. You can't look after her in this state and then I'm going to walk to the surgery to get you some help. It's non-negotiable.'

Aggie didn't have the strength to fight and nodded her understanding.

'Is there anything I can get you before I leave?'

Aggie shook her head and Esme peered back around the bedroom door. Aggie reached out her hand and the little girl grabbed it. 'Felicity is going to look after you today, Esme, while Nana has a little rest. Is that ok?'

Esme's eyes widened and looked towards Felicity who crouched down next to her. 'I'm going to take you to visit my mum, Rona.'

'Rona...' Aggie coughed and took a breath. 'Rona is the lady from Bonnie's Teashop.'

'The shop with the delicious sticky buns,' said Esme with delight.

'That's the one, but the teashop's been closed for a while so there won't be any sticky buns today.'

Esme looked a little disappointed.

'Fergus ... will you let Fergus know?'

Felicity could see the worry etched on Aggie's face.

'Yes I will, don't worry. And I'm going to leave the front door open so Dr Taylor can let himself in.'

'Thank you,' said Aggie. They locked eyes for a brief second before Felicity plumped up her pillows and made her as comfortable as possible before promising she'd be back very soon. After wrapping Esme up in her winter woollies and retrieving the wellington boots from the porch, she clutched the rest of the deliveries in one hand and firmly gripped Esme's hand with the other as they made their way up Love Heart Lane.

'The snow is coming over the top of my wellies,' giggled Esme. 'It's so cold.'

Felicity looked down. 'You can't walk in this. There's only one thing for it – piggy back time.'

Esme squealed with delight as Felicity hoisted her on to her back and she wrapped her arms tightly around Felicity's neck. Felicity liked the feeling of Esme holding onto her so tightly, it was comforting. A feeling she hadn't felt for a very long time. Her thoughts flicked back to the past and a deep sadness hit her once more.

'Why did the teashop close down?' asked Esme, trying to lean over Felicity's shoulder to make eye contact.

'Because my lovely grandmother...'

'Is that Bonnie?' interrupted Esme.

'Yes, Bonnie became poorly and unfortunately she is no longer with us,' answered Felicity, gripping Esme's body firmly so she didn't flail on her back.

'Bonnie made the best gingerbread men and sticky buns. She told me...' Esme stopped mid-sentence. 'She told me all about her secret recipe book too.' Esme's eyes lit up and she let go of Felicity for a second, bringing her finger up to her mouth making a shushing sound.

Felicity stood still. 'My grandmother told you about the secret recipe book? You must have been a very special customer.'

Esme nodded with a huge beam on her face. 'Every Saturday morning I went to buy a gingerbread man with my pocket money.'

'I used to help my grandmother in the shop when I was growing up and she let me help her bake some of those recipes from that very book.'

'Wow! So, you knew about the secret recipe book too.'

'I did, which means you and I are very special people.' Felicity turned her head, smiled and started trudging through the snow once more.

'Daddy always says I'm his special gorgeous girl.'

Felicity's stomach immediately flipped. Before she'd left Heartcross that had been Fergus's special name for her too. It had melted her heart every time the words had left his lips but now she felt a tiny sad pang that he'd never use those words about her again.

'And your daddy would be right. Here we are,' Felicity said, pushing open the garden gate. 'This is where I grew up ... Heartwood Cottage.'

'Do you know my daddy?' asked Esme with such innocence.

'I do, we went to school together when we were little, but then I went to live in London,' answered Felicity, keeping to the facts. Before turning the key in the lock, she placed Esme firmly back on the ground then opened the door. Felicity could hear her mum beavering away in the kitchen.

'One day, do you think we could bake something out of the secret recipe book?' asked Esme, following Felicity into the hallway.

'I'm sure we could.' She smiled. In spite of sounding confident Felicity's heart sank a little, unsure whether she could actually keep that promise. Fergus wouldn't be best pleased knowing Esme was here with her now, but surely he would have done the same under the circumstances.

Rona appeared around the living-room door.

Thankfully she'd kept the fire going and Felicity could feel the cottage was warmer than when she'd left this morning.

'I thought I heard voices – who have we here?' said Rona shooting Felicity a puzzled look.

'Why don't you take your coat off and go and sit by the fire?' said Felicity while Rona showed Esme into the living room then quickly reappeared and pulled the door behind her.

'What's going on?' asked Rona in a hushed whisper.

Felicity blew out a breath. 'I was delivering the goods for Hamish when I went over to Aggie's and found her ill in bed.'

'Ill in what way?'

'Coughing up mucus. She also has a fever from what I can tell.'

'She's not been right for a while.'

'I've promised to go and see Dr Taylor. Esme was there by herself, I couldn't leave her. Aggie was too poorly to look after her.'

'And she let you take her?' The amazement in her mum's voice didn't go unnoticed.

'I didn't give her much choice. Aggie needs help.'

Rona listened to her daughter. 'You've done the right thing. You stay here with Esme while I go to the surgery and get help.' Felicity was secretly grateful for her mum's suggestion. She'd been up since the crack of dawn and this gave her the perfect opportunity to spend a little time with Esme.

'Are you sure?'

'Yes of course, and after I've been to the surgery I'll go over to Aggie's cottage and check on her.'

Rona grabbed her coat from the banister, slipped her feet inside her boots and opened the front door. 'It looks like it's stopped snowing.'

'Only just. Mum, can you take this bag? This one's for the surgery, teabags and milk etc.'

Rona nodded, taking the bag from her daughter's hand and pulling the cottage door shut behind her.

When Felicity walked into the living room, Esme had made herself right at home; she'd discovered the box of old games stored in a box under the old dresser and was now sitting in front of the fire piecing together a jigsaw.

Felicity took a moment and watched her. She was beautiful, the vision of her dad, her nose and lips the same shape as his. Esme looked up and smiled.

'Do you want to help me to do the jigsaw?'

'I do, but how about I make us some hot chocolate first?'

Esme gave Felicity a look of approval as she disappeared into the kitchen and placed the kettle on the Aga. Five minutes later, Felicity was sat down on the rug alongside Esme, with two calorific hot chocolates on a tray alongside two spoons.

'What's it like in London?' enquired Esme. 'Do you live in a huge house and have you visited the Queen?'

Felicity gave a small chuckle. 'No, I don't live in a huge house, I have a flat but I've walked past the palace lots of times.'

'Daddy promised me he'd take me to London one day.'

'And I'm sure he will.'

'We could visit you.' Esme's voice was hopeful.

'You could,' answered Felicity, feeling a little guilty knowing that Fergus would never allow that to happen and she was making promises she wouldn't be able to keep. 'But London is a big place, there's lots to explore.'

'What are we going to do today?' asked Esme, fitting the last piece of the jigsaw into the puzzle before stirring the hot chocolate with the spoon around in the mug.

Felicity thought for a second; she knew she needed to phone the farm to let Fergus know that Esme was with her. But she also knew exactly how he'd react and she was enjoying spending time with the little girl; surely another hour wouldn't hurt and that would leave him to carry on with his work up at the farm.

'I know exactly what we could do this morning.' Felicity stood up and reached out her hand which Esme promptly took. 'Come on,' she smiled. 'I've got just the job.'

Felicity led Esme through to the kitchen and placed the kettle on the Aga to warm up the water and opened the door next to the pantry which led into the teashop.

Esme's eyes widened as she looked around. 'Are we going to bake?'

'This place has been closed for a while, so I think it's a little too dusty to begin baking, but all in good time,' answered Felicity as Esme jumped up on to one of the tables and swung her legs over the side.

'Firstly, we need music. We can't work without music.'

Over in the corner was Bonnie's old Roberts radio. She'd liked the simple things in life and wasn't into all the new technology of the day. She wanted a radio that she could switch on and tune in. Felicity plugged it in before rescuing the whistling kettle from the Aga.

As she poured the hot water into a bucket and grabbed a couple of sponges, Esme had jumped off the counter and was now singing into the brush handle pretending it was a microphone. Felicity couldn't help but smile. This little girl definitely had character.

'Being a popstar is exhausting,' Esme giggled as the song came to an end and she took a bow.

Felicity clapped. 'And I'll be the first one in the queue to buy your concert tickets. You are a very good singer.'

'Daddy says I'm the best singer.'

'What does Mummy say?' asked Felicity, the words leaving her mouth before she had time to think.

Esme just shrugged then glanced down at the floor. To this day Felicity could still recount every word of the phone call from her mum when she'd discovered that Fergus had moved on and was expecting his own child. It flashed through her mind now – the pain that had twisted in her heart, the indescribable feeling. It had hurt that much she'd needed to catch her breath. At the time, she hadn't wanted him to move on and had been jealous that he suddenly had everything they'd ever dreamed of together. She knew in time it was bound to happen but for her it was too soon, and she hadn't wanted to listen to any more details. It struck her now that she had no idea who Esme's mother was or whether Fergus was still in a relationship with her.

The only way she had been able to cope was to block Fergus and his new family out of her life. And now Fergus's little girl was here with her. She was everything that Felicity had once dreamed of, before it had all been smashed away.

Now, taking the broom from Esme's hand, Felicity quickly changed the subject. 'Today, Esme Campbell, we are on a very special mission.'

'We are?' she questioned, smiling up at Felicity.

'We are indeed, do you see this place?' Felicity flung her arms open wide and Esme nodded.

'How do you fancy helping me transform this place back into the old teashop we love so much?'

Since Felicity had been home she'd begun to think about her life in London. In the past six months things had changed for her; work was no longer fun, she'd split up with her boyfriend and she'd started to question whether it was time for a change. This morning, helping Hamish in the shop, she'd felt wanted and helpful and felt part of the community once more. What was actually waiting for her back in London? A one-bedroom flat that was ridiculously expensive due to its location, and a job that she'd begun to detest with a passion? Being back in the teashop suddenly made her think differently about everything. This little tearoom, opened by her grandmother, had been a special place for Felicity and the community of Heartcross, and it didn't sit right with her that it was now closed.

Felicity's mind had already begun to whirl. What if Felicity and her mum re-opened the place? Once the snow had thawed it would be a thriving business again, and Felicity was even considering suggesting that she and her mum work together, maybe in partnership. She knew her mum would welcome her back with open arms but with so many memories would Felicity be able to cope seeing Fergus on a regular basis? That was something Felicity wasn't sure about. Even after all these years, the memories still hurt.

Esme considered it for a second. 'Do the workers get drinks and biscuits?'

'Absolutely, without a doubt. I'll pour us a couple of drinks and fingers crossed there's still a secret supply of biscuits in the cupboard,' Felicity smiled and rummaged in the back of the cupboard. 'My grandmother always used to keep an emergency supply just in case all of her homemade delights were sold. She didn't want to let the passing ramblers down ... here we are.' Felicity checked the sell-by date and quickly rinsed a plate from the rack. 'Help yourself, but you have to promise to give your teeth an extra brush tonight.' She locked eyes with Esme who gave her a cheeky grin.

'I promise,' she said, adding a splash of cold water to the bucket before dunking the sponge into it and giving it a squeeze.

'Let's start at the back of the shop and make our way to the front,' instructed Felicity as the pair of them set to work. Esme mirrored Felicity. She watched and copied her every move which gave Felicity a warm glow inside. They scrubbed, cleaned, brushed and danced their way around the shop for over an hour, before the pair of them rested their foreheads against the glass window and giggled as their breath steamed up the window. All the cleaning was far from being a chore. It was fun and the room was soon spick and span. Leaning back from the window, Felicity gave Esme a high five before Esme wrapped her arms around Felicity.

Felicity felt a sense of pride as she cast a glance around the teashop; she knew this would be one less job for her mum and hoped she would be pleased. She felt guilty that she'd never had a clue this place had closed but hopefully now it was clean it might just nudge her mum in the right direction to think about re-opening it again very soon.

Thud ... thud ... thud.

Startled, they both jumped round to see a face staring back at them through the window.

Fergus.

'What the hell is going on here?' he shouted through the glass. 'Open the door.'

Felicity gulped. Fergus was angry, his face was red.

'Your dad will just be worried about you, he didn't know you were here,' said Felicity, thankful her voice sounded relatively normal even though inside she was trembling. She'd got carried away with the time and had broken her promise to Aggie about letting Fergus know she was looking after Esme.

Fergus was already rattling the door but Felicity knew the keys to the shop would be hanging up in the pantry as she hurried to retrieve them. Once the door was unlocked Fergus stepped inside, and Felicity knew he was annoyed because his top lip twitched.

'Would you care to explain what is going on here?' he demanded.

Felicity took a second; she was a little breathless from her quick dash to get the keys. She smoothed down her hair and wished Fergus hadn't spotted them through the window. Fergus was staring straight into her eyes, wanting answers.

She turned towards Esme. 'Esme, would you go back into the living room and put the jigsaw away for me, please? I just need a quick chat with your dad.'

Esme nodded and immediately skipped back into the main cottage.

'I'll ask again. What are you doing with my daughter?'

Felicity took a breath and tried frantically to keep her voice low.

'Your mum is ill and couldn't look after her.'

Fergus narrowed his eyes. 'What are you on about?'

'I was delivering the food for Hamish this morning up at the cottage when I discovered Aggie was ill. Mum has gone to see Dr Taylor and she's sitting with her until he arrives, or you get home.'

'And you thought it was okay to take my daughter without asking me?' Felicity could hear the irritation in his voice.

'That wasn't my intention. Time just slipped by and once we began cleaning this place, I got carried away. And anyway, you were at work.' Felicity knew that wasn't the point and she should have rung the farm to let him know. He had every right to be mad at her.

Fergus blew out a breath.

'Your mum is ill. Did you expect me to leave her there, to fend for herself?' Felicity asked, slightly annoyed that Fergus couldn't see her side to the story.

'No, I'd expect you to ring the farm, and bring her up there if that was the case.'

At first, that had been Felicity's intention, but she'd liked spending time with Esme. She was funny, kind and inquisitive and time had just run away with them.

At that second, Esme reappeared clutching her coat and her wellington boots.

'Daddy, I've had the best time. Can I come back tomorrow if Nana isn't feeling any better? Can Felicity look after me again?'

Felicity noticed Fergus bristle.

He regarded his daughter for a few seconds then smiled. 'Let's go and see how Nana is.'

As he led Esme out through the door he turned back towards Felicity. 'Please just leave me alone while you're here.'

Fergus and Felicity exchanged glances.

His words cut through the air. There was once a time when they had been so close and now it had come to this. They were like two strangers and Felicity didn't like it one little bit. She knew he was hurting. She'd upped and left Heartcross without talking it through with him. They'd been a couple and had been through so much together, but grief had swathed Felicity and she'd convinced herself she was never going to be enough for him. Fergus had always wanted a family; they'd spent many hours discussing how many children they wanted and even imagined what they would look like.

But after Felicity had miscarried their second baby and the doctor had confirmed that she was unlikely to ever be a mother, she had been completely devastated. At that split second her whole world had turned upside down.

At the time, she'd never taken into account Fergus's feelings. She'd been in turmoil, scared of the future, and had believed Fergus was better off without her.

She'd made the decision to leave the village on New Year's Eve through devastating grief, and even though it had hurt her to the core, she had seen it as setting Fergus free. There would still be a chance for him to have children and become a father, even if it wouldn't be with her like they had planned. And even though she'd tried desperately to build a future without Fergus, he was never far from her thoughts.

As soon as the teashop door shut behind Fergus and Esme, Felicity burst into tears.

Chapter 7

Isla's little get together that evening was like no other. She opened the door to Foxglove Farm with a beam on her face as Felicity followed her into the kitchen. Even though Isla was nearly nine months' pregnant she'd pulled out all the stops and the dinner table was set to perfection.

'Look at this lot, it feels like Christmas,' said Felicity kissing her on the cheek and accepting a glass of wine from Isla.

'I thought I'd best dazzle you with table decorations and chocolates because dinner is the leftover curry we didn't eat last night.'

'Are you hoping to entice that wee one out with spicy food?'

'Something like that,' grinned Isla.

Drew appeared in the doorway play-wrestling with Finn who said a quick hello to Felicity before giving his mum a kiss good night and scampering up the stairs.

'I'll put him to bed, you girls enjoy your night.'

'Thank you,' said Isla as both she and Felicity stood looking out through the window at the magnificent views across the fields – acres of untouched snow and the bare winter trees frosted with sparkles.

'There is something romantic about snow,' said Felicity, sipping her wine. 'I've not seen snow like this since I left Heartcross.'

'I could watch it fall for hours but it's not good for the community, especially when we are cut off from civilisation. Hopefully it will begin to thaw soon then the kids will be back to school.'

'How have you coped with Finn being off today?'

Isla rolled her eyes. 'It's tiring, especially being in this state. My ankles are swollen and the heartburn is driving me insane!'

To Felicity, Isla looked blooming. Her hair was just so, and her make-up was perfect. She had a certain glow about her – pregnancy suited her.

'But less about me. I've heard you've had an eventful day.' Isla changed the subject as Felicity followed her into the living room and sat down next to Isla on the settee.

'News travels fast.'

'Some things never change in this village.' Isla squeezed Felicity's knee and smiled.

'How did you hear?'

'Fergus was on the phone to Drew soon after. I think we were all surprised Aggie let you take Esme.'

Felicity knew Aggie didn't have much choice. 'Even though we both know I'm not Aggie's favourite person...'

'You wouldn't see her stuck,' interrupted Isla. 'Especially if she's poorly.'

'Exactly. And Esme was great fun. She's a great little girl. We gave the teashop a good spring clean and it got me thinking.'

'We all know it's dangerous when you start thinking,' said Isla. 'You disappear for years on end.'

'Very funny.'

'Go on. What have you been thinking?'

'That my life in London isn't all that,' Felicity admitted to her friend.

Isla shuffled forward on the settee and placed her hand gently on her pregnant stomach. 'What do you mean, it isn't all that?'

'Exactly that; I think I've had enough of trying to live the high life. The dream didn't exactly pan out as I'd expected. In fact, it was never really the dream.'

'Flick, what's brought this on?'

'Being home, Grandma passing away, seeing how Mum has been struggling – but most of all I've realised I've actually missed this place and my friends.' Felicity blinked back the tears that had welled up in her eyes.

'Don't you start getting emotional on me.' Isla flapped

a hand in front of her face. 'Anything makes me cry at the minute.'

'Sorry, I didn't mean to make you cry.' Felicity took a breath. 'But this morning ... Esme helped me to clean up the teashop which got me thinking.'

'About?'

'About my grandmother and her passion for the place. It's sad to see it closed and I know we only gave it a quick going over, but it brought the place to life for me once more. I could see Grandma behind the counter, chatting with the customers with a beam on her face. And then there's Mum. I feel so guilty for not being there for her. She must have really struggled for the teashop to be shut.'

'So, what are you thinking?'

'That maybe I could make it up to them both ... maybe this was the push I needed to come back home and face up to everything and by everything, I mean the future too.'

'Are you trying to tell me that you're thinking of coming home and opening up the teashop?' As the penny dropped, Isla couldn't help the smile that spread across her face.

Felicity nodded. 'I think that's exactly what I'm trying to say. Do you think it's a mad idea?'

'Mad?' exclaimed Isla, 'I think it's a brilliant idea and I'm sure Rona would snap your hand off. It must be quite daunting for her to think of re-opening by herself without Bonnie by her side. Have you mentioned it to her yet?'

Felicity shook her head. She'd been mulling it over in her mind and this was the first time she'd voiced it to anyone.

Just at that second there was a knock on the farmhouse door. 'That'll be Allie,' said Isla, attempting to push herself up off the settee. 'And don't worry, she's secretly glad to have you back.'

'Isla, please don't say anything about my plans, I should speak to Mum about it first.'

Isla patted her stomach. 'Mum's the word.' She grinned.

They both heard the front door open and Felicity felt secretly worried about how the night would pan out now Allie had arrived.

'Are my ears burning? Sorry, I let myself in ... I kind of knew you'd be stranded on the sofa, not wanting to get up.' Allie stood in the doorway, smiling at Isla, holding up a bottle of wine and sparkling lemonade. 'And I've brought supplies,' she said, placing the bottle on the table before turning towards Felicity with a hint of sarcasm. 'So, you're still here?' She looked straight at Felicity who felt a little uncomfortable. She knew Allie was never going to let the past go without getting a dig in. She always had to have the last word.

Isla shot Allie an exasperated look. All she wanted was a peaceful night and she was hoping all bridges would be mended.

'Of course I am,' Felicity replied, trying to smile.

Allie made herself comfortable on the chair opposite Felicity and tucked her feet underneath her.

'We do know you've been back over the years,' huffed Allie with a disgruntled look on her face. 'And you didn't think to come and say hello?'

Felicity instantly felt guilty. Allie was right, she had been back over the years, but it had always been a very short visit in fear of bumping into Fergus.

'I just wasn't ready to see anyone.'

'Not even your friends who have been there for you since primary school?'

Felicity knew Allie had a bee in her bonnet and wasn't going to let it drop but she didn't want a row with her either. It had been difficult for her, but she also knew Allie's reaction was entirely appropriate. At the time she'd left and tried to put Heartcross behind her, it had been about self-preservation and coping with her own tragedy. She hadn't meant to hurt anyone else, but she knew she had.

Felicity didn't know what to say, and an uncomfortable silence hung in the air.

'There we all were, enjoying New Year's Eve and the next minute you'd disappeared for almost eight years.

You didn't even tell us you were going.' Allie was not going to let the subject go easily.

'I wasn't thinking, I really wasn't thinking,' answered Felicity staring into her wine glass, wishing this conversation wasn't happening. What could she say? She couldn't change what had happened.

'I was hurt, Flick. We all were.' Allie said, staring at Felicity.

'I know Allie, and I'm sorry, but I was hurting too and I just couldn't face a future here. I didn't mean to make you feel that way,' offered Felicity.

'It wasn't about you, Allie,' chipped in Isla, shooting her a warning glance. 'We all know Flick had her own reasons for leaving the village and it's not for us to judge her or to make it about us.'

Allie stared at Isla.

'All I'm saying is...' Isla took a breath. 'All this happened a long time ago and it doesn't matter how often we see each other or speak to each other, I know we can just move on. We have been friends for such a long time.' Isla locked eyes with Allie. 'There's no point whatsoever anyone feeling hard done by or going over the past, it's not going to achieve anything. We all need to forgive and forget.'

Isla always had been the voice of reason.

Silence hung in the air for a moment, before Felicity spoke, 'I'm sorry Allie, I know I hurt you by not keeping in touch, but it was a difficult time for me and for Fergus – you know that. It's taken me a long time to try and come to terms with the situation and if I'm being honest, with every year that goes by it hurts a tiny bit more knowing that I'll never be...' Felicity's voice faltered.

Isla quickly squeezed Felicity's knee. 'You don't need to apologise to anyone. You needed to do what you needed to do at the time, and if fleeing the village to cope is what you needed to do, then so be it ... we understand, don't we Allie?'

'We were friends, shared everything. One minute you were here, next you were gone. We would have helped you get through it.' Allie's voice had now softened a little. 'What did we do wrong?'

'Absolutely nothing,' replied Felicity. 'I just needed to learn to cope with the consequences myself and get my head around it all.'

'Let's not go over old ground, the past is the past and unless we were walking in Felicity's shoes we can't begin to imagine.' Isla smiled towards Allie. 'Friendships like ours will always last forever. We are always here for you, even if we haven't seen you for years – that's a given.'

Felicity felt relieved to have Isla fighting her corner; she'd always been kind and compassionate and never judged anyone. Everyone knew Allie was a harder nut to crack but she always mellowed in the end.

'For the record, you pair will always be my best friends,' said Felicity, 'and sitting here with you now, as much as you are trying to give me a hard time Allie,' Felicity gave a small cheeky smile towards her, 'I've missed you.'

Allie was obviously thinking about what to say next and thankfully as the corner of her mouth lifted she smiled towards Felicity. 'I've missed you too, we've all missed you.' She flapped her hand between herself and Isla. 'And it's great to see you looking so well.'

'Thank you,' answered Felicity, finally feeling a little more relaxed now the conversation was moving on.

Each of them sipped their drink before Allie smirked at Felicity. 'And I hear you've only been back two minutes and are already causing chaos in the village today ... kidnapping children.'

Felicity's jaw hit the floor and she was about to protest. 'I'm only joking! Don't get in a flap! I passed Rona on the lane and she told me Aggie has taken a turn for the worse.'

'She's not been able to shake off that cold for a while now. Drew was saying it's a severe chest infection,' chipped in Isla with a look of concern on her face.

'Dr Taylor was leaving the cottage as I was walking here. She really needs to go to hospital but there's no getting over the bridge yet, the snow is too deep.'

'The thaw will start soon,' added Isla, 'but we all know that could be a number of days if the temperature stays below freezing.'

'What will they do with Esme tomorrow?' asked Felicity, knowing Aggie would be too poorly to look after her.

'I've offered to look after her for the day. If Finn's off school, I may as well have Esme too.'

Felicity didn't know why but her heart plummeted a little. She knew it was daft and Fergus would never leave his daughter in her care again, but she'd enjoyed their morning together; she felt she'd really connected with the little girl.

'Surely, that's going to be too much for you in your condition? What about Esme's mother, why can't she look after her? And where was she today?'

Both Isla and Allie spun round towards Felicity and stared.

'What ... what did I say?'

'You don't know?' Allie looked back towards Isla with a worried glance.

'Know what?' answered Felicity, with an uneasy feeling in her stomach.

Allie gave Isla a knowing look and slowly blew out a breath.

'Well, someone tell me,' insisted Felicity, not having a clue what was going on.

'Just after the birth of Esme, Lorna ... Esme's mum ... she ... she passed away.'

As Isla's words registered, Felicity had to take a moment before she spoke, 'How?' She couldn't quite believe it.

'Cardiac arrest. It was devastating and unexpected, and she couldn't be saved.' Isla's voice was low.

'The whole village was in mourning,' Allie added, grief-stricken. 'Lorna was a lovely person.'

Felicity's eyes glistened with tears. 'This is heart-breaking.' Thoughts of Fergus instantly flooded Felicity's mind. She couldn't even begin to imagine how he'd coped with such a devastating tragedy. 'How was Fergus?' Felicity's voice waned as she asked the question.

'How do you think?' Allie answered. 'Devastated.'

'But he coped really well,' added Isla, taking over the conversation. 'He channelled all his grief and energy into Esme, making sure she was loved and cared for. He's a wonderful dad.'

Felicity always knew that Fergus would be the most wonderful father. He was patient, kind and full of fun. Hearing the news, Felicity was overwhelmed with emotion. Why had nobody told her about this? But then, almost immediately she answered her own question – why would they? It had been her choice to run from Fergus's life and she'd insisted no one ever updated her on his life. But now she felt devastated all over again. She'd had no idea Fergus had been through even more heartache after what had happened to them, and she felt the familiar pang of guilt once more. She knew she'd left Heartcross to protect herself, but now knowing the grief Fergus must have gone through she wondered if she should have been back in touch sooner. She didn't like to think of him suffering even more heartache. But what could she have done?

'Were they married?' asked Felicity.

Allie shook her head. 'No.'

'But Fergus was planning to ask her, he'd mentioned it to Drew ... but then...'

Felicity didn't know how she felt about that – maybe a little saddened, but she knew she had no right to feel that way. As teenagers, she and Fergus had made promises to be together forever and at the time she'd believed it. Fergus had proposed to her and it had been the most romantic proposal she could ever have imagined. He'd written her a song and had played it on the piano in front of a packed pub. Everyone had thought they were the perfect match until Felicity had run away, leaving him behind. As the memories flooded her mind she felt a tiny pang of jealousy, knowing that he'd moved on and had fallen in love once more. But who was she to feel jealous after the tragedy he'd suffered? It had been over eight years since they'd been together. She'd had her chance to be with Fergus and had completely blown it. Things had changed and moved on but there was a feeling buried deep inside Felicity that she wasn't sure she could fight against. She knew that even after all this time, she was still very fond of Fergus.

Chapter 8

Felicity had tossed and turned all night, whether due to the freezing temperatures that were seeping through the cottage or the fact that Fergus was constantly on her mind. But the result was still the same, she'd barely had any sleep.

Shivering, she made her way downstairs and already could hear her mum bustling around in the kitchen. The fire was lit, giving off a welcome warmth as Felicity bent down on the rug and rubbed her hands together in front of the flames.

'Did you sleep well?' Rona asked, peering around the kitchen door.

'Not really and then when I finally went off to sleep I woke up feeling like a block of ice. We really need the snow to thaw so we can get the boiler fixed. We can't go on like this.' Felicity did everything in her power to stop her teeth from chattering as she thought back to the luxury of the heat in her tiny flat in London. But even though the thought of warmth enthralled her, the flat had just been a means to an end, it wasn't her home.

'Here, I've made you a warm drink, and boiled up the kettle for a wash.'

Felicity nodded gratefully. 'What's the weather like today?' she asked as she shot a glance towards the window.

'The snow has stopped and the sun is finally shining today, which means the thaw will begin.'

'Thank God.'

Rona cupped her hands around her mug of tea and stared out of the window onto Love Heart Lane. Rory was just leaving for work and she waved at him as he passed the window.

'What are your plans for today?' Felicity asked her mum.

'I promised Dr Taylor I'd call in on Aggie this morning and let the surgery know how she's doing.'

Felicity nodded. 'Pass on my best wishes.'

'I will. What are your plans for today?' asked Rona.

Felicity turned towards her mum. 'I think I'll go over to the farm to help Isla with Finn and Esme as the children are still off school.'

Rona eyed her daughter with suspicion. 'I'm not sure Fergus will think that's a good idea, especially after yesterday.'

Felicity already knew that Fergus wouldn't think it was a good idea, but something was drawing her in.

She knew she wanted to see Esme and spend more time with her.

'I'm helping Isla out. That's all there is to it,' Felicity replied, her response direct, even though she wasn't sure who she was trying to convince.

Rona wasn't a fool. 'Fergus has had enough to deal with in his life without you adding to his troubles whilst you are home.'

Felicity went red. She opened her mouth and shut it again.

'He won't thank you, you know,' added Rona, as she held Felicity's gaze.

'Isla and Allie told me about Esme's mum.' Felicity's voice was low.

'And that's exactly why he doesn't need you interfering.'

'Are you warning me off?' Felicity could feel a slight annoyance towards her mum's tone of voice. It reminded her of when she was a little girl, getting told off.

'I'm saying to you, don't go upsetting the apple cart. Time has moved on since you left and Fergus's life is finally back on some sort of even keel.'

Felicity chose to ignore her mum's suggestion. 'How did he meet Lorna?'

Rona exhaled. 'I thought you didn't want to know anything about Fergus ever again. They were your words.'

'Times change,' said Felicity rather sulkily, throwing a couple more logs on the fire from the basket.

Rona took a breath. 'There was a group of ramblers staying at Julia's B&B, and a bit like the weather now, there was a snowstorm and all of the ramblers were stranded ... Lorna was one of them. They'd all piled into the teashop; I can remember Mum's face now, excited by the sudden influx of customers and panicking as we only had two pairs of hands between us. Cutting a long story short, Lorna stepped behind the counter. She was a baker and was able to help us out. We soon had everyone fed and watered.'

Felicity was puzzled. 'What I don't understand is if she was just passing through, how did she and Fergus get together?'

Felicity knew that look on her mum's face; she was being super cautious. 'Just tell me, Mum.'

'Lorna fell in love with Heartcross and decided she wanted to stay.'

'You don't just decide you're staying in Heartcross, we are miles from normal life,' Felicity protested.

'Well, Lorna did. She lived in the city and fell in love with the Scottish Highlands.'

'And Fergus.' Felicity felt deflated. 'So, where did she work? You can't just up and leave without a job.'

For a second Rona remained quiet.

'What are you hiding?' urged Felicity, eyeing her mum carefully.

'I'm not hiding anything ... Lorna was genuinely a

lovely, down to earth girl, with a passion for baking.'

The gut feeling in Felicity's stomach told her she knew exactly what her mum was going to tell her next.

'Your grandma missed you when you left and having Lorna around the place was like a breath of fresh air.'

'You gave her a job in the teashop, didn't you?' asked Felicity wide-eyed.

'We did, we needed the extra help and she was the perfect assistant.'

Felicity let out a shuddering sigh.

Rona tried to smooth the way. 'Lorna was a beautiful girl, and what happened to her was a tragedy, leaving a little girl without her mother. Think about the bigger picture. Fergus was entitled to fall in love and find happiness again.'

Felicity knew her mum was right, but she couldn't shake off the tiny jealous niggles in the pit of her stomach.

'Where did she live?' Felicity knew the question was irrelevant but couldn't help wondering.

'At first, she rented a room at the B&B and then moved into the cottage with Aggie and Fergus when she fell pregnant.'

Felicity was quiet.

'Look, all I'm saying is, it was your choice to leave Heartcross. You are my daughter and I love you unconditionally, but please let Fergus get on with his life; he's got Esme to look after now.'

'I'm not here to cause any trouble, I was just a little shocked to discover that Lorna had passed away leaving Fergus with Esme.'

'I know ... but just tread carefully.'

Rona stood up, disappearing into the kitchen and putting an end to the conversation.

Felicity's mind was a whirl; she had a feeling of dread at the thought of Fergus's reaction if he saw her up at the farm but at the same time a tiny thrill of emotion passed through Felicity's body, knowing that Esme was going to be there and maybe she could spend a little more time with the little girl without a mother of her own.

Chapter 9

Felicity traipsed up the snowy drive towards Foxglove Farm. The rooftop of the farmhouse sparkled in the wintery light and the bare oak trees that adorned the path glistened in the early morning sunlight. She huddled deep inside her coat with her hands stuffed firmly in her pockets and shot a quick glance towards the barns. She could hear the noise of hammering and an engine being fired up but she hadn't set eyes on either Drew or Fergus yet.

As she rapped on the front door and waited she could hear the joyful banter of the children playing inside followed by footsteps. Isla soon appeared at the door, rosy-cheeked and wiping her hands down her pinny.

'You look kind of flustered,' smiled Felicity, as Isla flung the door wide open and ushered her into the hallway.

'Am I glad to see you! It's only 10 a.m. and I'm completely exhausted. We've baked cakes and played games. I'm ready for a rest.'

'The cavalry has arrived,' chuckled Felicity. 'You can sit and put your feet up for a while. I'll entertain the troops.'

'Who is it, Mum?' shouted Finn appearing at the top of the hallway quickly followed by Esme. As soon as Esme spotted Felicity she let out a squeal and ran towards her slipping her tiny hand inside Felicity's. A tsunami of warmth rushed between them and Esme's eyes sparkled as she led Felicity into the living room.

'Hi Finn,' said Felicity ruffling the top of his hair as she passed. He gave her a cheeky grin and ran back towards the living room.

'Come and help us build a Lego town,' said Esme, tugging on Felicity's hand. 'We are building Heartcross.'

Felicity followed Isla and Esme into the living room.

'Wow! Look at this,' exclaimed Felicity as her eyes scanned the floor. There wasn't an inch of floor that wasn't covered by a coloured brick of Lego.

'What are we building?' asked Felicity, gently pushing a pile of bricks to one side so she could sit down on the floor. She noticed Finn was already in the midst of building a fire station when Esme answered.

'A teashop.'

'A teashop,' repeated Felicity.

'Just like the one on Love Heart Lane.'

Felicity raised an eyebrow and smiled towards Esme. 'That sounds like the perfect plan. Let's get building!'

For the next twenty minutes, Felicity got to work building with Esme and Finn. Isla had brought out a tray of fairy cakes they'd already baked this morning with juice and a pot of tea. She now had her eyes firmly shut and had fallen asleep on the sofa.

'What do we think?' Felicity asked Finn showing him the white cottage they'd built with a teashop on the corner.

'Teashops are so girly,' he said, barely giving the building a second glance.

'I love it,' declared Esme. 'But before we can begin to serve tea and cake we need to write our secret recipe book,' she continued, completely ignoring Finn's reaction and staring up at Felicity. 'Just like Bonnie's secret recipe book in the teashop,' she added with a smile that melted Felicity's heart.

'She was a fantastic grandma,' replied Felicity, meaning every word and squeezing Esme's hand. 'She taught me everything I know about baking cakes.'

'My mummy was a baker,' offered Esme. 'Daddy told me she worked at the teashop, too, which means she must have known your grandma.' Esme's eyes met Felicity's.

'I believe so, my mum told me today.'

'Daddy said she made the best cakes.'

'I bet she did,' answered Felicity with a warm smile noticing the sparkle in Esme's eyes when she spoke about the mum she'd never known. Felicity felt a little pang in her heart because she felt saddened that Esme wouldn't ever know her mum, but Fergus was clearly doing a good job of keeping her memory alive. She wondered what Lorna had been like. Was she similar to her in any way, looks or characteristics? What had attracted Fergus to her?

They both watched as Finn wandered over to the dresser and pulled out sheets of paper and a box of felt tip pens. 'Here you go, use these to make your book,' he said, before promptly sitting back down amongst the Lego bricks on the floor.

'Shall we go over to the table?' suggested Felicity, standing up as Esme followed her. Felicity watched Esme settle at the table and fold the paper in half. She set the coloured pens out in front of her then started on the design of the cover. Felicity watched as Esme wrote, 'Esme and Felicity's Secret Recipe Book.' Esme caught her eye and smiled as she began to draw a delicious looking cake with a million love hearts scattered all over the page.

'What's the first recipe going to be?' asked Felicity, while Esme pondered.

'Carrot cake,' she announced after some thought. 'I loved Bonnie's carrot cake.'

'It was mouth-wateringly delicious,' Felicity answered, remembering her grandmother's carrot cake. 'Good choice.'

Felicity helped Esme write a contents page then they listed all the ingredients they needed to make the cake. They laughed and giggled as they worked and with Finn still building his Lego village and Isla having a nap on the settee, Felicity was unaware that the back door to the farmhouse had been opened until she heard Drew shout through to the living room.

'The workers are back for a cuppa, anyone want a drink?'

Immediately, Isla shot up at the sound of his voice. 'I'm so sorry, I must have dozed off,' she said apologetically to Felicity who was staring towards the door. She knew there was every chance she would bump into Fergus today but now she could hear his voice coming from the kitchen she felt anxious.

'I'll make you a drink,' called Isla hurrying through to the kitchen, 'The children have made cakes too.'

'Cake!' shouted Fergus. 'Where is my little superstar?' Felicity could hear his voice getting louder as he walked towards the living room; she shuffled nervously in her chair.

'In here, Daddy,' shouted Esme. 'I'm just designing a secret recipe with...'

Esme didn't finish her sentence.

'With Felicity,' interrupted Fergus, taken completely by surprise to see her.

'I've come to keep Isla company, while the children

are off school, give her a little respite,' said Felicity, quickly.

'Felicity has helped me to write all the ingredients ... look!' Esme proudly held up the book in the air for Fergus to see.

'It's looking mighty fine,' he agreed.

'If we don't finish it, can you come again tomorrow?' Esme's wide eyes turned towards Felicity who faltered, not knowing how to reply.

'Have you got a minute?' Fergus looked over towards Felicity before casting his eyes towards the hallway.

She stood up and followed him, pulling the door shut behind her.

'What is it?' asked Felicity as she noticed Fergus swallow.

'It's obvious to anyone Esme has taken a shine to you, but I don't want you getting close.'

'I'm only helping Isla to entertain the children, Fergus.'

Fergus locked eyes with her. She noticed they were watery but he didn't speak.

'What is it I'm doing that's so wrong?' Her voice was low so the children couldn't hear.

'I don't want Esme getting close to you.'

Felicity knew it probably wasn't the best time but she wanted to push the conversation. 'Why?'

'Because Felicity, you'll be leaving soon and I'll have

to deal with a little girl who will be upset, who will want to keep in touch and let's face it...'

'Let's face what?' she interrupted.

'You can break my heart but you aren't going to do that to Esme too.' Fergus's hurt floored Felicity for a moment. She had no intention of breaking Esme's heart and felt saddened Fergus would even think that of her. His words turned over in her mind.

'I didn't mean to upset you, Fergus,' she offered, touching his arm, but he pulled away.

'All I want and need is a quiet life. I appreciate Rona still lives in the village and you will come back from time to time but...'

'Actually, I might be staying around for a little longer than planned.' Felicity had no idea why she'd just shared that information but the words were now hanging in the air.

'What? ... Why? I thought you were a city girl now.'

'A girl can change her mind, can't she?' Felicity tried to make a light-hearted joke of it but the look on Fergus's face suggested he didn't find it funny.

'So after all this time Heartcross becomes good enough for you again?' The look on his face made her nervous.

She tried to betray no emotion on her face yet deep inside, her heart was hammering against her chest. 'That was never the case, and you know there was more to it.'

They stared at each other for a minute before Fergus turned to walk back towards the kitchen, leaving her standing there.

She had hoped Fergus might have softened by now but he'd made it very clear he didn't want anything to do with her.

Isla appeared and handed her a mug of tea. 'Everything okay?'

'Not really ... Fergus and I have just had words and I kind of let slip I was thinking of staying around.'

Isla touched her hand tentatively. 'He'll come round; it's a shock for him seeing you again after all this time.'

'I'm not sure he will come round,' sighed Felicity, following Isla into the living room and fixing her eyes on Esme who was still happily colouring away on her recipe book.

'Do you think we could bake the cakes from our recipe book?' Esme looked up towards Felicity the second she walked back into the living room.

'I'm sure one day, if you ask my mum, she'll let you bake them in the teashop.'

'Really, just like my mum?'

'Just like your mum.'

Felicity felt such warmth towards the little girl. She couldn't imagine ever losing her own mum at such an early age. It was heart-breaking. Felicity watched her as she began listing the ingredients for the next recipe.

Her brunette hair bounced just below her shoulders and her hazel eyes mirrored Fergus's.

'What if he doesn't come round?' Felicity looked at Isla but kept her voice low.

'He will. Are you definitely thinking of staying on?' Isla looked at her speculatively for a moment and Felicity knew right at that second that she'd made her mind up and wasn't going back to London.

Isla was very intuitive. 'You aren't going back, are you? You've made up your mind.'

Felicity blew out a breath. 'I don't think I am. What's there for me there now? A job I no longer like, night after night sitting on my own. Friends that are acquaintances, except Polly. Since I've been back...'

'You've realised you've missed us all that much you never ever want to leave us again,' chipped in Isla, with a warm beam on her face.

'Something like that and...'

'Go on.'

'And like I said to you, it's not sitting right with me that the teashop is closed. Maybe re-opening it can make it up to my grandma and Mum. I should have realised how difficult things were for them.'

'It's not sitting right with any of us, but it was a struggle for your mum to run it on her own ... it would mean you sticking around for some time to help her.'

Felicity acknowledged that. But suddenly the idea of

working in partnership with her mum to re-open the family business excited rather than scared her. She knew her grandma had made a decent enough living from the business and this would give her and her mum a new purpose, something to focus on. Felicity was genuinely excited by the idea.

'So,' said Felicity with a smile on her face, 'once this snow has thawed and the trucks are getting back through, I'm going to suggest to Mum we re-open the teashop, together.'

'And move back home into Heartwood Cottage?'

Felicity nodded. 'Yes, it will also give Mum some company too, especially now she's on her own.'

Isla gave Felicity a wide, reassuring smile. 'I actually think it's a perfect plan for you, and for Rona and then there's me. I'll have my friend back to lend a hand at the drop of a hat.' She grinned.

'Purely selfish reasons then!'

'Absolutely! Everyone will be glad to have you home.'

'Everyone except Fergus,' said Felicity glumly, taking a sip of her drink. She couldn't get him off her mind.

'Look, don't you go worrying about Fergus, we can work on him. He's just hurting.' Isla gave Felicity a warm, knowing look.

'I hope so, because believe it or not, I don't like the atmosphere between us. I really don't want to see him upset.'

'It's going to be okay, Flick. Trust me.'

Isla's words gave Felicity a glimmer of hope and her mouth lifted at the corners. If only she could turn back time and make everything better again.

Chapter 10

After the spectacular Lego town was finally built and the children had been entertained all day, Felicity kissed an exhausted Isla on the cheek and made the trek home back to the cottage. Everywhere was still a whitewash of snow but the sun had been high in the sky and thankfully the snow had started to thaw which meant the trucks and supplies to the village should be back on track in the next couple of days and hopefully the boiler in the cottage would be fixed too. On the whole, Felicity had enjoyed the day, except the conversation with Fergus of course, which had left her feeling glum. She shrugged off any residual guilt and tried to push it firmly out of her mind.

Swinging open the front door to the cottage, she shouted out to her mum. 'I'm home!'

Rona appeared with a smile on her face. 'Good day?' she asked.

Felicity stood still. The cottage was cool but not as

cold as normal and placing a hand on the radiator, Felicity was relieved to feel a blast of heat.

'What happened here? We have heat!' exclaimed Felicity slipping off her coat and kicking off her boots.

'We do! Leo came late this morning and fixed the boiler. The snow seems to be thawing fast now on the other side of the bridge, so he left his car and walked up here.'

Felicity was thankful. Boiling kettle after kettle just to get a wash had already become tiresome.

'I hate to ask—' Rona handed over the invoice '—but this will need paying.'

'It's really not a problem.' Felicity smiled at her mum.

'Any plans for tonight?' asked Rona, as she poked the log fire.

Felicity shook her head. 'No why?'

'Fraser and Meredith are putting on a pub quiz, trying to keep spirits high. Are you up for that?'

Felicity nodded, 'Of course, but any chance of a hot shower first?'

'Be my guest, the water has been heating all afternoon.'

Felicity disappeared upstairs towards the bathroom, while Rona pottered about in the kitchen.

Half an hour later, they traipsed down Love Heart Lane towards the pub. As they pushed open the door they could hear the welcome chatter inside. Allie waved from behind the bar and Felicity noticed Rory sitting next to Drew in the far corner, but she couldn't spot Fergus. He was more than likely at home looking after Aggie and Esme.

'Drink?' Allie bellowed over the bar towards Felicity.

'Two gin and tonics please,' she replied.

Fraser was to the left of the bar in a small alcove, trying to rig up the microphone which tended to let out a high pitch squeal every time he blew into it.

Allie passed the drinks over the bar. 'Whose team are you going to be on?' she asked as Felicity swung a glance round the pub.

'How many to a team?' she asked.

'No more than six,' answered Allie.

Heather, Hamish and Julia looked as thick as thieves on one table. Hamish was a man of nonsense knowledge and as far back as Felicity could ever remember, had always been on the winning team of every pub quiz she'd ever been at.

'I don't mind sitting at the bar and keeping you company,' offered Felicity thinking that was a better option but Rona was having none of it.

'Where's your community spirit? It'll be fun, let your hair down.'

'Okay, okay, whose team are we joining then?' answered Felicity not wanting to disappoint her mum.

But before they could make up their mind, Rory beckoned them over. 'Come and join us, we need all the
help we can get.'

Felicity chuckled. 'Considering you're a vet I'm sure
you are going to know a lot more than I can offer.'

'It's not about being academically clever, is it? Pub
quizzes are more about the useless bits of information
that you store up over time.'

As Rona and Felicity squeezed up next to them the
pub began to fill up. Teams gathered on tables and
Meredith handed out pens and paper. Felicity noticed
Hamish holding Heather's hand under the table and
smiled. He deserved happiness in his life and she hoped
their date went well.

Just at that moment a blast of air gushed through
the pub and everyone looked up to see Fergus coming
through the door.

Drew waved to him and Fergus smiled back before
he noticed Felicity sitting at the table.

'Good day?' asked Rory, patting him on the back. 'Let
me get you a drink.'

'Thanks pal.'

Rory stood up and disappeared towards the bar, while
Fergus sat down next to Drew.

'How's Aggie?' asked Rona, while Felicity remained
quiet. She felt a little awkward but she hitched a warm
smile on her face.

'She says she's okay but this chest infection has certainly knocked her off her feet.'

'Who's looking after Esme?' asked Felicity, the words out of her mouth before she could stop them.

Fergus looked at her.

'She's having tea with Finn and I'm going to drop her home after the quiz,' chipped in Drew, not noticing the slight tension between Fergus and Felicity.

'Rona, Rona,' a voice beckoned.

They looked round to see Hamish waving Rona in their direction.

'Come over on our team and leave the youngsters to it.'

'I might just do that,' said Rona, 'You'll be okay won't you?' she turned towards Felicity who resisted the urge not to pull a sulky face.

As Rona left the table, Rory sat back down and passed a pint of lager towards Fergus before Drew bellowed towards the door.

'Jess ... Jessica, over here.'

As Felicity looked over, Fergus was already up on his feet with his arms wide open.

'Jess, so glad you made it.'

Without warning Felicity felt a twinge of jealousy towards Jessica as she watched Fergus hug her tight and kiss her cheek before leading her to the chair next to him.

'Drink?' asked Drew, standing up and Jessica ordered a glass of red wine.

'Do you know Jessica?' asked Rory, looking at Felicity who could feel her cheeks turning a crimson colour.

'No, I don't think we've met before.'

'Finn's school teacher,' said Drew, passing Jessica a glass of wine and sitting back down.

Jessica smiled the most beautiful smile and held out her hand towards Felicity.

'This is Felicity,' introduced Rory.

Jessica's smile seemed to falter for a split second. 'Pleased to meet you,' Felicity said politely, as she shook the other woman's hand.

'Are you back for a visit? London, isn't it, where you live now?'

It was obvious to Felicity that some sort of conversation about her had taken place and she began to wonder what had been said about her and why.

'Yes, London at the moment. I'm back for a couple of weeks but who knows? I'm kind of missing this place.'

There was a look between Fergus and Jessica before Jessica spoke. 'I bet you don't see snow like this in London,' she said, keeping the conversation light.

'No, not as bad as this.'

'Any news on when the school is re-opening?' Drew asked, looking at Jessica.

'It's definitely closed for the rest of the week. I bet that's not what Isla wants to hear.'

Drew grinned. 'That's definitely not what Isla wants to hear in her condition.'

Jessica swung around towards Fergus, 'And you tell our gorgeous Esme of course I will look after her tomorrow. I can't wait to spend some time with her.'

The word 'our' pulsated inside Felicity's mind.

'I can even look after Aggie tomorrow too.'

Fergus leant over and kissed Jessica's cheek, 'Thank you, you're the best. That's a weight off my mind.'

'In fact, let me look after Finn too, give Isla a rest.' She smiled towards Drew who promptly accepted on Isla's behalf.

Felicity felt saddened. She thought she'd made up her mind to come back to Heartcross and as much as Isla had welcomed her back with open arms, watching her old friends talk and laugh amongst themselves she suddenly felt out of the loop. There had been a time when she would have been the centre of attention, the one leading the conversation between her friends, but now she felt like an outsider watching from the sidelines, no one including her in their conversation.

She'd no idea how Fergus had met Jessica but anyone could see they got on like a house on fire. They were more than friendly and Felicity really didn't like the feeling in the pit of her stomach. It suddenly hit Felicity that life in Heartcross had carried on without her. Fergus had kept the bond with her old friends, and they all had their own place in the community. But even though she was Heartcross born and bred, Felicity knew that her place here had long been lost.

Just at that second, Fraser blew into the microphone, making everyone jump. He ordered quiet and the chatter died down as he explained the rules of the quiz.

Hamish was muttering under his breath and the table next to him shushed him in a good-natured, friendly way as Fraser began to read out the first question.

Everyone was in good spirits except for Felicity who wasn't concentrating on anything at all. Her gaze was fixed firmly on Fergus and Jessica, and feelings of jealousy were creeping through her body. She suddenly wanted to be anywhere else but here. She attempted to paint a smile on her face, but deep inside she felt sad knowing someone else now had that playful connection with Fergus that she'd once had.

Rory and Drew argued over who was writing the answers down when Jessica took control of the pen.

Felicity wasn't much help at all. In fact, the way the others interacted with each other only made her feel like even more of an outsider.

'No! That's not the answer,' laughed Rory, playfully bickering with Drew.

'It's only a suggestion, I wasn't born in the 1930s. I've no idea.' He threw his hands up in defeat.

'Any ideas, Felicity?' Jessica turned towards her.

Felicity knew she hadn't even heard the question, never mind know what the answer would be.

'No, sorry, I'm not much use, am I?'

Jessica scored a line through the number and they all waited for the next question.

Allie suddenly appeared at the table and slipped into the seat next to Felicity.

'You okay?' she whispered, realising that Felicity didn't look like she was enjoying herself.

Felicity took a sip of her drink. 'I'm actually feeling very tired. I don't know what's come over me. I think I may just go and get an early night.'

Allie cocked an eyebrow.

Just at that moment, Fraser declared that the round had come to an end; there was a brief pause and once everyone swapped their papers the chatter began once more.

Rory clapped his hands together. 'More drinks?'

'I'll get these mate, you're always getting the round in,' insisted Fergus, standing up and reaching for his wallet. 'Same again?'

Everyone nodded except Felicity, who was still thinking about leaving.

Fergus turned towards her. 'Same again, Flick?'

Felicity's heart skipped a beat at the sound of Fergus using her nickname and was completely taken by surprise for a moment. It reminded her of old times, when they'd been close, the times she missed. 'Thank you,' she replied and watched as Fergus disappeared towards the bar.

Allie smiled at her. 'We both know he's a decent guy and wouldn't leave anyone out. He's bigger than that.'

Felicity was about to answer when Fraser blew on the microphone and every head turned towards him.

'I have news,' he declared gleefully, with a huge beam on his face. 'We've had confirmation that the supply trucks will be crossing the bridge in the morning. The shelves will be restocked!'

The whole pub erupted in cheers and clapped.

'Thank God that crisis is over,' said Allie. 'The food stocks here were basically non-existent.'

The pub was again full of joyful chatter and Felicity glanced over towards the bar. Fergus's hand was placed in the small of Jessica's back. Leaning in towards each other they were laughing about something and seemed close. She remembered the way she'd laughed with Fergus, the closeness between them and the plans they'd once made for the future. Felicity felt a pang of regret – if only she'd been able to cope, think clearly at the time and stayed to talk things through with him, maybe it would have been okay? But then she felt anxious and remembered Esme. Things would have never been okay between them because Felicity knew she would have always tortured herself, wondering if she would be enough for Fergus. She'd never want to hold Fergus back because she was unable to have children. And even back then, she'd known he'd make a wonderful father, and, of course, now she knew that to be true. If she'd stayed around at least one thing would have been different for Fergus – he wouldn't have had Esme.

She suddenly thought back to the day she'd discovered she was pregnant with Fergus's baby. They had been so young but so much in love and Fergus had been over-joyed. They made plans to get married and had decided once the baby was born that Felicity would move into Aggie's cottage while they saved for their own place.

Things had been perfect, but then just before their first scan, Felicity had felt a terrible pain and had collapsed. Within an hour she had been under anaesthesia, with the surgery revealing that she had a torsion alongside a giant cyst on her fallopian tube – a rare but serious condition.

She'd lost the baby and had been told her chances of getting pregnant were greatly reduced but that there was still hope. Fergus had looked after her, loved her and they'd clung to each other and the dreams they had made together.

Six months later, Felicity had fallen pregnant again,

but this time with another devastating outcome. Her pregnancy was ectopic, and her remaining tube had erupted, resulting in that too being removed. Even after all these years, it still felt like yesterday to Felicity when she remembered the consultant standing by the side of her bed as he'd delivered the terrible news.

At first Felicity had blamed herself. What was wrong with her body? Why couldn't she have a simple pregnancy? Then the anger came, as she'd lashed out at everyone who tried to help her – especially Fergus who had been by her side through it all. Then, finally, the fear had kicked in and she ran from Heartcross. As much as it hurt to the core, even now after all this time she knew Fergus was still the love of her life. No one had ever come close to what they'd once had. And although, she knew she'd done the right thing at the time, now she was back and faced with him once more, she was more certain than ever that her heart still very much belonged to Fergus Campbell.

Chapter 11

It was 6 a.m. when Felicity prised her tired eyes open and peeped at the clock. She was woken by the whistling wind and the rain hammering against the window. With all that torrential rain the snow would soon disappear, and she smiled from under the comfort of her duvet as she heard the drone of the trucks passing the bottom of Love Heart Lane towards the heart of the village. After the extreme weather conditions, supplies were finally being delivered and normality would once again prevail in Heartcross. Hamish would soon have the shelves re-stocked and normal business resumed.

As she lay there, Felicity thought more and more about her return to London. She didn't relish the idea one bit and the more she thought about the opportunity to re-open the teashop and work alongside her mum, the more she was filled with excitement. She made the decision there and then that she was going to talk to her mum today about moving back home.

The comfort of Heartcross was drawing her back in, and she wasn't sure how or why but something was telling her the time was right to come home.

She thought about the teashop and could picture her grandma bustling around the place with a huge smile on her face. Not once had Felicity ever heard her grumble or not enjoy a day's work in the teashop. She'd put her heart and soul into running her empire and Felicity had butterflies in her stomach thinking about how she would carry on with her grandmother's legacy. Even though her return to Heartcross had been under sad circumstances maybe the timing had been right. Working in partnership with her mum to run her grandma's teashop would give her a project to focus on, and maybe give both of them a new zest for life. Felicity was even more determined to run the idea past her mum the second she set eyes on her, and with the snow thawing and supplies being delivered to the village once more, they could even be up and running by the end of the week.

Felicity was thankful to hear the clanging of the radiators which meant the boiler and heating were back to full working order.

Hearing a rap on the door, Felicity sat up in bed as her mum appeared around the door holding a mug of tea.

'Just what I needed,' said Felicity, plumping up her pillows and sitting up in bed.

'The rain and the trucks woke me up.'

'This rain is horrendous,' agreed Felicity, 'but at least the trucks have managed to drive over the bridge and up the hill.'

Rona perched on the end of the bed. 'Aggie's been taken to hospital. The ambulance came late last night.'

'Oh no,' exhaled Felicity.

'Pneumonia, I think.'

'Is there anything we can do?' asked Felicity, thinking of Fergus and Esme and feeling worried for them both.

'I'm sure Fergus has everything under control.'

Felicity nodded, but she knew she'd be hot-footing it over to Isla's today at some point to hear all the news.

'I'm going to pop over to Hamish's when this rain eases and pick up some fresh bread.'

Felicity chewed on her bottom lip then opened her mouth to speak.

'I know that look, what are you thinking about? Is there something you need from the shop?' asked Rona, standing up.

'Not right at this minute, but there's something on my mind.'

Rona eyed her daughter. 'Go on, it's better out than in as your grandma used to say,' she encouraged, waiting for Felicity to speak.

'What happened to the suppliers that delivered to the teashop?'

Rona blew out a breath, 'I had to cancel them when your grandma got ill.'

'And what are your plans for re-opening?' probed Felicity, gauging her mum's reaction.

'It's quite daunting to think I'd have to re-open without your grandma by my side.' The tears welled up in Rona's eyes. 'I'm not sure...'

'What about...' Felicity interrupted then paused while she fixed her gaze on her mum. 'What about if I come home and we took on the shop together?'

Rona let out a tiny gasp and narrowed her eyes.

'Of course, that would mean putting up with me every day,' added Felicity with a cheeky grin.

'What about London?'

'This girl has had enough of the bright lights of the city.'

Rona's face brightened. 'Really? You actually want to come home and run the shop with me?'

'Really,' replied Felicity with a full-on beam.

A flush of warmth flooded through Rona as she flung her arms open and Felicity bounded out of bed straight into them.

'But what's brought this on all of a sudden?' asked Rona.

'I know I've let you and Grandma down ... I should have been around more to help and support you both especially near the end.' Felicity's voice wobbled. 'I am sorry, Mum ... and in a way I suppose this is my way of trying to make everything right ... make it up to you and Grandma.'

Rona cupped her hands around her daughter's and studied her face. 'You have to do what's best for you, Flick. What about your job?'

Felicity snuggled back under her duvet and pulled it up to her chin. 'It's time for a change,' she revealed. 'It's just not the same job anymore and I'm ready to come home. I've been thinking about it for a while now Mum, and since I've been back in the village, it's only grown stronger, especially when I discovered the teashop was shut but then there's...'

'There's what?'

Felicity sighed, 'At the quiz, I actually felt like I'd lost my place here, does that sound silly?'

'What do you mean?' asked Rona.

'When I was sitting there and everyone was so at ease in each other's company, laughing and joking – I felt like an outsider.'

'You've been away for a long time, Flick,' said Rona softly. 'But you are definitely not an outsider.'

'I felt like they'd all left me behind.'

Rona could see that Felicity was upset. 'Once you settle back in you'll feel a part of your old friendship group again, part of the community. Heartcross will always be your home, you know.'

Felicity nodded and sat thinking for a second. She wanted to fit back into the community and be part of the village once more but knew it would take time.

'I have a suggestion,' she said. 'Working in the teashop is going to be a new start for me and hopefully for you too, Mum. We will be keeping Grandma's business alive … so how about we become partners?'

Rona's eyes lit up. 'That is the best suggestion. Partners!' she repeated, as the two of them stared at each other with huge beams on their faces. Felicity felt excitement bubbling inside her and Rona felt the same for the first time in a long time.

'And thank you.'

'What are you thanking me for?' asked Felicity.

'Because after losing your grandma, I didn't know what to do. I wasn't sure I was strong enough to walk back in there without her by my side. It feels lonely enough without her conversation every day. But now I have you and that means a lot.'

Felicity took both of her mum's hands and squeezed them tight. 'We are going to do this as a team.'

'Your grandma would be so proud of you,' said Rona, with such affection.

Immediately, Felicity's eyes brimmed with tears. 'Mum…' Her voice wavered. 'I'm sorry I wasn't around … at the end.' The tears flowed freely down Felicity's cheeks and Rona gently brushed them away.

'It's okay, don't cry. You had your own life in London. Your grandma didn't want to draw you away from that.'

'But I could have come back.' The guilt kicked in again for not supporting her mum through such a difficult time.

'Look, let's look to the future. And being partners. Doing what Bonnie would have wanted us to do.'

Felicity hugged her mum again. 'So, when shall we get up and running?' she asked lightening the mood.

'There's no time like the present. Shall we have a look at menus and what ingredients we need, then we can give the suppliers a ring and get them back on track?'

'Sounds like a plan,' answered Felicity enthusiastically, wanting to throw herself wholeheartedly into the day. 'No time like the present,' she sang, throwing back the duvet and jumping out of bed.

'How about a bacon sandwich to cement our new partnership?' smiled Rona.

'Yes please.'

Felicity followed her mum downstairs and took a swift glance out of the living-room window.

'Have you seen the weather out there? It may have stopped snowing but my gosh ... that wind.' Felicity watched as the gale force winds shook the lamp post outside.

'It's from one extreme to another,' Rona shouted from

the kitchen. 'That's the joys of the Scottish Highlands for you.'

Just at that second, the rain began falling in even more heavy chaotic drops, the gusting wind pelting the rain against the window. It sounded like bullets being fired from a machine gun and took Felicity by surprise.

'Have you seen the water running down Love Heart Lane, it's like it has its own river.'

Rona hovered behind her daughter. 'I bet the river will be high today,' she said, switching on the TV before attending to the sizzling bacon in the pan on top of the Aga.

Felicity curled up on the settee and watched as the local news played out. The Met Office had issued a severe weather warning and people were advised to stay indoors if they didn't have to travel. Felicity watched in horror as she saw cars being overturned in high speed winds and trees strewn across roads. Houses were being tested, roof tiles blown off and windows broken, and most schools remained closed.

'I think the best place for us today is the teashop; we can fire up the ovens and switch on the heating while we plan the new menus.'

Felicity nodded, flicking a glance towards the window. She'd wanted to pop up to the farm – firstly, to check on Isla and secondly, to see if there were any updates about Aggie. She knew Esme wouldn't be at the farm today as Jessica was taking care of her and Finn. As the rain grew heavier and heavier and the angry black clouds surged through the sky she didn't want to venture out anytime soon.

'I think you're right,' agreed Felicity as she stood up and began to throw some logs on to the fire.

'Here you go, one bacon sandwich, one fresh cup of tea, but don't think you are getting this kind of service every morning.'

'I wouldn't dream of it,' replied Felicity, with a cheeky grin.

They ate in silence, listening to the wind rattling the windows whilst watching the chaos of the weather unfold on the TV.

'How are things with Fergus?' asked Rona tentatively, risking a tiny glance in Felicity's direction.

Felicity shrugged and placed her sandwich back down on her plate. 'It was a little tense when he saw me up at the farm, but I think he was trying hard to include me at the pub. He didn't leave me out of the round anyway.'

'It will be a shock seeing you after all this time,' said Rona softly. 'Fergus has had a lot to cope with over the years, especially with Esme's mum passing away.'

'I thought I was doing the right thing at the time by leaving,' said Felicity, with a twinge of sadness in her voice. 'But now, I'm not so sure.'

'It was difficult for both of you, you were both young and you dealt with the grief the best way you could.'

Felicity was tearful and swallowed down a lump in her throat. 'One thing I do know is that if I hadn't have gone Fergus wouldn't have had Esme. I knew I would never have been enough for him.'

'You were enough for him. But seriously, you couldn't have expected him to put his life on hold and wait to see if you ever came home?'

'I suppose not,' said Felicity a little sulkily but knowing her mum was right.

They sat in silence for a moment while they finished their breakfast. Felicity's mind flicked back to the pub quiz, her thoughts filled with Fergus and Jessica. Jessica was pretty with her blonde hair and her bright blue eyes, and even though she must have known that she was Fergus's ex she hadn't made Felicity feel unwelcome in the slightest.

'How long has Fergus been seeing Jessica?' Felicity asked, knowing it was absolutely none of her business but letting curiosity get the better of her.

Rona looked towards her daughter. 'Jessica?'

'Yes, Finn and Esme's school teacher.'

'I know who Jessica is. What makes you think they're together?' Rona held Felicity's gaze.

'In the pub, they seemed very close.'

Rona gave a small chuckle to Felicity's annoyance.

'Jessica isn't Fergus's girlfriend, Jessica is Lorna's sister.'

The words took a second to register. 'Lorna's sister?' Felicity repeated.

'Esme's aunty,' replied Rona simply.

Felicity blew out a breath and a huge part of her felt relieved. 'So, is Fergus with anyone now?'

'Not to my knowledge,' Rona answered, and the corners of Felicity's mouth began to lift.

'So how did Jessica end up in Heartcross too?'

'A vacancy came up at the school when Lorna was pregnant with Esme so Jessica decided to follow her sister. She's been a great help to Fergus, great support. I think you'll like her.'

'Esme seems a great girl too,' Felicity added.

'She is,' said Rona, 'and now you've decided you're staying, maybe you and Fergus will become friends again.'

Felicity hoped so and she'd already made her mind up to go and talk to him to try and smooth over some of the past issues between them.

As they both drained the dregs of tea from their mugs, they sat in silence for a few minutes watching the TV before Felicity pondered whether to go and get ready.

'Five more minutes and I'll jump in the shower,' she said.

'I'll fire up the ovens and put the heating on in the shop when you go up.'

Felicity looked confused and was suddenly distracted by shouting. 'What's that noise? Can you hear shouting?'

Rona wasn't convinced. 'Shouting? Isn't it just the wind howling outside?'

'No, that's not the wind. I can definitely hear shouting.' Felicity leapt to her feet and peered out of the window. 'What's going on?'

Immediately Rona stood up behind Felicity and looked perplexed, 'Look, there's Allie, Drew and half the village running down the lane.' Felicity pointed before spinning back round towards her mum. 'What's going on?'

Felicity and Rona exchanged looks as Love Heart Lane began to hum with the arrival of even more villagers.

'I'll get my coat on and see what all the commotion is about,' said Felicity.

'You're still in your PJs, the weather is brutal out there. Put some warmer clothes on first,' insisted Rona.

Felicity knew her mum was right. She raced upstairs and quickly pulled on her jeans and thermals before thrusting her feet inside her boots and grabbing her hat and coat.

'Keep me updated,' Rona shouted after her as a gust of cold air blew in from outside when the front door opened.

As Felicity stepped outside, the wind nearly knocked

her straight off her feet. The rain stung her cheeks and she bent her head low and let the wind carry her down Love Heart Lane, the stream of water from the storm and thawing snow swirling quickly underneath her boots.

At the bottom of the mountainous terrain she could already see a group of people huddled together, standing back from the banks of the river shouting and pointing.

As Felicity got closer the chaos unfolded before her eyes. She could see the rising river was running wild, turbulent and unforgiving, swilling over the side. She hurried to where she spotted Fergus, Allie and Drew standing, shouting towards the bridge where Felicity noticed a van stranded which was swaying wildly.

The storm was blowing virtually at right angles to the bridge, the wind speed hitting over 65mph.

Felicity narrowed her eyes. 'Is that...'

'Yes ... it's Rory,' cried a panicked Allie. 'He went out early to pick up some veterinary supplies and now he's stuck in the van on the bridge. The wind is too strong.'

Drew cupped his hands around his mouth and began to shout. 'Drive ... get off the bridge.'

Rory couldn't hear him due to the shrilling winds and he looked petrified inside the van clutching the wheel as he rocked from side to side.

Everyone looked on, the wind slamming into their faces. The force of the water was racing against the side of the bridge and spilling over the banks.

Allie grabbed Felicity's arm. 'He's not going to make it, he's going to be blown into the water.'

Felicity could feel her shaking.

'Please ... someone help him,' Allie shouted, there was no mistaking the fear in her voice.

At that second Felicity felt a swift movement at the side of her followed by a loud gasp from the villagers. She looked towards the bridge and her heart dropped out of her chest.

'Fergus ... NO!' Felicity shouted with all her might. Her pulse quickened and she felt like she was watching a scene from a movie in slow motion. Fergus battled against the weather as he ran towards the bridge like his life depended on it. The rain hit him hard and was unforgiving, his body bent over. He struggled to keep walking, fighting with every muscle against the wind as it whipped against his body. He staggered, it was nearly impossible to stay upright, and with one gust, the wind swooped him near to the edge of the bridge as he pushed back with all his might. The villagers screamed.

'He's going to be blown into the water,' said Felicity, her eyes wide and her heart thumping fast.

Everyone had their eyes firmly fixed on Fergus and Rory when Felicity took a sudden intake of breath and pointed to the far side. She could feel her shoulders shaking with fear and could barely dare to look.

Hundreds of years ago the bridge had been built with skill and precision, but right before everyone's eyes, the bricks of the old bridge began to crumble.

Felicity tried to run forward but Drew swiftly pulled her back. 'You can't go on to the bridge, Flick, it's too dangerous.'

'Someone needs to help them both!' Felicity's voice was earnest. Fear engulfed her body as she looked at Fergus.

'He's nearly at the van.'

The river was rising and hurling over the top of the bridge, at a faster pace.

With one last surge against the wind, Fergus was at the van gripping tightly on to the door handle as the wind and the rain tried one last time to knock him clean off his feet.

Another violent gust of wind shook the van, and Felicity was filled with dread as trepidation ran through her body.

'Get out of the van,' shouted Drew from the river bank but of course Fergus and Rory couldn't hear him.

Fergus managed to pull open the van door and grabbed onto Rory, pulling him free from the van just as it was hurled over the side of the bridge and sent crashing into the water. Everyone screamed and Felicity watched in horror as, soaked through to the skin and clutching on to each other for dear life, Fergus and Rory began to fiercely struggle against the weather back to safety.

'Come on ... keep walking ... please don't let anything happen to them,' Felicity mumbled under her breath. Her heart felt like it was pounding out of her chest.

They were only metres from safety when everyone screamed again. Felicity screwed up her eyes and couldn't bear to watch as the apex of the bridge went crashing into the river.

'It's okay, they've made it,' screeched Allie letting go of Felicity's arm and running towards Rory with her arms open wide.

'Thank God,' Felicity muttered under breath, her heart still thumping against her ribcage. Fergus was safe. Everything was going to be okay.

But just then the riverbank burst and people watched in horror as the bridge collapsed completely, leaving Heartcross cut off from civilisation.

Chapter 12

Allie was standing with her arms wrapped firmly around Rory's neck, tears rolling down her face. 'I thought you were going to end up in the river.'

'Me and you both,' answered Rory visibly shaken.

Drew and Felicity were soon standing by their side and everyone was in complete shock. Where once had stood a Grade II listed bridge that gave access to Glensheil from Heartcross, there was now nothing but a roaring river. Any sign of the bridge was now non-existent.

Fergus's eyes were wide and he shivered and paled as he realised that he had been only seconds away from being hurled into the violent water just like the van.

Feeling emotional, Felicity turned towards Fergus and without thinking hugged him. 'Are you okay?' she asked, her voice wobbling.

A white-faced Fergus didn't push her away but the only thing he could manage was a nod in reply.

'You saved my life,' Rory blew out a breath before thrusting out his trembling hand towards Fergus who shook it.

'Don't be daft, all I did was run on to the bridge.'

'I honestly thought I was a goner...'

'And vans can be replaced—' Drew patted them both on the back '—but my best mates can't. Come on, you pair need to get warmed up.'

As they turned to walk back up the hill the villagers had gathered around them and let out a rapturous cheer.

Fergus raised his hand in acknowledgement as he walked through the crowd before taking one last look back towards the river.

Felicity watched him shudder as he took in the sight and thought how very different things could have been.

As the cheers died down an eerie feeling rippled through the villagers. Everyone appeared paralyzed not knowing what to do or where to go, after watching their only access to the rest of the world disappear. Felicity seized the moment to take control. Shaken still, but thinking calmly now that Fergus was safe, she ordered everyone back to the teashop. Cold and wet, they huddled outside the doorway whilst Felicity nipped through to the cottage calling out to her mum as she grabbed the teashop keys.

'Mum ... MUM! We need you in the teashop now.'

Felicity could hear her rummaging around upstairs in the bedroom.

'MUM!' Felicity bellowed again before she rushed through the door into the kitchen and towards the villagers who were patiently waiting outside.

As she flung open the door the bell welcomed each and every one of them as they fell into the warmth.

Felicity shouted above their chatter. 'You all sit down and I'll get some hot sweet tea on the go.'

The villagers appeared grateful and began to scrape the chairs back as they settled around the tables. They all look shell-shocked.

Felicity set to work unloading the cups and saucers from the cupboards and lining them along the counter top next to the teapots. Thankfully her mum had switched on the urns whilst she'd been out and the water was already heating. As Felicity began to rummage around for teabags she felt a gust of wind from the open door and looked up to see Hamish scuttling towards her.

'Here,' he shouted, holding up numerous carrier bags full to the brim. 'Milk, tea and sugar.'

'You Hamish are a lifesaver,' she replied with a smile. Glancing behind her, she saw her mum standing in the doorway looking around the room in puzzlement at the cold, wet villagers sitting there.

'What's going on?' asked Rona, 'Why is everyone here?'

'The bridge has collapsed,' answered Rory, peeling

the wet coat from his back and hanging it over the back of the chair. He sat down next to Fergus and Drew who were busy tapping on their mobile phones.

Rona looked momentarily confused. 'The bridge has collapsed?' she repeated, looking for clarification.

'The river has burst its banks and the storm has brought the bridge down,' confirmed Fergus.

Rona looked startled. 'Are you serious? But that means…'

'We're stranded,' answered Rory. 'There's no way in and there's no way out.'

'Rory was stuck on the bridge in his van and it's been blown into the water, and Fergus battled the high winds to rescue him,' chipped in Felicity proudly.

Rona looked shell-shocked. 'The van's in the river?'

'It is,' confirmed Rory. 'Blown off the bridge … before it collapsed.'

'Oh my, you must all be in shock. Never mind tea, they need something stronger.' Rona flapped her hand at Felicity. 'Whisky from the cabinet.'

Felicity disappeared inside the cottage while Allie took over throwing a couple of teabags in the teapot before passing out the teacups to the villagers.

'What are we going to do now? Has anyone got any ideas?' asked Julia, who'd watched the commotion unfold alongside a few of her guests from the B&B's top window. She was hoping someone was going to come up with a magic solution or wave a magic wand.

But nobody had an answer.

Within minutes, Fergus and Rory had swigged back a neat whisky while the rest of the traumatised villagers hugged their warm drinks and were chatting amongst themselves. The mood was low.

Once everyone had a warm drink inside them Felicity took control and clapped her hands to get everyone's attention.

She smiled, trying to remain positive but inside felt far from optimistic and had no clue what to really say or do.

All eyes were on her. 'I know we are in shock,' she began, thankful her voice sounded relatively normal even though inside she wasn't feeling very calm. 'But, we are all going to have to pull together and support each other through this. With the bridge gone this means ... well, I think we all know what this means.'

There was an undercurrent of chatter.

'What about food and supplies to the village?' Meredith shouted out. 'What are we going to do?'

Drew piped up, 'There is another way into the village...'

'But that's a twenty-mile round trip over the mountain,' exclaimed Rory, 'and it's treacherous.'

Once more alarmed chatter filled the room.

'We might not have much choice,' replied Felicity,

putting her hand in the air to bring the room back to some sort of order.

'We can't get any vehicles over the mountain top,' said Drew.

Felicity didn't like the worry etched on Drew's face nor did she like the dread that washed over her. She knew the bridge couldn't be fixed overnight. It wasn't going to be that simple. It could take months, even years to rebuild that bridge – how was everyone going to cope in the meantime?

Supplies in the village would run low very quickly, businesses would be affected. People were going to have pull all resources together and work together.

'At least this morning the trucks have already delivered to the shops, so we can ration the food and try and make it last as long as possible,' said Hamish, with a little hope in his voice but unable to hide the look of concern on his face.

'How about we set up some sort of food kitchen, use the teashop to feed the whole village,' suggested Rona.

'I was going to suggest something similar with the pub,' piped up Allie looking teary. Both Meredith and Fraser were nodding their heads in agreement.

'I definitely think it's a good idea, if we can pool all the food together until we know what's going on,' confirmed Rona.

'We can use all the perishable food first from each

household, cook up soup and stews and have various sittings throughout the day,' added Felicity.

'The elderly and children need to be fed first,' offered Allie to a room of consensual nods.

Just at that second, they all looked up to see Jessica bursting through the door, 'Have you seen the floods? And the bridge ... it's gone!' Her face paled as Fergus pulled her out a seat and sat her down. 'Where's Esme?'

'With Isla. I was just collecting Finn when I saw all the commotion.'

Rona hurried over with a cup of tea and placed it on the table in front of her.

'We were on the bridge when it began to collapse,' said Fergus.

'WHAT? Was anyone hurt?'

Fergus shook his head. 'No, thankfully, but Rory's van was blown over the edge of the bridge and was swept into the river by the storm.'

'And Fergus rescued him,' chipped in Felicity once more. Her stomach did a flip as she remembered his heroic rescue.

'Thank God everyone is okay but that's the village cut off.' Jessica's voice was shaky. 'And what about Aggie?' Her worried eyes looked towards Fergus.

Aggie was in the local hospital on the other side of the collapsed bridge.

Fergus blew out a breath. 'It didn't cross my mind.

How are we going to visit? We need to get word to her. She'll think we've abandoned her.'

Heather, the postmistress, was sitting at the back of the teashop flicking on her mobile phone. 'There's a possibility Aggie will already know about the bridge, looking at this.' She held up her phone in the air.

Everyone looked towards Heather. 'The news reporters are on the other side of the bridge. Heartcross is plastered all over the news.

Heather turned up the volume and the whole room hushed to listen.

'The scene behind me is what residents of Heartcross village have woken up to this morning. The River Heart has flooded, with businesses and houses being cut off, leaving villagers undoubtedly worried about the next steps forward.

'The army and the environmental agency have been in attendance and will begin to clear the mud and rubble brought up by the rising waters as soon as the storm subsides.

'We've not managed to reach the residents of Heartcross or interview anyone from the village as yet. There is no direct route into the village. If you are watching, please contact our help desk; the number is currently on the bottom on the screen.'

'Quick write the number down,' urged Felicity,

throwing a pad and pencil towards Heather who eagerly scribbled down the number.

'Shh,' said Meredith, still trying to listen to the news report.

Once more, the tearoom fell silent.

'The video footage you are about to see shows a local Heartcross resident battling the storm to rescue local vet Rory Scott who was stranded in his van on the bridge before the archways begins to crumble.'

'It's Fergus!' exclaimed Heather.

Rona hurried over to watch the video, quickly followed by Felicity who peered over her shoulder.

Rona gasped as she watched Fergus struggling to keep on his feet, as the wind howled and the rain battered his body. Felicity could feel her eyes watering and her heart was in her mouth as she held her breath and re-lived the moment Fergus had nearly been blown off the bridge while the van swayed from side to side.

'Oh my...' said Rona bringing her hand up to her chest as she watched the van crashing into the river. 'You boys are both lucky to be alive.'

'Very lucky...' Felicity blew out a breath. 'It doesn't bear thinking about.'

Everyone in the tearoom could hear the gasps from the villagers on the river bank as the archways began to crumble leaving Fergus and Rory running for their lives when the bridge collapsed.

'Who took the footage?' asked Rory.

'It was me,' piped up Stuart turning to his son Rory. 'I sent it over to the news desk, I hope no one minds.'

'I'm sorry about the van, Dad.'

'Don't be daft, vans are replaceable, my son isn't.' Stuart patted Rory on the shoulder.

Everyone hushed once more and listened.

'*The Environmental Minister Annie Boyd is due to arrive at the scene today but has already pledged she'll do everything she can to get supplies through to help the residents of Heartcross, and that this is now a priority for the government. This is Aidy Redfern reporting for BBC Scotland.*'

Once the news report had finished, Heather switched down the volume on her phone and looked towards Felicity. 'You should phone the helpdesk and speak to them on behalf of the residents. Give them an update from this side of the bridge.'

Felicity brought her hand up to her chest. 'Me? Why would I speak to them? There are more upstanding members of the community to talk to them. Drew, Rory, Fergus, Fraser or Meredith. Just to name a few.' She pointed around the room.

'I think you'd be perfect,' seconded Meredith, followed by a muttering of agreement.

Rona placed a hand on her daughter's shoulder. 'I think it's a good idea too.'

'Why?' asked Felicity, feeling confused.

'Because at the moment you are less emotionally involved than all of us. I think you'll make a good spokesperson for the village and be able to communicate clearly for all of us.'

'I agree too,' added Fergus. 'You were always good at organising and getting things done.' He locked eyes with Felicity for a split second as she felt her heart give a little leap that he trusted her to be the spokesperson for the village.

'Put your hand up if you agree?' bellowed Allie as everyone in the room thrust their arm high into the air.

'That's that then,' said Hamish, 'Felicity is the village's spokesperson, our chief communicator.'

Felicity smiled at everyone. Her heart was hammering against her chest, but she was secretly pleased that the villagers thought she was the best person for the job. 'I'll promise I'll do my best.'

Even though it wasn't under the best circumstances she felt a flutter of excitement that the community had put their faith in her, but also anxious in case she let them down.

'There will be some villagers who haven't woken up yet or have any idea that the bridge has collapsed,' said Rona, walking towards the window and staring out.

Outside the storm was still raging, the trees were

swaying, and Love Heart Lane had a real doom and gloom feeling about it.

'How about I nip up to the school? I've got a set of keys, I could print out a quick flyer letting everyone know the teashop is going to be our base for updated information and meetings. Once the rain has stopped we can start pushing them through the doors?' suggested Jessica.

'And we could set up a Facebook page to keep everyone updated on social media too?' chipped in Allie.

Everyone nodded.

'Shall we say all meet back here tonight at 6 p.m.? Once we've got over the shock and are able to think a little clearer, we can put together a list of tasks and jobs. We need to get in touch with the council. The community really needs to pull together now,' said Felicity as she began to gather up the cups and saucers.

The bedraggled villagers began to gather up their belongings and slide on their wet coats. Everyone was glum; they were all worried about what was going to happen and no one had a clue how long it would take to repair the bridge.

'Spread the word too, bring all perishable goods, vegetables, fruit anything, so we can begin to plan meals for the next few days,' shouted Felicity over the scraping of chairs.

Everyone bobbed their head before they began to

reluctantly disappear back out into the miserable weather.

Allie, Rory, Fergus and Drew stayed behind. Felicity threw them each a tea towel. 'Mum and I will wash, you lot can dry,' she ordered.

'You're very strict,' Drew teased. 'That's what we like in a spokesperson.'

'Right woman for the job then,' joked Fergus playfully while Felicity rolled her eyes at him but was secretly thrilled at his teasing.

As Rona began to fill the sink with hot soapy water and load in the cups and saucers, Felicity checked her phone.

'I've twelve missed calls and one voicemail,' she said in astonishment.

'Who from?' asked Allie with intrigue.

'Isla,' answered Felicity, as she listened to the message. 'She'll have seen the news and will be worried about everyone.'

As Felicity heard Isla's voice she gasped out loud.

'Whatever is the matter? You've gone a peculiar colour.' Allie was standing by her side.

'It's nothing to do with the bridge at all. It's Isla, she's gone into labour.' Felicity's voice rose an octave. 'We can't get her to hospital, there's no way out of the village.'

Drew looked panic-stricken as he threw down the tea-towel and raced through the door.

'You go with him,' Rona ordered her daughter. 'She's going to need some help.'

Felicity turned towards Allie. 'Come on, she'll need both of us.' Allie didn't need asking twice as she threw her tea towel towards Fergus and grabbed her coat.

Felicity's pulse was racing, thinking of the pain Isla must be in, not to mention the worry. There was no way they could get her to a hospital.

'What about the air ambulance?' suggested Felicity thinking out loud.

'I'm not sure that'll even be an option in this storm,' answered Rory, 'but leave it with me, I'll contact Dr Taylor.'

Felicity nodded, flinging open the tearoom door and stepping outside into the stormy weather.

Immediately Rory picked up the teashop's phone and began to dial the number of the surgery.

In less than a minute, Felicity and Allie were following behind Drew, battling the high-speed winds trying to get to Foxglove Farm and Isla as fast as they could.

Chapter 13

'Isla,' bellowed Drew, his heart thumping fast as he stepped into the hallway. 'Where are you?'

He heard footsteps running across the landing and at the top of the stairs Finn's wide eyes appeared with Esme standing at the side of him.

'Mummy's not well. She's up here.'

Esme flapped her hand. 'Come on.'

As fast as he could, Drew's fumbling fingers untied his boots. 'You come down here and watch the TV now. I'll see that Mummy is okay.'

Finn and Esme did as they were told and skipped down the stairs. As soon as they disappeared towards the living room Drew leapt up the stairs towards the bedroom.

'Isla, I'm here,' he said, pushing open the door.

A flustered looking Isla was lying on the bed, sweating profusely and looking in complete agony.

'Thank God, what took you so long?' she said breathlessly.

'Don't worry about that now, I'm here,' he said, taking his wife's hand.

'The contractions are getting closer, you need to drive me to the hospital.'

Drew was rooted to the spot as he stared at Isla. He didn't know how to tell her she wouldn't be going to hospital anytime soon. He started to panic – he'd no clue how to deliver a baby.

'Drew, you look like you've seen a ghost. What's the matter? Don't just stand there. Grab my bag and help me down the stairs. I've texted Jessica to come and get the children, she should be on her way.'

Drew faltered. 'I can't drive you to the hospital.' But before Isla could question why, they heard hurried footsteps up the stairs.

Isla looked towards the doorway to see Felicity and Allie fall into the room. 'I've seen it in the movies, we need hot towels,' said Felicity. 'Can I be chief midwife?'

'What are you pair doing here?' Isla looked perplexed. 'In fact, can you look after Finn and Esme until Jessica arrives? Now help me up and get me to that hospital.' Isla tried to push herself up in the bed, but then came a contraction that dominated her entire body. She let out an almighty scream that made Drew jump out of his skin before taking his wife's hand once more. Isla's pain lasted for what seemed infinity.

'Breathe through it,' offered Allie, 'I've heard them say that in the movies too.'

Isla closed her eyes, waiting for the agony to pass.

As soon as it did, she exhaled, then her eyes met Drew's. 'Please just get me in the car before the next contraction comes, they are getting nearer and nearer.'

'You haven't told her, have you?' said a wide-eyed Felicity looking in Drew's direction.

'I've not had a chance yet,' he replied, risking a tentative look towards his wife.

'Told me what?' she said with a guttural grunt clutching her stomach once more. 'What do you need to tell me?'

'We can't get you to the hospital,' answered Allie in a sympathetic tone. 'But we are here to help.' She raised her eyebrows and rubbed her hands together.

'What do you mean? You either drive me there or ring for an ambulance.'

'Isla, we can't. The bridge has collapsed in the storm. We can't get out of the village. We are stranded.' Drew watched as the words registered.

'And no one can get in,' added Felicity.

'Are you serious? What about the air ambulance?'

'Rory's looking into that and alerting Dr Taylor. But with these winds it's going to struggle to land safely. It looks like we need to prepare to deliver the baby here.'

'We can't deliver the baby here,' she screamed, as she clutched her stomach again.

'Mummy, are you okay?' They all heard Finn's voice call out from the top of the stairs.

'I'll occupy the children until Jessica arrives,' said Allie, swiftly turning and taking what seemed like the easy option. She firmly closed the bedroom door behind her.

'Come on Finn, let's go and watch a film. Mummy is absolutely fine.' Allie took him by the hand and led him swiftly downstairs into the living room.

'Is the baby coming out of Mummy's tummy?' he asked, giving a quick glance towards the closed living-room door.

'Yes, Finn. The baby's on his way.'

Felicity could hear her phone ringing as she delved inside her bag. 'It's Rory,' she said, quickly swiping the screen.

'What's he saying?' flapped Drew.

A minute later Felicity hung up the phone. 'Well?' urged Drew.

'It's not good news. The air ambulance was called out on another job but due to the storm, it's stranded somewhere on the other side of the mountain. Rory has tracked down Dr Taylor and he's on his way over.'

Isla let out a hysterical laugh. 'So you pair are telling me I'm having the baby here? With no pain relief?'

'That's about the size of it,' confirmed Felicity, sucking in a breath before taking off her coat and throwing it over the chair in the corner of the room. 'We are stranded, the village even made the news headlines.'

Isla couldn't believe it. 'And there's really no way out of the village?'

'Only the twenty miles over the treacherous terrain but I don't think you're up to trekking over the mountain top just at the minute.'

'What are we going to do?' said Drew, looking between the both of them.

'Luckily for you, you don't have to do much.' Isla's tone was a little sarcastic. 'Right,' she said, suddenly sounding in control. 'I've done this before and I can do it again.'

'That's the spirit,' exclaimed Felicity spurring on Isla.

'We can do this,' Isla spluttered as another contraction tightened across her stomach and she controlled her breathing.

'How long have you been having contractions for?' asked Drew.

'On and off for the past few days but they've become more frequent since about three o'clock this morning,' she admitted through gritted teeth.

'And you let me go to work and you didn't think to tell me?'

Isla couldn't answer but let out another scream.

'Okay. I need a bowl of warm water, some towels, in fact as many as you can find,' Felicity instructed, locking eyes with Drew who saluted. He was thankful Felicity was there and rushed towards the airing cupboard where he grabbed a handful of towels before filling up a bowl of warm water.'

'I want to push,' exclaimed Isla.

'We need to get you comfy and out of these clothes,' said Felicity, sounding calmer than she actually felt. She helped Isla wriggle out of her maternity jeans.

'Have you got a loose-fitting nightie?'

'In that bag.' Isla pointed towards her overnight bag in the corner of the room that she'd packed ready for the hospital.

Felicity quickly rummaged through it and pulled out a white cotton nightie. 'Not the best colour of clothing for giving birth,' she smiled, trying to make a joke before handing it to Isla. 'You slip that on, while I wash my hands.'

Drew returned to the room and placed the towels on the bed and the bowl of water on the dressing table.

'What's next?' he asked sitting on the edge of the bed.

'You need to hold your wife's hand and take all the abuse she's about to throw at you.'

Drew smiled. 'That's no change from normal then,' he joked placing a kiss to Isla's cheek.

'It's coming again,' said Isla, gritting her teeth. She felt pressure to her back and heard a loud pop, followed by a gush of fluid that soaked into the sheets.

'My waters have broken.'

Drew jumped up and grabbed a towel. 'Can you lift yourself up so I can slide a clean towel underneath you?'

Isla couldn't speak. She was scrunching her eyes shut as she grabbed Drew's arm. She tried her best to concentrate on her breathing but the pain was becoming unbearable. Drew mopped her brow with a sponge to soothe her.

'Breathe through it, it will soon stop,' said Felicity, breathing in and out in an exaggerated way, hoping Isla would copy her.

'I don't feel well,' Isla cried out in pain.

'You're doing brilliantly, honestly I'm so proud of you,' encouraged Drew.

'It feels like it's all going too fast, this is so much quicker than having Finn,' she panted.

'They say second babies are always quicker than the first,' said Drew, once again mopping her brow as the contraction came to an end.

'Are you comfy?' asked Felicity.

'As comfy as I can be. But I've got the urge to push.'

Drew shot up from the edge of the bed and stood up by the side of his wife.

'Can you take a look?' he asked Felicity.

'Do you mind?' Felicity turned towards Isla.

'There's no point me being modest now, is there?'

Isla brought up her knees and Felicity took a swift look. The next contraction came, though it seemed like only a matter of seconds since the last one.

Isla cried out, 'It's coming!'

'Take short breaths,' ordered Felicity. 'You are doing really, really well.'

'I can feel the head,' panted Isla.

'Are you sure?'

'Yes,' she screamed.

Felicity took another look under her nightie. 'I can see the head, it's crowning.' Felicity's heart was beating nineteen to the dozen.

'I need to push again.'

'This baby is nearly here.' Felicity glanced over at Drew; the colour had drained from his cheeks.

'This baby isn't hanging about. With the next contraction, push down,' ordered Felicity, encouraging Isla to push hard. 'You can do this.'

Despite the pain and giving it everything she'd got, Isla pushed with all her might. The perspiration was running down her forehead as she clutched Drew's hand so tightly he thought he may pass out.

Isla let out an almighty scream just as a beautiful slithering bundle of life slid right into Felicity's hands and Drew let out a joyful cry. 'He's here!'

Drew quickly wiped the mucus from the baby's mouth and nose. Joyful tears were cascading down Felicity's cheeks, the emotion surged through her body as the baby let out a cry and the relief was instant. Immediately Felicity placed the baby on to Isla's chest.

'He's beautiful. Welcome to the world, baby Angus.' Tears of relief were streaming down Isla's cheeks as Drew wrapped his arms around his wife and baby son.

'I'll leave you to it and congratulations to you both,' Felicity stood up, and quickly hugged both Isla and Drew.

'Hello, can I come in?' Hearing a knock on the bedroom door, and recognising Dr Taylor's voice, Felicity opened the door.

'Angus has arrived,' exclaimed a delighted Felicity who stepped out of the way to let Dr Taylor into the room.

Both the proud parents beamed towards him.

'How's mother doing?' asked Dr Taylor placing his bag on the floor then looking directly towards Isla.

'She's doing just fine,' answered an exhausted Isla.

'Can I just check over the little fellow?' he asked stretching his arms out and taking hold of Angus.

Isla looked towards Dr Taylor.

'All is good with this little man, I suggest we get you both cleaned up and this little one dressed.'

'I'll leave you to it,' said Felicity, 'but shall I let Finn know the good news?'

'You tell him and I'll come and fetch him as soon as we have Isla and Angus ready,' beamed a proud Drew.

Felicity excitedly bounded down the stairs and opened the door to the living room to find six pairs of eyes staring back at her.

'When did you lot sneak in?' asked Felicity, amazed that Jessica, Rory and Fergus had now joined Allie, Esme and Finn.

'Never mind that,' said Allie, flapping her hand towards Felicity. 'Any news?'

Felicity couldn't contain the excitement any longer and perched on the arm of the chair next to Finn.

'I'm over the moon to announce you have a brand new baby brother called Angus, who is absolutely perfect!'

The whole living room erupted in cheers and Finn jumped to his feet. 'Can I go and see him?'

Felicity was just about to answer when Drew appeared in the doorway. 'You sure can!'

Finn squealed as his father was met with a barrage of congratulations and everyone jumped to their feet. Finn launched into his dad's arms who hugged him tight.

'Are you ready to meet your new baby brother?'

The huge beam across Finn's face said it all as he clutched his dad's hand.

As a proud Finn disappeared up the stairs to meet his new brother everyone else began reaching for their coats.

Allie blew out a breath. 'Are you thinking of changing careers to midwifery?' she joked, looking at Felicity.

'I noticed you took the easy option,' Felicity replied, as she rolled her eyes at Allie.

'I'm not good with all that squeamish stuff,' Allie said, hugging Felicity.

'Congratulations to you,' said Fergus, standing up. For a moment Felicity thought he was actually going to hug her but he touched her arm tentatively. 'That's a huge thing you've just done,' he exclaimed, leaving Felicity beaming with pride.

'It's just an average day in Heartcross ... bridges collapsing, babies being delivered,' joked Felicity, suddenly remembering the chaos of the morning which had passed her by for the last hour.

'The press have been in touch,' said Rory, slipping his coat on. 'They want to interview you, this afternoon.'

'We've given the reporter your number,' chipped in Allie. 'They just want to talk to you about how the village is feeling and what's the plan from here.'

Felicity didn't know how she felt about this even though she knew she'd agreed to be the spokesperson for the village. All she wanted to do was return to the cottage and grab a cup of tea. 'I'll await the call then. I'd best get back to Mum, see what's going on. What's the plan for you lot now?' asked Felicity.

'We'll be off. We can nip back and see the baby once

they've had some time to themselves,' answered Allie.

Not wanting to crash their family time the gang shouted up the stairs to Isla and Drew with the promise they'd visit soon.

As everyone got ready to leave, Felicity sank into the chair in front of the fire. She actually felt quite emotional and drained. As she'd been helping to deliver the baby she'd felt scared, even though she'd tried her best not to show it. What if something had gone wrong? But luckily for everyone, Dr Taylor had arrived just at the right time and baby Angus was more than perfect.

'Penny for them?' Rory looked over towards Felicity. 'You look exhausted.'

'I feel it to be honest,' she replied, tucking her feet underneath her.

'Are you coming?'

Felicity shook her head. 'I'm going to stay here and gather myself,' she said. 'In fact, I'm in need of a drink. It's not every day you deliver a baby.'

'Do you want me to stay with you?' asked Allie.

'No, you get off, I'll catch up with you later, and we have that meeting at six o'clock in the teashop.'

'You've been amazing today.' Allie said, giving her a quick hug, and Felicity felt a warmth run through her body at being congratulated by her friends. Maybe this was the start of her feeling less of an outsider?

As she sat on the chair a lonely tear slipped down

her cheek. Of course, she was over the moon for her friend; it would be selfish for her not to be happy for Isla and Drew, but she was deeply saddened knowing she would never give birth, never have her own child that she'd love with all her might, that no one was ever going to call her Mum. And try as she might to imagine her future without children, the pain never went away. Fergus's words still echoed around her head, words from the past. 'I love you, only you, instead of thinking what we should have or could have been, let's focus on what is and what can be.'

Felicity pushed herself up from the chair, feeling emotional, and poured herself a stiff drink from the decanter on the sideboard. Swirling the amber liquid around she immediately drained the glass feeling the whisky burn the back of her throat. The memories from the past whirled around in her head as the tears cascaded down her cheeks.

Delivering Angus had brought back painful memories, and even after all this time, she still yearned to be a mother.

She stood and watched her friends walking away from Foxglove Farm, her gaze fixed on Jessica and Esme. Rory and Allie were in front holding hands, and she noticed Fergus stop and say something to Jessica who nodded then carried on walking clutching Esme's hand. Fergus turned and began to walk back towards the farmhouse. Felicity's heart jumped. Why was he coming back?

Quickly, she wiped away the tears with the back of her hand and moved away from the window. She heard the click of the door, and Fergus appeared in the doorway of the living room.

'Did you forget something?' asked Felicity, her heart hammering against her chest as he walked back into the room. Her eyes shifted towards the floor as she didn't want him to notice her bleary eyes.

'Are you okay?' he asked tentatively. 'I kind of got the feeling…'

Before Fergus had even finished his sentence, Felicity couldn't hold the emotion back and the tears cascaded down her face.

She locked eyes with him and for a moment they stood in an awkward silence until he opened his arms and did what felt the most natural thing in the world. He hugged her.

Felicity buried her face into his shoulder taking in the spicy aroma of his aftershave, a closeness she had missed so much.

'I know how difficult it must have been for you delivering a baby … after everything.' Fergus pulled away gently and perched on the arm of the chair.

'You have no idea…' Her voice faltered. 'But we both know…'

Fergus could see Felicity was upset and still very much trying to come to terms with the past. 'Flick, there are other options available and when you meet someone...'

'No, Fergus,' interrupted Felicity. The thought of having another man's baby when all she'd longed for was his too much. 'A baby of my own is all I've ever wanted. It's all right for you.' She knew as soon as the words left her mouth that they seemed unkind. 'I'm sorry ... I didn't mean...'

'I know you didn't ... I lived through it too, remember,' he said tenderly. 'I know exactly how you feel.'

'But you have your family now, you've moved on. I'll never have that.' She knew her emotions were running away with her, but she couldn't help it. It wasn't his fault she'd left for London, in fact he had been the one begging her to stay.

'That doesn't mean to say I will ever forget the past or not care,' said Fergus, his voice soft.

Felicity looked up through her fringe and slowly sat down on the settee. 'Care about the past or care about me?'

The question hung in the air.

Fergus didn't answer it.

'I'm just making sure you are okay.'

'And if I said I wasn't?' Felicity felt saddened and vulnerable as she thought about her lost chance at being a mother. She remembered her own childhood, how she'd splashed in puddles in her bright red wellington boots, how she'd danced a jig every time her grandmother had pulled the gingerbread men from the oven and how her mum would curl up with her every night and read her a bedtime story. Those moments were precious and were ones she'd wanted to share with her own children. With her and Fergus's children.

Their eyes fixed intently on each other for a moment before Fergus spoke. 'Then I'd walk you back to the cottage and deliver you into the safe hands of Rona.'

Felicity was hoping for more; she was hoping he'd say that he would sit with her until she was feeling better, as long as it took, but she knew that would be difficult for him too.

She nodded, shaking herself from her painful memories. 'Honestly, I'm okay ... you go and catch up Jessica and Esme.'

He hesitated before standing up, then raked his hand through his hair. Her stomach slumped and she felt shattered as Fergus moved towards the door.

'You take care of yourself.'

As she watched him walk out of the farmhouse and stride up the long driveway she swallowed down a lump in her throat.

Upstairs she could still hear the joyful chatter from Finn, who was absolutely made up with the arrival of his new baby brother. Felicity knew that even though she'd never have her own child, she was going to embrace baby Angus and make sure that she helped Isla at every possible opportunity. She'd decided she was going to be chief babysitter. She couldn't turn back time but Fergus coming back to see she was okay gave her a glimmer of hope for a friendship that she'd thought was unfixable. She'd worried about how he was going to react to her homecoming, but now believed that they had a real chance at being friends, which would only make it easier for her to fit back in with the community. They still had a long way to go, and Felicity wasn't sure she would ever get over what happened between them, but Fergus had shown he still cared and she felt happy about that.

Chapter 14

'Felicity, it's the phone for you,' Rona shouted up the stairs towards the locked door of the bathroom.

After Felicity left the farm, she'd wandered up to the village shop where Hamish had already organised a bundle of food to deliver to the teashop. He told Felicity that the mood in the village was one of worry which was understandable. The whole village was shrouded in uncertainty. No one knew what was going to happen or how soon the bridge could be repaired or when any further supplies would get through. The impact on the village was huge and only time would tell how everyone would be affected.

Hamish told Felicity that Meredith and Fraser had already transported huge aluminium pots to the teashop to make it easier to prepare the food in huge quantities. Meredith, of course, had offered to help Rona. In fact, it was going to be all hands on deck feeding the masses in the coming days, maybe weeks.

And now Felicity was soaking in the bath with bubbles up to her neck thinking about the village and how everyone was going to cope. She knew things wouldn't be that different for the first few days but once the food began to dwindle, people would be pushed to their limit and tempers could fray.

'Who is it?' she shouted, as she swirled the warm water around her body.

'Aidy Redfern, reporter from the BBC,' her mum bellowed back as Felicity quickly slipped out of the bath, towelled herself down and pulled her bathrobe tightly around her body before hurrying downstairs. Rona handed her the receiver as she sat down on the bottom stair.

'Hello, Felicity Simons here,' she answered in a posh telephone voice which made her mum smile as she disappeared towards the kitchen to make a cup of coffee. She could hear Felicity chatting away and as soon as she hung up she shouted to her mum, 'Switch on the TV. Apparently, I'm on the news in a moment.'

Rona thrust a mug of coffee into Felicity's hand before immediately switching on the TV.

They watched and waited patiently until they saw the collapsed bridge flash before their eyes with news-reader Aidy Redfern poised with his microphone, ready to start talking.

'I'm still standing near the flooded banks of the River

Heart where earlier this morning the bridge collapsed, isolating the village of Heartcross. Severe weather warnings remain in place with further rainfall forecast for later on this afternoon making homes and businesses still very vulnerable and at the mercy of the next storm. The army and RAF are currently dropping sandbags to limit any further damage to the area, but normality will take a long time to return. We have managed to speak to local resident Felicity Simons who is the dedicated spokesperson for the village of Heartcross. What's the general feeling in Heartcross at this moment in time, Felicity?'

'One of shock,' Felicity heard herself say.

'Eww, my voice sounds weird. I don't sound like that.' She grimaced at the TV screen.

'That's exactly how you sound,' chuckled Rona, still staring at the TV. 'And look, there's your name in the banner across the bottom! Felicity Simons ... spokeswoman for Heartcross Village,' said Rona with importance.

'Everyone is doing their best to comfort one another. We don't know what's going to happen, or when the bridge will be repaired. The mood in the village is very sombre at the moment.'

'Environmental Minister Annie Boyd has promised Heartcross is her first priority, how do the villagers feel about this commitment?'

'Everyone is grateful for all the help we can receive. The village had supplies delivered just before the storm hit and we've held an emergency meeting of the residents to pool our provisions and open up a food kitchen which will be run by myself and other villagers.'

'We also have Glensheil's local councillor standing here next to me.' Aidy turned the microphone towards a stout man in his early sixties, dressed in a flat cap, waterproof coat and trousers with green wellington boots. His cheeks were rosy, and his spectacles perched on the end of his nose. 'What is the first plan to help Felicity and the residents of Heartcross?'

'We are holding an emergency meeting tomorrow morning with the Environmental Minister. We need to discuss the repair of the bridge and the cost.'

'Surely the first priority is to make sure the bridge is repaired as soon as possible? And that normal service is resumed for the residents of Heartcross?'

The local councillor seemed to hesitate. 'The bridge is Grade II listed, the actual cost to rebuild it will be phenomenal, but we are currently working with the military, the Scottish highways and the department of transport on the best way forward.'

Aidy turned back towards the screen. 'We will keep you updated on events throughout the day. This is Aidy Redfern reporting for BBC Scotland.'

*

'Look at you, on the TV,' exclaimed Rona.

'It was only my voice and they cut loads of the interview out,' replied Felicity, still staring at the screen.

'That's what they always do.'

They both watched the rest of the news in silence. The storms and unruly weather were affecting the entire country.

'The bridge repair isn't going to happen overnight, is it?' sighed Felicity, thinking about the news report and the look on the councillor's face.

Rona shook her head. 'The cost is going to be astronomical, and in the meantime, the long trek over the mountain top might be the only access in and out of Heartcross.'

Felicity knew there was no way they could rely on that route. Trucks wouldn't be able to use that pass and it would take people hours to walk it. They'd need a temporary footbridge that could be erected straight away even if it meant no vehicles could travel over it. Then at least they'd have access to the other side. She picked up her iPad and logged on to Facebook and was amazed to see that villagers were marking themselves safe in the Heartcross Bridge collapse. She clicked on her notifications and saw she'd been invited to like a Facebook page which had been set up by Allie. There was a photo of Felicity, with the title Heartcross Spokeswoman. Other residents had already liked the page and tonight's meeting had already been posted inviting all the residents to attend the teashop at six o'clock.

Felicity noticed some of the questions and comments that had been posted too. One was from Julia at the B&B, aimed at the council. She wanted to know the answer to the question that was on everyone's mind – how much it would cost to erect a temporary bridge across the river. An answer had been posted which suggested in the region of £300,000. Reading through the questions, Felicity tried to catch her breath; she wasn't sure how they'd even be able to raise that sort of cash unless the government offered to fund it.

'What are you looking at?' asked Rona, noticing Felicity had gone quiet.

'It looks like Allie has set up a Facebook page, so we can keep all updates on Heartcross and questions in one place.'

'That's a good idea,' exclaimed Rona, who wasn't hot on technology and would rely on Felicity to keep her updated.

'I think, looking at some of the questions, people want answers and things to move right away, but according to the council it isn't going to be that easy.' Felicity scrolled through some more of the comments.

'It really isn't going to be that easy,' answered Rona. 'Money and manpower won't come cheap.'

Hearing the iPad ping, Felicity clicked on the notification and saw it was a message from Polly.

Flick...Waving hello from London and sending you lots of hugs. We've just heard you on the TV in the pub and can't believe what's happening up there in Heartcross.

Everyone sends their love and we hope to see you back in London very soon! Take care.

Love Polly x

'It's Polly, she's seen the news.'

'Your friend from London?'

Felicity nodded. 'Hoping to see me back in London very soon.'

'You'll need to email your boss,' said Rona. 'Let her know you won't be back when you're meant to be.'

Even though Felicity had made her mind up that she wasn't going back to work in the department store she knew she needed to email Eleanor Ramsbottom ASAP. It wasn't as though she'd be getting out of Heartcross anytime soon anyway. She opened her email and began to type.

Dear Eleanor,

As you may have seen on the news, the Heartcross Bridge has collapsed in the storms and unfortunately I am currently stranded in the village with no way out. Therefore, I won't be returning to work as planned next week.

Yours sincerely,

Felicity Simons.

The email was short and sweet.

After hitting 'send' Felicity scrolled through the rest of her emails and noticed a rather official one sitting at the top from Councillor Smith. She opened it up to find a virtual invitation to a meeting being held by Skype in the morning to discuss the way forward for the residents of Heartcross. This would give her direct insight to how the Environmental Minister would help them. She immediately accepted the invitation and posted on the Facebook page of the newly formed group to let them know that she would be attending.

Almost immediately, a barrage of questions was put forward from residents who were carefully watching the page. Felicity began to write them down.

'I'm not sure if I've bitten off more than I can chew,' sighed Felicity. 'Everyone seems to think I've got a magic wand and by end of tomorrow another bridge is going to be erected.'

Rona raised her eyebrows. 'They are in for a shock.'

'I hope they don't go blaming me if things take a little time.'

'They won't, and anyway Annie Boyd, the environmental woman, said she was making Heartcross a priority. They can't ask for more than that.'

'Let's hope so, because Bert from the care home is holding no prisoners on this Facebook page.'

Flicking through the rest of Facebook, Felicity turned the iPad towards her mum. 'Isla and Drew have welcomed Angus to the world with their first official family photograph … take a look.'

Rona flapped a hand in front of her eyes as they welled up. 'He's gorgeous. He's definitely got Drew's nose.'

'How can you tell, he's only a few hours old,' chuckled Felicity, who'd promised Isla she'd try and nip back later today.

'You can always tell,' stated Rona, meaning every word. 'And how are you? That must have been a bit of shock delivering the baby.'

Felicity felt that familiar twinge of sadness.

'I'm okay, honestly I am,' she answered. 'I just went into autopilot and did what anyone else would do … well, everyone except Allie,' laughed Felicity. 'I've never seen anyone move so fast when the options were looking after Finn and Esme or delivering a baby.'

'Was Fergus there with Esme?'

Felicity nodded. 'He left with the others but came back once they'd gone to check I was okay.'

Rona raised an eyebrow. 'That was very kind of him.'

Felicity agreed. 'It was... the storm has died a little, I'm going to go and get changed then nip back up to the farm and see if there's anything I can do for Isla and Drew,' said Felicity, standing up and pulling the belt tight on her dressing gown.

'Pass on my best wishes, and I'll be up to give the little man a wee squeeze very soon.'

Within five minutes, Felicity was on her way to Foxglove Farm. She noticed a cluster of villagers standing on the hill looking over towards where the bridge had once stood. There were now helicopters circulating up above that had dropped sand bags all along the burst river banks which would help keep the flooding under control. The only saving grace for the residents of Heartcross was that their dwellings and businesses were up the mountainous track so at least they weren't flooded too. As Felicity carried on past the school she noticed the sign pinned to the door: 'closed until further notice.'

She stopped walking for a moment and leant against the fence. Taking in a breath and closing her eyes, she tilted her face towards the sky. Without warning, her thoughts filtered back to the past and all of a sudden her legs took her off in another direction to a place where she'd spent a lot of time as a child and through her teenage years. With the wind in her hair she scrambled over the stile at the top of Love Heart Lane and began to climb the small incline towards the pass, where she stumbled along the rocky path for approximately ten minutes. The view from up there was one of outstanding beauty, where you could see for miles and miles. This was a place she hadn't walked for over ten years, off the beaten track, untouched by time amongst the majestic mountain-scape, yet it was all still so familiar to her.

Then she saw it, up in the distance, the small brick building that, as kids, she and the others had spent many a summer holiday hanging out in. She felt a flutter of excitement inside her stomach, remembering the time Fergus had entwined his fingers around hers inside the hideaway and gently kissed her for the first time.

As she continued to walk towards it, she noticed the windows were now broken and it looked weathered, but there was still something magical about the old place that brought back good memories. Felicity twisted the knob on the door and pushed it open, feeling a little anxious as she looked around.

The place only consisted of two small rooms. There was an old battered musty sofa in the corner and litter strewn over the concrete floor. She guessed someone had been sleeping rough here, maybe sheltering from the chilling winter weather. She stood for a minute remembering all the times as a child that she'd brought picnics up here with Isla and Allie and they pretended it was their house, occupying themselves for hours before returning down the rocky mountainous terrain towards home.

Felicity knew the last time she'd been here and blinked back the tears in her eyes – it only seemed like yesterday. She went back outside and took the shingle path to the back of the small brick building and exhaled as the view took her breath away. There was a bench and somehow the snowdrops on the ground hadn't been destroyed in the wind. Instead they stood proud and danced in the breeze.

Felicity had no idea why this building was even here. She'd no clue what it had ever been used for but she remembered the day she'd discovered it alongside Isla and Allie. They'd been splashing around in the narrow stream that ran down the mountain when Isla had decided they were going to discover where the water began. The three of them were forbidden to venture up this rocky terrain without an adult, but with the sun beating down on their backs one summer's day they had set off on their little adventure. And once they'd discovered the building they'd played in it all day, until time had run away with them. For the rest of the school holidays they'd always disappeared to their new den, just the three of them, until the boys had spotted them vanishing upstream and followed them, soon joining their summer holiday gang. That was when Felicity and

Fergus had become inseparable, and each morning of the school holidays had made her heart leap, knowing they'd be hanging out together. As they'd messed around in the water and hung out in their hideout, they'd shared their dreams and planned to live happily ever after, together forever.

As Felicity found herself swathed in happy memories of her childhood, she wondered why adult life wasn't as easy and carefree. She wandered over to the huge tree that had shielded them from many an afternoon sun; now its wintery bare branches waved madly above her. This tree was special to Felicity, and as she stood in front of the trunk she swallowed a lump in her throat. There, carved in the tree, was a heart with the words *F & F forever* etched inside it. Felicity traced the heart with her finger, 'Fergus and Flick ... blooming memories,' she said to herself, brushing away a tear with the back of her hand.

A snap of a twig behind Felicity caused her to spin round, breaking her reverie. For a moment, she thought she was still dreaming. Fergus looked as handsome as ever standing in front of her. He swept his hair out of his eyes leaving them fixed on her.

'What are you doing here?' Her heart thumped faster as the question left her lips.

'I saw you climb over the stile.'

'And you followed me?' Felicity narrowed her eyes.

'Well, I'm here,' he answered, digging his hands into the pockets of his coat. 'I knew this was where you'd be heading.'

Felicity watched as he walked over to the tree and he too traced his finger around the heart. 'It's still there ... young love, eh,' he said softly, turning back towards her.

Felicity sat down on the bench, not knowing what to say. In the past she'd planned out so many conversations in her head with Fergus, but now she didn't know where to start. She was lost for words.

'What are you doing here?'

Fergus was looking up at the sky. 'I wanted to make sure you were okay.'

Numerous questions were swimming around in Felicity's mind and she didn't know which one to ask first. She took a minute then spoke. 'Do you ever think about us?'

She noticed Fergus taking his hands out of his pockets and rub them together, something he did when he was nervous.

'Sometimes,' he admitted, still looking up at the sky. 'But times have moved on, Flick.'

'Have they?' The words had slipped out of Felicity's mouth before she could stop them.

Fergus looked towards her. 'What do you mean?'

'Nothing, it doesn't matter,' she answered, knowing

deep down inside she wanted to tell him she still had feelings for him, even after all this time.

Again, they sat in silence staring into space.

'I didn't mean to hurt you.' Felicity finally broke the silence.

'It was a long time ago.' His voice was steady.

She looked in his direction and noticed his eyes were bleary.

'I couldn't have given you what you wanted,' she said softly.

He held her gaze. 'You tried to second guess what I wanted, I told you at the time all I wanted was you. It was your choice not to believe me and run.'

'Do you blame me?'

He looked towards her in puzzlement. 'Blame you for what? The miscarriages? Of course I don't. Why would I? I loved you.'

The pain twisted in Felicity's heart when she heard the word loved. 'No, for running away,' she stuttered.

He stole a second to answer. 'It took me a long time to get over it, a very long time. You left me. I was grieving for our loss and you. At the time I thought we were a team. We would have got through it together. I would have made sure we did. But you didn't trust what I was saying to you. You made the decision to leave and I had to somehow pick myself up, brush myself down and carry on existing. I learnt to move on.'

'Which you obviously did.'

Fergus gave her a look that was far from impressed. 'That's really not fair, Flick. Put yourself in my shoes. Walk those months, those first six months, hoping and praying each day you'd walk back into my life.'

Felicity looked at the ground and didn't speak.

'What did you expect me to do, wait around forever? Wait until you gave me the time of day, remembered I was here suffering as much as you ... just put my life on hold?'

'I was the mother,' she replied.

'And I was the father who loved the mother with all his heart.'

Felicity didn't reply; she felt sad knowing what she'd put Fergus through. He was one of the good guys and look how she'd treated him.

'I never thought I would ever get that feeling back. And then Lorna walked into my life.' He took a breath. 'I never thought I'd be able to trust another girl; I didn't want to get close to anyone in case they abandoned me again. The fear of rejection was way too much to bear.' Fergus sniffed, and Flick handed him a tissue from her pocket.

'When Lorna came along she taught me how to love and trust again. She gave me a new zest for life and I loved her.' He wiped away his tears.

Felicity felt a tiny pang of jealousy hearing those

words, even though she knew it was ridiculous. She still didn't want to think of Fergus loving anyone else.

'And Esme is the best thing that could have ever happened to me.'

Felicity couldn't help herself. 'So I did do the right thing by leaving.'

Fergus shook his head. 'That's a little unfair, how am I meant to answer that? It's been hard Flick, Esme losing her mother ... it's been difficult for me too, ensuring she doesn't feel different from her friends and giving her the love and attention of both parents.' Fergus's voice wobbled.

'I'm sorry,' she said. 'It was never my intention to hurt you.' She closed her eyes and took a breath.

'I know ... but you did Felicity, you did. I thought my world had ended.'

'Mine too,' breathed Felicity, moving her hand to his.

He shook his head, realising his mistake. 'I shouldn't have followed you.' He moved his hand away and Felicity's heart came crashing down.

'We can't turn back time.' He looked directly at her. 'You broke my heart, Flick. I was hurting too, but you abandoned me without a second thought. I truly believed we would have been together forever but now...'

'It wasn't like that.' Her voice faltered.

'Why couldn't you just trust me and let me love you? Like I promised.'

'I'm back now.' Her voice was shaky. 'I still love—'

'Don't say that, Flick. We can't just turn back time.'

'We could see how it goes?'

'Why now, after all this time, have you decided this is for you? You had me and didn't want me. It took me a long time to get over you.'

'And are you over me?' She briefly closed her eyes, waiting for him to answer.

He took a breath. 'Yes, I'm over you.' The truth of his words cut through her. 'Things have moved on in my life. Esme is my priority, she comes first ... and how could I ever know that you wouldn't leave me again at the drop of a hat?' Fergus stood up, his admission breaking Felicity's heart, shattering again into tiny pieces.

'That's not going to happen, I'm back to stay.' Her thumb skimmed over the pulse in her wrist.

'How could I ever know that?' His voice was soft as he turned to walk away from her, like she had once done to him.

It was only as she sat and watched him walk slowly along the pass that she knew she'd made the biggest mistake of her life leaving Heartcross. Once he was out of sight she allowed the tears to flow. The pain made her chest heave as she tried to inhale enough air to breathe. Why did it hurt so much? She hugged her knees to her chest. Every muscle in her body ached. She bitterly regretted leaving Fergus. He'd meant everything to her. He still did mean everything to her.

Her heart still soared with love for Fergus.

Chapter 15

Felicity put her hand in the air to fend off the multi-tude of questions being fired at her. Inside she felt close to tears. She wanted to be anywhere but here right at this very minute. Not only had she had the run in with Fergus but now most of the village seemed to think she was wholly responsible for erecting a bridge and getting it built ASAP so Heartcross could get back to normality.

The room was packed to the rafters; there were even villagers standing against the back wall armed with notepads and pens, and Felicity was standing right in the line of fire at the front of the teashop.

Everyone seemed a little on edge, and they all wanted answers to their questions, but it wasn't as easy as that.

'Please, please speak one at a time,' insisted Felicity, still holding her arm in the air and trying to bring some order back to the room.

'What if the council refuses to erect a temporary

bridge?' shouted Louis, a local farm labourer, from the corner of the room. 'What are you going to do about it?'

There was angry muttering in the room which unnerved Felicity. 'We are losing our livelihood. We can't get across to Glensheil,' he continued, and there were jeers from the back of the room.

Hearing a scraping of a chair, Felicity looked over to see Fergus jump to his feet and wave his hand above his head to calm everyone down, much to her surprise. The room fell silent. 'Can we just stop and take a moment? Felicity has agreed to be our spokesperson, not to take on the job of building the bridge single-handedly by herself.' He cast his eye around the room. 'The way you are speaking to her is out of order. It's for all of us to pull together, support each other and be kind to each other. That is the only way to get through this. Felicity, Rona and Meredith have all agreed to open up this place as a food kitchen and prepare all our meals and ration the food until we know how we are going to transport supplies. We've had tough times before with the weather; granted, we haven't been totally cut off, but what we need now is solutions, not shouting at each other.'

'It may be the case that once the river dies down we can transport supplies by boat ... maybe?' offered Felicity as a solution.

'See, this is what we need, ideas we can take on board, positive suggestions without pointing the finger,' encouraged Fergus sitting back down and catching Felicity's eye who mouthed 'thank you'.

'First things first, I'll attend the virtual meeting in the morning and will post an update for you all on the Facebook page. Does that sound fair to everyone?'

Felicity followed the nods around the room and was thankful that the majority of villagers had calmed down.

Rona was flitting from table to table filling up cups with tea and generally chatting to keep the mood uplifted.

'And we will start the food kitchen tomorrow lunchtime, feeding the children and the elderly first. I'll devise a rota with different meal times for each street in the village and post that on the Facebook page as well as pinning a poster to the window of the teashop.'

'Excellent plan,' shouted Allie. 'And don't forget to pool your supplies of food, anything perishable we will use first. You can either drop them here, to the pub or into Hamish at the village shop.'

The chairs began to scrape as people gathered their belongings. There was nothing more they could do until after the meeting tomorrow.

'Well, I'd best get back to Isla,' said Drew. 'I left her with the wee man screaming the house down.'

'Ah bless.' Allie smiled, wrapping a scarf around her neck and pulling on her coat.

'I'll drop off all the eggs from the farm in the morning.' Drew turned towards Felicity and Rona. 'I'm not going to market any time soon and there will be plenty to go around for everyone.'

'Excellent, thank you. That's so kind,' smiled Rona, touching his arm. 'What a day everyone has had.'

'I'm in need of a stiff drink,' declared Meredith, 'but there'll come a time when the pub will run dry too, if we don't sort out access very soon.'

Rory looked horrified at that remark. 'That can't happen ... remember the time when we brewed our own beer?'

Now it was Fergus's turn to look horrified. 'Things are never going to get that bad again,' laughed Fergus, slapping him heartily on his back. 'I'd go teetotal, you nearly poisoned us all.'

'It wasn't that bad,' argued Rory.

Fergus nodded encouragingly while he was speaking but then cocked an eyebrow and found himself grinning. 'I think you'll find it was more than terrible.'

Everyone laughed and as they all turned to leave, Felicity found herself tugging at the arm of Fergus's coat. 'Thank you,' she said immediately when his eyes locked with hers.

'Thank you for what?'

'For sticking up for me against the masses.' Her voice sounded weaker than usual.

'I'd do the same for anyone that I thought wasn't being treated fairly.'

'Of course,' she answered, feeling like a fool.

He followed the gang and she found her heart speeding up a fraction when he hovered by the doorway and turned back towards her. She was rooted to the spot and her eyes darted all over his face.

'Take no notice of Louis,' he said. 'His bark is worse than his bite. Everyone is just worried about their livelihood.'

Felicity nodded, then Fergus gave her a smile she wasn't expecting, the same smile he'd once given her in the past. Her heart lifted, and she knew that no matter how many times he tried to convince himself that he didn't still have feelings for her, that he did. She could feel that the connection between them that hadn't gone away, but she knew she had to convince him that he could put his trust in her once more.

Chapter 16

When the crowd finally ebbed, Felicity began to help Rona clear the empty cups away and load them into the sink. They were silent, lost in their own thoughts while Rona washed and Felicity dried.

'It's going to be a mammoth task you know, cooking for two hundred households,' said Rona, wondering if they'd bitten off more than they could chew.

'Huge pots of stew, we can peel vegetables, potatoes etc. Allie and Meredith will help and I'm sure Jessica will too,' said Felicity, neatly stacking the cups and saucers onto each table ready for the next day. 'And there's the children.'

'Children?' asked Rona in puzzlement.

'Esme and Finn ... I'm sure Isla will need a rest and with Aggie in hospital it's one less thing for Fergus to worry about. They could pitch in here for the day. We'd keep them occupied.'

Rona stopped and stared at Felicity.

'I've not sure that's such a good idea Felicity.'

'What do you mean?' asked Felicity, even though she knew what was coming next.

'Just that I'm worried you are trying to ease your way back into Fergus's life.'

Even though she knew her mum was right, she still felt annoyed at her assumption. 'I'm just saying...'

Rona gave her daughter a knowing look.

'All I did was thank him for sticking up for me.'

'If Fergus still has feelings for you, don't push it, let it happen naturally, let him come to you.'

Felicity knew her mum was right but she wanted to give it a little push in the right direction.

'He has a lot on his plate with Aggie on the other side of the water in hospital too.'

Felicity felt her mood slide after suddenly feeling elated by Fergus's smile.

Hearing a knock on the window they spun round to see Allie mouthing at them through the window. Felicity hurried over to the door. 'Have you forgotten something?'

'No, spur of the moment thing. Fancy a drink in the pub? Everyone's coming.'

'Everyone?'

'Well, except Isla ... obviously. A quick wet of the baby's head.'

Felicity looked towards her mum.

'You go, enjoy yourself,' she said. 'I can start prepping the vegetables ready for tomorrow.'

Felicity pressed a quick kiss to her mum's cheek. 'Thank you, I won't be late.'

She grabbed her coat and linked her arm through Allie's as they began to walk. 'Will Fergus be there?'

Allie squeezed her arm, 'Jessica has Esme so he's coming to the pub for one.'

The corners of Felicity's mouth lifted.

'Don't think I haven't noticed that smile,' teased Allie.

'I have no idea what you are talking about,' replied Felicity bringing up a hand to her chest in mock protest.

Allie rolled her eyes good-humouredly. 'I'm sure you don't.'

Chapter 17

The gang were sitting at the table next to the roaring log fire when Allie and Felicity walked into the pub. Nell, Allie's trusted golden Labradoodle was stretched out in front of the fire. With one beady eye on the door she spotted Allie and thumped her tail on the floor, but other than that, didn't attempt to move.

'She's a total darling, isn't she?' said Allie, rubbing her tummy before sitting down next to Rory and kissing him on the cheek.

'Drink?' he asked.

Allie nodded, and waved to her mum behind the bar who promptly brought over a couple of gin and tonics.

Felicity sat down next to Drew, who was already wetting the baby's head. 'The delivery was like a dream,' he boasted. 'I was hands on all the way through.' He gave Felicity a mischievous grin who shook her head in disbelief then laughed.

'No, honestly ... I was a wimp. It was thanks to Felicity

keeping everyone calm that Angus arrived safely. Firstly, I'd like to propose a toast to my gorgeous wife who is currently feeding the wee man while I get to drink beer, and secondly to Flick, we couldn't have done it without you. Isla and Flick!' he toasted, and everyone chinked their glasses together.

Felicity felt the burn of crimson to her cheeks as all eyes were on her. 'Anyone would have done the same.'

'Well, except me, I ran for the hills,' Allie chuckled to herself. 'I'm no good with all that blood and stuff.'

Felicity grinned and leant over and gave her a tentative hug which was reciprocated.

'Are you pair planning on having children?' asked Drew innocently.

Rory choked on his beer, then spluttered, feeling like he was under some sudden spotlight. Allie raised her eyebrows at him. 'I think that question kind of shocked Rory.' She squeezed his knee. 'Who knows … one day … still early days for us.'

The chatter died down and everyone took a sip of their drinks. As Felicity drained the dregs from her glass she felt Fergus watching her. She caught his eye and immediately looked away, only to find herself staring back at him. 'You okay?' he mouthed.

But before she could answer Allie clocked them both. 'I'm sorry Flick, all this baby talk, are you okay?'

'I'm absolutely fine, honestly, don't worry about me.'

She smiled, brushing it off and wishing Allie hadn't asked that question in front of everyone. She didn't want anyone to feel uncomfortable, least of all Drew who was merrily drinking his second pint and celebrating the birth of his son.

'Whisky is what we need.' Rory banged his hand on the table. 'WHISKY.'

'Oh no, is it going to turn into one of those nights?' teased Allie, once again waving towards her mum who gave her a stern look to suggest she had no intention of being at Allie's beck and call all night.

'I think I'd best get the drinks,' Allie giggled, standing up. 'Whisky chasers all round?'

'No! Not for me,' exclaimed Felicity. 'I'm the one who needs their wits about them ready for morning ... don't forget I've got this Skype meeting with the officials.'

'I've got every faith in you that you'll get that bridge rebuilt by the end of the day,' winked Allie, before wandering off behind the bar and pouring the drinks.

'I think that's what everyone is hoping.' Felicity rolled her eyes, suddenly feeling nervous for agreeing to be the village spokeswoman, so much was resting on her shoulders.

'You'll be okay,' said Fergus. 'And surely the council and officials can't leave us stranded for too long?'

'I bet they actually can. It depends on how much money they have in their budget, I suppose. It's not going to be easy. The cost will be phenomenal,' added Drew taking a drink from Allie who'd returned to the table. 'I've said that bridge would crumble at some point and I was right.'

'There's one for you Felicity, don't think you are getting out of it that easily!' Allie slid a tumbler over towards her.

Felicity didn't argue and everyone picked up their glass at the same time, looked at each other, and swigged back the amber liquid.

'Ew, it never tastes any better.' Allie grimaced as the liquid burnt the back of her throat. 'Here's to new baby Angus.'

'Baby Angus,' everyone repeated in unison.

'Could you imagine if Isla had left for the hospital before the bridge had collapsed? What a nightmare situation that would be,' said Allie.

'Tell me about it,' replied Fergus. 'That's exactly the situation I'm in.'

Everyone looked towards Fergus momentarily confused until the penny dropped.

'Aggie!' exclaimed Felicity. 'How is she? Have you spoken to her?'

'Not directly ... I was going to take her mobile phone next time I visited and of course now I've not got any direct contact.'

'So, have you spoken to the hospital?' chipped in

Rory, flipping a beer mat over and over in his hand.

'Yes, I've spoken to the hospital, they'd seen the news and of course I know she's in the best place but to have no visitors anytime soon ... Esme is already asking to see her nana.'

'We always have the boat?' joked Drew. 'The one in the old barn. We could row you across the water once it's calmed down. In fact, I think that sounds like an excellent plan.'

'I might hold you to that.'

'I can see a new business venture evolving,' laughed Rory, 'Drew's boat trips.'

'Hey, don't jest, it may be the only way to get to the other side.'

'Another round?' asked Rory, standing up and placing his hand on Allie's shoulder. 'Your mum won't shout at me if I nip behind the bar?'

'If you're feeling brave you go for it!'

'Surely, he's practically family now?' winked Drew teasingly.

'Actually, not for me. Sorry to break up the party,' claimed Felicity suddenly feeling guilty. 'I need to make sure Mum is okay. I think she's already started peeling the veggies ready for tomorrow. I can't leave her to it all night.'

'And I'd best head home too,' said Drew, with a goofy smile. 'Well, maybe just one for the road. It's not every day you welcome your new son into the world.'

Everyone cheered and patted him on the back. The gang knew Drew from old, there was no way he was going home anytime soon and before Felicity slipped her arms into her coat he was already ordering tequila.

Felicity popped a kiss on the top of Drew's head. 'Make sure you don't get too drunk. Isla will murder you.' She winked at him before turning and making her way to the door. As she stepped over Nell who was still lying in the same place and hadn't moved a muscle all night, she waved at Meredith and Fraser who were still serving behind the bar.

'I'm coming over in the morning to help with the food,' shouted Allie after her. 'Good luck with the meeting.'

'Thank you,' answered Felicity as she zipped up her coat. The fresh air hit Felicity as she stepped outside the pub. Even after just a couple of drinks she felt a little tipsy. She stumbled down the step and felt a hand steady her.

She looked up to see Fergus's dark eyes gleaming under those eyelashes.

'Thank you,' she said.

'I'll walk you back, I need to get home to Esme and relieve Jessica of her auntie duties.'

They walked in silence for a little while. Even though Felicity felt her heart flutter, like a teenager again, she felt surprisingly relaxed walking next to Fergus and didn't feel nervous in the slightest.

He walked her up Love Heart Lane. 'So what's it like to be famous?'

'Famous?' repeated Felicity perplexed.

'The main lunchtime news.'

'Hardly famous; a telephone interview doesn't warrant that much fame and they cut out half of it.' She smiled. 'I didn't like the sound of my voice. Do I really sound like that?'

'You do.' He gave her a cheeky smile that melted her heart.

They carried on in silence and Felicity noticed that his elbow gently brushed against hers, sending shivers down her spine. She glanced ahead and could see Heartwood Cottage at the end of the lane, the light was still on in the teashop which meant her mum was up pottering around. She didn't want this walk with Fergus to end, but each step she took, she knew Fergus would be turning around and going home very soon.

They stopped just under the street lamp only a stone's throw away from her garden gate. 'At least the storm seems to have passed,' said Fergus.

'Thankfully, but more rain is forecast for tomorrow,' answered Felicity looking up at him as he looked back.

Her eyes flickered towards his perfect lips and she moved a step closer to him, until they were inches apart. She could smell his aftershave and the closeness to him made her pulse quicken. She leant up and Fergus placed a hand on her shoulder. He held her gaze and what she saw was a flicker of panic in Fergus's eyes.

'Flick, I can't,' he said and hesitated. 'I'm sorry, I really can't. It will only end in tears and pain.'

'It won't, I promise,' she murmured, attempting again to lean forward but Fergus held her at arm's length.

'You've made promises before that you couldn't keep and now I have Esme to think about.' His voice was shaky.

Felicity felt close to tears as well as embarrassed at her mistake. She didn't like the feeling of rejection at all.

Unsure what to say, she took a step backwards, away from Fergus.

'I can't have her world upset any more than it has been. We are both in a good place now.'

'I understand,' said Felicity, thinking of all those years she was hiding away in London from reality. 'But I'm not looking to hurt anyone.'

'It's a chance I just can't take, Flick,' Fergus said softly as he broke free. 'I really have to go.'

As Felicity stood and watched him walk away, her heart plummeted to a new low.

Chapter 18

It was just before 9 a.m. when Felicity's iPad began to ring out. She'd got up at the crack of dawn, showered and eaten her breakfast, before nervously sitting in the living room watching the clock.

She imagined the council offices in the middle of town and could picture everyone sat around a huge table each with a glass of water and pen and paper poised in front of them. She had no idea how this meeting would pan out or even if she really needed to participate. Felicity had never been involved in anything like this before and she felt anxious as she accepted the Skype call.

'Felicity, welcome,' a voice boomed, and that's when she saw Councillor Smith and what seemed like every other Tom, Dick and Harry sitting around the table. All eyes were on her. 'Let me introduce you to everyone,' continued Councillor Smith as he went round the table. Felicity nodded along, but by the end of the introductions she couldn't remember anyone's names except the councillor and Annie Boyd the Environmental Minister who looked extremely important at the head of the table.

Felicity sat back on the settee, tucked her feet underneath her and watched as Annie Boyd ordered the woman on her left to take the minutes before she kicked off the meeting. First, she began to talk about how the village had been cut off from the main town of Glensheil and how the army had dropped sandbags to minimise any further flooding. She then moved on to the best way to reconnect the village. Everyone began chipping in with costs and timings and Felicity felt like she was watching a fast-paced tennis match as the conversation batted back and forth across the table.

'I just don't think it's feasible for a temporary bridge,' a voice chipped in, 'and how much will that cost?'

'By my reckoning—' a stern looking man shuffled some papers at the far end of the table '—in the region of two hundred and fifty thousand pounds ... maybe more.'

Everyone was silent.

'Our main priority in the short term is to transport food and medicine to the villagers, especially the vulnerable. Maybe we could set up boats to cross the river?'

'Boats? We can't load rowing boats with food,' someone sniggered.

'A temporary bridge will need to be erected ... the

Grade II listed bridge could take years to rebuild. A temporary bridge is really the only way forward.'

Annie Boyd shuffled some papers in front of her and shot a quick look around the table. 'I deem the temporary bridge essential. The money needs to be found from somewhere.'

'There aren't enough funds in the pot.' A worried man was now frantically looking down at a series of numbers on a spreadsheet.

'How about...' said Felicity, speaking for the first time.

All heads turned towards the screen.

'Go on,' encouraged Annie.

'How about we look to raise the money?'

Felicity heard a stifled giggle and one councillor scoffed at Felicity's suggestion, but she wasn't deterred by his less than positive attitude.

'We have a Facebook page. Maybe we could set up a fundraising page, asking for help?'

The stern-looking man that was sitting to the right of Annie now smirked. 'There is no way on this earth that those kind of funds will be raised,' the councillor said in a condescending tone.

'Surely, it's worth a go? Every little helps, doesn't it?' suggested Felicity.

Annie frowned towards him. 'I think it's a fantastic idea Felicity, and every little certainly does help.' She gave her a warm encouraging smile.

'We need to make the money available and I'm appointing you, Councillor Smith, to find it. Organise, implement and instruct the workers as a main priority.'

All Councillor Smith could do was nod and try his best to look enthusiastic.

'I want daily updates. Keep me in the loop.' And with that Annie stood up and gathered her papers in her arms before turning towards the camera. 'You have my personal assurance we will not leave you and the village stranded for too long, Felicity.'

Felicity watched as Annie left the room and everyone else remained sitting around the table. Felicity was still looking at the screen and didn't know whether to end the Skype call or wait until they did. They all began chatting amongst themselves in a rather disgruntled manner especially Counsellor Smith, who didn't seem pleased at all. 'How do you just magic up the funds or move money about to erect a temporary bridge that will cost the earth and serve no purpose in the future?'

'A complete waste of money,' another man agreed shouting over the table at him. 'It would be easier to buy a fleet of dinghies and employ someone to keep ferrying them across the river.'

'And who chooses to live up the side of a mountain anyway?' spouted Councillor Smith. 'And really, that villager thinking a Facebook campaign would help … absolutely deluded.'

Felicity felt her cheeks begin to burn and her blood boiled. She was livid. How dare he ridicule her in front of a room full of people. Who did he think he was? Immediately, she ended the Skype call. She didn't want to listen to any more.

'I'll tell you who wants to live up a mountain … me!' She shouted at the blank screen and tossed the iPad on to the table.

'Who are you shouting at?' asked Rona, appearing in the doorway of the kitchen. She'd been up at dawn beavering away in the kitchen of the tearoom. She'd set the places, laid out the cups and saucers and already there were huge pots of beef stew simmering on the stove.

'Those councillors are up their own backsides,' Felicity huffed and Rona cocked an eyebrow at her daughter. 'What's going on?' she asked, sitting down on the arm of the settee.

'I've just hung up from the Skype meeting. Annie Boyd told them to find the funds to build a temporary bridge. However, the local council weren't as supportive as her.'

'What do you mean?'

'The suits were complaining that it would be cheaper to set up boats across the river than to construct a temporary bridge and when I offered to try and raise funds they kind of ridiculed me.'

'How much would we need?'

'Probably in the region of two hundred and fifty thousand.'

Rona gave a low whistle. 'They have a point.'

'Mum...'

'And how long will the original bridge take to repair and be up and running again?'

'That could take years ... maybe a couple of years, because it's listed.'

Rona blew out a breath. 'So what was the actual outcome?'

'Annie Boyd said without a doubt we needed a temporary bridge erected and to keep her in the loop. She delegated the task to Councillor Smith who was far from pleased about being left to find the money to fund it. As soon as she left room he began moaning that it was a waste of money and ridiculing anyone who would choose to live in such a remote place up the side of a mountain. He was downright rude.'

'And he forgot you were still watching?'

'Yes ... but I'll show him,' she said with sheer determination in her voice.

'What are you going to do?'

'I'm going to go viral.'

'That sounds painful.'

Felicity smiled at her mum. 'No, I'm going to make a video and upload it on to the Facebook page.'

'And say what?'

Felicity was turning it over in her mind. 'I'm not sure yet, but I'm going to show that councillor what I'm made of. How dare he scoff that we'd never raise that amount? The fact is we shouldn't have to...' She took a breath. 'But he's put goddamn fire in my belly.'

'Councillor... what's his name?'

'Smith,' said Felicity.

'Doesn't know what he's let himself in for.' Rona finished off her sentence before standing up and smoothing down her pinny. 'But in the meantime, we need to prepare the food to feed the village.'

Felicity watched her mum return to the teashop and quickly picked up her phone and began to text Allie. 'Are you on your way over yet?'

Within a matter of seconds her phone pinged. 'On my way.'

'Good, we are on a mission and you are my right-hand woman.'

'Sounds ominous.'

Felicity was suddenly full of determination, and she wasn't going to let some old councillor stop her. She was going to show him one way or another that the village of Heartcross was not to be laughed at!

Chapter 19

When Meredith and Allie came through the door of the teashop, Allie didn't even have time to take her coat off before Felicity was ushering her through to the main cottage.

'Don't mind us,' Rona shouted after her daughter. 'We'll carry on with the food preparation.' Even though Felicity knew her mother was only half-joking, Felicity wanted to tell Allie about her idea.

'Why are you acting all cloak and dagger?' asked Allie with intrigue, throwing her coat over the back of the settee.

Felicity updated her about the meeting and Councillor Smith's reluctance.

'He wasn't very encouraging towards the idea of us raising money towards the bridge.'

'And what might those efforts be?' asked an alarmed Allie, wondering what she'd managed to rope herself into.

'I'm not actually sure. But I've set up a fundraising page on Facebook and thought about creating a video with owners of some of the local businesses with a few heartfelt comments to connect us back with the outside world, asking people to donate funds.'

'And that's your plan?' replied Allie, not looking at all convinced.

The pair of them stared at each other for a moment. Felicity took a second. 'You know what, you are absolutely right,' said Felicity, her mind in an absolute whirl. 'I need more.'

'I know that look from old, what are you thinking?' urged Allie.

Felicity didn't look Allie in the eye as she continued to go through possible ideas.

'Come on, spill.' She swiped her arm playfully, and Felicity took a deep breath. 'What are the two things that people say you should never work with?'

Allie screwed up her face. 'Children and animals.'

'You've got it!' Felicity clapped her hands together like an excited child as a look of puzzlement appeared on Allie's face.

'Come on, let's get back to the kitchen,' insisted Felicity, with a big smile on her face.

'Is that all you're going to say?'

'For now!' Felicity linked her arm through Allie's and led her back into the teashop.

Meredith and Rona were standing side by side stirring the huge pots of stew and singing along to the radio. The tables were laid with cutlery, and teapots stood in the middle of every table ready to be poured. Rona looked down at her watch and right on cue the bell above the door tinkled as the first sitting began to file through the door. The children were excited as their mothers led them to the tables at the far end of the tearoom decorated with the colourful tablecloths. From the look on their faces they thought they were attending a birthday party. Felicity was relieved to see Finn and Esme walk through the door alongside Jessica. For the last few minutes Felicity had had a plan hatching in her mind, but she wasn't quite sure whether she was going to be able to implement it today.

As soon as everyone was settled, Felicity and Allie began to serve up bowls of the stew. The second the food was served the room fell silent and everyone began to eat. The first sitting was a success and the four of them gave each other a secret high five behind the counter.

'We have thirty minutes to wash these bowls and cutlery and turn it around for the next sitting,' said Rona.

'How many sittings altogether?' queried Allie.

'Five ... I think ... then we have two hours to produce the next meal and do it all again.'

'I feel like I'm a part of *MasterChef*, or the *Great British Bake Off*. Will I get the Rona Simons handshake?' teased Felicity.

'The what?' Rona asked in puzzlement.

'*Great British Bake Off*. When the baking is out of this world you get the Paul Hollywood handshake ... to say you've smashed it.'

'Oh, I see,' replied Rona, still none the wiser.

Jessica stood up from the table and brought Finn and Esme's plates over to the counter.

'All finished and delicious. Thank you. But Esme needs the toilet,' said Jessica.

'I'll take her through to the cottage,' insisted Felicity, knowing full well that the teashop ladies' room was spotlessly clean and in full working order but she seized the opportunity to put her plan into action. Taking Esme by the hand, Felicity led her through the cottage and showed her the way to the bathroom then waited for her in the living room. When Esme reappeared, she gave Felicity a beam. 'I like you,' Esme said out of the blue, taking Felicity completely by surprise. 'You have a nice face.'

Felicity felt a surge of warmth through her body and bent down in front of Esme, taking hold of her hands. 'I like you too, Esme.'

'I heard Jessica say you're going to re-build the bridge,' Esme said, and Felicity chuckled.

'Not quite re-build it by myself, but I'm hoping to raise some money to help with the cost of re-building it.'

'How are you going to do that?' asked Esme.

'Well, I'm thinking of making a short video asking for people to donate money.'

'I hope they give plenty of money,' said Esme, 'because until the bridge is fixed Grandma is all on her own in the hospital. Uncle Drew said he was going to get his old rowing boat and row us across to the other side.'

'That sounds like a lot of fun.'

'Are you pair okay in there?' Felicity heard her mum shout from the teashop.

'Yes, all's good. We'll be through in a minute.'

Felicity took the mobile phone out of her pocket and placed it on the coffee table.

'Do you want to help me?'

Esme's face lit up. 'With the video?'

'Yes, with the video.'

Esme let out a tiny squeal.

'We need a sign to hold up,' instructed Felicity.

'I'm good at drawing and colouring.'

Felicity directed her eyes towards the dresser. 'In the bottom over there, there's some old card and pens.'

Esme skipped over to the dresser and opened the door, grabbing a piece of white card and a box of pens.

Felicity began to draw a bridge alongside huge letters: SAVE HEARTCROSS – DONATE NOW.

'What do you think?' enthused Felicity, opening the box of coloured pens and passing one to Esme.

'I love it,' she answered, busily colouring in the letters. When they finished, Esme looked pleased with herself.

'Will you record me from my phone,' asked Felicity, 'while I make a short video?'

'Can I be in the video too?' Esme's pleading eyes locked with Felicity's. 'Pleeease.'

'I don't see why not. Let me set the phone up over here and we can sit there.'

Felicity set the timer on the phone and when she turned around Esme was already sitting upright on the settee, proudly clutching the poster. Felicity slipped into the space next to her. 'I'll talk and you hold the poster,' Felicity said and Esme nodded her understanding.

As the phone beeped Felicity stared towards it and began to talk.

'As you have all heard, the bridge between Glensheil and Heartcross collapsed yesterday, leaving our tiny village completely cut off. The Grade II listed bridge could take many years to repair and the Environmental Minister has deemed a temporary bridge essential, but it comes at a cost. Soon the food supplies in our tiny village will run out so we need your help. Please, please donate and help us raise funds to erect a new temporary bridge.' Felicity looked down at Esme who held the poster up high. 'Save Heartcross,' she shouted. 'And please donate as I need the new bridge to visit my grandma who is in hospital in Glensheil. She will have no visitors until the bridge is up and will be really sad. Save Heartcross!' Esme chanted once more before Felicity switched off the recording.

'I think we did all right there, don't you?' Felicity gave Esme a high five and smiled before taking a look at the video.

'What do you think?' Felicity showed Esme who grinned from ear to ear.

'I take it you approve?' laughed Felicity, as she logged onto the Facebook fundraising page. She was just about to upload the video when she thought of Fergus, and she knew she'd better check with him first before posting it.

'Felicity, where are you?' shouted Rona from the teashop.

'Just coming,' bellowed Felicity, placing the phone on the table. 'I'll just use the bathroom and I'd best get back to work. Can you put the pens back for me?'

Esme bobbed her head with approval and they shared the same gleeful expression.

Back in the living room Rona was standing in the doorway with a frown on her face when Felicity arrived back from the bathroom.

'What's taken you so long? Jessica was wondering

where you'd both got to. Come on ... we need help out here, the next sitting will be along shortly,' she insisted, hurrying them both along.

Felicity slid the poster down the side of the dresser before grabbing Esme's hand as they walked back into the teashop.

'There she is,' said Jessica. 'We were just about to send out a search party. Did you get lost?'

Esme obviously took this cue to try and explain in great detail, 'No ... we were trying to save Heartcross.' But before Esme could explain any further the teashop door swung open and the next lot of villagers began bustling through the door.

'You can tell me later,' answered Jessica, ushering Finn and Esme through the crowd of hungry villagers.

'What took you so long?' Rona said in a hushed voice, narrowing her eyes at Felicity who quickly slid her phone into her apron pocket.

'What do you mean?' asked Felicity, knowing full well what her mum was insinuating.

'You, Esme...'

'We were talking about the bridge ... and...'

'And?'

Felicity felt her shoulders tense. 'And time just ran away with us,' she answered, a little on the defensive side.

Felicity didn't know why but she didn't want to tell

her mum about the video just yet, she wasn't sure how she was going to react knowing Esme was in the video and Felicity didn't want to antagonise her any more. She already looked a little stressed. And Felicity needed to check Fergus was happy with it, before she posted it online. He might hate the idea.

'Well, no more sloping off and get these bowls of stew on the tables.' Rona's tone was firm as Felicity took the steaming bowls from her hands.

She placed the bowls down on the table in front of Aida and George, who had lived right at the other end of Love Heart Lane in Butterfly Cottage for over fifty years. George had been the caretaker at the school all his working life until he'd retired and Aida had been the school cook.

'We could do with your help in the kitchen, Aida.' Felicity smiled, nodding towards her mum, Meredith and Allie who were busy dishing up the stew and pouring cups of tea.

'I cooked for the masses day in and day out, it's nice to be waited on even though not under the best circumstances ... but I'm always here dear, you tell me when and I'll be there. At times like this we need to pull together.'

George leant across the table and squeezed Aida's hand. 'We do; remember the floods over forty years ago? It was Glensheil that was affected then. Homes were evacuated and families actually moved across the river and lodged with families of Heartcross for months until the houses by the riverbank were renovated and refurbished. I'm surprised it's not happened more over the years. Those river banks are fit for bursting every time there's a spot of rain.'

'We had that lovely family come and live with us, didn't we George, but we lost touch over the years, they moved out of Glensheil,' chipped in Aida.

Felicity smiled at Aida and George and turned to see Allie looking down at her mobile phone much to Meredith's dissatisfaction. 'What is it with you youngsters and mobile phones ... put it down, we've got work to do here.'

'It's just ... actually you aren't going to believe this...' Allie locked eyes with Felicity.

'What is it?' she asked, pulling a strained face.

Rona and Meredith were now standing by her side looking intrigued.

'According to Rory, who's just texted me ... you just posted a video on the Facebook page and it's spreading like wildfire.'

Felicity stopped dead in her tracks. 'What are you talking about? I haven't posted anything.'

'Wildfire,' repeated Allie. 'Yes, apparently a few hundred shares already.'

'Stop winding me up.'

'I'm not … here, look.' Allie handed over her phone to Felicity.

'Bloody hell, I didn't post this.' Felicity's voice was heavy with worry as the video she'd taken played out right in front of her very eyes.

'Seriously, everyone seems to be smitten with Esme's contribution. They want to reunite her with her grandmother. Everyone seems to have taken pity that her grandma is in the hospital on the opposite side of the river. Rory said donations have already come flooding in.'

'I hope you ran it past Fergus before putting his daughter on the internet?' said an alarmed Meredith. 'You can't be too careful with kids on the internet these days.'

Suddenly, a wave of panic hit Felicity, 'Fergus…' she said out loud. 'He won't be happy, but I didn't post this.'

Felicity had a very uneasy feeling in the pit of her stomach.

Allie's phone was still in her hand and it began to beep. Sure enough, as the Facebook page moderator her notifications exploded. She pressed on the video once more and gasped.

Rory was right, the video was being shared and donations were already coming into the fundraising page to support the temporary bridge with lots of goodwill messages wanting to reunite Esme with her grandma.

Felicity looked up, alarmed.

'You haven't asked him, have you?' said Allie, clearly sensing a modicum of awkwardness and taking the phone from her hand.

'What am I going to do?' stuttered Felicity. 'I didn't post it ... honestly, I don't know how...'

Then she stopped in her tracks. She'd left her phone on the coffee table when she went to use the bathroom, leaving only Esme in the room. Surely she hadn't posted it?

'I wouldn't like to be in your shoes when Fergus finds out,' said Allie.

Felicity hadn't anticipated it would find its way on to Facebook before she'd spoken to Fergus or that the video would have escalated so quickly. To her dismay, Allie's phone was still pinging with notifications and the video was still being shared to the masses.

'There's another residents' meeting here early evening, but you need to tell Fergus about this before he sees it for himself,' suggested Rona, with a look that knew best.

'It's going to be okay, isn't it?' Felicity didn't know who she was trying to convince.

No one spoke.

A nagging doubt told Felicity her mum was right, she needed to tell Fergus – but even though this wasn't her fault, she wasn't sure that he would believe her. And by the time she'd finished here today it would be time for the meeting. She just prayed Fergus wouldn't stumble over the video before she spoke to him.

Chapter 20

Felicity busied herself in the kitchen all afternoon and early evening until the last villager had been fed and watered, but her mind wasn't really on the job. Her mobile phone had been permanently attached to her hand and she couldn't believe the video was still being shared such a ridiculous amount of times. She'd thought about deleting the video but it had already been shared that many times that even the hashtag #SaveHeartcross was now trending on Twitter too. The collapse of the bridge was getting more attention than any international popstar releasing their latest song, and the donations were flooding in. Already in one afternoon the fundraising page had received over five thousand pounds to help fund a temporary bridge to connect them back to Glensheil. It was unbelievable.

Felicity glanced up at the clock; it was just before 7 p.m., and the residents would start to arrive very soon. She looked over at her mum who for the umpteenth time today was making the tea ready for the villagers. With a sodden tea towel resting on her shoulder, Felicity noticed how tired her mum looked. She hadn't stopped all day and hearing the bell tinkle above the teashop door Rona automatically sprang into action once more, plastering a huge beam on her face.

Felicity was amazed to see Isla walking through the door with both Finn and Esme clutching the side of the pram.

'Wait there, let me help you.' Felicity rushed to hold the door open. 'What are you doing here?'

'It's our very first outing and we thought we'd come and see you and what state of crisis the village is in,' said Isla. 'Even though I'm absolutely shattered – this little one kept me up all night and now look at him.'

Felicity peeped into the pram to see Angus all bundled up in a tight woollen blanket wearing a blue hat and mittens. 'He is absolute gorgeous,' said Felicity softly stroking his mitten.

'Oh he is, especially when he's asleep,' smiled Isla.

Felicity chuckled before turning to Finn and Esme. 'And would you like a hot chocolate? I'm sure if you ask my mum nicely...' Before Felicity had time to finish her sentence they both ran off towards the counter.

'Here, sit down.' Felicity gestured towards the table in the corner which had space to park the pram. 'Can I get you a drink?'

'I've already got Isla one,' said Rona, placing a steaming mug of tea down on the table alongside a plate of biscuits before taking a peep at sleeping Angus. 'He's got that baby smell, smells of newness. Congratulations ... he's gorgeous.'

'Thank you. It already feels like I've had him forever,' replied Isla, breaking a biscuit in two and popping it into her mouth after dunking it in her tea.

Rona walked back to the counter, clapping her hands. 'When you've finished those hot chocolates—' she playfully swiped them with the tea towel '—I've a few jobs for you children.'

They both nodded eagerly, as they spooned cream and marshmallows into their mouths.

'I didn't get to thank you properly,' said Isla with a smile. 'Thanks for everything you did at the birth. I couldn't have done it without you and I know it must have been difficult for you with everything...'

'Honestly, anyone would have done the same, well, except...'

'Allie,' they both said in unison then laughed.

'Are my ears burning?' said Allie, walking into the tearoom at that very moment. She sat down opposite Isla.

'I'm saying nothing.' Felicity giggled then stood up. 'I'd best go and help Mum before the masses begin to arrive.' She shot a glance out of the window and could already see the villagers trudging up Love Heart Lane towards the teashop. 'Here we go again.'

'I bet you've been run off your feet feeding the villagers. I don't envy you at all.'

'Yes busy, but it was great to reconnect with the community. I saw some faces today I've not seen for a while.'

'I'm thinking there's going to be a big turnout tonight especially after your little stunt today.'

'Huh?' said Isla, oblivious to all the fuss that Felicity had created online. She shot a glance at them both while gently rocking the pram.

'Is Fergus still up at the farm?' asked Felicity with caution.

'Yes,' replied Isla, sipping her tea. 'He'll be here soon, why?'

'No reason,' replied Felicity, as the teashop door swung open and she hurried back behind the counter.

One by one the villagers filed through the door, and Felicity began to busy herself to try and take her mind off Fergus's arrival. A shiver ran down her spine and she closed her eyes for a brief second.

'I'm not sure we are going to fit everyone in here,' exclaimed Rona with a hint of worry in her voice. The tables were already packed and people were shuffling themselves into any space they could find.

'I was thinking the same,' chipped in Meredith who

appeared by Rona's side behind the counter. 'We can see how it goes and if need be, we can swap the meetings to the pub.'

As the door opened, one last time Felicity heard the church bells in the background chime seven o'clock.

'We've seen the post on Facebook and we don't understand,' a voice shouted from the back of the room. 'Are we getting a new bridge?'

She looked up to see Ethan, the owner of the local skip hire firm, staring back at her and by the look on his face he was spoiling for a fight.

'Our businesses are suffering here.'

There was a mumble of agreement around the room before everyone hushed and all eyes were on Felicity, leaving her completely on the spot.

'As you all know, this morning I virtually attended the council meeting regarding Heartcross and I'm pleased to say it was all very positive,' spouted Felicity, trying to forget Councillor Smith's comments and his unhelpful manner as she tried to put a confident spin on the situation.

'How can it be positive?' Alfie, a construction contractor, shouted. 'And why have you set up a fundraising page unless that means the council aren't prepared to fund a temporary bridge?'

There were disgruntled mutterings all around the room.

'The Environmental Minister Annie Boyd has deemed a temporary bridge a must.'

'So, what's with the fundraising page if a temporary bridge has been given the go ahead?'

Felicity stared at him; he had always been a sanctimonious idiot at school.

'They really want to reconnect us as soon as possible.'

'So, basically what you are saying is you have nothing to tell us. We could be stranded here for weeks before there's any hint of a temporary bridge being built?' His voice was raw and he emphasised each word which signalled fury beyond his control. He leaned back in his seat, a smirk curving on his lips. He was enjoying putting Felicity on the spot and now the whole village seemed to be nodding in agreement with him.

She felt under pressure, her heart was thumping. 'Can we just all calm down? I can't physically build the bridge myself.' The annoyance now showed in her voice.

All eyes were fixed on Felicity, and she rubbed her sweaty palms on the side of her jeans, her body a jumble of nerves.

'And as some of you will have noticed, every little helps ... and that is why I set up the fundraising page.'

Felicity spotted Allie out of the corner of her eye waving her mobile phone in the air, trying to catch her attention.

'The video is still spreading like wildfire. Everyone

seems to be jumping on the #SaveHeartcross band-wagon. The donations today alone have already reached just under ten thousand pounds,' Allie shouted.

Felicity's jaw fell to somewhere around her knees. 'No way ... that's absolutely amazing!'

'What video?' asked Isla, unknowingly.

But Felicity didn't answer; she shivered and her skin prickled as she spotted Fergus strolling up Love Heart Lane towards the teashop. Time felt like it had slowed for her and she was rooted to the spot, waiting. Did he know or didn't he? She'd no idea what to expect, but in approximately three seconds she would have her answer.

Fergus burst through the door. Her heart sped up and she tried to slither discreetly behind the counter but there was no escaping.

'Felicity!' he bellowed, and she was more than confident that he was fully aware of the video.

She reluctantly turned around. Fergus looked dishevelled, his eyes were bloodshot. He'd come straight from the farm, his overalls were dirty and his wellington boots left a muddy trail over the white tiled floor.

'Sorry ... sorry Rona,' he muttered, looking down at his feet before catching Rona's eye.

'Don't you worry about that, I'll clean it up later.'

After muttering further apologies, he turned his attention back towards Felicity.

'We need to talk now. For God's sake, what did you think you were doing?'

The pink flush to Felicity's cheeks ramped up to cerise.

'Come through to the cottage.' She glanced at her mum who nodded; no one wanted to air their dirty laundry in public and judging by the sudden hush in the teashop everyone was waiting to see what would happen next.

Felicity felt herself shaking as Fergus quickly took off his boots and left them by the side of the counter. As soon as they were inside the kitchen, she closed the door to the teashop behind her.

'Well?' he said impatiently.

The silence hung between them, and what seemed like minutes passed.

'I didn't know anything about it, I promise.' Felicity was hoping her voice sounded convincing.

'Well, you were in the video unless you are about to tell me you've had a twin sister hidden away all these years?'

'No ... I mean, I didn't post it ... I was going to ask you first then the next thing I know it's ended up on...'

'And you expect me to believe that?' Fergus interrupted her.

'Honestly, I'm telling the truth.'

Anger was carved in Fergus's face. 'My phone hasn't

stopped ringing. I've had newspapers and radio stations all asking for interviews with me and Esme,' he said, thrusting his hands in the back pockets of his overalls and staring at Felicity.

'You've put my daughter on the internet, the video has gone viral and now the whole world wants to see her reunited with her grandmother.'

'Fergus, I'm sorry, but surely it's not that bad? Look at the donations that have already come flooding in.' Felicity knew those were the wrong words as soon as they'd left her mouth.

Fergus locked eyes with Felicity, who could see the fury in his eyes, 'You posted a video of my daughter on the internet without parental permission.'

'I'm sorry, I really am … yes I took the video, but I didn't upload it.' Felicity attempted to smooth the way.

'Then who did?'

Felicity didn't know what to say. She wasn't a hundred percent sure who had uploaded it, even though she had her suspicions. There had only been Esme left in the living room with her phone.

Felicity just stood there.

'And what gives you the right to think you can even video Esme without my permission?'

Felicity knew Fergus had every right to be mad with her. She'd just got carried away in the moment and hadn't thought about the consequences for him or Esme.

'Don't think of doing anything like this again, you are not her mother, Flick.'

The words cut through the air and Felicity held onto her tears. She was shocked that Fergus could say something so cruel to her, but before she could reply, the kitchen door burst open.

'Why are you shouting at Felicity?'

They both spun round to find a wide-eyed frightened looking Esme standing in the doorway. She looked like she was on the verge of tears and she stared at them both before turning around and fleeing.

'Now see what you've done, just stay away from us,' Fergus growled as he turned away, disappearing after Esme. Felicity felt utterly deflated as she wiped a frustrated tear from her eye. She hadn't set out to hurt Fergus, or upset him, but clearly she had. She felt she'd bonded with Esme and would never have uploaded the video without asking Fergus's permission first, but she should have been more careful.

She walked into the living room and slumped into the chair and flicked on to her phone. She didn't know what to do as her finger hovered over the uploaded video. Should she delete it? But now it had that many shares and comments, it had taken on a life of its own. Esme was the star of the show and donations were still flooding in.

And now Esme was upset because she'd seen them

arguing. For the hundredth time since she came back to Heartcross, Felicity wished that she could turn back time. She wiped away the tears with the back of her hand feeling completely drained.

Chapter 21

Felicity climbed out of bed and pulled back the curtains.

She'd barely slept a wink and had tossed and turned all night with thoughts of upsetting Fergus firmly on her mind. She'd made her mind up to hot-foot it over to the farm after breakfast and try and put things right as best she could. She was hoping Fergus had calmed down a little after he'd slept on it.

Rona was already up making breakfast. 'We are on the last of the bread but there's enough for a wee bacon sandwich if you fancy it,' she said, rolling up her sleeves before tying on her pinny.

'That'll be good,' replied Felicity in rather a subdued tone.

'Are you still worrying about Fergus?' Rona asked, throwing the bacon in the frying pan and placing it on top of the Aga.

'A little ... in fact a lot,' she admitted.

'He will have calmed down now. It would just be a shock finding out and receiving all those calls asking for an interview when he knew nothing about it all.'

'I hope you're right.'

'And how is the campaign going today?'

'I've no idea, in fact I daren't even look.'

Felicity had left her iPad charging in the living room overnight and after grabbing a mug of tea, she sat down and took a deep breath. First, she checked her emails. Yesterday, before Fergus had arrived at the teashop, Felicity had taken great pleasure in emailing Councillor Smith and informing him that the #SaveHeartcross fundraising page had been set up and donations were already pouring into the pot. But now she felt quite disappointed. Sitting in her inbox was an out of office reply for Councillor Smith, announcing he would be out of the office for two weeks.

Surely not? Who was going to organise the rebuilding of the temporary bridge now?

'He's not in the office for two weeks,' shouted Felicity to her mum who was still beavering about in the kitchen.

Rona appeared in the doorway, drying her hands on a tea towel, 'Who, Fergus?'

'No, Councillor Smith. How can anyone take a holiday now when Heartcross needs their bridge? Who's going to manage the project?'

'Well, superwoman, that'll be down to you then,' joked Rona before she disappeared back into the kitchen, unaware that Felicity had a bee in her bonnet about something.

She clicked on the Facebook app and once more her notifications nearly exploded. She stared at the video and couldn't believe how many times it had been shared; her jaw dropped open. The number of comments from the general public was unbelievable. Felicity began to read through them. All of them were in support of Heartcross and reuniting Esme with her grandma and clearly Esme had become the main focus of the campaign. When Fergus logged on to Facebook this morning and saw this, she knew his anger would only be reignited.

The nation had begun to fall in love with his little girl and wanted to see the temporary bridge rebuilt immediately. Felicity clicked on the link that took her through to the fundraising page.

'Christ on a bike!' she screeched as Rona immediately appeared in the doorway once more.

'What's up with you now?'

'The fundraising page has exploded, donations are coming in from all over the world and there's twenty thousand pounds in the pot.'

'Really, are you sure?' asked Rona, in utter amazement as Felicity turned the iPad towards her. She let out a low whistle. 'That's not bad going at all. In fact, that's incredible. I'm proud of you,' she said, switching on the TV and sitting down with her breakfast.

Felicity texted Allie. 'Have you seen the fundraising page?'

Almost immediately a text pinged back and Felicity swiped the screen.

'Yes! Are you watching the news?'

Felicity read the message out and Rona quickly switched channels. There was Aidy Redfern the news reporter standing by the collapsed bridge in Glensheil with a huddle of people standing behind him with placards.

Felicity squinted at the screen and drew a sharp breath. 'O-M-G! Can you read those?'

Rona grabbed her spectacles from the table and took a closer look at the TV.

'Save Heartcross … Reunite Esme with her grandma … Support Felicity Simons' fundraising page.'

'Fergus is going to hit the roof,' muttered a horrified Felicity, knowing full well he would clock the news at some point today. Her heart was in her mouth as she watched Aidy Redfern live on the screen.

'As the Environmental Minister Annie Boyd deemed the temporary bridge a must, local resident Felicity Simons has taken matters into her own hands to reunite Esme Campbell, age 6, with her grandma, Aggie Campbell. Aggie

was rushed to St. Mary's hospital, here in Glensheil, the night before Heartcross Bridge collapsed, leaving her isolated from her family in a time of need.

We are led to believe the estimated cost of building a temporary bridge over the river to reunite the community is in the region of two hundred and fifty thousand pounds according to sources. The reconstruction of the original bridge could take years according to the department of national heritage.

Councillor Smith who was put in charge of the project is unfortunately unavailable to comment.'

'He picks his moments to be unavailable,' said a disgruntled Felicity under her breath.

'A video posted to a Facebook page that the local residents had set up to keep everyone informed of the construction of the temporary bridge has gone viral with donations to the fundraising page now flooding in.'

Aidy Redfern turned towards the group of people standing behind him holding the placards. He held the microphone towards a lady.

'What brings you here today?'

'We came across the video on Facebook and Esme stole our heart. She's a gorgeous little girl and everyone is hoping the temporary bridge is constructed sooner rather than later, not only to reunite the community with the outside world but so Esme can visit her poorly grandmother in hospital.'

'*Save Heartcross!*' The rest of the group shouted.

'*We will keep you updated on developments. This is Aidy Redfern reporting for BBC Scotland.*'

Felicity and Rona just stared at each other, speechless for a minute before Felicity broke the silence. 'If Fergus wasn't mad at me before he will be now with Esme's name plastered all over the news. What am I going to do?'

Ping ... ping ... ping ... ping ... ping...

'What the heck is going on?' Felicity looked down at her phone and swiped the screen. 'It's Facebook again, even more people are donating to the page.'

'That'll be down to the news. Are you sure you don't want the councillor's job? I reckon you could have those funds by this time tomorrow.' Rona smiled at her daughter while finishing her breakfast.

'I'm actually going to telephone the council this morning, in fact now. We need to know who has taken over the project and who our first point of call is. They can't just leave us stranded.'

Rona stood up. 'You make your call but I need you in that kitchen as soon as. These meals aren't going to cook themselves. Drew transported all the food needed today from Hamish's at 5 a.m. this morning, so we are all ready.'

Rona walked into the kitchen leaving Felicity dialling

the number for the council. Slowly losing her cool, it took her nearly ten minutes to be transferred to the right department.

'Hi, this is Felicity Simons,' she said in her best telephone voice. 'I'm the spokeswoman for the residents of Heartcross.'

'What can I do for you today?' the voice asked on the other end.

'Councillor Smith was put in charge of funding and organising the temporary bridge between Glensheil and Heartcross but I've received an email this morning stating he is out of the office for two weeks.' Felicity took a breath.

There was a hushed silence. 'I'm afraid Councillor Smith is no longer working for this department.'

Felicity made a puffy sound through her lips as she was taken by surprise. According to her email and the news report there was no evidence he had left the council.

'Who is in charge of the project now?'

There was a long pause and she could hear the woman on the other end shuffling some papers.

'No one has been appointed yet,' she said.

'But someone needs to be appointed ASAP. What about the organisation of the new bridge?'

'They are currently looking into it,' she replied, even more non-committal.

'Who are "they"?' queried Felicity, not in the least impressed with the lack of information.

'The committee.'

Again, there was a long pause.

'There really isn't anything else I can tell you at this time.' She now sounded huffy as Felicity hung up the call and let out a frustrated squeal.

Standing up, she flounced into the teashop and sniffed. 'There's no one in charge. The committee are appointing someone but they have no idea when or who.'

Rona could see the annoyance written all over Felicity's face. 'That doesn't sound good in the slightest. The community needs some answers, worry isn't good for anyone.'

'If you want a job doing, do it yourself.'

'Exactly,' said Rona, waving the potato peeler in the air. 'I'm trying to make lunch for the masses, are you going to give me a hand anytime soon?'

Felicity didn't hear her mum's words as her mind was turning over her own words. 'If you want a job doing, do it yourself.'

She stared at her mum, then flicked on her mobile phone once more; the donations were increasing by the second.

An idea leapt into Felicity's head.

'I'm going to take matters into my own hands,' she declared.

'I'll be happy if you take a potato peeler into your hand,' teased Rona, but with a stern undertone.

'Mum, I'm being serious. With this amount of money already flooding in, I'm going to contact Annie Boyd and tell her I'm going to hire a contractor to get this show on the road.'

'And I'm serious ... get peeling.'

Felicity took the peeler from her mum's hand thinking about the temporary bridge and the donations. The community couldn't wait for the project to be allocated to someone else – that could take days and they could all lose precious time. Every day they were stranded in the village, the businesses were losing their livelihood. Someone had to do something to get the ball rolling and Felicity decided it was going to be her.

Chapter 22

After spending the morning helping her mum to peel what seemed like every perishable vegetable left in the village, Felicity's hands were red raw, but for the past hour she had been quiet whilst Meredith, Allie and her mum had been happily chatting amongst themselves and singing along to the radio.

Jessica had arrived at the teashop with the news that the primary school was to remain shut for the time being.

Unfortunately the headmistress and the majority of the teachers lived over in Glensheil and it was impossible for them to cross the river. The secondary school was also situated across the river which meant the older children were stranded in Heartcross too.

'Which means I'm an extra pair of hands if anyone needs any help? Chief dishwasher, tea maker?'

Immediately, Rona threw her a tea towel and nodded towards the pots that needed drying. 'Welcome to the team!'

They began to work side by side, but within seconds Jessica had noticed Felicity wasn't her usual self and assumed her slumped mood was something to do with Fergus. 'He'll get over it, you know. He's just a little over protective,' she said, sympathetically, throwing an arm around Felicity and giving her a squeeze.

Felicity heaved a sigh, but with the video now being shared on the news too, she was certain Fergus was definitely *not* going to be happy.

Meredith gave her a tentative smile and rubbed her arm gently. 'Jessica is right. He is a little over protective but that's his right. He does the job of two parents and Esme is his world ... give it time, he'll come round.'

The news report wasn't sitting well with Felicity. In fact, the churning feeling in the pit of her stomach was making her feel queasy. She had no clue whether Fergus had seen the news but her gut feeling was telling her to go and tell him even if it meant having another argument.

'Have you seen him this morning?' Felicity turned towards Jessica.

'Yes, he was a little subdued when he left for the farm. He's taken Esme to play with Finn. Don't worry about it ... look at the donations that are flooding in. The public love Esme and that cheeky little smile is wooing people to donate.'

'Did he see the news this morning by any chance?' Felicity's heart sped up waiting for the answer.

'The news? No, why?'

'Because the latest news report was all about reuniting Esme with her grandmother.'

Jessica's eyes widened at the information.

'Maybe it's a good idea to go and see him now? Before everyone begins to arrive for the first sitting?' Rona took a quick glance up at the clock. 'You'll have time, if you go now.'

Felicity wasn't relishing the idea of another confrontation with Fergus but after his reaction to the video yesterday, she knew she needed to go and see him. Slipping her arms inside her coat she took a deep breath. She walked down Love Heart Lane towards the farm, her shoulders slumped, her face unhappy knowing that she needed to grovel like her life depended on it. Even though it was for a good cause and the donations were flooding in, she knew for whatever reason Fergus didn't quite see it like that.

Reaching Foxglove Farm, she heard banging from the far barn echoing all around. She took a deep breath and reluctantly began to walk in that direction. Drew and Fergus were bent over the bonnet of an old tractor tinkering with the engine. The smell of diesel fumes hit Felicity as she nervously walked towards them. Drew spotted her first. 'Good morning. What, no coffee for the workers?' he teased, wiping his hands on an oily rag.

'I've only just arrived but I'll make sure that's next

on my list,' she replied with a smile, noticing Fergus had avoided any eye contact with her up to now.

'I see the fundraising page is going great guns,' said Drew oblivious to any tension in the barn.

'Yes, apparently so,' Felicity replied trying to play it down, even though she knew the exact amount that had been donated so far, to the penny. 'Is it okay if I have a quick word with Fergus?'

Drew flicked a glance between them both. 'Of course, I'll go and collect the rest of the tools from the shed. We'll get this beauty up and running in no time.' He affectionately patted the tractor with his hand before strolling towards the open barn door.

Felicity shuffled her feet then took a deep breath. Fergus was not making this easy for her. He leant against the tractor, his arms folded tightly across his chest and his face thunderous. Felicity already knew there was only one way this was going to play out – with another blazing argument by the look on Fergus's face.

'Have you seen the news this morning?' she asked cautiously.

'Is this just a general chat about my morning routine? Are you going to ask me if I had jam on my toast next?' His eyebrows furrowed as he stared at her.

'There's been a further development.' Felicity ignored his sarcasm and was relieved her voice sounded a lot calmer than she actually felt.

'What do you mean, a further development?' He scowled, not taking his eyes off her.

She swallowed. Her palms were sweaty as she dug them into her pockets.

'I know you weren't happy about the video,' started Felicity, her voice was quiet now. 'But with the appointed Councillor disappearing, the general public are really getting behind the Heartcross campaign and the donations are flying in and that's all thanks to Esme. She's crept into the people's hearts.'

Fergus blew out a breath. 'Felicity, what is it? You're stalling. Just spit it out.'

For a brief second, she closed her eyes. 'I'm sorry,' she started, 'and it's more than likely you aren't going to be happy with what I tell you, especially after your reaction to the Facebook stuff...'

Fergus looked like a cartoon character now; his face was reddening by the second and she was sure he was going to have steam bursting out of his ears any second. 'But BBC Scotland have aired the video on TV, there's a camera crew on the other side of the river. The community of Glensheil are fully behind us. They've made placards and the number of shares on social media is now phenomenal. Donations are flooding in, which is fantastic,' she said, trying to keep everything positive.

'Are you telling me Esme has been on TV?'

'Not in person ... but the video was shown on the

news. Esme has become a little celebrity. Everyone wants to reunite her with Aggie as soon as possible,' she replied, barely taking a breath.

There was no denying Fergus looked panic-stricken. He raked his hands through his hair. 'What the hell have you done, Felicity?' His tone was severe. He was shaking his head and looked like he was about to explode. 'I don't want Esme in videos or appearing on the news. Do you understand me? She's my daughter, not yours, and now look what you've done.'

As much as she knew Fergus from old, Felicity had never quite seen a reaction like this from him before. She was flummoxed. In her mind, he was blowing all this out of proportion. Yes, she should have asked his permission, but it was only a short video and it was helping the community. In the grand scheme of things, it was madness, but if Heartcross could be reconnected again sooner rather than later than maybe businesses and people's lives wouldn't suffer too much. Surely Fergus could see that?

'Why are you overreacting?' She narrowed her eyes at him. 'What's going on?'

'Why does there have to be something going on?' Fergus wouldn't meet her gaze, and he looked shifty which puzzled Felicity.

'Because this doesn't make sense. It's just a video...'

'Don't interfere Felicity, this is nothing to do with you.'

'So there is something going on?' she probed, trying to keep her voice calm and get to the bottom of what this was actually about.

Fergus was clearly agitated.

'Look how much money we have raised now.' Felicity dug into her pocket and retrieved her mobile phone. 'I'm going to organise a meeting with a contractor once I've got the go ahead from Annie Boyd. My aim is to get this temporary bridge up and running as soon as possible. You'll be able to visit your mum...'

But Fergus wasn't listening, his mind was elsewhere.

'Fergus ... what is going on? Talk to me.'

'I need to collect Esme and go home,' he said, turning and grabbing his coat that was slung over the hay bales.

'Fergus!'

But he didn't answer.

Drew walked back into the barn, juggling a bag of heavy tools. 'Here, grab these, mate,' he said. 'Who's that shouting?'

'Shouting?' replied Felicity.

'Yes, listen.'

All three of them stood quietly and listened.

'Drew! Fergus ... where are you?'

'That doesn't sound good, I know that tone,' said Drew dropping the bag and rushing towards the barn door.

'Isla,' he bellowed, who spotted him immediately. She

ran towards him, baby Angus swathed in her arms, while Finn was crying clutching on to her skirt. The distress clear on her pale face.

'What is it? Is it the baby?' asked Drew, immediately taking Angus from her arms.

'No, he's asleep.' Her voice faltered.

'Then what's wrong?' Drew passed Angus to Felicity before draping his arm around his wife's shoulders. A tear-stricken Isla looked over towards Fergus. 'It's Esme … she's gone.'

They all fell silent as the words registered.

'What do you mean, she's gone?' asked Felicity, rocking Angus gently who was now beginning to stir.

'One minute she was there and then she wasn't!'

Fergus was beside himself. 'What do you mean Isla? How long since you've last seen her?'

Isla looked down at Finn who shrugged, 'Maybe about an hour ago?' said Isla knowing that wasn't what Fergus wanted to hear.

'An hour … and you've only just noticed she's missing?' Fergus was now shouting and baby Angus woke and began to scream.

'We were in the kitchen having a snack and drinks before I put a film on the TV for them both whilst I went upstairs to bath Angus.' Isla looked down at Finn. 'Tell them what you told me,' Isla soothed. Finn looked too frightened to speak.

'You aren't in any trouble, just tell Fergus what happened next.'

'Esme told me she didn't want to watch Star Wars, it was boring—'

'And?' interrupted Fergus impatiently.

Drew put a hand on his shoulder. 'And then what, Finn lad?'

'She said she was going upstairs to help Mummy bath Angus. So, she did.'

'Only she didn't appear,' said Isla. 'We were up there for an hour, and after I bathed Angus I've been so tired recently, we fell asleep for a wee while.'

'And Esme didn't come back to watch the film,' added Finn.

'Have you checked the farmhouse from top to bottom?' urged Drew.

'Yes, every inch, then I noticed Esme's shoes were gone.'

Fergus was now puffing out air, both hands raking through her hair. 'It's taken you an hour to notice she's missing?'

'It's not Isla's fault mate. Let's not panic,' said Drew, trying to restore some calm.

'I've got you posting videos of her—' Fergus stared at Felicity '—and you not keeping an eye on my daughter.' Fergus was beside himself.

Felicity thought about saying again that it wasn't her

who had posted the video but it wasn't the time to argue about that. She took his accusation on the chin.

'I'm so sorry Fergus, I really am,' said a distraught Isla.

'It's not your fault,' Drew said again as he pressed a swift kiss to his wife's head and gave Fergus a look telling him to pull himself together.

'She can't have gone far. I'll ring Mum at the teashop. We know how much she loves the teashop, she may have gone there. Someone will have spotted her. Get Jessica on the phone too.'

'Did anything happen this morning between you to make her want to run off, Fergus?' asked Isla tentatively.

'We had an argument this morning on the way to the farm. A silly argument,' admitted Fergus, still pacing around.

'What about?'

He looked directly at Felicity. 'About you.'

Felicity was shocked at the anger and upset in Fergus's eyes. Clearly he was still furious with her, even after her recent attempts to smooth over the past.

'It doesn't matter now,' said Drew, trying to diffuse the situation a little. 'All that matters is we find her. It's freezing out there but at least we know there's no getting out of Heartcross. She can't have gone too far.'

'Isla, you go back to the house with Finn and Angus. I'll check the barns and Felicity, you start ringing around. Fergus you get yourself back to your cottage, check there first and let's say we meet at the teashop in fifteen minutes?' ordered Drew.

Felicity could see Fergus's turmoil and she was on the verge of tears. Even though things were fraught between them she just wanted to put her arms around him and make everything all right, but she knew she couldn't. She knew he would push her away.

Drew hurried from the barn whilst Isla took the children back to the farmhouse.

As Fergus headed out of the barn, Felicity shouted after him, 'We will find her!'

He stopped and spun round. 'My life was fine until you turned back up,' he yelled, kicking his boot in the ground in fury.

Felicity ignored the scatter of earth and spoke calmly. 'She can't have gone far. Ring me as soon as you know something.'

Fergus gave out a sound, like a wounded animal. 'This is YOUR fault! If you hadn't posted that video, this would never have happened.'

Felicity's body felt heavy with emotion. Her heart shattered and she felt broken.

He staggered, and with a choice word righted himself and took off down the drive of Foxglove Farm.

Half blinded by tears, Felicity ran too, pushing her legs to run faster and faster. Somehow, they managed

Christie Barlow

to carry her all the way back along Love Heart Lane without buckling underneath her, the anxiety swirling in the pit of her stomach.

Felicity burst through the teashop door. When she opened her mouth, the words came out fitfully. She was half-sobbing, 'It's Esme … she's gone. She's run away.'

Chapter 23

Immediately, Rona went into robot mode, asking all the relevant questions before organising Allie and Meredith. Felicity felt sick to her stomach with guilt; if she hadn't taken that video this would never have happened and if she and Fergus hadn't argued then Esme wouldn't have run away. She looked out of the teashop window and dark clouds began to loom overhead. 'What's the weather forecast?' she asked in horror, thinking about Esme being caught in a storm.

'It's not good,' replied Allie, grabbing her coat. 'But on the plus side, the whole of Heartcross will be out looking for her.'

Emotion swarmed Felicity, as her body began to shake and the tears began to cascade down her cheeks. 'This is all my fault.'

Immediately, Meredith pulled her in for a hug. 'There's probably nothing to worry about. Jessica nipped back to the cottage over half an hour ago. We'll probably discover they are sitting there enjoying a hot chocolate without a care in the world.'

Felicity shook her head. 'No, because Jessica would know she shouldn't be on her own and would have phoned Fergus as soon as she turned up.'

'She might already have rung ... let's not panic. Did you say everyone was meeting back here?'

Felicity nodded. 'I think so, but I can't remember now,' she answered, taking a worried glance out of the shop window.

'We know she can't go far. Do we know why she'd decided to run away ... what's happened?' asked Meredith.

'I'm what's happened ... Fergus hates me,' sobbed Felicity, feeling absolutely distraught.

'He doesn't hate you,' reassured Allie. 'He's always been overprotective, it's just his way. Don't worry, we'll find her.'

'Here they come now, but she's not with Jessica.' Meredith spotted Drew, Fergus and Jessica running towards the shop. Fergus was tapping on his mobile phone as the door swung open.

'Anything?' asked Felicity hopefully.

'Nothing,' replied Drew. 'Rory's rounding up the troops and they should be here in a minute. Hamish and Heather are currently checking their end of the village and Julia has been out and about all morning but hasn't seen her.

Fergus cast his eyes upwards. 'We need to find her,' his urgent voice rang out.

'Here's Rory now,' nodded Meredith. He was marching up the lane with Fraser by his side and an army of villagers right behind them.

Allie pulled open the door and Rory pecked her on the cheek before turning towards Fergus. 'How long has she been gone mate?'

'Nearly a couple of hours now.'

Rory cleared his throat and took control. 'We need to split up into groups, that way we'll cover ground more quickly.'

Everyone agreed and Rory and Drew organised everyone into groups with specific areas to cover.

Just before they left, Fergus turned towards Felicity. 'If anything has happened to her...' His voice was shaky and his eyes brimmed with unshed tears.

The intensity of his gaze made her shiver and tears pricked Felicity's eyes. A huge dollop of fear descended over her. Nothing was going to calm her beating heart until Esme was found.

'As soon as you find her, ring me or Fergus,' instructed Drew, wearing an anxious expression as he raked his hand through his hair.

The villagers muttered their understanding.

Everyone spilled out of the teashop onto Love Heart Lane and went their separate ways.

Felicity had been instructed to walk the path down to the river and check along the river bank. In a daze she rushed down the rocky path towards the water's edge. It was all her stupid fault. Why hadn't she thought about her actions more? But she genuinely couldn't see why Fergus had been so opposed to it.

What if she'd fallen in the cold water? Once Felicity had reached the riverbank she stared across the now tranquil river, a far cry from the raging waters of the storm. She could still see the film crew in the distance on the opposite side of the river, keeping the world updated on the collapsed bridge. She peered up at the sky, praying Esme would be found safe. There was no way across the river, but Felicity pounded the riverbank scanning every inch of the area looking for Esme.

'Come on, where are you?' muttered Felicity under her breath. The fear was now stabbing in the pit of her stomach as she checked her mobile phone, but there was nothing from anyone.

Her knees trembled as she turned back and walked the path back to Heartcross. She spotted Rory and Drew up ahead and shouted towards them. 'Anything?'

'Nothing,' Rory shouted back whilst Drew hurriedly shook his head.

Felicity couldn't see Fergus but now the villagers were out in force. She pushed forward towards the teashop. Her hands were numb with the cold and her cheeks were stinging so goodness knew how Esme would feel if she'd been out in the cold for nearly two hours now.

Felicity choked up thinking about it as she headed back into the teashop. Meredith had dropped off some polystyrene cups that were left over from the hog roast during the summer and Rona was currently handing out cups of tea to the searchers to keep them going.

'There's no sign of her by the river,' said Felicity. 'Where can she be?'

Allie and Jessica thundered through the door. 'Anything?' asked Jessica.

Reluctantly Rona shook her head and handed them both a warm drink.

'Has anyone thought to ring the police?' asked Allie, sipping her drink.

'Constable Lees has radioed the station, which of course is over in Glensheil. They've asked to be kept informed. If there's nothing in the next hour they'll launch a boat across the river to help with the search but they are confident she'll turn up.'

'I'll get back out there,' said Felicity, giving her mum a quick hug before walking back outside into the cold. She hovered on Love Heart Lane. At first she thought she'd head towards the heart of the village, but she saw people were already checking cars and outhouses.

Felicity racked her brains – which way to go now?

She'd covered the riverbank and the village was being scaled with no stone left unturned.

Felicity glanced over to the stile, the one that took the ramblers over the top of the mountain. Maybe Esme had decided to climb the pass to try and reach Aggie that way?

Without thinking, Felicity hurled herself over the stile and after landing on the other side with a thud she began to stumble along the rocky terrain. 'Esme!' she shouted out, cupping her hands around her mouth. 'ESME!' But there was no answer.

Felicity searched every inch of the area but there was no trace of the little girl. She didn't like the thought of Esme all alone, clambering over the rocky ground. Standing still, Felicity checked her phone and exhaled. Quickly she texted Allie, who replied instantly; still, there was nothing.

She was just about to turn around when she remembered the little hut where she'd sat with Fergus only a couple of days ago. Maybe she would just walk as far as there, then turn back. She continued to shout out Esme's name into the wilderness.

Felicity could see the building in front of her and noticed the door was slightly ajar, but that didn't mean anything. The wind could have blown it open.

'Anyone there?' called out Felicity. She thought she heard movement inside. The door creaked as she pushed it open but there was no one inside. The litter and the old battered sofa remained untouched. Dismayed, Felicity was just about to pull the door shut when she thought she heard a sniffle. She stopped dead in her tracks to listen and heard the sound again. She pushed the door open a touch further and stepped inside fully, peering behind the back of the door. A pair of teary alarmed eyes locked with Felicity's, who exhaled and held a hand to her chest, her heart pounding. There was Esme, looking frightened and cold and Felicity's heart soared with love for the little girl. Thank God she was safe. The feeling of relief was instant and immediately she scooped Esme up into her arms and hugged her tight.

'Jeez, you frightened the life out of me.' Felicity forced herself to breathe normally. 'How long have you been here? You're freezing.' Felicity took off her coat and draped it around Esme's shoulders to give her some extra warmth.

Esme shrugged and carried on sniffling.

'Why have you run away?' asked Felicity softly, leading Esme by her hand to the battered old sofa and gently sitting her on her knee. 'Everyone is so worried about you.' She squeezed Esme once more. 'I need to let your dad know you're safe,' Felicity punched a text to Fergus's mobile to let him know where they were.

Esme clung on to Felicity. 'I'm sorry,' she sobbed, her voice wobbly.

'Do you want to tell me what made you run away?' asked Felicity tentatively.

Esme looked like she was about to say something but changed her mind.

'There must be a good reason?'

Esme shrugged. 'Daddy's angry. He's been different.'

'Did you argue with him?'

Esme nodded. 'After he shouted at you, he told me I had to stay away from you, but I like you and I said no. Why does Daddy not like you?'

Felicity smiled at Esme. 'I think your daddy does like me, but he's just a bit angry with me too. He thinks I posted that video without asking his permission and that was wrong of me.'

'But Auntie Isla said we'd raised lots and lots of money for the new bridge which means we can get Grandma home when she's better.'

'We can, the donations are flooding in.'

'That means we've done a good job. So why is Daddy so mad with us?'

'Well, I think you need to have a chat with your daddy about that. Sometime adults get it wrong too and I know for a fact he's been so sad since you've been gone. He'll have the biggest hug for you ever.'

The hut door burst open and the look of relief on

Fergus's face was instant, the second he lay eyes on Esme. Scooping her up from Felicity's knee, he hugged her like his life depended on it.

'Thank God, thank God you're safe,' he murmured over and over, kissing her hair. 'I'm sorry I shouted at you, I'm sorry we argued.' He sat down on the mouldy damp sofa next to Felicity and smoothed down Esme's hair. 'What made you run away, I've been very sad without you.'

Esme swung her legs and looked at the ground. 'You were really mad, and I didn't like you arguing with Felicity.' She took a breath. 'You shouted at her for posting the video and it wasn't her.' Esme looked down to the ground. 'It was me...'

'You?' said Fergus in disbelief.

Esme nodded. 'Felicity's phone was on the table and I picked it up and pressed something, and the video sent but I didn't think it would matter until you started shouting. I'm sorry I made you mad.'

Fergus glanced over towards Felicity who was looking at Esme. He didn't know what to say.

'And I didn't like you telling me I couldn't see her anymore. I like Felicity.' Esme looked up through her fringe and gave Felicity a smile before looking back down at the ground again.

Fergus took hold of his daughter's hands. 'I didn't mean to shout, and I certainly didn't mean to upset you.'

'But we're raising money for the bridge, to see Grandma. It's a good thing isn't it?'

Fergus nodded. 'It is a good thing,' he said, not wanting to rock the boat. He had his own reasons for not wanting Esme to appear on the internet, but he'd never shared that insecurity with anyone.

Felicity sat quietly throughout it all and watched the interaction between Fergus and Esme without interruption. He absolutely doted on his little girl; the love and warmth oozed out of his every pore.

'What made you come to this place?' asked Fergus, looking around the room then back at Esme.

'Grandma tells me stories about the hut on the hill and the adventure always begins at the stile at the top of Love Heart Lane.'

'She does now, does she?'

'She told me you used to come here in the summer and hang out with Uncle Drew and Rory.'

'We did, and Auntie Isla, Allie and Felicity too.'

Esme's wide eyes looked towards Felicity. 'You've known my dad a really long time!'

'I have,' she answered with a smile. 'Now shall we get you back down the mountain and see what my mum has to offer in the teashop to eat? You must be hungry?'

Esme looked up at Fergus. 'I am hungry.'

'Come on, let's go and get you fed but you have to promise never to run away again. You've given everyone the fright of their lives! And Auntie Isla and Finn were upset too,' said Fergus, standing up. Felicity copied his lead.

'I'm sorry Daddy.' Esme cupped one of her tiny hands in her dad's and the other one in Felicity's as they began to walk back down the mountain.

'Can we all be friends again?' asked Esme, with hope in her voice.

'Of course,' answered Fergus, ruffling the top of his daughter's hair. Esme skipped between them both and Felicity took a moment to reflect on the last few hours. She felt shattered and emotionally drained and had never been so frightened in her life. She'd experienced emotion like she'd never felt before and never ever wanted to experience again. Was this what it felt like to be a mother? The feeling of fear that had surged through her body when discovering Esme had disappeared was one she wouldn't wish on her worst enemy.

Felicity smiled over at Fergus, but he looked away. That feeling of dread that had lifted from her stomach after finding Esme was back. She knew that look on his face; Fergus was worrying about something. She didn't know what, but she knew even though she might be over-stepping the line, she was going to tackle Fergus about it as soon as possible.

Chapter 24

The next morning, Felicity was sitting in the living room with her ear to the end of the receiver waiting for the phone to connect. She'd no idea what Annie Boyd's reaction was going to be to her suggestion, but she was about to find out. Since the last news report everyone had been flabbergasted by the donations they'd received and the total was hovering near one hundred thousand, which was unbelievable in such a short space of time. Huge businesses were donating all over the country and the response was overwhelming.

'Annie Boyd speaking.' The voice on the other end of the line spoke with authority.

'Hi, this is Felicity Simons, spokeswoman for the residents of Heartcross.'

'Hello, Felicity, how are things at your end?'

Felicity took a breath and began to explain all about the video and how it had gone viral. There was no denying Annie Boyd was impressed and even more so when Felicity shared the news of the fundraising total.

'And that's why I'm ringing,' continued Felicity. 'I'm aware I can't be involved in the reconstruction of the original bridge, due to the many departments that need to be involved etc. But I was hoping with Councillor Smith now out of the equation and while you appoint someone else in his position, I could crack on?'

'What do you mean?' asked Annie with intrigue.

'With the funds sat there, I could organise a meeting with the contractors and facilitate the go ahead for the temporary bridge to be erected – sooner rather than later for the residents of Heartcross.'

For a moment Annie Boyd was quiet on the other end of the line. 'And you think you can do that single-handedly?'

'I can give it my best shot and I'm sure you can steer me in the right direction.'

'I can indeed, I'll email you a list of contractors we use alongside some other vital contacts. You really have done amazingly well raising that amount of money in such a short space of time. I'll be employing you as a chief fundraiser!' she said and gave a little chuckle.

'That's settled then,' said Felicity, wearing an enormous grin. 'I'll get to work as soon as I receive the email.'

'I'll send it now and please keep me in the loop, Felicity.'

'I will,' and with that Felicity hung up.

With a spring in her step she fired up her laptop and waited for the email to land in her inbox. True to her word, Annie Boyd had sent it immediately and had included a list of contractors, some of whom were based over in Glensheil and some even further afield. Maybe Felicity would need to take Drew up on his offer of launching his boat across the river to meet up with some of these people. There were approximately twenty names on the list and it was more than likely most of them were in the middle of projects already. Who knew when they could begin work on the temporary bridge? There was only one way to find out; she grabbed the phone and made herself as comfy as she could be on the bottom stair before she began to ring the names starting at the top of the list. But with every contractor she tried, she discovered that most already had work on for the next few months and couldn't juggle their workload to help the residents of Heartcross. This wasn't going to be as easy as she'd thought.

Felicity crossed off the next name with a pencil and let out a sigh; she wasn't going to be beaten. The next name she stared at was ... surely not ... Alfie Wilson.

Felicity remembered back to the meeting in the teashop where Alfie had tried to ridicule her in front of everyone. He hadn't changed from school, and he wasn't a person that Felicity had ever warmed to, but maybe on this occasion she could muddle along with him for the sake of Heartcross? He must be good at his job if he had contracts with the council.

Felicity pondered for a minute before popping back through to the teashop. 'Have I got time to nip out?'

Rona looked towards her daughter. 'You have ... is this to do with the phone call?'

Felicity tapped her chest and grinned. 'You are looking at chief temporary bridge erector ... not that that is the most glamourous title I could have given myself.'

'Annie Boyd went for it?'

'She did. She was amazed by the amount of donations and gave me the go ahead to get the show on the road, and the bridge over troubled waters.'

'So, what's the plan now?' asked Rona, adding a pinch of salt to the pot simmering on the hob.

'Well, I've started to ring around a few contractors, but so far no one could help due to their own workload. But then an interesting name came up on the list.'

Rona raised an eyebrow. 'Who?'

'Alfie Wilson – not my favourite person in the world...'

'Yes, but needs must, and that's definitely his line of work. Is that where you are going now?'

Felicity nodded. 'Wish me luck.'

Strolling down Love Heart Lane, Felicity noticed Drew and Fergus trundling along in a nearby field in the tractor.

She hadn't seen Fergus since they'd walked Esme back to the teashop, but she'd made her mind up to go and call in at the cottage later that evening to see how the land lay. She spotted Heather cycling through the village past the pub and she waved at Felicity who waved back.

Despite the cold weather, there was Alfie, sitting outside the pub at one of the picnic tables with a full pint of beer in front of him, reading a newspaper.

'Just the man,' said Felicity, forcing a bright smile and trying not to hold a grudge at the way Alfie had tried to stitch her up in front of the other residents at the meeting.

Alfie Wilson's large-lidded eyes looked up with suspicion, and he took a glance behind him before turning back towards Felicity. 'Are you talking to me?'

'Yes,' she answered brightly. 'You are just the man I need.' She regretted those words as soon as they'd left her mouth.

'Really?' he sniffed.

'Have you got time for a chat?'

Alfie shifted uncomfortably on the bench and moved his newspaper to one side.

'I suppose,' he answered disgruntledly, taking a sip of his pint and not looking happy at all.

'I've got a proposition for you.'

A sly smile slid across his face and again, Felicity regretted the words as soon as they left her mouth.

'How's work?'

'Work?' he replied in puzzlement. 'Proving a little difficult with the bridge collapse.'

'That's what I thought. How do you fancy being Heartcross's knight in shining armour?' Felicity trilled, sliding her legs under the bench opposite him.

'Huh?' he huffed, not having a clue what Felicity was leading to.

'The video...'

'The one with you and Fergus's kid?'

'That's the one ... it's had a huge impact on raising the funds to erect a temporary bridge across the river. In fact donations are pouring in all the time.'

'What's that got to do with me?'

'I've had the go ahead from Annie Boyd to recruit a contractor to manage the build.'

It was only then that Alfie Wilson sat up straight and began to take notice of Felicity.

'That's going to be a big deal.'

'It is indeed. How are you fixed?'

'Me?' He put a hand to his chest.

'Well, you are on the council's books and why not? It's not as though you're run off your feet at the moment, and this is your type of work, isn't it?'

'And you thought of me?' He cocked an eyebrow.

Felicity didn't want to admit that actually she'd rung quite a few numbers on the list before she'd gotten around to him. Alfie didn't need to know that.

'You have to look after your own in this village, and as you are born and bred Heartcross, you are the best man for the job.' Felicity didn't know why she was blowing smoke up his backside, it wasn't as though he was going to turn her down. What else did he have to do at this moment in time? 'Your name will go down in the history books,' she added, trying to seal the deal.

The corners of his mouth turned up even more. 'Let's go and talk in my office,' he suggested, standing up and swilling his pint down at record speed.

Felicity didn't even know he had an office or where it was, but she stood up and followed him down the lane anyway.

As a child, she remembered Alfie and his family lived off the High Street in a two-up two-down, and that's exactly where it looked like they were heading to now.

'Here we are,' he said pushing open the garden gate. Felicity followed him down the shingle path that led around the side of the house and towards the bottom of the garden. In front of her was a ramshackle shed that look like it had seen better days.

'Come in,' he said, pushing open a creaky door. Felicity had no idea how it was still standing after all the recent storms. She followed him inside and noticed the place was cold, his desk was stacked high with papers and there was barely any light shining through the grimy windows, which at a guess had never been cleaned in their lifetime.

'Have a seat,' he said.

Felicity stole a glance around the small space but couldn't see a place to sit.

'Sorry,' he said, shifting some paperwork off an old camping chair in the corner of the room. 'Sit here.'

Felicity carefully lowered herself into the chair and prayed it wouldn't collapse underneath her.

'It's looks like quite an empire you have here,' she said, eyeing up the most gigantic spider in the corner of the shed and praying with all her might it wouldn't drop on her head anytime soon.

'Yes,' he replied, 'it all goes on in here.'

Felicity was in no doubt whatsoever and shivered at the very thought.

'So, what happens now?' she asked, keen to move things along quickly.

'I'll draw up the contract and get the team in place, and you will need to transfer the money into the business account, so I can pay wages etcetera,' he said, handing Felicity a folder that contained the banking details. 'I'll also liaise with Annie Boyd, as she's actually a good friend of mine. We tend to use the same men for each job, and the majority of them live over in Glensheil which will make things a little easier on that side at least!'

'It sounds like this will begin moving forward quickly.' Felicity said in hope.

'I'm on it now,' replied Alfie, opening the filing cabinet and pulling out some papers. 'We need to reunite this community with the outside world and thank you for thinking of me,' he said with sudden sincerity. 'Things have been a little difficult for me recently and this has given me a purpose again.' His face softened and for the first time ever Felicity saw his hard exterior disappear.

'Like I said, if the community can help each other, then let's make sure we support each other.'

Alfie nodded, and held her gaze for a moment longer than necessary. 'You know at school, I always had a bit of a soft spot for you.'

Felicity was taken back. 'Actually, no I didn't know that.'

Alfie Wilson had always been one of those lads, the class clown. The guy who sat at the back, disrupting lessons and always being sent out of the classroom. As far as Felicity could remember, Alfie had fallen into a bad crowd at secondary school, whilst the rest of the gang from Heartcross had stuck together.

'You were the prettiest, the funniest, the brainiest, everyone wanted to be your boyfriend.'

'Don't be daft,' she said and found herself blushing.

'It's true, but you only ever had eyes for Fergus.'

Those words rung true. Felicity knew that was the case – after those summer holidays hanging out at the hut there was never going to be anyone else for her.

'That is true,' she found herself saying. 'So why have things been difficult for you?' she asked tentatively, changing the subject.

Alfie blew out a breath. 'Remember my brother ... Lucas?'

Of course, Felicity remembered Lucas, he was a few years older than them.

'Yes. Didn't he move to London too?' Felicity loosely remembered her mum saying something in passing.

'Yes, he met his wife on a training course and fell deeply and madly in love. He left Heartcross and moved to London to be with her and bring up their family.'

'That doesn't sound a bad thing?' queried Felicity.

'They have one daughter. My niece, she's gorgeous but then...'

'But what?'

'My brother's wife, she became ill ... she was diagnosed with cancer...'

Felicity felt a surge of emotion. 'That's awful. I'm truly sorry, Alfie.'

Alfie swallowed. 'The good news is she's come through it. I wanted to help more but I'm too far away, although I've spoken to my brother most days.'

'And I'm sure he appreciates that. It is difficult when

you live so far away.' Felicity felt for Alfie, having been in a similar situation.

'Why don't you go and visit them?' she suggested.

Alfie sighed. 'I think we need to build a bridge first to get me out of Heartcross.' He gave a small chuckle.

'Oh, there is that,' said Felicity trying to lighten the mood.

'And London is such a long way from Scotland.'

'Opposite ends of the country,' joked Felicity. 'But on a serious note, don't leave it too long. If you want to go and spend some time with them, just do it. When my grandma was dying ... I regret not coming home, spending more time with her. I was caught up in my own problems and before I knew it, it was too late. Grandma passed away and I never got to say goodbye. That's something that is going to live with me for the rest of my life.'

Alfie thought about it for a second. 'You know what, I think I will go and see them, just as soon as we get this temporary bridge up and running. Otherwise it might be years before the people of Heartcross can escape to the other side.'

'That sounds like an excellent plan.'

'Felicity ... I'm sorry for being a pain in the backside in the teashop.'

'Don't worry about that, it's forgotten.'

Felicity left the shed seeing Alfie in a new light. Maybe his overzealous personality was a front, but he seemed caring and genuine enough and Felicity was pleased she'd approached him for help with the bridge.

She glanced at her watch and hurried back towards the teashop. Hamish had already dropped off the food for the day and now the village shop was closed until further notice. She could see her mum and Allie busying themselves in the kitchen. Felicity pushed open the door and took her coat off and safely tucked away the bank details Alfie had given her behind the counter.

'How did it go?' asked Rona, stirring the huge pans of soup of the stove.

'Pretty well, Alfie's jumped at the chance and is confident he's got just the right men for the job. So, it's all systems go.'

Meredith suddenly popped her head around the door from the cottage. 'I thought I heard your voice,' she said to Felicity. 'I was taking a quick break, but I think you all should come and see this.'

They quickly followed Meredith into the living room where the TV was switched on and there was Aidy Redfern interviewing Aggie from her hospital bed.

'At least she's got some colour back in her cheeks,' said Rona, perching on the edge of the chair.

Aidy had the microphone held near to Aggie's mouth and was sat at the side of her bed.

'Your granddaughter has been causing quite a stir on the internet, Mrs Campbell!'

Aggie smiled. *'I'm very proud of her and of course Felicity too. I believe the donations to build the temporary bridge are flooding in thanks to the video they made.'*

'How are you coping being away from your family?'

'It's a little difficult. When I first saw the news that the bridge had collapsed all that was going through my mind was when I would see them again.'

'Hopefully, it won't be too long before you are reunited with your family, but in the meantime you are in the best place to recuperate. Thank you for talking to us today Mrs Campbell. This is Aidy Redfern reporting for BBC Scotland.'

'Look at Aggie getting in on the action,' chuckled Rona. 'Even though it must be awful stranded in the hospital all by herself, she's definitely looking better.'

'She is,' replied Meredith, 'but how are they going to get her home? How long will it take for the temporary bridge to be built?'

'God only knows. Hopefully with Alfie, things can get moving along really quickly but I would still estimate maybe a few weeks,' answered Felicity, standing up and switching the TV off.

'Maybe it's going to have to be Drew's boat to ferry her across the river when the time comes.'

'Talking of Drew...' said Rona, taking out a picnic basket from underneath the counter and handing it over to Felicity.

'What's this?'

'The lads can't get down for lunch today and I promised Isla one of us would take them up a picnic basket full of food, save her bundling Angus in the pram ... do you mind?'

'Of course not,' replied Felicity, placing it on the table while she slipped her coat back on. 'I won't be long.'

Felicity made her way over to Foxglove Farm, feeling a little nervous. She hadn't spoken to or seen Fergus since Esme was found and she was unsure how things stood between them, especially now Aggie was getting in the act on the TV. Would he be cross with his mum too?

She ambled up the driveway but there wasn't any sign of the boys out in the fields or in the barns. She knocked on the door and Isla opened it within seconds, looking relieved and taking the picnic basket from Felicity. Angus was strapped to her front in a baby sling, fast asleep.

'You are a life saver, I'm exhausted with this little one. Luckily for me Finn has just fallen asleep which gives me a little time to try and eat my lunch in peace.'

'No Esme today?' Felicity asked.

Isla shook her head. 'Jessica's looking after her. Are you coming in?'

Felicity shook her head. 'No, I'd best get back and help Mum dish up the food.'

'Thanks for bringing this over.'

'You're welcome.'

Felicity dug her hands in her pocket and strolled quickly back towards the teashop, a little disappointed that she hadn't managed to see Fergus until, a little further on, she noticed him opening the door to his cottage and disappearing inside. Without thinking Felicity found her legs walking in that very direction and before she knew it she was knocking on his door.

Within seconds the front door swung open and Fergus was standing there. 'What are you doing here?' he said sullenly, looking like he had the weight of the world on his shoulders.

Felicity really didn't know what she was doing there but thought quickly on her feet. 'I've just taken your lunch up to the farm.'

'Thank you,' he said, but still looked distracted. Clearly he wasn't in the mood for making conversation. He looked like he was about to close the door on her.

'You don't seem your usual self,' Felicity pushed on. She might have been stating the obvious, but she needed to get to the bottom of why he was so upset about the video. She was sure there was more to it than he was telling her.

'And how would you know what my usual self is?' He turned away from her but left the door open and Felicity took this as her cue to follow him.

The cottage with its low ceilings and traditional fittings had always felt homely to Felicity and she relaxed slightly as she followed Fergus into the living room. He seemed agitated, and she watched as he quickly walked over to the corner of the room to a simple desk and closed the lid of his laptop. Immediately, she got the impression there was something to hide, something he didn't want her to see.

'How's Aggie?' asked Felicity. 'Have you spoken to her recently?'

'Apparently, she made her TV debut this morning,' he answered, not sounding the least bit impressed. 'Is there anything in particular you wanted, Flick?' he asked, staring at Felicity.

'No,' she answered. 'I was just seeing how you are.'

Despite her best efforts to be friendly, Fergus wasn't having any of it.

'I'm fine, I just need to nip to the bathroom and get back up to the farm.'

He left the living room and Felicity heard the bathroom door click open at the top of the stairs. She took a swift glance back towards the laptop and without giving it a second thought, she opened it. A webpage was open, and Felicity cast a glance over the screen. She felt puzzled. Why was Fergus googling DNA testing?

Hearing the chain flush and feeling guilty for

snooping, she quickly closed the lid again and made her way to the front door.

'I'll be off!' she shouted up the stairs, and before Fergus could answer she hurried out of the cottage and back towards the teashop, thoughts whizzing through her brain.

Chapter 25

When Felicity arrived back at the teashop, the room was already full with the first sitting of villagers spooning their homemade soup from their bowls. She scanned the room and spotted Jessica and Esme sitting in the corner. The second Esme saw Felicity she scraped back her chair and came running over, flinging her arms wide around her waist.

'Now there's a welcome,' smiled Felicity. 'How are you today?'

'I've been into school this morning and helped Jessica tidy up the stationery cupboard.'

'Sounds like fun.'

'And I picked some books from the school library that we are going to read this afternoon.'

'Perks of the job,' said Jessica, now standing behind Esme.

'Baking books,' added Esme. 'I want to be a baker like Mummy and own my own teashop, just like this one.'

'And I'm sure you will,' said Felicity, loving the little girl's enthusiasm. 'One day, we can have a look at my grandma's secret recipe book and bake something out of there.'

'Promise?' Esme's wide eyes looked up at Felicity.

'I promise.'

Esme gave out a little squeal. 'I'll need my own apron, I can't be a baker without my own apron.'

Felicity bent down in front of Esme. 'Do you see that old dresser?' She nodded to the far corner of the teashop. 'If you go into the left-hand drawer, in there will be my old apron from when I was a little girl. You can borrow that for a while.'

'Can I?'

'Of course, you can't be a baker without an apron.'

Excitedly, Esme skipped off towards the dresser and pulled out the drawer. Felicity and Jessica watched as she rummaged inside and found the old apron. She hurriedly put the loop over her head and tied it around her waist. 'Ta-dah!' Esme grinned. 'I am now a proper baker.'

'Why don't we go and have a look through those books?' suggested Jessica, beaming at Esme's enthusiasm.

Esme nodded before turning and hugging Felicity so hard she nearly toppled backwards. 'And I'll look forward to hearing all about those recipes.'

As a content Esme skipped out of the teashop, a pristine-looking Alfie sauntered in through the door. His hair was combed and parted, his shoes were polished, and he was dressed in a navy-blue suit, which completely took Felicity by surprise.

'You look very smart,' said Felicity, doing a double take.

'Thank you, I'm just going to grab a bite to eat before I set to work on rounding up the architect and engineers for the temporary bridge by a virtual meeting, but have you seen the donation page today?'

Felicity hadn't checked since last night, but she knew the donations had continued to rise rapidly. Everyone had been so kind and the response was overwhelming. In the last twenty-four hours over another fifty thousand had been donated from corporate companies all over the world. Quickly checking on her phone she was astonished.

'If we receive another fifty thousand, we'll have raised the funds needed for the temporary bridge,' she shouted towards the teashop kitchen. 'How is that even possible?'

'What? ... That's amazing, absolutely amazing! We knew you came back to the village for a reason, Felicity!' chuckled Meredith. 'But now get serving!' She thrust two bowls into Felicity's hands.

As she hurried to serve the hungry villagers, something caught Felicity's eye. There was Fergus hurrying up Love Heart Lane again. He looked anxious and Felicity knew that look of worry from old. He was up to something, especially if he wasn't up at the farm. She eyed him as he disappeared back inside the cottage. Something was telling her to go and speak to him again, but she knew he wouldn't welcome her interference and she couldn't disappear from the teashop until everyone had been fed and watered.

Alfie was on his phone and making notes on his pad; he caught her eye and smiled.

'Your phone is about to explode,' remarked Allie, who was filling up the teapots. 'You are certainly in demand.'

Felicity hummed her way over to the counter and swiped the screen of her phone. 'Five missed calls from Aidy Redfern, the news reporter.'

'Ring him back?' suggested Rona, who was busy mopping up a spilt drink.

Felicity hit his number and waited patiently for him to answer.

'Felicity! How are you feeling right now?' His voice was jovial.

Felicity had no clue how she was meant to be feeling but judging by the sound of his voice she was missing something.

'We've launched a boat from Glensheil and the news team want to come and interview you, as soon as … now in fact,' he said, completely taking Felicity by surprise.

'Why?' she asked, completely perplexed.

'The donations! You, Felicity Simons, have single-handedly raised over two hundred and fifty thousand pounds in a matter of days. How does that make you feel?'

Felicity was absolutely flabbergasted; she'd only checked the donations a matter of minutes ago. 'Really? We've hit the target already?'

'You have, we've noticed in the last half an hour or so that a donation for over fifty thousand pounds has landed on the page.'

'What! That's amazing ... who?'

'We don't know, it's an anonymous donation, we hoped you might know?' replied Aidy.

Felicity could feel a goofy grin spread right across her face before she let out a squeal. Everyone in the teashop turned and stared towards her as Felicity began jumping up and down like an excited child at Christmas.

'Heartcross must be so proud of you Felicity. It is all down to you and the video you posted. Would Esme be available to be interviewed with you?'

Felicity knew that was more than likely going to be a no, especially with the way Fergus had reacted to the whole thing, 'I'm not sure, I'll have to check with her dad.'

'That will be very much appreciated, we will be with you hopefully very soon. Where shall we meet you?' he asked.

'Bonnie's Teashop on Love Heart Lane.'

When Felicity hung up, her mum, Meredith and Allie gathered around her. Felicity was feeling proud; her actions had raised the funds for the temporary bridge to reconnect them with the town of Glensheil which meant the construction could begin immediately.

'What's going on?' asked Rona, wiping her brow with a tea towel.

'You are not going to believe this. There's been a secret donation given, taking us up to our target of over two hundred and fifty pounds... Alfie did you hear me?'

Alfie looked up. 'What's going on? You look like the cat that's got the cream.'

'We've just hit our target!'

'You're kidding me?' he said, flicking straight to his phone then exhaling. 'That is amazing.'

'Who would donate that much money?' asked Allie.

Felicity shrugged. 'No idea, an anonymous donation apparently. I can't believe we finally have enough money!' Felicity's heart swelled with pride and happiness. 'Our community is going to get their temporary bridge.'

'It's wonderful news, you must be so proud of yourself.' Alfie stood up and hushed all the villagers in the teashop who looked in his direction. 'Felicity has gone and done it. She's raised the funds for the temporary bridge.' Alfie grinned towards her and began clapping.

The villagers followed suit and burst into rapturous applause.

Felicity felt overwhelmed, 'Thank you, thank you ... I'll update the Facebook page and let the whole community know.' She turned towards her mum. 'Aidy Redfern has launched a boat across the river along with the news team and he's coming to interview me now.' Felicity took a tentative look towards the mirror on the wall in the teashop. 'I'll need to brush my hair and at least put a little make-up on.'

'You look fine,' smiled Rona, ignoring Felicity's vanity.

'And they want to interview Esme too,' said Felicity, not knowing what to do about that.

'All you can do is ask Fergus,' said Allie. 'He might have mellowed a little?'

'I thought I saw him going into the cottage, I'll go and ask him before they arrive,' said Felicity, using that as an excuse to go and see Fergus once more.

Outside, the sky was grey and heavy. It looked like it was going to rain any second as Felicity strolled down the lane towards the cottage. In her heart she knew exactly what Fergus would say about Esme being interviewed but she wanted an excuse to go and see what he was up to and thanks to Aidy Redfern, she had the perfect one.

Feeling apprehensive she knocked on the cottage door and waited. She could hear no sound or movement, so she knocked again. Felicity was certain that Fergus was still inside. Taking the plunge, she twisted the knob of the front door and immediately it clicked opened. Feeling like an intruder, but curious, she stepped into the hallway.

'Fergus, are you here?' she said softly, pushing open the living room door. The curtains were drawn and the lighting was low. It all seemed very strange for the time of day.

Fergus was there, sitting on the settee, and it looked like he'd been crying. By the side of him was a stack of photos and the small cardboard box.

'What are you doing here ... again?'

Without being invited Felicity sat down on the chair opposite. He raised his eyebrows then looked away from her stare and began to place the photos back inside the box.

'What have you there?' she asked, sensing the strange tension in the air.

'Nothing,' he answered, 'and you didn't answer me, what are you doing here?'

She took a deep breath and knew this wasn't the right time to say anything but she went ahead anyway. 'We've raised the total amount of money for the temporary bridge to go ahead and the news reporter was wondering if he could interview myself and Esme. They are actually arriving by boat from Glensheil any minute now.'

She slowed down her words towards the end of the sentence because she noticed Fergus's face turn a deep beetroot colour.

Without warning, he banged his fist down on to the settee sending the cardboard box into the air, then he straightened up his body to catch his breath.

'No!' he spat. 'You should never have put Esme on there in the first place without my permission. It's just what I didn't need.'

Felicity didn't have a clue why he was behaving this way, but she took this opportunity to try and understand him better. 'Fergus, you are acting very strange. What's going on? You can trust me, you know.'

'Trust you? Don't make me laugh ... I did trust you and you were the one who left me after we'd made plans to stay together for the rest of our lives.' He exhaled sharply then rubbed a hand over his face, trying to calm his outburst.

'The video ... it was only for fundraising purposes ... to raise awareness. There was no harm done.'

'You have no idea about the harm it could have done, or still might do.'

Felicity narrowed her eyes at him. 'What are you hiding?' she asked, holding his gaze.

'You need to mind your own business. You've come back here, potentially opening up a right can of worms.'

For a moment silence hung in the air.

Felicity felt she had nothing to lose and asked the question that was burning inside of her. 'Why do you need a DNA test, Fergus?'

Fergus's face plunged into despair and Felicity's stomach churned as she waited for him to answer.

He stared at her like a rabbit caught in headlights and couldn't quite believe his ears.

'What do you know about that?' His voice faltered. 'Tell me what you know,' he said, staring at her. She knew that he wasn't going to let it drop until she came clean.

'I took a look at your laptop.' As soon as she told him she felt underhanded, but it had felt like the only way to understand what was going on for Fergus – why he was behaving so out of character.

'How ... how dare you ... I leave you alone in here for a split second and you think you have the right to go snooping?'

She nodded. 'Yes, I'm sorry. I shouldn't have, but I was worried about you. You've been acting really strange lately and this isn't like you. Why are you googling DNA testing? Come on Ferg...' she pressed, her voice soft. 'Has this got anything to do with your reaction over the video?' She noticed Fergus bristle at the very mention of the video. 'It has hasn't it?'

Fergus held Felicity's gaze, his own eyes brimming with tears.

'What is it? If you don't want to tell me about it, talk to Drew if something is bothering you.'

Fergus shook his head. 'I can't ... I've never told a soul. A secret only stays a secret if you keep it to yourself. I can't risk anyone else knowing.'

'Surely it can't be that bad? A problem shared and all that.'

Fergus didn't answer her, and she watched his shaky hands open up the cardboard box. He grasped an envelope and held it out to Felicity. 'Go on ... read it.'

Her pulse doubled, and her palm felt sweaty as she took the letter from Fergus. 'Read it, before I change my mind.'

Carefully, Felicity opened up the letter and began to read, taking a moment to digest the information on the letter.

As she read, her pain for Fergus hammered against her chest, 'Have you done anything about this?'

He shook his head. 'I was hoping it would all go away.'

'Esme isn't your child?' said Felicity, the words echoing around the room.

'According to that letter, she's not my child.'

Felicity was shocked to the core. She really hadn't been expecting that.

'Where did you get this?' she asked, looking at the envelope. It was addressed to Fergus but had never been posted and had been written by Lorna to Fergus, telling him the devastating news that he was not the father of her baby.

'After Lorna died, I found it amongst her things but as you can see she never posted it. The letter is dated before Esme was born, so I guess she changed her mind about telling me and then she passed away.'

'Have you told Aggie ... Jessica ... shown them this letter?'

Fergus broke down and shook his head. 'No, I couldn't. What if this was true? I couldn't bear the thought of losing her. I love Esme with all my heart. I haven't told a soul about this ... until now ... until you.'

'And what are you planning to do with this information?'

Fergus took a moment. 'Absolutely nothing.' He wiped his eyes with back of his sleeve. 'But it's killing me inside.'

'Was it an affair?' Felicity asked, trying to piece everything together in her mind.

Fergus shrugged. 'I've no idea.'

Lorna had written in the letter that she didn't deserve Fergus's love and that every day the truth was eating away at her. That she was sorry for the hurt she was going to cause him, but that she couldn't live with the lie any longer. There was no mention of who Esme's real father might be.

'Do you think Jessica knows?'

He shrugged. 'I've no idea, but she's never given me the impression she does.'

'And is this anything to do with the reason you reacted the way you did about the video?'

Fergus fought back more tears. 'I know it sounds daft but what if...' Fergus took a deep breath. 'What if Lorna told Esme's father the truth before she died and he knows she exists? He might realise that was her on the TV or on social media. I couldn't bear it if he came looking for her, if he took her away from me. And what would that do to Esme? Not only has she lost her mum in tragic circumstances but then all the security she has ever known is taken away from her too. What rights would I have? I'm not her dad.'

Felicity could see he was visibly shaken and tried to smooth the way. 'She *is* your daughter. You are the one that's brought her up, that loves her and has been there for her all these years. No one can ever question you aren't her dad.'

'I'm not her biological father though ... according to this. Every day, Flick, I live in fear, fear that the truth will come out. What if her real dad knows and is already looking for her? Or the worst case scenario – what if Esme gets ill, God forbid, and needs a biological parent to help her live?'

'I've no idea, but you are just panicking now,' said

Felicity sympathetically. 'This man hasn't turned up yet, has he? My guess would be he probably doesn't know anything about her.'

'And the only person who has all the answers to any of this is dead. I can't believe she could do this to me. I thought we were in love but all the time there was this betrayal. How could she live with the deceit and let me love that girl like my own, knowing she wasn't mine?' His voice cracked.

Felicity had no words, but she was deeply distressed to see Fergus hurting this way.

'Maybe speak to Jessica?' Felicity softly offered. 'Maybe she knows something?'

'Maybe, but if she doesn't and I tell her, that's another person who knows the truth. Flick, I love Esme ... I love her so much it hurts. I don't want her to have to deal with any more trauma in her life and I don't want to lose her. She is my child Flick, no matter what this letter says. She's mine! Things are good just the way they are ... and you have to promise me Flick, you can't tell anyone.' His voice was passionate, earnest.

'I won't tell anyone, I promise. You can trust me Fergus,' she whispered softly. Their stupid row evaporated as Felicity took Fergus in her arms and cradled him. Her heart went out to him as he let out a shuddering sigh then wept.

'I'm so scared, Flick,' he whispered.

'It'll be okay.' She kissed the top of his head gently. She knew some of the blame laid at her door for his distress, and she felt her own guilt rise again. If only she'd checked with Fergus before even taking the video with Esme. Felicity had never anticipated this was the reason he didn't want Esme plastered all over the internet and her heart twisted for him as she rocked him gently, promising him that everything was going to be all right. In that moment it hit Felicity fully that her feelings for Fergus had never gone away. In fact, she knew without doubt that this was the man she would always love. And as she held him tighter, she wished with all her heart, that she could take away his pain.

Chapter 26

Half an hour later it seemed every villager was crammed outside the teashop to see what was going on inside. The film crew had arrived and there was an air of excitement around the place.

As Felicity weaved her way through the crowds towards the teashop door, everyone began to pat her on the back and the sound of rapturous applause echoed all around.

She smiled at the sound of cheers and villagers shouting, 'Well done Felicity! You've saved Heartcross!'

The community was out in full force praising her, and she recalled how only a few days ago she had worried that she would never fit back into the community. But now she knew she'd been welcomed back into the fold with open arms. Feeling like royalty, she waved a hand above her head and pushed the door open to the teashop which was packed to the rafters with the TV crew. How they'd lugged their equipment from the river up the hill Felicity would never know, but at the moment they were enjoying a well-earned tea break and chatting with Rona.

Allie was the first to notice Felicity. 'You look dreadful,' she whispered. 'Is everything okay with Fergus?'

'Everything's fine,' Felicity lied, hoping for a change in subject, even though he was firmly on her mind.

'I'm assuming interviewing Esme is a no-go?'

'You assume right,' she answered, as Rona appeared at her side.

'Go and touch up your make-up and at least pull a brush through your hair,' she suggested, shuffling her daughter through the film crew towards the back of the shop and into the cottage, 'and hurry.'

Felicity risked a tentative look in the mirror; Allie was right, she did look dreadful. She'd wanted to stay comforting Fergus but with Aidy Redfern being shipped across the river she didn't have much choice. The timing couldn't have been worse. Inside she felt sad for Fergus but knew there was nothing she could do to help him, except keep his secret like she'd promised.

Pulling a brush through her hair and dabbing lip gloss on to her lips she declared herself ready. Walking back into the teashop, her stomach started fluttering as she spotted Aidy Redfern who was currently being pampered by a make-up artist whilst tapping on his mobile phone.

'We will be going live in ten minutes!' the floor manager shouted before ushering Felicity over in Aidy's direction.

Felicity held out her hand. 'We've spoken on the phone. Hi, I'm Felicity.'

Aidy gave her a smile, instantly putting her at ease. 'Congratulations! In all my time as a news reporter I've never known anything quite like this. A local girl back from the bright lights of the city, stranded in a village after the bridge collapses then raises the money for a temporary bridge within record time. Well done, you.'

'Thanks,' she replied, slightly blushing. 'But I really didn't do much.'

'You posted a video that went viral. You won the heart of the nation alongside Esme. Those donations came flooding in and in such a short space of time too. Any clues to the mystery donation that helped reach the final target? It's a hell of a lot of money.'

In all honesty, Felicity had forgotten all about the mystery donor; all that was firmly planted on her mind was Fergus.

'I've no idea,' she replied. Felicity didn't know anyone with that sort of ready cash.

'How did it feel when you knew the video had gone viral? In fact, don't answer that ... I'll be firing all those sorts of questions at you in a minute,' he said, checking his face in the mirror and ruffling the front of her hair.

Felicity started to panic a little. Of course she felt proud, but she knew that in no time at all the conversation and questions would be steered towards Esme and she really didn't want to upset Fergus any more. She knew he would be at home watching the news report go out live.

After the floor manager gave Felicity the once over, they positioned themselves in front of the counter. She began to feel nervous seeing all the faces pressed up against the window watching her, but taking a deep breath she waited for the filming to begin. Aidy was talking to someone through an earpiece then he switched on his microphone. Just at that second, Felicity saw Esme press her small hands against the pane of glass and then begin waving. Jessica was standing behind her. Her breath caught in her throat as Aidy also spotted Esme in the window. 'Sorry to interrupt—' he pressed his hand to his earpiece before touching a hand lightly to Felicity's arm '—is that Esme? The public would love to see her again. Can we get her on this interview too?'

It felt like time had slowed as Felicity watched Aidy walk towards the shop door. 'No,' she said abruptly, grabbing his arm. 'We can't.'

Taken aback, he spun round. 'It will make great viewing.'

Felicity couldn't risk going against Fergus's wishes, after the fragile trust they had built this afternoon. She knew he would never forgive her if Esme appeared on TV for a second time.

'I've already spoken to her dad and he doesn't want her to be interviewed.'

Aidy didn't have time to question Felicity further as the floor manager shouted, 'Take your places, nearly ready to go.'

Aidy stood back next to Felicity while Rona, Allie and Meredith huddled in the corner of the room. Allie gave Felicity a thumbs up and a huge grin.

'Good afternoon,' said Aidy as the babble of voices outside the tearoom began to hush. He waited for them to settle then he counted himself in. 'Going live in five … four … three … two … one…'

He turned towards Felicity. 'This afternoon we are live from the village of Heartcross. We are currently standing in the heart of the community inside Bonnie's Teashop situated on Love Heart Lane.'

Felicity stole a furtive glance towards the window, where Jessica and Esme were now nowhere to be seen, much to Felicity's relief.

'We are chatting with Felicity Simons, the woman who has stolen the nation's heart with her plea to raise money to build a temporary bridge between Heartcross and Glensheil after the original Grade II listed bridge collapsed during the recent storms. Felicity, what do you think about the local villagers hailing you a hero?'

'They are too kind,' Felicity felt herself blush and briefly lowered her eyes to the floor. 'I really didn't do much.'

'Your video went viral,' interrupted Aidy, 'with now over five million views. What do you think prompted such a response from the general public?'

Felicity knew he was steering the conversation towards Esme, but she was going to do everything in her power to steer it in the opposite direction. 'The fabulous community spirit.' She felt her voice go up an octave. 'During the storm, we were all shocked to see the bridge collapse. At first there was panic in the village about how we'd ever manage with no supplies being able to cross the bridge but we've all supported each other. Hamish, the local shopkeeper has donated freely the food that's left in his shop and this place, Bonnie's Teashop, founded by my late grandmother Bonnie Stewart, has been catering for the village, rather like a soup kitchen making sure everyone is fed and watered.'

'Very commendable. Tell us more about this amazing community you live in. What makes Heartcross such a special place?'

'I think we all look out for each other here, and we always have really. We even managed to deliver a baby safely into the village without the emergency services. This whole situation has brought us all much closer together.'

'Very, very commendable! Tell us about your relationship with Esme Campbell.'

The microphone was poised towards Felicity who felt her heartbeat quicken.

'She's a local girl who I had the pleasure of meeting after I returned from London.' Felicity kept it brief.

But Aidy Redfern didn't stop there, 'The night before the storm—' he turned straight towards the camera '—Esme's grandmother Aggie was taken into hospital in Glensheil and found herself stranded from her own village and family, is that right?'

Felicity found herself nodding.

'Everyone fell in love with Esme's plea to be reunited with her grandmother and this was obviously a motivating factor for people to donate to your appeal. How did you feel seeing the funds beginning to mount up?' He turned back towards Felicity.

'Astonished, it all seemed to happen so quickly. One minute there was ten pounds on the fundraising page and the next minute, two hundred and fifty thousand pounds thanks to all the kind people out there.'

'Felicity, you've certainly put Heartcross on the map and in the hearts of the people! But then another extraordinary thing happened, with a mystery donation of fifty thousand pounds, the amount needed to reach the final target. Have you any idea where – or who – the mystery donation could be from?'

Felicity shook her head. 'Honestly, I've no idea, but I want to say a huge, huge thank you to everyone who has made a donation. I've had a meeting with a local contractor, Alfie Wilson, who is putting together the team to begin the construction of the temporary bridge until the original bridge can be restored.' Felicity smiled at the camera. 'Which hopefully will connect us back with civilisation very soon.'

'I've information just in ... that the team will actually start work on the project tomorrow,' announced Aidy.

The villagers outside began to cheer which brought a smile to everyone inside the shop.

'But we have one last surprise for little Esme.'

Felicity's heart began to hammer against her chest. 'A special message for her from her grandmother, Aggie.'

The TV screen switched over to Glensheil and Felicity was amazed to see Aggie perched on her hospital bed with a smile on her face. Another reporter was poised with a microphone and as soon as they got the green light they were live on TV and Aggie began to speak,

'I'm so full of pride. The amount of money raised is astronomical. Who'd have thought one video could cause all this publicity, I feel like a minor celebrity,' chuckled Aggie. 'A huge thank you to everyone who has taken the time out to wish me well.'

'We have another little surprise for you and your granddaughter, Mrs Campbell. We are currently shipping her across the river with her Auntie Jessica to visit you!'

Aggie gasped and brought her hands up to her face, clearly delighted.

Felicity's jaw dropped to somewhere near the floor as the picture now switched to the side of the river bank and she saw Esme climbing into a speedboat at the edge of the water with Jessica right behind her. All Felicity could do was stare at the footage and force herself not to gasp out loud, her heart in her mouth. That was why Esme had disappeared from the window, she'd been taken down to the river to meet the boat.

She watched as the boat took off across the river, the wind blowing in Esme's hair and her eyes wide with excitement. She looked like she was having the time of her life, but Felicity felt sick to her stomach. She'd promised Fergus this wouldn't happen, that Esme was to go nowhere near the cameras, but she'd had no control over this situation. Surely Jessica had checked with Fergus first? She had a horrible feeling he was going to blame her for the entire situation.

The crowd had dispersed now from outside the teashop. They must have hurried down the track towards the riverbank to wave off Esme. Felicity felt paralyzed, rooted to the spot. She didn't know whether Aidy Redfern had finished interviewing her, but she tried to force a smile on her face as best she could, even though inside she was far from happy.

She watched the TV screen, where another reporter was standing at the side of the river waiting for Esme's boat to reach him. Felicity watched as Esme and Jessica climbed out into an awaiting car as people all around them clapped and waved them off.

Felicity's legs felt like they were going to give way and fear stabbed her entire body. She wanted to run as fast as she could to see Fergus, who she knew would be watching this from the cottage. She shivered and felt devastated, knowing that it was she who had dragged Fergus into this unholy mess.

Aidy Redfern wrapped everything up in the teashop before turning towards Felicity. 'You are a natural on screen! Congratulations again on such amazing fund-raising efforts.'

'Thank you,' she managed to say.

The TV crew chatted amongst themselves as they packed up all their equipment, and Allie walked over to Felicity. 'You are quite the local celebrity and look at Esme being whisked off to see Aggie. I've never been in a speedboat, I'm rather jealous. Did Fergus change his mind then…?'

Felicity was speechless, her mind in a whirl.

'Flick, are you okay? You look like you've seen a ghost?'

Felicity didn't answer; already her legs were thundering down Love Heart Lane towards Fox Hollow Cottage. All Felicity could think about was finding Fergus as soon as possible.

Chapter 27

Felicity swung open the garden gate and burst through the front door of Fergus's cottage without knocking. The TV was still on and Fergus was pacing up and down the carpet like a wild animal. Tears blurred his eyes and he was frantically raking his hand through his hair.

'I'm sorry Fergus, I didn't know they were going to whisk her off in a boat. I promise it has nothing to do with me.'

'I know,' he said. 'Jessica called me and Esme was that excited, I couldn't say no.'

This took Felicity a little by surprise. 'You knew?' she asked hesitantly. 'Did you think about going with them?'

'For a second.' His voice was shaky. 'But look at the state of me. I've got myself into a right mess ... I can't think straight and didn't want Esme seeing me like this.'

'Come on sit down, let's try not to blow this out of

proportion ... let's think rationally.' Her voice was soft and her eyes were kind. 'Try not to get worked up.'

Fergus seemed to calm for a minute. 'I've really no idea what to think or do, Flick.'

'Well, do nothing then. Burn the letter and try and forget about it.'

'Don't you think I've tried? It's been nearly six years since discovering the letter and it's always there—' he tapped his head '—somewhere in my mind. I can't believe Lorna would do this to me. If she didn't give me the letter, then why keep it? Why not destroy it?'

'I don't know the answers,' said Felicity sympathetically.

'After you left me, and Lorna came into my life, I started to look forward to the future again. And then Esme came along and I couldn't have loved that little girl more. But now it's all changed in the blink of an eye.'

'Has it changed though?' offered Felicity, softly.

'What do you mean?'

'What makes a good father? Biology or commitment? Maybe Lorna got it wrong.' Felicity took a deep breath. 'Maybe ... she didn't send the letter because she wasn't a hundred percent positive you weren't Esme's dad. Have you thought more about having a DNA test?'

Felicity could see the sadness in Fergus's eyes and it was his turn to take a deep breath before speaking.

'That thought swims around in my mind all the time but I'm not sure what's worse, the knowing or the not knowing ... what would you do?'

Felicity mulled it over, unsure what she would do in the circumstances. She knew she still yearned to be a mother, but now knowing Fergus's predicament and how much he loved Esme, had her views changed? How would she feel in Fergus's shoes? She'd always thought that what made a parent was the biological DNA, but now she knew that wasn't true. Fergus loved Esme, even faced with the prospect that she wasn't his biological child. Whatever the outcome, Fergus was Esme's father, he was committed to her and loved her unconditionally no matter what, and a piece of paper wouldn't change that.

'Fergus, I don't know what to tell you...'

'We lost two babies Flick, and the pain was unbearable. I can't lose Esme as well.' His breathing became erratic and he took a few deep breaths. 'Just thinking about it makes my chest feel tight and...'

Felicity wrapped her fingers around his, interrupting his words. 'It will be all right. Go and see Dr Taylor ... talk it over with him. See what the process is. It will all be confidential. And you don't have to decide anything straight away.'

Felicity could see that Fergus was considering her suggestion.

'If by any chance Lorna has got it wrong, all this anxiety, uncertainty will go away,' added Felicity.

'And what if the information in the letter turns out to be correct?'

'Then you can make a decision based on the facts and decide what you want to do next. One step at a time.'

Fergus nodded and seemed a little calmer. 'Thanks Flick. Thanks for being here for me.'

'We'll get through it,' she reassured him, holding out her arms and Fergus fell into them.

Fergus's phone vibrated and he pulled away, looking at the screen. 'It's a FaceTime call from Jessica,' he said quickly, wiping his eyes with his sleeve. 'Do I look okay?'

Felicity ruffled the front of his hair and gave him a smile. 'You look damn fine to me,' she said holding his gaze.

He swiped the screen and painted a smile on his face. 'Hi Jess!'

Jessica was smiling back at him. 'We are here!'

'How was the crossing and how is Mum?'

'Why don't you ask her yourself,' smiled Jessica, turning the phone towards the hospital bed where Aggie was sitting up with a very smiley Esme perched on her knee.

'You certainly look better, probably enjoying all this attention,' he teased.

'Yes, I feel better,' she answered, 'and what a lovely

surprise, the TV crew shipping this one over the river for a quick visit.' She patted Esme's knee – the little girl was beaming.

'Yes, a surprise for all of us.'

'I'm missing you all.'

'We miss you too, Mum.'

'The staff have been brilliant, and I'm allowed home in a few days. I just need to work out how that's going to happen, but I can't wait to be back. Jessica has been filling me in on all the goings on in the village. I believe the teashop has been going great guns feeding everyone?'

'Yes, they've been doing a marvellous job. In fact, Felicity is here with me now.'

Fergus swung his phone in Felicity's direction who gave Aggie a small wave. 'You are looking better!'

'I feel it ... but what's the food situation like in the village?' asked Aggie with concern written all over her face.

Funnily enough Hamish had rung the teashop earlier today and informed them that supplies were already running low. Felicity was going to ring Annie Boyd to see if there was anything they could do to help. Maybe they could drop food supplies by helicopter or even transport across the river. By Hamish's reckoning they could maybe stretch for another week.

'It needs looking into straightaway,' confirmed Felicity. 'In fact, I'll make a few phone calls this afternoon.'

Aggie nodded.

'And when am I getting my beautiful daughter home?' asked Fergus.

'Soon,' smiled Esme. 'But the boat, Dad ... was amazing. It zoomed across the water. Can we get a speed boat?' Esme gave Fergus such an adorable smile it melted his heart.

'Uncle Drew has a boat and I'm sure we can take you and Finn out in it very soon. It's not a speed boat mind, you'll have to row.'

'We are heading back over the water in around twenty minutes,' said Jessica, glancing at her watch. 'Is that okay with you?'

Fergus nodded and after saying goodbye to everyone, he hung up.

'How are you feeling?' asked Felicity.

A tear ran down Fergus's face and he brushed it away.

'Why me Felicity, why do I always have to deal with upset Look at Drew and Isla, they have no worries, a beautiful family, two gorgeous children. Rory and Allie are head over heels in love ...'

'And you have a gorgeous daughter who loves you with all her heart.'

'It's just such a mess.'

'If you want me to, I'll come with you to see Dr Taylor, or I can wait outside. For what my opinion is worth I don't think you'll settle until you know one way or the other.'

Christie Barlow

Fergus paused for a moment and took in a deep breath, filling his lungs with air. 'I think you're right. It's been eating away at me for far too long and I'm always on edge, feeling anxious.'

'I'm sorry you are going through this, I really am,' said Felicity slowly. 'You don't deserve this.'

'Someone thinks I do, otherwise it wouldn't be happening to me.'

Felicity pulled him gently towards her and he didn't object. 'You do know I never meant to hurt you, don't you?' Gripped by sudden emotion she looked up at Fergus with bleary eyes. 'If I could change what I did back then, the way I ran ... I would in a heartbeat. I was an idiot.' She was conscious her heart was pounding, and a feeling of trepidation ran through her entire body. 'You hate me, don't you?' she pressed.

The silence echoed all around them and she felt a tear roll down her cheek that Fergus brushed away tenderly.

'How could I ever hate you? Now it's you that's being daft. I didn't like you for a very long time,' he admitted with sadness. 'And you hurt me, but at the time I know you had your reasons. I just thought we'd get through it together. I was crushed when you left me, Flick.'

Felicity rested her head on his shoulder, the warmth and smell of his body sending a tingle up her spine.

Felicity knew he was still hurting, she was hurting

too. She should have trusted him at the time and believed that she was enough for him. They were enough for each other.

'I'm sorry,' she said under her breath. 'I'm really sorry.' She tilted her head up towards his. The familiarity of his lips were staring her straight in the face and she had to do everything in her power not to lean in and kiss them tenderly.

He rested his forehead against hers. 'I know. We were young, scared, and unsure of the world,' he said softly. 'But just for the record you were always enough for me and that would have never changed.'

'I still love you, Fergus.' The words were out there before she could stop them. She looked deep into his eyes and willed him to kiss her, but he didn't.

His eyes stayed locked on hers and her heart gave a little bounce until Fergus spoke. 'Flick, I can't have my heart broken again. I just can't.'

She'd let him down, everyone had let him down.

Fergus leant back on the settee and she automatically rested her head against his chest just like they had done in the past. Tears threatened to spill over as she closed her eyes and listened to his heartbeat. She knew she wanted him back and loved him with all her heart, but maybe too much time had passed between them. Maybe she had left it too late to come home...

Chapter 28

The next morning Felicity awoke to the sound of rustling coming from the bedroom opposite. Taking a quick look at the clock she noticed that it was just before eight o'clock. Throwing back the duvet, she slipped her feet into her slippers and pulled her dressing gown tightly around her body and padded across the landing. A soft glow came from the room opposite that had once been her grandmother's bedroom. Felicity sneaked a peek through the crack in the door and could see her mum sitting on the bed with a drawer laying on the duvet in front of her. She noticed her mum wiping away tears. The door slightly creaked, and Rona looked up startled and brought a hand to her chest. 'You frightened me then, what are you doing up so early?'

'I could ask you the very same question ... I heard you rustling about in here. What are you up to?'

Felicity perched on the end of the bed and looked

inside the drawer. It was like a treasure trove, full of knick-knacks, cinema tickets, photographs and old letters.

'Your grandmother's life.' Rona smiled up at Felicity. 'Here, look at this.' Rona passed Felicity a photograph.

'Wow, Grandma looks so young.'

Bonnie was proudly standing outside the tearoom in a long black skirt and a white blouse. Her hair was tied up in a neat bun and she wore the most beautiful smile. She was pointing up at the newly painted sign, 'The Old Teashop', and alongside her stood two gentlemen dressed in hiking gear holding up mugs of tea.

Felicity turned the photograph over and scrawled on the other side were the words: 'My very first customers'.

'Grandma definitely saw an opportunity.' She reached over and giving her mum's knee a squeeze followed by a smile.

'She did. I've lived in this cottage all my life and I can remember all those years ago, ramblers knocking on the door and asking Mum where the nearest toilet was. She always invited them in and gave them a cup of tea and a slice of homemade cake, and that's how her idea was born ... "we don't use that front parlour",' Rona mimicked Bonnie's voice. '"all it's doing is gathering dust, and I'm going to turn it into a tearoom."'

'And so she did,' smiled Felicity, remembering the times she'd spent baking with her grandma.

Rona fanned her face with her hand, trying to keep the tears at bay. 'Don't mind me, I'm just having a wee moment.'

'Have all the moments you want, I miss her too.'

'It's a strange feeling when someone has been a part of your life for all of your life, and then they are no longer there. Some days are a struggle and in a funny sort of a way the bridge collapsing has helped me to cope.'

'What do you mean?' asked Felicity tentatively.

'It's given me a purpose again, to get back in that kitchen and reconnect with the villagers ... and it's brought you back home.'

'It has,' said Felicity with a smile.

'It's good to keep busy.'

'It's always good to keep busy when you've got something on your mind,' agreed Felicity.

'Is there something going on between you and Fergus?' Rona probed gently, placing the photograph back in the drawer.

'What gives you that impression?'

'You are distracted, all over the place and I saw you running off in the direction of his cottage yesterday after the interview. Then when you came home, you went straight to your room.'

'It's complicated,' admitted Felicity, not wanting to talk about it in case everything came spilling out.

'You still have feelings for him?'

Felicity nodded. 'Of course, he's always been the man for me. I just lost my way for a time.'

'Are you at least friends again?'

Felicity nodded. 'I hope so.'

'Time will tell.' Rona patted her daughter's knee and stood up. 'Hamish and Drew will be arriving soon with the food supplies, I'd better get down to the kitchen.'

Rona slid the drawer back into place and took a battered old looking book from the dressing table.

'Do you recognise this?'

Felicity smiled, taking the book from her mum's hand. 'Of course I do, Grandma's recipe book.'

Felicity carefully opened it up. All of the recipes were neatly written in Bonnie's handwriting.

'You keep that, she'd want you to have it.'

'Are you sure?' asked Felicity, feeling privileged that this special book was being handed down to her.

'Of course, I'm sure.'

Interrupted by a knock on the door, Rona and Felicity both hurried downstairs to let in Hamish and Drew who were standing outside with the day's food supplies.

'Good morning, lads, how are you?' chirped Rona, holding the door open wide. They placed two boxes full down on the table and Rona peered inside.

'Supplies are getting low,' said a worried Hamish. 'In fact, the shelves are already becoming quite bare. Any ideas what we can do, Flick?'

'It's going to have to be the boat.' Felicity turned towards Drew.

'I'm not sure we are going to fit many supplies in that rickety old thing.'

'I was going to contact Annie Boyd yesterday to see what she suggests, but I forgot. Is it too early to ring now?' Felicity's mind flicked back to a programme she'd once watched where there were people stranded on an island after a flood and helicopters swooped in dropping parcels of essential foods.

'You can always leave her a message,' suggested Rona.

Felicity left them unpacking the boxes and grabbed the phone from the hallway. She dialled the number and waited to be connected to Annie Boyd.

'Hi, it's Felicity Simons.'

'Felicity!' her voice trilled. 'Marvellous, marvellous fundraising for the temporary bridge. I'm in awe of your efforts ... and the good news is you chose the right man for the job. Alfie has the team all in hand and work will start as soon as ... well, as soon as today I believe!' She finally came up for breath.

'That's good to hear but we have a slight problem looming over us.'

'Which is?'

'The food supplies here are diminishing fast. The villagers pooled together their resources but now even the local shop is running low. We've even thought of taking a rowing boat across the river but that would take so many trips and there is very little space to store much food in the boat anyway.'

'We can get the army involved,' said Annie without any hesitation. 'I'm in no doubt the supermarket in Glensheil will help out with supplies. I'll get back to you sometime this afternoon,' she declared before hanging up.

Hamish and Drew were just finishing unloading the tins when Felicity walked back into the tearoom. They all looked up at her hopefully.

'Annie Boyd will be getting back to me this afternoon,' she said while tapping on her mobile phone and updating the Facebook page to let everyone know. 'She said something about enlisting the army to help.'

'Good, good,' muttered Hamish. 'The only upside to empty shelves is I can give them a damn good clean before they begin to get stocked again.'

'Right you pair, you get out from under my feet.' Rona shooed a tea towel at Hamish and Drew before flinging it over her shoulder.

'We're going!' grinned Drew, quickly standing up.

'Have you seen Fergus today?' chipped in Felicity, trying to drop the question into the conversation without causing any suspicion.

'He's at home today with Esme, she's feeling a little under the weather.'

'Why, what's the matter with her?' quizzed Felicity while filling up the water jugs for each table.

'Not sure, but I can cope up at the farm today,' he answered before waving a hand above his head and disappearing out of the shop quickly followed by Hamish.

'I wonder what's wrong with Esme?' said Felicity out loud.

'It'll be something and nothing,' replied Rona, currently opening the tins of veg and pouring them into the huge stew pots on the stove.

Felicity scrunched up her face. 'A girl can get sick of stew, you know.' She stirred the pot.

'Needs must for now and at least it's good wholesome food for the pensioners and a warm meal.'

The door to the teashop opened and Felicity was expecting to see the smiles of Allie and Meredith but instead was surprised to see Fergus standing in the doorway holding Esme's hand.

'Good morning,' chirped Felicity, throwing Fergus a smile before bending down in front of Esme. 'A little bird told me you are unwell.'

'Really?' answered Esme wide-eyed.

'Well, maybe Uncle Drew told me when he dropped off today's supplies.' She gave a hearty laugh, gently tickling Esme's stomach. 'Are you okay?' She stood up and looked at Fergus.

'Could you possibly look after Esme for me, say for about half an hour or so?' he asked.

'Of course,' said Felicity without hesitation, thrilled that he trusted her to look after his little girl.

Rona walked over. 'What do you have there?' she asked.

Esme was proudly clutching her apron. 'I've brought my apron, so I can help.'

'Excellent, you go and hang your coat on the back of the door and I'll help you tie it on.'

Felicity watched Fergus who kept his eyes on Esme as she skipped off happily.

'Where are you off to?' asked Felicity.

Fergus lowered his voice. 'I've got an appointment with Dr Taylor. I'm taking your advice ... I need someone to talk to.'

Felicity gently touched his arm. 'Take your time, Esme will be fine here.'

'I know, and thanks Flick.'

Felicity watched him walk down Love Heart Lane and her heart gave a little leap. Fergus had actually asked her to look after Esme. He was beginning to trust her again, letting her back in and as Esme walked towards her smiling, Felicity glowed inside.

Rona was busy in the kitchen and Felicity took Esme by the hand. 'Guess what my mum gave me this morning? A very special present that belonged to my

Grandma Bonnie. Do you want to come and see?'

'Yes please!' said Esme with delight.

Felicity led an excited Esme through the teashop into the living room and sat her down on the settee. She walked over to the dresser and grabbed the old recipe book.

Esme's eyes grew wide as Felicity passed the book to her and rested it cautiously on her knee. 'Is this the secret recipe book?' she said in awe, not taking her eyes off it.

'Go on, open it, but be careful, some of the pages are very old and delicate.'

Esme nodded, and gently began to turn the pages.

The book contained every delicious recipe Bonnie had ever made, from Victoria sponge to blueberry muffins, from mouth-watering pies to scrumptious pastries.

'I'm going to bake all these recipes in my own shop when I grow up,' said Esme with such passion.

She smiled up at Felicity and it melted her heart. A sudden surge of emotion flooded through Felicity. This gorgeous little girl had brought a new kind of happiness to her life, one she'd never experienced before. In the past she'd tended to shy away from children and had always felt tearful and maybe even jealous when she'd seen families laughing and joking and enjoying time together. But meeting Esme and getting to know her had changed things for Felicity. She enjoyed Esme's company, her kind nature and the way the little girl made her feel gave Felicity some purpose in her life. Felicity realised that she couldn't change the past and maybe now was the time to learn to love and focus on the things she already had in her life. It made her think about Fergus. No matter what the outcome of the DNA test, he would always be Esme's dad. She was learning slowly what it really meant to be a parent and she had Esme to thank for that.

'I've got an idea, how about we bake a recipe from the book this morning?'

'Can we, can we really?'

'Of course we can. Your Uncle Drew has already dropped off a supply of eggs and milk. What do you fancy baking?'

Esme's face turned serious while she thought for a moment. 'Daddy said Mummy's favourite cake was Victoria sponge.'

'We can certainly bake one of those.'

Esme passed the book back to Felicity before standing up and tightening the apron around her tummy. 'I'm ready, Chef,' she said, giggling, with a salute. 'I've seen that on TV.'

'I think we'd best bake in the cottage kitchen today as the gang in the teashop will already be preparing lunch for the villagers, is that okay with you?'

'Yes, Chef!' came the loud response once more with a huge grin.

Felicity couldn't help but smile. She sat Esme down at the table while she popped her head around the door to let her mum know what she was doing.

Despite the concerns over the food shortage, everyone was being their best and brightest self. Allie was humming a tune as she laid out the cutlery on each table, Meredith and Rona were sharing memories of Bonnie while stirring the pots of stew and Felicity couldn't help feeling the love and warmth in the room. She paused for a moment and leant against the doorframe listening to Meredith reminisce about the time over thirty ramblers turned up at the teashop unexpectedly, due to a charity walk, leaving Bonnie completely flummoxed. They laughed at the memory. Rona looked up and caught Felicity's eye. 'What're your plans with Esme? Does she want to help serve the villagers?'

'We've decided to bake a cake out of Grandma's recipe book; we'll do it in the cottage kitchen … if that's okay with you?'

'Of course,' Rona nodded, giving her daughter a warm smile. 'There are some baking tins in the pantry.'

Felicity grabbed the ingredients and Esme's eyes lit up when she walked back into the room.

'We need the scales,' said Felicity, taking them from the windowsill and placing them in front of Esme who was perched on the kitchen chair with a cushion under her knees.

'Can you measure me out 225g of flour?'

'I can, Chef,' answered Esme with determination but then looking at the scales in wonderment.

'Here, let me show you.' Felicity carefully explained the numbers on the front of the dial before sliding the bag of flour towards Esme.

'Go on, you can do this,' encouraged Felicity.

Esme tore open the bag only to find it mushroomed out into a huge snowstorm in front of her covering her face and hair in flour.

'Yikes!' exclaimed Esme, her eyes wide.

Felicity burst out laughing. 'Oh my! I'm going to be sending you home looking like a snowman at this rate.' Esme couldn't help but giggle when Felicity passed her a mirror. She fell about in fits of laughter.

'Next we need the eggs.'

Felicity cracked the first one and Esme mirrored her actions and dropped three more into the bowl.

'Well done!' cheered on Felicity. 'You are a natural at this.'

For the next fifteen minutes, with huge smiles on their faces, they laughed and sang while Esme beat the mixture with a whisk and then divided the mixture into two. She then spooned it into the cake tins.

Felicity took them both and opened the Aga door.

'I'll pop them in here … we don't want you burning yourself.'

Esme watched with delight as the Aga door shut.

'Not long to wait, but then we need to let them cool,' confirmed Felicity, setting a timer on her phone.

'Here, take these, we need to wash up.' Felicity piled the dirty dishes on top of the worktop while Esme pulled the chair over to the sink, stood on it and turned on the tap.

Felicity watched Esme as she busily set about washing up. She smiled to herself, feeling a flurry of happiness and a rush of affection towards her. She'd had the best morning and truth be told, didn't want it to end but glancing up at the clock she knew Fergus would be back very soon to pick her up.

After a quick drink and a biscuit, the timer began to beep. Esme jumped up with excitement and waited patiently by the Aga door while Felicity slipped her hands inside the oven gloves.

'Ta-dah!' exclaimed Felicity, sliding the cake tins out of the Aga and placing two golden sponge cakes on the cooling rack. 'What a success!'

'Wow! It looks a-m-a-z-i-n-g! And smells—' Esme squealed sniffing the air '—like … like a proper cake.'

'It is a proper cake! And we need to let them cool before we whip the cream and spread the jam on.'

Felicity held her hand up for a high-five but taking

her by surprise Esme flung her arms around Felicity and plonked a smacking kiss right on her cheek.

'What was that for?' asked Felicity, feeling all warm and fuzzy inside.

'Because, I've had the best time.'

'That's good to hear, and are you feeling better now too?'

Esme looked a little shifty. 'Can I tell you a secret?' she said, bringing her finger up to her lips and making a shush sound.

'Of course, you can.'

'I'm not really poorly.'

'Any particular reason you would say you were when you weren't?' asked Felicity, screwing up her eyes.

'Because I didn't want to go to Finn's, I'm fed up with playing with Lego and soldiers.'

Felicity ruffled her tummy. 'Well, I think you should probably tell your dad that, he's worried you are feeling under the weather.'

'Then do you think he'll let me stay with you in the teashop?' smiled Esme.

'That's always an option.'

Esme turned and looked at the cooling cakes once more. 'Do you think my mummy would be proud of me?'

Felicity felt the tears prick the back of her eyes. 'Without a doubt and once they've cooled we will finish it off ... a special surprise for your daddy.'

Felicity clasped Esme's hands and with a lump in her throat, she led her back into the teashop knowing she was beginning to feel real love for the little girl.

Time had flown, and it was suddenly midday and everywhere was a hive of activity. The villagers filed through the door, unravelling their scarfs and hanging their coats on the back of the chairs. Felicity smiled. Everyone seemed to have gotten themselves in a little routine and each day they sat in the same seats. She could hear the conversation from the table in the corner, most people chatting about Aggie's appearance on TV. Suddenly the chatting stopped as an overcast shadow fell on to the teashop, taking everyone by surprise.

'What's that noise?' Meredith asked, with horrified look. A loud whirring sound could be heard as she placed the bowl down on the counter and quickly moved towards the window, her eager eyes looking up to the sky.

Rona clapped a hand over her mouth. 'Look at that sight!'

Felicity grabbed Esme's coat and slipped her arms into it and led her outside the shop door. The breeze lifted Esme's hair from her face as she too looked up at the sky.

'Look at those,' said Esme in amazement.

The sky was filled with helicopters hovering in the air above the fields of Foxglove Farm. Felicity saw the pilot in the first helicopter hunched over the controls, lowering the aircraft, its blades beating the air. As it came lower, Esme covered her eyes, held her breath and watched through her fingers. The villagers joined Felicity, all standing on Love Heart Lane looking up at the sky.

Everyone watched the magnificent sight as the helicopters lined up in the sky. Then the first one edged forward and began to descend, its side doors opening.

Over the field Felicity spotted Drew's farm truck bouncing over the uneven ground. She squinted and noticed Rory was alongside him, strapped into the passenger seat. They parked up and jumped out, bending their heads low, the gush of wind from the helicopter's blades blowing their hair. Everyone watched as the helicopter hovered above Drew and Rory and a large box was lowered right to their feet where Drew took a knife and slit the rope. He gave the co-pilot a thumbs up and immediately the rope began to lift. Within seconds the door had shut, and the helicopter soared through the sky back towards the airbase in Glensheil. Rory and Drew lifted the box and loaded it straight into the back of the van. The next helicopter loitered over where Drew was standing and exactly the same happened again.

'What are they doing?' asked Esme, still staring up into the sky.

'My guess, it will be food parcels. What do you reckon?' Felicity turned towards her mum.

'Absolutely!' replied Rona, slipping her arm around Felicity's shoulder and giving it a quick squeeze. 'And that's all down to you.'

'All I did was make a phone call ... Annie Boyd organised all this in record time.'

Everyone watched until the last helicopter had flown off and was just a dot in the distance.

'For a small village in the middle of nowhere, it's never quiet here,' exclaimed Meredith walking back into the warmth of the teashop and hanging up her coat.

'Those helicopters were amazing,' exclaimed Esme, slipping on to a spare chair just in front of the counter.

'It was an incredible sight,' chipped in Allie, who was standing behind the counter checking her mobile phone.

'Yes, it's definitely supplies of food! Rory has just texted me,' she said, showing her phone to Felicity. 'They are going to unpack the boxes at Hamish's. Apparently, all the food has been shipped from the local super-market in Glensheil.'

'At least that's one worry off everyone's minds,' replied Felicity, before turning towards Esme. 'I think that cake will be cool now; shall we go and decorate it quickly before your daddy arrives?'

Esme eagerly nodded and leapt out of the chair,

skipping in front of Felicity as she led the way back to the cottage kitchen.

Fifteen minutes later the cake was oozing with cream and strawberry jam and Esme proudly sprinkled icing sugar on the soft sponge to finish it off.

'It looks absolutely delicious and you are BRILLIANT,' said Felicity taking the cake into the teashop and placing it on top of the counter. 'Wait until your daddy sees and tastes that.'

'Did I hear my name being mentioned?'

Esme squealed and ran to Fergus who lifted her up in the air. 'You seem to be feeling better,' he exclaimed in amazement, placing Esme's feet firmly back on the floor.

'That's all because of Felicity.'

'Does Felicity have a magic wand to make little girls feel better?' he teased, giving Felicity a warm smile.

Esme slipped her hand inside Felicity's and looked up at her with the sweetest smile that melted Felicity's heart.

'I think I've managed to take Esme's mind off feeling poorly.' She winked down at the little girl, keeping her secret.

'We've baked a cake.' Esme dropped Felicity's hand and took hold of her dad's. She led him to the counter and pointed up at the cake.

'You've not made that, have you?' he teased.

Esme put her hands playfully on her hips. 'I have.'

'I can confirm that Esme was chief baker,' said Felicity, taking the cake down from the counter and placing it carefully into Esme's hands. 'Don't drop it,' she joked.

'Daddy, you take it.'

Fergus took the cake from Esme's hands. 'Well, I am impressed, very impressed but I have a very important question to ask. Can I be chief taster?' Fergus kept his face completely serious.

Esme looked towards Felicity. 'What do you think?' she asked before giggling uncontrollably.

'I think your dad will make the perfect chief taster,' replied Felicity with a wink.

'This has been the best morning ever,' said Esme, swiping her hands together in a triumphant way then wiping her hands on her pinny. 'Can I come back and help you in the teashop until I go back to school?'

Felicity cast her eyes towards Esme then Fergus, and her heart skipped a beat at the thought of spending more time with Esme, laughing and baking. Her eyes welled up with happy tears.

'I'm sure you can't be under Felicity's feet in the teashop.' Fergus looked down at his daughter.

'She's a hard worker, I don't mind in the slightest.'

'I have my own uniform!' Esme pulled at her apron then tilted her head to one side and gave Fergus a winning smile. He switched his gaze towards Felicity and her heart jolted.

'Well, if it's all right by Flick and Rona, then it's okay by me. But you have to promise not to get under anyone's feet.'

'Yes Dad!' Esme saluted, and everyone laughed.

'Now go and get your coat.'

Both Fergus and Felicity watched Esme skip happily over to her coat.

'She wasn't ill, was she?' asked Fergus quietly but not looking at Felicity.

'I couldn't possibly say.'

'She just wanted to come and see you.'

'I think that was the case.'

'Thank you for this morning,' said Fergus with such warmth that Felicity could feel her heart beat faster. She pressed her lips together to try and suppress her smile.

'You're very welcome, Fergus.'

Fergus's eyes met hers and sparkled. It was then Felicity reminded herself to breathe normally.

'I'm ready,' said Esme looking up at Fergus then Felicity with a wide smile. 'Thank you for having me,' she said.

'You're very welcome and I hope to see you soon.'

'Would you like to join us for dinner at the cottage tonight?' asked Fergus with hope in his voice. 'I think it's only fair you should sample this wonderful cake too, after all you did help to make it.'

Esme's face lit up, her excitement about to bubble over. 'Please say yes!' She put her hands together in a prayer-like stance.

They both smiled at her enthusiasm.

'It would be my absolute pleasure.'

'Around seven?' added Fergus.

'Sounds perfect,' Flick replied.

Fergus turned quickly, and Felicity caught the scent of his aftershave, her stomach fluttering instantly. She snagged her mum's eye who gave her a knowing look – a look that meant, even though things always took time, everything was going to be okay. She hoped so, this was a major step for both her and Fergus. She knew under the circumstances Fergus wouldn't let just anyone get close to Esme.

Chapter 29

Felicity spent most of the day watching the clock and trying to keep the bubble of nervous butterflies in her stomach under control, which was daft as she'd known Fergus for such a long time. As soon as the last shift in the kitchen was over and the teashop was spick and span, she skipped up the stairs with a spring in her step. She stood for a moment, looking out of her bedroom window, and caught her breath. She could see Foxglove Farm in the distance, and it still looked bright on such a grey day. The branches of the willow tree hung over the pond and she watched a mallard with its brown speckled plumage bobbing its head under the water. Felicity was longing for warm summer days to arrive.

She turned and opened the wardrobe door, flicking up and down the rails deciding on an outfit. She knew it was silly worrying about what she was going to wear. After all, it was only dinner at the cottage but she still wanted to look her best. In the end, remembering Fergus always complimented her when she wore blue she plumped for skinny jeans and a navy cashmere sweater.

Once she'd pulled a brush through her hair and swept blusher across her cheeks, she declared herself ready. After giving her mum a kiss on the cheek she set off towards Fox Hollow Cottage.

Considering the high winds and snow recently, everywhere was peaceful but chilly as she ambled along Love Heart Lane. She noticed Allie settling down on the settee in Rory's living room to watch TV, and Hamish disappeared inside Heather's cottage a little further down.

Felicity dug her hands deep inside her pockets and within no time at all, she pushed open the garden gate to Fergus's cottage. She knew the log fire was lit as there was a woody scent in the air and wisps of silver grey smoke curled and danced their way from the chimney.

Her stomach gave a nervous flip as she walked towards the door. 'Come on Felicity, be brave, it's only dinner!' she said, giving herself a talking-to which didn't do much to calm her nerves.

Within seconds of knocking, Fergus opened the door. Her eyes lifted towards him, and she held her breath. He looked perfect, the cobalt blue shirt suited him and he had it tucked into a dark blue pair of Levi jeans that fit him snugly.

There was something about the way he smiled at her that made her heart skip a beat but before she could say good evening, she heard a squeal from inside the house. 'Is that Felicity?' Esme shouted, before thundering down the stairs. She jumped straight off the bottom step and launched herself into Felicity's arms.

'I'm here,' she smiled. 'Now that's what I call a welcome!' She laughed, placing Esme's feet back on the floor.

'Let Felicity get in and take off her coat,' Fergus joked at Esme's enthusiasm.

Felicity unbuttoned her coat and passed it to Fergus who hung it on the coat stand in the hallway.

'You look lovely, Flick,' he said, flashing her the most gorgeous smile. 'But then, you always did look good in blue.'

His words made every part of her tingle.

'Thank you,' she replied, thankful her voice sounded relatively normal. 'You don't look too bad yourself, Fergus Campbell.'

'We've saved the cake for after dinner,' Esme chipped in with a huge beam.

'Excellent, I can't wait to have a taste,' answered Felicity, meaning every word. She watched Esme run off into the living room. The TV was on in the corner and the log fire was flickering away bringing a welcoming warmth to the room. Felicity could see through to the dining room. The table was set and it all looked very posh with a couple of crystal wine glasses standing tall – glasses she knew only came out on special occasions.

'Drink?' asked Fergus.

'A glass of wine would be nice, if you have any?' answered Felicity, following him into the kitchen.

'Funnily enough, Mum had a bottle in the fridge.'

'How is Aggie?'

'Hopefully coming home tomorrow if she can stomach the rocking of Drew's boat.'

Felicity chuckled. 'She's a braver woman than me. Remember that time we had that mini-break ... Windermere, wasn't it? You managed to get us stranded in that rowing boat after dropping the oar in the water.'

'Hey, that wasn't me, that was your fault! You declared you could row faster and stop us from going round in circles then dropped the oar into the water.'

'Oh yeah!' she grinned. 'I'd forgotten that part.'

'I bet you had.' Fergus laughed, hitting her playfully on the arm before handing her a glass of wine.

'I bet it'll be good to have Aggie home though,' said Felicity.

'It's certainly been quiet without her and don't tell her this, but I've actually missed her,' he admitted, leaning against the kitchen table.

Felicity took a quick glance towards the door. There

was no sign of Esme so she took her chance to ask Fergus about his doctor's appointment. 'How did you get on with Dr Taylor?'

'I've told him everything,' he sighed. 'It seems so much more real now an outsider knows, but to be honest I feel like a weight's been lifted off my shoulders.'

'Have you made any decisions?'

He nodded. 'I can't live with all this uncertainty hanging over my head, I'm ... we're going to take a DNA test but I'm going to have to wait until the postal system is back to normal in the village.' His voice was low and a huge dollop of fear descended all around. Fergus raked his hand through his hair, an anxious expression written all over his face.

Felicity squeezed his arm. 'It's going to be all right, I'm here for you.' She smiled towards him.

Tears were pricking Fergus's eyes at the obvious fear of this next step he was taking. 'I know and thank you,' he said, pulling Felicity in for a hug. She rested her head against his chest, inhaling his woody aftershave.

She pulled away as the kitchen door opened and Esme was standing there. 'You're taking ages, is dinner ready now?'

'It is! Go and wash your hands and sit yourself down at the table,' Fergus ruffled her hair before she ran off in the direction of the bathroom.

'Do you need help with anything?' asked Felicity.

He shook his head. 'No, I've got everything under control, you go and sit down too.'

Felicity made her way through to the dining room, feeling indecisive about where she should sit. In the past she used to sit on the far side of the table towards the door, but what if that was Esme's spot now?

'Why don't you sit in your usual place?' Fergus appeared behind her carrying two bowls which he put down on the table.

It had been over eight years since she'd sat in her usual place and she felt a rush of warmth towards Fergus for even remembering. The last time she'd sat at this table had been on Christmas Day, alongside Fergus, Aggie, her mum and gran. She remembered the day like it was yesterday. It was strange to think that a week later she'd left for London.

She pulled out a chair, looked down at the bowl and chuckled. 'I recognise this food, prepared and made by my own fair hands ... you invite me around for dinner and I'm the one who cooked it! Such cheek,' teased Felicity.

He laughed. 'What can I say, there's a shortage of food in the village ... Rona kindly gave us ours. You and your mum make a good team.'

Felicity thought back to her childhood for a second. She'd been brought up by two strong women. Her mum and Bonnie. The love and warmth they'd both provided her with had given her a happy childhood. Her relationship with her mum was one of friendship, and growing up they'd enjoyed shopping trips and lunches together.

'We do make a good team and I can't wait to get the teashop up and running again once normality is regained in the village,' she said, meaning every word.

'Is that it then? You are definitely not going back to London?' Fergus asked tentatively.

'I don't think I can face another day of Eleanor Ramsbottom.'

'Huh?' said Fergus.

'My not-so-nice boss ... let's just say working for myself alongside Mum in Grandma's teashop has given me new hope for the future. I'll send my resignation email soon,' she said, noticing the corners of Fergus's mouth lift.

Esme skipped into the room and settled on the chair between them. She picked up a fork and took a mouthful followed quickly by another one.

'Slow down ... you'll give yourself tummy ache,' pointed out Fergus with a slight frown. 'And remember your manners.'

'The quicker I eat this the quicker I get a piece of cake.' Her eyes were wide as she stared at the Victoria Sponge that was sitting proudly centre stage on the table.

'Fair point,' grinned Fergus.

'Did you tell your dad about all the helicopters today?' prompted Felicity, taking a small sip of wine.

Esme immediately put down her fork on the table and her eyes danced with excitement as she re-told the story of the helicopters dropping boxes on to Uncle Drew's field.

'They were boxes of food from the supermarket so the village doesn't starve. In fact, Annie Boyd sent me an email this afternoon to say there will be two drops every week until the temporary bridge is up and running which is fantastic news ... at least that's one less thing to worry about.'

'That is good, what happened to the boxes?' asked Fergus.

'Rory helped Drew load them on to the truck and they whizzed them off to Hamish's shop to sort and ration. I think Hamish is glad of the responsibility; it's keeping him busy with the shop being shut and the amount of livelihood he must be losing at the moment is a worry for him.'

'It doesn't bear thinking about. The farm is losing money too. Drew can't get to market etc ... it's actually having a massive effect on everyone. I bumped into Julia in the doctor's and she's having the same problem. With the bridge collapse the B&B is empty. There are no passing ramblers through the village and again ... another business that is losing money.'

'I think everyone is suffering, but thankfully Alfie has organised a great team for the temporary bridge construction really quickly. He sent me a detailed schedule through and fingers crossed if all goes to plan the bridge should be up and running in approximately three weeks' time. But until then there isn't a lot we can do,' said Felicity.

'All finished,' beamed Esme, placing her cutlery down on the table with a clatter.

'Have you licked that bowl clean?' laughed Fergus, amazed at how spotless it was.

'Don't be silly,' she said with a grin, folding her arms and staring at the cake.

'Why don't you go and get us all a clean plate from the kitchen? I've left them on the side by the kettle.'

Esme didn't need to be asked twice. She saluted and scooted off quickly towards the kitchen.

'She's adorable,' said Felicity, watching her disappear through the door. For a moment Felicity wondered about the children they might have had together. What would they look like? What would their personalities be like?

'She is that,' replied Fergus, moving all the empty bowls out of the way and sliding the cake towards him.

Esme returned in record time and placed the plates down on the table.

'Now young lady, I've already sliced up the cake, so

which piece would you like?' He looked at Esme who was studying every piece. 'Mm, I think that one,' she said, pointing to the larger slice in the middle.

Within seconds and after numerous appreciative noises of delight, the slice of cake had been devoured. Esme had demolished every last crumb and with a satisfied look on her face and her hand placed on her very full stomach, she slumped back in the chair. Fergus couldn't help but laugh at the jam and cream smothered all over her face and the dusting of icing sugar on her nose.

'Now that was the best cake I've ever tasted. You are the best baker.' Fergus stood up and plonked a kiss on the top of Esme's head before collecting up the empty plates. 'You need to bake more often.'

'I second that,' said Felicity with a smile. 'I think there'll be a job waiting for you in the teashop when you're older.'

'Do you really?'

'Absolutely!'

Esme's face beamed. 'Can I have another piece?'

Fergus laughed. 'Not on your Nellie, that'll be way too much for your wee belly to handle.'

Esme rolled her eyes in jest.

'Why don't you go and get your PJs on and give those teeth a very good clean.'

Esme pushed back her chair and her footsteps could be heard echoing up the wooden stairs.

'I'll help you wash up,' said Felicity standing up, collecting the empty glasses from the table.

'You will do no such thing, go and make yourself comfy in the living room. That's what dishwashers are for.'

With a spring in her step Felicity walked into the living room. Feeling happy but sentimental, she plumped for the settee and tucked her feet underneath her, staring contently into the flames of the fire. She'd missed all this, she thought with a slight pang – the closeness of family life, having someone she trusted by her side, the feeling of being part of a couple with a man you love. She'd missed the warmth and contentment of curling up at night with good company and not having a care in the world. For a long time, she'd felt like a shrunken version of herself and it was only now she was starting to feel like her old self again. When you're hurt and confused, it's sometimes easier to retreat and run from the people you love the most. Maybe if she hadn't been so young at the time she would have handled the past and the situation better.

'Penny for them.' Fergus placed the wine bottle on the table before throwing another couple of logs on the fire and settling on the rug in front. He stretched his legs out in front of him and Felicity's heart constricted at how gorgeous he was.

He looked up and caught her watching him. The two of them exchanged a look.

Suddenly from nowhere a little sadness crept in. 'Sometimes ... I wish I could turn back time,' she said softly, leaning forward and topping up her wine.

Fergus smiled knowingly at her. 'I know what you mean.'

'I was just thinking how lovely it is to be back sitting here ... with you and with Esme.'

'I was thinking the same.'

His words touched her heart. 'I know I've said it before, but I am sorry for everything, Fergus,' she admitted, 'running like I did ... back then.' Her voice faltered a little.

'Hey, don't dwell on it ... it can't be changed,' he said sensibly. 'And, if all that hadn't have happened, I wouldn't have that little ray of sunshine upstairs.'

'I know ... everything happens for a reason.' Felicity sipped her drink while Fergus picked up his phone from the table which had just beeped.

'Anything important?'

'A text from Isla asking if I can join them in the pub?'

Just at that very second, Felicity's phone beeped too. She glanced at her screen. 'I've just got the same message. I wonder what that's all about.'

'I'm not sure ... I can't go, I've got Esme to look after. But maybe you should?'

Felicity looked up and chewed on her lip while she deliberated; she didn't want to go without Fergus, she was having a really lovely evening and didn't want it to end. Felicity was still staring at the message as Esme bounded down the stairs and into the living room in her unicorn PJs holding out a brush in her hand. Her gorgeous wavy hair bounced just below her shoulders. She weaved around the coffee table and stood in front of Felicity holding the brush towards her.

'Would you brush my hair for me?' she asked.

Felicity glowed inside at being asked. 'Of course I will,' she answered, taking the brush from her hand as Esme knelt down in front of her. She gently pulled the brush through her hair and caught Fergus watching her. As they gazed at each other, a feeling of peace washed over Felicity, and her heart swelled with love for Fergus and Esme. She knew she wanted them both in her life for a very long time. She smiled shyly at Fergus and saw the feeling of warmth in his eyes reflecting back at her.

'I think you're all done,' said Felicity, just as there was a knock on the cottage door and Esme shot to her feet to answer it.

'You're a natural with her, she really likes you,' said Fergus as he hot-footed after Esme.

Felicity glowed with delight at his words and a smile played across her lips.

The blast of air from the front door was cool as Esme squealed, 'Auntie Jess, what are you doing here?'

'Hurry up and let me in, I don't relish the idea of standing out in the cold for very long.' She grinned, stepping into the hallway. 'Hurry up summertime,' she said, tickling Esme's tummy.

'What are you doing here?' Fergus asked. 'Not that you're not welcome,' he added quickly.

'You're wanted in the pub, and ta-dah! ... I'm your babysitter.'

Fergus narrowed his eyes at her. 'What's going on?'

Jessica's eyes twinkled at him. 'Isla and Drew are waiting for you and you need to track down Felicity and take her with you.'

'Felicity's already here,' said Esme, dragging Jessica into the living room where an intrigued Felicity uncurled her legs from underneath her and looked up.

'Perfect, that solves that problem then.'

'What's going on?'

Jessica shrugged modestly before pressing her lips together to hide her smile.

Fergus and Felicity exchanged glances. 'It looks like we'd better go and find out,' said Fergus.

Felicity stood up. 'Come on then, grab your coat.'

Fergus disappeared into the hallway while Felicity bent down in front of Esme. 'I've had a lovely time this evening ... in fact the best time, and your baking is going to win awards one day. Maybe you could offer your Auntie Jess a piece of cake and let her taste how scrumptious it is.'

'Did someone mention cake?' grinned Jessica, as an excitable Esme led her into the kitchen while Fergus and Felicity slipped on their coats. As the front door closed behind them they walked up the path to the garden gate. Felicity paused for a second and stared up at Fergus to find his gaze boring deep into hers.

'Thank you for tonight.' Her words were soft. Feeling brave, she closed the distance between them and leaned up on her tip-toes and planted a kiss lightly to his cheek.

'You're very welcome ... you should come again sometime soon.'

Felicity pressed her lips together with a secret smile. 'That would be lovely.'

As Fergus shut the garden gate behind them, he gave Felicity a sheepish smile before slipping his hand inside hers, completely taking her by surprise. She basked in the pleasure of his touch. Her heart was beating nineteen to the dozen at how good it still felt, even after all these years. She knew it had been wrong to run, leaving him coping alone, but maybe that was what had needed to happen to bring them back together. Her heart swelled with happiness as they walked in silence towards the pub ... together at last.

Chapter 30

Fergus held open the door for her and walking into the pub, Felicity felt like she was walking on cloud nine. She spotted Isla and Drew in the far corner sat at the table alongside Allie and Rory. Isla looked up and waved them over.

'Drink?' asked Fergus disappearing towards the bar.

Felicity nodded. 'Gin and tonic please.'

As Felicity walked over to the table, Isla looked between Fergus and Felicity in wonderment.

'What's going on here? Did you two arrive together?' Isla narrowed her eyes at Felicity who snagged a glance towards Allie, who was looking on in amusement.

'There's nothing going on,' answered Felicity, shocked at the sudden change in her voice as it went up an octave.

'Leave the girl alone,' said Rory and pulled out a chair.

Felicity mouthed, 'Thank you', and hoped the crimson blush to her cheeks would disappear soon.

Thankfully Allie came to the rescue. 'Come on then, what's going on, why have we all been summoned to the pub ... not that I'm complaining.'

Fergus parked himself on the chair next to Felicity and Isla gave her another knowing look. Felicity shook her head in jest then grinned.

'Now we are all here ... we have news,' said Isla, not able to hide the excitement in her voice.

Allie and Felicity exchanged glances and both shrugged.

'Things have been a little glum in the village since the bridge collapsed but thanks to Flick enlisting Alfie's help, the rebuild will soon be up and running—' she took a breath, '—but Drew and I thought we all needed something to look forward to.'

Drew reached over and took her hand.

'A christening!'

Allie clapped her hands together. 'A christening for Angus!'

'A christening for Angus,' Isla repeated. 'We can't thank you enough for being such amazing friends. And thank you Flick for helping to bring our wee man into the world. I actually don't know what I'd have done if you weren't there.' Isla was getting emotional at the thought of it.

'You don't need to thank me.' She reached over the table and squeezed her friend's hand. 'So, what's the plan? The village church?'

Isla nodded, 'Yes, we've booked it for the middle of March, so hopefully everything in the village will be back to normal by then.' Isla stopped talking and looked between her friends. 'So, you all need to save the date because none of you could miss it for the world.'

'We wouldn't want to miss it,' chipped in Allie, taking a sip of her drink.

'Well, you can't miss it … because… gushing friend moment coming up.' Isla flapped her hand in front of her face then beamed at Drew before turning back to her friends. 'Because Drew and I would like you all to be godparents.'

There was a colossal gasp around the table. Allie squealed, her smile turning into a huge grin.

Fergus leapt to his feet and patted Drew on his back before kissing Isla on the cheek; Rory mirrored his actions.

Felicity was over the moon to be asked to be Angus's godmother, but knew there would have been a time, not so long ago, that the offer would have caused a momentary flicker of pain to surface, knowing that she'd never have a biological child of her own. But since being back in Heartcross she'd begun to let go of the past and embrace life again. Esme had helped to change her view on motherhood without her even knowing it.

Even though she swallowed a lump in her throat she knew she was going to embrace this chance and would wholeheartedly take on the role. After only being back in the village a short time she felt honoured to be asked and the feeling of being loved by her friends enveloped her. It didn't matter that she'd taken herself away to heal her pain, these were her friends, her true friends and the emotion surged through her body. Her eyes brimmed with happy tears. She would never let Isla, Drew or baby Angus down.

She pulled herself together. 'Let's raise a toast,' ordered Felicity, picking up her glass. 'To baby Angus.'

Everyone chinked their glasses together.

'To baby Angus,' everyone repeated, taking a swig of their drink.

As the excited chatter filtered around the table, she felt Fergus place a hand on her knee. 'You okay?' He kept his voice to a whisper.

'I am … honestly. Sometimes the memories just creep up on me.'

He squeezed her knee and snaked an arm around the back of her chair.

Felicity felt an overwhelming feeling of contentment, not just at being with Fergus, but with the old gang all back together. They spent the next hour or two reminiscing about the past, and between them they raked up every funny story from their school days up until Drew's stag do where he'd accidently climbed on to a train bound for London. If it wasn't for a little old lady waking him up due to his snoring, he might never have made the wedding.

Fergus checked his watch and even though it wasn't quite closing time he announced he had to get home to Esme. The night had been perfect, and Felicity wished it would go on forever.

'I'd best get back too,' she said standing up.

'I can walk you home,' said Fergus, which was exactly what Felicity was hoping for. After they said their good-byes they hovered on the steps outside the pub. It was a clear night and the view was magnificent. The sky was littered with stars that looked like beautiful flashing fairy lights. They both looked up at the illuminated darkness and the past seemed to linger at a distance, an excitement for the future suddenly gripping her.

'Everything will be okay, you know,' said Felicity noticing that Fergus had gone quiet.

'As long as we look after each other, everything is going to be more than fine,' he replied, leaning forward and dotting Felicity's nose affectionately with his finger. 'Come on, let's get you home.'

Fergus linked his arm through hers as he walked towards Love Heart Lane and there was no denying Felicity shimmied with happiness.

Chapter 31

Felicity finally located her mobile phone on approximately the fifth missed call after frantically searching under her duvet. It felt like she had only just gone to sleep. She'd been messaging Allie, who'd been grilling her about Fergus, until the early hours and once her head had finally hit the pillow she'd fallen into a deep sleep. Whoever was ringing her now wasn't giving up, and she peered at the screen with blurry eyes.

'Alfie, you've woken me up. Where's the fire?' asked Felicity, in a complete daze.

'Sorry ... sorry ... sorry ... but I thought you might like to get yourself down to the river.'

Felicity glanced at the clock. 'It's 6.30 a.m. Why would I want to get myself down to the river?'

'Because all the plans have been drawn up, and approved thanks to Annie Boyd and the construction of the new temporary bridge is about to begin. Granted, they are starting from Glensheil but the press are down there. You'll be able to catch a glimpse from Heartcross.'

'Thanks Alfie,' she said, hanging up the call and quickly pulling on a jumper and a pair of socks. She tip-toed downstairs hoping not to wake her mum and pulled on her boots. She buttoned up her coat and carefully closed the door to Heartwood Cottage behind her.

There wasn't a soul in sight as she hurried down Love Heart Lane but she noticed the light on in Rory's living room; even with the isolation of the village he still religiously opened up the veterinary practice every day.

Felicity walked the half-mile to the river. Even though there was an icy chill in the air the unspoilt early morning view was outstanding. There were heather-clad, mist-filled hollows that sloped up over the mountainous terrain, picturesque by any standards. Felicity wondered how she'd ever given all this up to escape to the city smog. She didn't yearn for the noise or crave the fast pace of the city anymore, it was well and truly out of her system.

As she reached the end of the path, she saw the river in sight. It was still strange to see the view without the original bridge arching over the river.

There was a hive of activity on the other side of the river, and Felicity felt a flutter of pride as she could see the army of yellow-hatted workmen and the machinery on the opposite side. With Alfie's input things were beginning to take shape quickly and she watched for a minute, feeling a tiny bit emotional. She'd made this happen, obviously with the help of the general public donating so generously, but it had been her idea to do a video in the first place. She thought for a second about the mysterious donation that had pushed them over their target. Still no one knew where that had come from but whoever it was, Felicity knew both she and the villagers were extremely grateful.

'Wow, I can't believe they've started already.'

Felicity jumped out of her skin and spun round. 'What are you doing here?' she asked watching the breath swirl around her face in the cold air.

'Jogging,' laughed Fergus, standing in front of her dressed in sports gear.

Felicity felt a slight blush to her cheeks. 'Ha! Yes! Silly me.'

'But you don't look like you're jogging?' Fergus flicked a curious glance at Felicity then grinned. 'In fact, I would say they were PJs under your parka.'

'Busted!' laughed Felicity, trying to brush it off but feeling a little embarrassed. 'Alfie woke me up, told me the construction had started in case I wanted to witness the start and before I really thought about it I found myself here. But I am regretting not putting anything warmer on.' She shivered, feeling the cold. What on earth had she been thinking?

'The villagers are going to be glad it's all happening so soon. The funny thing is everyone has taken that bridge for granted for all these years; it was inevitable it wasn't going to last forever especially with the wild weather up on these mountain tops.'

'I'm sure it's going to take years to reconstruct the old one again, but at least we will soon have access to the town and normal life can resume.'

'There's nothing normal about Heartcross, for such a small village in the Scottish Highlands there's always a drama.' Fergus looked down at his watch before touching Felicity's arm. 'I need to jog on and get ready for work.'

'Where's Esme?'

'Jessica stayed over last night so I took advantage of her good nature and thought I'd try and get this body back into some sort of shape.'

'It looks fine to me.' The words were out of Felicity's mouth before she could stop them.

Fergus tried to hide his smile.

'Are you coming tonight?' she probed, with her fingers firmly crossed in her pockets.

'What's tonight?'

'I take it you aren't keeping up with the village Facebook page?'

'I try and stay away from social media at all costs.'

'Sorry ... I didn't mean...'

'Don't be daft ... what's tonight?' interrupted Fergus, steering the conversation back on track.

'Yesterday, we got talking to the pensioners in the teashop and they began reminiscing about past times and the annual bingo night in the village hall which they'd enjoyed. So, Allie mentioned there was still the old machine stored in one of the sheds at the back of the pub.'

'You've decided to put on a bingo night?'

'Absolutely, a little bit of light-hearted fun, to keep everyone entertained.'

'You, Felicity Simons, are a woman of many talents.' He grinned, now shuffling from foot to foot to try and keep warm. 'From bridge constructor to bingo caller.'

'So, are you going to come over?'

'I've had some offers in my time ... but bingo,' he teased.

'Bring Esme, she'll have fun.'

He cocked an eyebrow. 'Okay, it's a date,' he said, before turning and powering his legs up the hill.

It's a date. Felicity turned the words over in her head before pulling her lapel up tight around her neck. Fighting the icy winds, she walked as fast as she could back up the track towards Love Heart Lane. Even though the early morning chill was cutting right through her, her heart was warm with love for Fergus. Everything in her life was coming together and she felt happy strolling back towards Heartwood Cottage until she suddenly remembered Eleanor Ramsbottom, her boss from the department store, who no doubt would be expecting her back in London very soon. She couldn't put it off any longer. She knew she needed to send that email terminating her employment and that she would now have great pleasure in doing so.

Chapter 32

As Felicity and Rona pushed open the double doors of the village hall, Allie and Rory were already inside. They'd set out the tables and chairs and erected some sort of prehistoric looking machine at the front of the room. Rory had plugged in a microphone and was currently blowing into it, sending a high-pitched squealing sound through the room.

Allie gave them a welcoming smile. 'Have you brought your dabber?'

'Funnily enough ... no!' laughed Felicity.

'You can have one of mine,' she said waving a neon-pink stick in the air.

'Thanks, just what I've always wanted!'

'It's amazing what you find in the shed, and we've even got a pile of bingo books from a fundraiser we did years ago.'

'Well, that's a result, shall I put them in a pile by the door? So everyone can grab one when they come in?'

'Yes please.'

Rona walked over towards Rory who had finally managed to work the microphone without deafening everyone.

'I thought you'd be wearing a pristine white jacket with a black shirt and bright red bow tie if you are our bingo caller for tonight,' teased Rona.

Rory cringed. 'Woah! I'm doing no such thing. I've set this wee lot up but there's no way I'm calling out the numbers ... that's down to you, Allie.'

Allie looked panic-stricken, 'I can't do it! I'm not confident enough.' She smiled sweetly towards Felicity. 'It was your idea.'

Felicity threw her hands in the air. 'I don't mind.'

'Do we have any prizes?' asked Rona. 'Or is it just for fun?'

'We can do a free meal at the pub and afternoon tea at the teashop once everything gets back to normal ... but I think everyone is out for some light-hearted fun this evening.'

The village door opened, and everyone looked round.

'Look who's home!' Esme came flying through the door and as soon as she spotted Felicity, ran straight into her arms. Following right behind her was Aggie and Fergus.

'Well, you look better,' exclaimed Rona, walking over towards her. 'Welcome back!'

'Thanks, it's great to be back,' said Aggie, wearing a huge smile.

'When did you get home?' asked Allie.

'Drew came and got me in his boat. I have to say I never thought I got seasick, until I had the misfortune of sitting in a rowing boat over the choppy river but great progress is already being made on the bridge from Glensheil.'

'That's great news,' replied Felicity, and everyone agreed.

'What's that machine?' asked Esme, suddenly fascinated by the old bingo machine rigged up at the front of the room.

'Come on ... I'll show you.' Felicity took Esme by the hand and led her towards it while the village hall doors opened and everyone filed through the door and settled down at the tables.

Felicity switched on the machine and showed Esme how it worked. She was captivated watching the tiny balls float and dance in the air before being sucked up into the tube and pop out of the top. 'And see that number on the ball—' Felicity showed the ball to Esme '—you read that number out and cross the number off on the tiny books and once all the numbers are crossed off you shout Bingo and are the winner!'

'That's so cool,' said Esme. 'Can I help you call the numbers?'

'I don't see why not.'

'Daddy ... Daddy.' Esme turned and ran towards Fergus. 'I'm going to help Felicity call the numbers.'

'Make sure you call my winning ones.' He smiled at his daughter before sitting down next to Aggie and Rona.

They all watched as Esme ran back to Felicity.

Within ten minutes, every seat in the place was filled and the room was full of chatter with everyone raring to go. Felicity placed a stool next to the machine which Esme perched on and she switched on the microphone and blew into it.

The room fell silent.

'Welcome everyone! I hope you've all got your books and a pen ready to hand but before we begin I would like you to put your hands together and give a huge bingotastic welcome to Esme, my helper for the evening.'

Esme grinned like the Cheshire Cat while the room erupted into rapturous applause.

Felicity started the first game and each time gave Esme the number to read out. The game was in full flow and the only sound that could be heard were the dabbers thudding on the table until there was a gasp and Aggie shouted, 'HOUSE.'

'Grandma's won!' cried Esme, then flew off her chair towards Aggie and gave her a huge hug.

'I said my numbers, not your grandma's!' winked

Fergus at Esme before she ran back off towards her stool ready for the next game.

After an hour of fun, the games came to an end. Everyone seemed to have a good time and spirits were lifted. Felicity had had a wonderful time and had enjoyed every second with Esme. Once the villagers had gathered their belongings, everyone seemed to head towards the pub.

'Well, that was a success and good light-hearted fun,' exclaimed Rona who joined Aggie and Fergus. They began to collect up the used bingo books while Rory packed up the microphone.

'I'll put away these table and chairs etc.' Felicity turned towards Allie. 'You were the one who got them all out. Get yourself to the pub and I'll join you when I'm done.'

'Are you sure?'

'Absolutely sure.'

Felicity began to stack the tables and chairs as everyone walked towards the doors. Fergus stopped, and Felicity saw him kiss Aggie on the cheek. She took Esme by the hand and Fergus turned back towards her.

'I'll help you stack all these up.'

Felicity was secretly pleased, and they began to work together to put the room back to normal.

'I have to admit I quite enjoyed that,' grinned Fergus, taking hold of one end of the table while Felicity grabbed the other.'

'Can't beat old-fashioned fun.' She laughed as they stacked the tables.

'You are really good with her, you know,' said Fergus warmly, holding Felicity's gaze. 'Esme has really taken to you.'

'I've really taken to her and you know whatever happens with all your tests, she is a special, amazing girl and that's all down to you ... you should be proud, Fergus.'

He leant against the stacked tables and Felicity did the same. 'I am so sorry you can't become—'

'Hey,' interrupted Felicity. 'Let's not go there. It's something I can't change and as much as I wish things were different there are so many positives in my life – Mum, the teashop, Heartcross, my friends, and of course there is Esme ... and I'm glad me and you are friends. We are friends, aren't we?' she quickly added.

Fergus opened his arms wide, gesturing towards her, and Felicity slipped into them and rested her head against his chest. They stayed like that for a moment in silence and Fergus gently stroked her hair. 'I have missed you, you know.'

Felicity's heart skipped a beat at his words; being in Fergus's arms felt like the most natural thing in the world. She tilted her head towards his and they held each other's gaze. She studied his beautiful eyes as he brushed his finger across her lips and she willed him to kiss her. He tipped his head forward and pressed his lips lightly on hers. Neither of them spoke, but Felicity's head whirled as his arms tightly wrapped around her body.

'I'm glad you are staying in Heartcross,' he mumbled.

'Me too,' she answered, their eyes never leaving each other, knowing that she was never going back to London. She wanted Fergus full stop and from that kiss alone, she knew he was beginning to feel the same. She made a promise to herself there and then that she wasn't going to rush Fergus. She was going to let him take things at his own pace but make sure she was always there for him. Since she'd left Heartcross, his life hadn't run smoothly. And once the bridge was up and running and the postal system back to normal, he had the worry of the results of the DNA test still to come – but whatever the outcome, Felicity knew they were in this together and she was going to be by his side no matter what.

Fergus couldn't deny his feelings any longer. 'I'm sorry I gave you a hard time when you turned up ... I knew I'd see you again one day but didn't quite expect it to be in the middle of a snowstorm when I was attempting to rescue a Shetland pony.'

'Don't worry about it, I never expected to see you again in such circumstances either. I'd played the situation over and over in my head for years and none of it played out like I expected.'

'You had now, had you?' He tilted Felicity's chin up.

'There's never been anyone else that has come close to you, Fergus,' said Felicity, raw emotion taking her by surprise. She blinked away a tear and glanced nervously into his eyes and took a deep breath. 'There's only ever been you.' Her heart was clattering, and she could barely breathe, her pulse was racing.

Fergus traced his finger under her chin, and she could feel his breath on her face and the hairs on the back of her neck prickled. Their eyes stayed locked and neither of them faltered. Fergus grasped the back of her head lightly and pulled her in closer and then their lips met and sparks flew like she hadn't felt in such a long time. They kissed slowly at first, the tingle in Felicity's body immense.

'I want you,' he mumbled,

'Is this what you really want?' Felicity asked, pulling gently away.

'Yes ... I've missed you so much. I want you back in my life for good.'

'I want that too.'

'And Esme?' Fergus held her gaze.

'That beautiful little girl is just an added bonus.' Felicity leant up and kissed him once more. 'I won't let either of you down ... I promise,' she whispered.

Fergus took her by the hand and they walked towards Heartwood Cottage, both knowing that they'd fallen madly and deeply in love with each other once more.

*

Five weeks later...

There was a loud knock on the door and Felicity and Rona immediately spun round. Aggie was standing outside next to Fergus who had a huge grin on his face and Esme had her nose pressed up against the window.

With a spring in her step, Felicity quickly opened up the teashop and spun an excited Esme who'd launched herself into her arms.

'It's today!' squealed Esme. 'It's today you get to open the bridge and cut the ribbon ... you are sooo famous!' she emphasised, making Felicity giggle.

'I'm not famous, all we did was raise a few thousand pounds ... and you had as much to do with that as me!'

Fergus was hanging back looking very shifty. 'And what are you doing?' asked Felicity, narrowing her eyes at him. 'What are you hiding behind your back?'

'These are for you ... I know they aren't real as it's very difficult to find real flowers in the village at the moment, but Esme and I have made you these as we think you are very special.'

From behind his back he produced a small posy of handmade flowers from different coloured tissue paper. Felicity's heart swelled at the sight of them. She took them from his hand, planting a kiss on his cheek, then automatically went to sniff them which made everyone laugh.

'Thank you, they are gorgeous, I will treasure them forever.' She turned and pressed a kiss to the top of Esme's head before placing them in a jam jar on the counter. 'They look perfect there.'

'This one has barely slept,' chipped in Aggie. 'Honestly, you'd think Father Christmas was visiting Heartcross today.'

Esme gave a cheeky smile before sitting down at the table with a drink of juice.

'But it's not only the bridge that is re-opening today ... is it?' Aggie held her arms open and gave Rona a hug, before moving on to Felicity.

Instantly, Rona welled up with tears and cast a glance around the teashop. In the past couple of weeks, Hamish's shelves had been fully stocked from the twice-weekly food drops by the army which meant Rona and Felicity didn't have to feed the villagers en masse, and everyone had begun to take care of themselves. Over the past few days Felicity had worked really hard and had set to work giving Bonnie's Teashop a fresh lick of paint, with new menus printed and the transformation was incredible. Felicity had taken down all the old frayed, discoloured bunting and created new ones from scraps of material found in the bottom of Rona's sewing basket with the help of Esme. They criss-crossed them around the ceiling. She'd even taken the old plush velvet sofa that was gathering dust in the back room, hoovered it down and dressed it with throws and cushions creating a work area in the back of the teashop for anyone who wanted to sit with their laptop and enjoy an afternoon tea. The teashop had sprung back to life.

'I know,' said Rona, taking Felicity by the hand and giving it a quick squeeze. 'Today we re-open this place ... together.'

'How are you feeling about it all?' asked Aggie.

Rona took a breath and composed herself. 'A little sad Mum isn't here to see us working together, in partnership. There was a time I thought I wouldn't step foot inside this place again without her but even though I'm feeling emotional I'm on top of the world ... with Felicity by my side I know we will do Mum proud.'

'We will. Grandma's teashop will be up and running once more,' agreed Felicity, her eyes welling up with happy tears as she shot a quick glance towards the photograph of Bonnie and her first customers hanging proudly on the wall.

'How did it go when you sent the email resigning from your post at the department store ... any reply yet?' asked Fergus, grabbing himself a drink of water from the jug on the table.

Felicity had left it until the very last minute to email Eleanor Ramsbottom tendering her resignation.

The second she pressed send a huge weight had lifted off her shoulders. That part of her life had finally come to an end but she knew she would have to return to London one last time to empty her flat.

She flicked on to her phone and checked her inbox.

'Yes, she's replied.' Felicity quickly scanned the email and gasped. 'You aren't going to believe this,' she said pulling out a chair and sitting down.

'What is it?' asked Fergus, with a sprightly raise of his eyebrows.

'The money, the final donation ... the fifty thousand pounds was from Eleanor Ramsbottom...' Felicity looked up at everyone who had gathered around her.

'You're kidding me?' said Fergus.

'Honestly, I'm not ... look,' said Felicity, passing the phone to Fergus.

'Well, would you believe it? She wasn't as bad as you thought!' exclaimed Fergus, handing the phone back to Felicity.

'I actually feel awful now,' replied Felicity re-reading the email, not only taken aback by the grand gesture from Eleanor and the company she'd worked for, but by the tone of the email, which was extremely sincere. Eleanor not only wished her well but claimed Felicity was an extremely valued member of staff who would be welcomed back at any time if she ever changed her mind.

'She's even wished me all the best for future and offered to give me a reference if I ever needed one ... I just can't believe it was Eleanor who donated the money.'

'You need to thank her,' said Rona.

'Absolutely, I will,' Felicity replied still flabbergasted.

'She's not even making me work my notice ... in fact, it's like someone has hacked her email,' joked Felicity.

'I'll look forward to reading that reference,' teased Rona grabbing her bag from the counter. 'Look...' She nodded towards the windows. The majority of the villagers could be seen ambling down the track towards the river.

There was an air of excitement and Felicity couldn't believe today was the day the temporary bridge was opening. At eleven o'clock the whole of Heartcross would be re-united with the outside world again.

In the last few weeks everything had continued to go from strength to strength. Felicity and Fergus's relationship was getting stronger every day and she had been spending a lot of time at Fox Hollow Cottage with him and Esme. The teashop was about to re-open its doors and Felicity was feeling content with life again.

Everyone grabbed their coats and they followed the masses down to the water in the sunshine. The past weeks had been tough, but thankfully it seemed the winter days were behind Heartcross and the warmth was drifting in. How things had changed since Felicity had arrived during that winter snowstorm.

As they reached the bottom of the track, Fergus gripped Felicity's hand and they hovered by the river bank. Her heart thumped with excitement as she took in the view. There was lots of activity on the water with press boats and cameras bobbing around and people on rowing boats joining in the fun.

'I can't believe this is going to happen, that the bridge is actually opening today,' she gasped.

Esme ran off towards Hamish who was handing out balloons, quickly followed by Aggie.

They spotted Finn up high on Drew's shoulders and Isla was gently bouncing Angus in the pram as they stood and watched the activity on the water. People had already started to form a queue to walk across the bridge as soon as it was declared open.

Felicity tried to hold back her tears. She couldn't believe she felt so emotional. 'This is all amazing,' she said, wiping her bleary tears.

Fergus put his arm around her. 'You did this, you raised the money to make this happen and I'm sorry I gave you a hard time about the video.'

'Don't be daft,' she replied, fully understanding that was a situation that still needed dealing with. Fergus was still struggling with the bombshell in Lorna's letter, undecided about what to do for the best.

Fergus looked out across the river and took a minute then shook his head. 'You know what Flick ... I'm not going to do it. I'm not going to take the DNA test.'

Felicity looked up at him.

'Having Esme and you back in my life, I've realised that no matter what, I'll always be Esme's dad. Biology doesn't matter, it's all about care, love and security and as far as I'm concerned, she's my daughter, I love her and nothing will ever change that.'

'I agree,' said Felicity, snaking her arms around his waist and hugging him tight. Felicity whole-heartedly agreed.

'And I'm hoping you are going to be a part of our lives for a very long time.'

'I think you can both count on that,' said Felicity feeling the warmth of love rush through her body, as she reached up to plant a kiss on his perfect lips.

'And now look at this,' Fergus said as he took a step back, reluctantly breaking the moment. 'All these people are here because of you.'

Alfie clapped his hand on Fergus's back and appeared at their side. 'Look at the turnout, it's truly magnificent, the whole village has come down to see the bridge open. You should feel proud of yourself, Flick,' he said as he turned towards Felicity.

'It's not just down to me, you organised the best team, Alfie. Thank you. Now that the bridge is about to be opened, there's no excuse not to go to London and visit your family.'

Alfie beamed. 'I plan to do just that!'

They all watched the BBC boat moor at the edge of

the water and Aidy Redfern climbed out. He scanned the crowd and spotted Felicity, then beckoned her over.

'This is your moment, enjoy it,' Fergus whispered into her ear.

Her eyes shone. 'Thank you.'

Fergus squeezed her hand reassuringly before Felicity walked towards the edge of the bridge, the crowd behind her following closely.

The BBC camera crew had already set up their equipment and the opening of the bridge was being televised.

As Aidy Redfern shook Felicity's hand she stood in front of the red ribbon that was draped from one side of the bridge to the other and the crowd behind her erupted in cheers. She spun round and took in the view. The whole of Heartcross had turned out and Felicity's eyes brimmed with unshed tears. She swallowed down a lump in her throat and could feel the emotion rising inside.

The press photographers began to snap her photo and Fergus was smiling proudly, clutching Esme's hand.

Aidy Redfern put his arm in the air and the crowd hushed.

'Going live in five, four, three, two, one...' He brought the microphone up to his mouth.

Felicity's body trembled as he began to speak.

'This morning we are live from the village of Heartcross where just weeks ago disaster struck and the Grade II bridge that linked Heartcross to the town of Glensheil collapsed in the ferocious storms. Local villager Felicity Simons took matters into her own hands with a community appeal that went viral and the funds to construct the bridge were raised in a matter of days. Environmental Minister Annie Boyd has invited Felicity here today to cut the ribbon and open the new bridge linking Heartcross back to Glensheil.'

Everyone cheered.

'Would you like to say a few words?' Aidy poised the microphone not far from Felicity's lips.

'The morning the village woke up to discover the bridge had collapsed was a shock to the whole community with potentially a devastating effect on our livelihood and businesses.' Felicity felt her voice wobble; she glanced towards Fergus who gave her a quick thumbs up to settle her nerves. Allie and Rory were standing behind him next to Drew and Isla, all of her friends beaming.

'As a community, we all came together to make sure everyone in our village was fed and we looked after each other, we all pulled together. I would just like to thank everyone that donated to the cause, we have had donations from all over the world and all those funds raised have been pulled together to build this amazing temporary bridge.' The crowd cheered once more.

A member of the film crew passed Aidy a pair of scissors. 'Felicity, would you do your community the greatest honour and cut the ribbon for village of Heartcross?'

Felicity nodded and took the scissors from his hand. 'We finally declare the new bridge open,' she said with pride, before snipping the ribbon.

Aidy gestured for Felicity to step onto the bridge first, and she was soon joined by Fergus and Esme.

The sound of clapping echoed all around as soon as they stepped onto the bridge. The crowd of villagers followed behind.

'You did great!' Fergus hugged her.

'Thank you ... but I still can't believe it,' said Felicity stopping in the middle of the bridge. 'I can't believe one video could have raised the funds to construct this bridge. It's just amazing.' Fergus lifted up Esme so she could take a closer look at the river flowing under the bridge as they moved with the crowds. Vehicles were now beginning to drive slowly across the bridge from Glensheil and toot their horns; drivers and passengers were waving out of their windows.

Aggie and Rona caught them up. 'Back to normality,' said Rona kissing her daughter on the cheek.

Fergus placed Esme back on the ground and Aggie cupped her hand. Alfie too stood by their side as they all watched the happy faces driving through in their cars and people walking from one end of the bridge to another.

'Felicity ... Felicity,' a voice hollered.

Felicity spun round and squinted. 'Surely not ... it can't be.'

'Who's that?' asked Fergus, not recognising the woman hurrying towards them pulling a suitcase.

'Polly ... it's Polly, my friend from London!' Felicity squealed as they ran towards each other and hugged.

'What are you doing here? You're a very long way from home,' said Felicity, hugging her friend to make sure she was real.

'Everyone ... this is Polly my friend from London. What are you doing here?'

'It's a long story ... but basically the pub has been sold and I decided I needed a holiday before I look for work. Then I thought who better to visit than my best friend, who actually I've missed like crazy! And I'm hoping you can put me up?' She screwed up her face in hope waiting for Felicity to answer.

'Absolutely, yes ... I can't believe you are here! Mum, it's okay if Polly stops with us?'

'Of course, any friend of yours, is a friend of mine.' Rona welcomed Polly to Heartcross.

'Let me take your case.' Alfie stepped forward.

'Pol ... this is Alfie.'

Polly smiled up at him. 'Well, thank you.'

Felicity noticed that Alfie blushed.

'Shall we start walking back?' asked Aggie as Rona glanced at her watch.

'We best had, we need to get back to the teashop to open up.'

Everyone began to weave their way back across the bridge, and it certainly felt like a carnival day, with everyone wearing a smile and music playing from the banks of the river.

Fergus hung back and chatted with Alfie while Felicity walked alongside Polly.

'I've been following the Facebook page,' said Polly. 'I can't believe the amount of money you raised ... you are a superstar.'

'I wouldn't go that far.'

'I couldn't quite believe it when I saw the bridge collapse on the news then when I saw your video, and the attention it brought ... and when you told me you weren't coming back...'

'I know, but once I was home I realised I'd missed this place and everyone here.' Felicity looked over her shoulder and smiled at Fergus. 'To open up my grandmother's business again and work alongside my mum ... it's a dream come true.'

'I can't wait to see the teashop.'

'You are going to love it, and we re-open in approximately thirty minutes.'

'Well, I just arrived at the right time ... will there be cake?'

'There's always cake,' laughed Felicity, 'and you my friend can have a slice on the house.'

As they walked up the track back towards the village with their faces tilted up towards the sky enjoying the atmosphere all around them, Felicity knew she'd made the right decision to come home, there was nowhere else she wanted to be.

'Now tell me all about Fergus, is that *the* Fergus? Old flame Fergus?' Polly asked in a hushed whisper.

'It is but shh, not now, he'll hear us!'

They both giggled as they sauntered up Love Heart Lane. 'We have so much catching up to do!' said Felicity.

As they reached Heartwood Cottage, Felicity and Fergus hung back while Rona and Alfie showed Polly into the cottage and dropped her suitcase inside.

All the other villagers were forming an orderly queue along the pavement waiting for the teashop to open its doors.

'What a day,' said Fergus. 'The bridge is open and now the grand opening of the teashop.' He narrowed his eyes at her and pressed a soft kiss onto Felicity's lips.

'You know whatever happens in the future, I will always love you,' she whispered.

'You sounded rather serious there, Felicity Simons.'

'I am being serious and don't you ever forget it.'

He wrapped his arms around her waist. 'Good, I'm glad. You are an amazing woman,' he said, with an intensity that made her whole body quiver.

'You're not so bad yourself, but carry on saying things like that and you'll make me cry ... I'm an emotional wreck today.'

Fergus pulled her in and hugged her. 'I do love you, Flick.'

'I love you too.'

'Come on, you've got a teashop to open,' he said, turning and slipping his arm proudly around her shoulder. 'Your customers await.'

Esme was running around at the top of Love Heart Lane, holding a balloon and laughing with Finn. Isla and Drew were standing next to the pram and the entire village of Heartcross oozed with happiness.

'We have a very special girl there,' said Fergus, squeezing Felicity's hand and glancing towards Esme. His words brought tears to Felicity's eyes.

'We have.'

'Together forever.' Taking her by surprise Fergus scooped her up in his arms and kissed her passionately sending her heart soaring. When they came up for air they realised that everyone standing on the pavement of Love Heart Lane was clapping and cheering them.

'Come on,' said Fergus, giving her a gooey smile, 'let's

get you to work. I'm hoping Esme and I can be your very first customers in the teashop.'

'Without a doubt.' She grinned, taking him by his hand.

'Daddy ... Felicity ... come on!' shouted Esme, running towards them. 'There's going to be cake and Rona has promised me a sticky bun too.'

Esme grabbed each of their hands and both Fergus and Felicity swung her in the air as she giggled.

'Well, if there are sticky buns,' giggled Felicity, 'let's get that door open.'

They all walked through the teashop door together, holding hands, a new family unit, taking their first steps towards a new life together.

A Letter from Christie

Dear all,

Firstly, if you are reading this letter, thank you so much for choosing to read *Love Heart Lane*.

I sincerely hope you enjoyed reading this book. If you did, I would be forever grateful if you'd write a review. Your recommendations can always help other readers to discover my books.

I can't believe my eighth book is being published; writing for a living is truly the best job in the world.

I'm particularly proud of this novel, the characters of Felicity Simons and Fergus Campbell have been a huge part of my life for the last five months but the good news is I won't be leaving them behind just yet! There will be more books to come based around the little village of Heartcross in the Scottish highlands.

I want to say a heartfelt thank you to everyone who has been involved in this project. I truly value each and every one of you and it's an absolute joy to hear from all my readers via Twitter and Facebook.

Please do keep in touch!

Warm wishes,

Christie x

Acknowledgements

I really can't believe my eighth book has been published and there is a long list of truly fabulous folk I need to thank who have been instrumental in supporting me in crafting this novel into one I'm truly proud of.

Huge love to my crew – Emily, Jack, Ruby and Tilly. I couldn't do it without any of you.

Woody, my mad cocker spaniel and my writing partner in crime, who is always by my side and unquestionably the best company ever.

Nell, my lass – my labradoodle puppy that has disrupted my work without a doubt these last few months but is already a member of the fam I couldn't ever imagine being without.

The clever team at HarperImpulse, Charlotte Ledger, Claire Fenby and Eloisa Clegg who are all utterly fabulous. I still pinch myself that I'm a part of this fantastic publishing family and am grateful for all your hard work turning my stories into books.

My editor, the wickedly smart Emily Ruston – thank you for your wise words of encouragement throughout the year and keeping me writing when times were tricky.

My agent Kate Nash, for your energy, vision and continuous support in me.

My second family, Anita, Aidy, Jenna and Kimberley Redfern who are simply the best and make me a happier human. I love you all dearly.

Big Love to my soul sisters, Jenny Berry, Lisa Hall, Natalie Emmerick and Charlotte Seddon. You lot rock!

Team Barlow! Huge love to my merry band of supporters and friends, Louise Speight, Catherine Snook, Suzanne Toner, Sue Miller, Sue France, Bella Osborne, Bhasker Patel and Sarah Lees who provide oodles of laughs along the way when I'm locked away in my writing cave for hours on end. I am truly grateful for your support and friendship.

Thank you to Rachel Gilbey who provides the best blog tours.

Finally, high fives to everyone who enjoys, reads and reviews my books especially Claire Knight, Lorraine Rugman, Sarah Hardy, Noelle Holten, Annette Hannah and Joanne Robertson. Your constant sharing of posts has never gone unnoticed and your support for my writing is truly appreciated.

I have without a doubt enjoyed writing every second of this book and I really hope you enjoy hanging out on Love Heart Lane with Flick and Fergus. Please do let me know!

Christie xx

HELP US SHARE THE LOVE!

If you love this wonderful book as much as we do then please share your reviews online.

Leaving reviews makes a huge difference and helps our books reach even more readers.

So get reviewing and sharing, we want to hear what you think!

Love, HarperImpulse x

Please leave your reviews online!

amazon.co.uk·   **kobo**..   goodreads   L♥ve**reading**   iBooks

And on social!

f/HarperImpulse   **🐦**@harperimpulse
📷@HarperImpulse

LOVE BOOKS?

So do we! And we love nothing more than chatting about our books with you lovely readers.

If you'd like to find out about our latest titles, as well as exclusive competitions, author interviews, offers and lots more, join us on our Facebook page! Why not leave a note on our wall to tell us what you thought of this book or what you'd like to see us publish more of?

🅵/HarperImpulse

You can also tweet us 🐦@harperimpulse and see exclusively behind the scenes on our Instagram page www.instagram.com/harperimpulse

To be the first to know about upcoming books and events, sign up to our newsletter at: http://www.harperimpulseromance.com/

Coming soon by

Drew Karpyshyn:

CHAOS UNLEASHED

Torn apart by the horrors they have witnessed — and
caused — the Children of Fire are more vulnerable
than ever. The fanatical armies of the Order
march across the land, trying to preserve the Legacy
with a bloody Purge of any who have the ability
to call upon the power of Chaos.

And behind the Legacy lurks Daemron the Slayer
and his armies of Chaos Spawn, eagerly awaiting their
chance to be unleashed upon the mortal world . . .

Coming soon from Del Rey

DEL REY